The door slid open and Wendy stepped inside. She closed it again without a click, then turned into the darkness, the familiar compassion starting its slow fire.

Something wasn't right. She stood, reluctant to try a light, feeling into the space. It smelled like any other patient room, old perfume and old body fighting it out over the background of institutional carpet and drywall. What she could see appeared normal. The feel of the room was nothing special.

It felt empty. Like there was nobody here.

Fighting a growing confusion, she placed the syringe back into her skirt and slapped on the lights. Her adjustments had been undone. The bed was made. Delores Kilborn was already gone.

And she'd taken her pillow with her.

"Mrs. Kilborn is not in her room," she announced a minute later at the nursing station. That brought Sandy up out of the pages of Freewheel Monthly in a hurry.

"What?"

It took them three minutes to find the sticky note, on Tooly Carleton's file and not Delores'. 'Mrs. Carleton will be having a sleepover tonight with Mrs. Kilborn and Mrs. Howe.' "Whew!" said Sandy, "thought we had a runner there for a minute. Not that I'd ever expect 114 to run anywhere."

"Hmm." Wendy was already past the crisis, her nose deep into the back pages of Delores Kilborn's chart. There it was, plain as day. She had a massage therapist.

The heat of her compassion settled into a slow, deep burn.

TONY BERRYMAN

THE NIGHT NURSE

Twintree Books

THE NIGHT NURSE

a massage therapy thriller

Paperback original published by Twintree Books / May 2020

ISBN: 978-1-7771335-0-4
Also available in ebook

Cover design: Shawn Wernig, Eggplant Studios
Cover photos: Shutterstock.com
Back cover photo: Lions Gate Bridge by Adam, Flickr.com

Printed in the USA
1 3 5 7 9 10 8 6 4 2

For Juanita
my First Reader

One Month Before

Wendy stood by the meds cart in the quiet of the darkened hallway and waited while the other nurses drew straws. The three of them huddled behind the nursing station, not fighting over actual straws but deep in the kind of tense and whispered argument Wendy had seen plenty of times before. She tapped the cart's handle. This sort of thing was getting old.

The 3 a.m. rounds needed to be done, whispers or no. "I'll be doing the east wing, then," she said to the quiet, and started the meds cart moving. The whispers cut off with a short, sharp command from Gloria, the floor supervisor.

"I'll come with you." It was Esther, the skinny, young one with no discipline and disgracefully sloppy pink scrubs, who scurried to Wendy's side without meeting her eye. That left Maria for the west wing, and dried-up Gloria to stay and monitor the station. Wendy gave Esther a sweet smile, and they turned the corner. Gloria's gaze burned into her back as they went.

The thick, moist fug of Oregon in April flowed like a river through the White Shores Medical Center's air conditioning. She would miss that. Still, the Third Rule was humming its low note at the bottom of her mind: When They Suspect, Move West.

Mr. Orland in 703 needed some oxycodone from the narcotics drawer. "I'll take the evens," said Wendy, heading into

702 with a tray of paper cups. She made it three steps before she heard Esther gasp out a bad word. The girl was holding her hand and staring at a growing stream of blood pouring out of a fingertip.

"The drawer bit me!" she murmured. They both bent over to look. Jammed up under the curved handle was a jagged syringe needle, several inches long and glistening red. "Well how the hell?" said Esther, staring at it in disbelief.

"That's going to need disinfecting," Wendy told her. "You'd better hustle back to Gloria and let her take care of it. You'll have to do some incident reports, no doubt. I can handle the rest of the wing."

The girl's eyes got round. "No, I can – I mean, what if you need help?"

As if this child would be able to help with anything Wendy couldn't handle. "Every room has a call button," she said. "You go on, you're starting to drip. I'll be fine." She carefully opened the narcotics drawer, added Mr. Orland's meds to her tray and went into 702. When she came out, Esther was gone and she was alone.

A quick yank freed the broken needle, removing the evidence. She abandoned the meds cart and strode to 714, where a single nameplate on the wall read Micheline DuBois. Wendy had spent time with the sweet, sharp-minded, retired librarian the day before, making sure. The old woman was recovering from an obstructed bowel operation and had been denied the strongest narcotics because of their tendency for constipation. She'd been given a private room to shield other patients from the moaning. The doctors assured Mrs. DuBois that the pain would subside in another few days, but Wendy knew better.

Mrs. DuBois would be beyond her pain much sooner than that.

"It's me," she murmured into the dimly lit room, "nothing to worry about."

"Nurse Wendy? I'm so glad. I wish I could get some sleep, but it - hurts too much." The words came in a ragged, papery voice from the middle of the room. Mrs. DuBois was centred on the bed, poor thing, unmoved from where she'd been placed an hour before.

A spike of hot compassion lanced through Wendy's insides. "I've come to make it all better. You'll see."

Mrs. DuBois laughed, a dry huff from a pinched face. "You're good, girl, but not that good. I – mmmh – I can feel myself getting older, you know. Like it's taking my years from me. Don't have that many to spare."

Wendy looked around the room. They always tried to make it their own. The obligatory vase of flowers was on the dresser, towering above a hinged three-photo spread of the grandchildren. The night table sported a seated Buddha. A porcelain statue of Charlie Chaplin and a small, exquisite girl doll reading a book decorated the windowsill.

A nice try, but it didn't feel right. The arrangement made the room feel closed in. Like nothing could escape.

She picked up the Chaplin. "My granddaughter's studying theater," said Mrs. DuBois. It changed nothing, so she put it back. She tilted the photos of the grandkids so they smiled at empty space, then turned the Buddha so he was blessing the wall. The little girl doll she moved right next to the bed. Wendy stood for a moment, feeling for it, and there it was. Like a cool breeze blowing out the window, taking everything with it.

There was movement behind her. Mrs. DuBois was trying to rise, her face white with the pain it caused. "Please don't re-arrange my – ohhh – things. That doesn't feel good. Put them back." Her strength drained, she withered back into the mattress.

The First Rule shone bright in Wendy's mind: Ease The

Suffering. She nudged Mrs. DuBois into the right position. "There, hush now, I've made it better in here. You'll see."

For this occasion she had chosen a new method. The phenomenon was well known, but finding out exactly how to cause it had cost her many hours of study in medical libraries, blowing dust off old books about thoracic neurology and synaptic impulse and the chemistry of nerve conduction. Finally she'd found it for anyone to see on the Internet, of all places. She took up Mrs. DuBois' thin wrist, feeling for the telltale drumbeat of life under her fingertips. There it was, a rhythmic surge of systole and diastole marking the precise flashes of bioelectricity that flexed the powerful ventricles and pushed blood to the very end of Mrs. DuBois' wrist. The heart was built to be the most durable organ in the body, its electrical system practically unstoppable. Except during the 30 milliseconds when it was gathering strength for the next ventricular thrust.

Wendy reached over the bed and balled up her fist. "What are you –" Mrs. DuBois tried to demand, but she didn't have the chance.

Pulse, rest, pulse. The next rest, then the barest edge of the next pulse. Wendy brought her fist down with a hard, sharp tap on the center of the thin chest. A light but fast blow, 40 miles per hour on impact for best results, stopped just short of bruising.

Mrs. DuBois' eyes bugged out and her face flushed deep red. After a beat of complete stillness she caught her breath, shuddering in a deep lungful and wheezing out, "You – no, you're trying to – nurse!"

Wendy gasped. Shame flooded through her; she had caused more pain with her bumbling. Of course, there was a momentary delay between the wrist pulse and the actual physical heartbeat. She'd been stupid. Before Mrs. DuBois could gather another breath she curled her fingers, carefully timed, and struck a second thump to the frail chest, again stopping short of leaving a mark.

Mrs. DuBois' body jerked in a wave.her eyes got large again, this time with the fixed stare of the final astonishment. No breath came to replace the last one. The thrum in the wrist was still.

Wendy's compassion lit her up from the inside. She leaned close, beaming. "That's better. You don't have to suffer anymore, Mrs. DuBois. Good night now." She watched as the body slowly relaxed. The eyes dropped, their last look of reproach a minor pain Wendy would gladly endure in the face of her great joy. The job was done, and none the wiser.

Except she could hear hallway sounds. Esther was standing in the open doorway, her finger hastily wrapped and her mouth forming a rosebud of alarm. "I heard a noise and came straight in, but I found her like this," Wendy said, properly hushed and respectful. "She's passed."

Esther rushed over, grabbing for a carotid pulse. "She's near normal temp, we should – " Her hand was reaching for the code button. Wendy covered her hand and brought it down.

"No, too late for that. Let her go. It's for the best." Stupid girl, sloppy in her technique, sloppy in her uniform. She didn't care.

Esther stepped back from the bed, taking her hand out from under Wendy's. "I'll go alert the team and get things going, then," she said. She paused in the door, far enough away to find her courage. "You've been on the night shift here for six months. This makes, what, five?" Then the door hushed closed.

There it was. Wendy would never again be alone on the floor and free to give her mercies. It was time to move. She was ready, but a cold rush of frustration ruined the warmth of her accomplishment. She pocketed the girl doll reading the book and left the bedside.

As the night's activity faded back into the cool quiet, Wendy slumped into a chair. She was tired. The Third Rule had taken her all the way to the Oregon coast, but now there was no more west. In a departure from the Rule she'd sent inquiries north to Vancouver, where a new job already waited for her.

Maybe things would be different in a whole new country. Maybe she could practice her skill in peace. Surely that wasn't too much to ask, after all this time.

Chapter 1

The mellow sunshine of late May in Vancouver had teased open the peonies and rhododendrons, turning the tidy rows of small, postwar houses along the back streets of Dunbar into a postcard. Jackson idled his Subaru down to his first stop of the day, the six-room bungalow where Emily Shrop had lived for the past 45 years.

The flower boxes needed weeding and a few shingles on the roof were succumbing to the West Coast moss, only to be expected since Mr. Shrop had gone to his reward some six years before and Emily was in no shape to take over the chores. The concrete walkway was in fine form, though, leading up to the front door in an undamaged series of white slabs.

His eyes tracked along the twin edges of the walkway. The symmetry was perfect. The grass verge looked like it had been trimmed with a ruler. His gaze was caught by the lines and swept up towards the door, skipping along the regularity of the cracks between the slabs. A small bit of him thrilled at the wonderful pattern.

Knock it off, he told his head. The fascination faded away.

A twenty-ish woman with toffee skin and bright, dark eyes answered the doorbell. "Hi, Dahlia," Jackson said. "How're things?"

Dahlia's white teeth didn't flash into a big smile today, a first as far as he could remember. She was wearing the cornflower yellow version of the uniform, with Arbutus Home Care stencilled in blue above the polo shirt's pocket. Since Jackson's career choice to be a traveling massage therapist had made him an accidental specialist in geriatric and palliative care massage, they'd crossed paths at a number of houses and developed something more than a nodding acquaintance.

"Oh, Dr. Jackson, not so good today, I think," she replied in Filipino-accented English. "Mrs. Shrop hasn't been feeling good for a couple days now. She is in bed. She is always in bed, never in her chair anymore."

"I see." Something had happened, then. It was the usual way of things in palliative care, and they'd both seen it before - a brief illness or small injury would come along to break the fragile status quo and precipitate the last decline. "So, what was it?"

Dahlia's face, already serious, grew darker. "Nothing, Dr. Jackson. Nothing." They left the door and stepped through the foyer into the small living room.

"It's just Jackson, Dahlia, I'm not a doctor." It was an old joke between them, and brought a tinge of smile back to the care aide's face. "Well, let's see what I can do for her today. Is she still loving your jasmine ..." He faded to a stop in the living room doorway and felt his insides clench. His face grew cold, like he'd stepped in front of an open freezer.

The living room was spectacularly awful. Shelves and tables lined the confines of the ten-by-twelve space, loaded down with Hans Christian Anderson collectible plates, a massive porcelain doll collection and a long line of single-malt whiskey bottles from probably every distillery in the Highlands. There was only a small walking space to the hall and a big hole for Mrs. Shrop's easy chair.

Jackson found it difficult to push into the room. He felt like he was being shoved back, by what he had no idea. The room didn't feel right. His mind tried to find the room's natural geometry, the comfortable coexistence between furniture and walls and mementos that inevitably coalesced over the years. It was gone, replaced by a weirdness that made him want to leave.

Not now, he told his condition. The feeling subsided and he stepped into the room.

"Has anything changed here?" he asked.

Dahlia's eyebrows rose. "No, nothing has changed. Mrs. Shrop has not been to her chair since your last visit. She is in bed, waiting."

He made it through the objectionable space and down the hall to Emily Shrop's bedroom. His nose registered the usual smells of body, soap, medicine and the indefinable smell of age, this time tinged with the peaty scent of fine Scotch.

"About time, young man," came the voice from a mop of white sticking up in all directions out of deep feather pillows. "I know she's cute, but remember you're here to see me."

"Mrs. Shrop," blushed Dahlia, and left the room laughing. Jackson grinned. Dahlia might be cute. She was also married, with two kids and a husband back in Manila waiting for her sponsorship paperwork to bring them over.

The bedroom was cluttered, too, with more trinkets and the accoutrements of illness. A huge porcelain doll, two feet high and neatly dressed in a Scottish pinafore beneath a mass of red curls, stood on the seat of the platform rocker in the corner. A new addition, it ate up the space on that side of the bedroom. By rights it should be in the living room with the rest of the collection.

"Enough about my love life," he said, turning back to his patient. "I hear you're not well. Getting old, or something."

"Nonsense and balderdash," Mrs. Shrop announced, but there was the smallest wheeze to her voice. "So long as the girls keep my medicine coming I'll be fine."

At least they knew enough to keep the Glenlivet out of the bedroom. "Still three shots a day?"

"Prisoner's allowance, but it's all the doctor will prescribe. Makes the pills go down easier." Emily Shrop was, not to put too fine a point on it, a whiskey-soaked alcoholic. The small forest of pill bottles on the night table were propping up her hard-pressed liver, and the three shots staved off a shuddering withdrawal that would have been the end of her.

"All for the best," he said, and stepped up to the bedside. "Let's have a look at you, then." She was like one of her dolls. Emily Shrop had been blessed with clear, porcelain skin over fine features pared to their essentials by advancing age, the hair of a bleached-white kewpie doll, and eyes like tiger-eye beads, bright and startling blue.

Usually bright eyes. Usually clear skin. Today she was cloudy and pale, like he was seeing her through a mist. She said, "Quit staring, you're just like Dahlia. I haven't felt so good in weeks. My aches and pains are practically gone."

"Great to hear." Or not, he thought to himself.

He put his oil bottle and appointment book on the side table, stepped up to the bed and took a breath. He loosened his guard over the fascination inside his head and let it out a tiny bit. Then he drew back the bedsheets and looked.

Mrs. Shrop lay in her knee-length nightie and glowed. The clean lines of her face and head stood out in sharp relief. Her skull sat square and level on top of her spine, and then all hell broke loose. He could see it, all the way down, the brittleness of severe osteoporosis. Three failed thoracic vertebrae had collapsed her chest into a deep inward curve, and he could almost feel the bright sparkles of pain that emanated from the breaks. Her ribs bumped and rubbed into each other as she breathed. Below her ribcage it was like her body was barely held together, so weak were the connections of her spine and pelvis.

"What do you mean, your aches are gone?"

She lifted a hand to grasp his arm with a surprisingly strong grip. He could hear her shoulder creak. "I mean, I don't hurt, not hardly. Best I've felt since my last bender."

He frowned. "Then why aren't you getting up and around?"

Mrs. Shrop let her arm fall. "I don't feel like it. The pain's not holding me back, but I'm, I don't know, drained." For the first time a vague worry crossed her face. "Like somebody's pulled a plug somewhere and I can't get it back in."

He squinted and tried to figure out what he was seeing. It was a diminishment of sorts. Something was stealing her away.

She looked at him with those misted tiger eyes. "Yep, you see it, all right. What's the verdict, Dr. Jackson?"

The bed joined the wall at a pleasing angle that meshed with the night table and the door. Jackson closed his eyes and refused to be caught. It felt good to be so dangerously open. Go away, he told the thing in his head. He pushed against the inner door and tried to lock it down. He opened his eyes on the platform rocker in the corner and saw it was skewed. It begged to be nudged a hair to the right so the chair would line up with the corner and the big red-headed doll would face the bed.

The fact that he could see this – feel it, even – scared him. After three years, his hold on his condition was slipping.

Go away, he growled, closing his eyes again. Please.

When he opened his eyes he was back, and Mrs. Shrop was gazing at him. He reached for the oil bottle. "Dr. Jackson, yeah right. Roll onto your side, please. Your spine needs help, whether you feel it or not."

On the sidewalk, he turned once to look back at the neglected planters and the perfect walkway. He'd enjoyed his time with Mrs. S, and had done some good work with her. He didn't think he would be seeing her again. It was how the job rolled when you worked with the elderly. You got used to saying goodbye.

Still, he didn't leave with an easy heart. Emily Shrop shouldn't be that sick. She shouldn't be dying quite yet.

Taking the long way to her desk at the start of shift was almost a regular thing for Marilyn. Most days she came to work at Vancouver Police Headquarters a few minutes early so she could walk past other departments on her way to Community Policing. Covert Operations, Major Crimes and Organized Crime were interesting. Today she was taking a stroll past her favourite, the Emergency Response Team.

All the sections hummed with activity these days. One of the major companies in the West Coast energy industry had decided to allay concerns about the safety of liquefied natural gas exports by running an LNG tanker ship right into Vancouver's inner harbour. The PR stunt was due to take place in a few weeks and every environmental group, alternative energy lobbyist and professional protestor in the Western Hemisphere was gearing up for the event. The Vancouver Police Department had spent months trying to convince the city not to allow it. Now the whole building was running simultaneous planning sessions on everything from traffic management to riot control to full-bore terrorist attack. The tension of a coming storm was palpable in the air and quickened Marilyn's steps.

Briefing Room C was full of people. As Marilyn approached the windows looking into the long room she recognized officers from Organized Crime and Major Crimes. A few men and women in street clothes and visitor badges were deeply involved in the conversation, suggesting involvement from other agencies. She saw Inspector Takeda's trademark steel-grey buzz cut in the middle of one knot of people, the Emergency Response Team commander obviously playing a central role in whatever this was.

A constable she didn't recognize hustled past and into the room with a stack of photographs. Marilyn paused by the open doorway as he pinned a series of mug shots and long-lens surveillance images on the far wall. Some of the men in the photos looked mean enough to eat children for breakfast; others sported suits and briefcases like businessmen on their way to their first latte. It was a safe bet these were all bad guys, so she started at the top left and began scanning the faces into her memory.

"Constable Mathers!" Inspector Takeda's voice cracked through the room and two dozen sets of eyes swivelled towards the door. Takeda was staring at her, and he knew her name. She braced herself and returned his gaze. He pointed a finger. "I see you." He lowered his finger and turned back to the visitor next to him. The conversations restarted.

Unsure if she'd just been rebuked or rewarded, Marilyn headed for the elevator and up to Community Policing.

Wendy glowed with high purpose as she emptied the tiny packet of pure acetaminophen into the shot of Scotch. So much more powerful than ordinary Tylenol, she was certain this last dose was more than Mrs. Shrop's liver would take. Later tonight the old woman would be stepping out of her ruined body, and that was wonderful.

"Don't you be delaying my medicine," called Mrs. Shrop from her bedroom. It was so perfect that the death she'd chosen should also relieve this poor woman's terrible pains, if only for the last few days while it ate out her liver.

She hurried over to the bedside. Mrs. Shrop was in a full-blown sweat now; it wouldn't be long. The beautiful old woman grabbed for the glass. "Slàinte mhath!" she toasted. Wendy smiled, and glanced over at the porcelain Scottish doll to make sure it could see everything.

By happy coincidence Borden was standing on Wreck Beach looking right at the target when his cell phone growled into the first few bars of Yuve Yuve Yu. The LNG tanker was cruising up and down Georgia Strait beyond the mouth of Burrard Inlet, waiting for the last bureaucratic squabbling to settle down before sailing in to prepare for her big day. He let the phone thrash out more Mongolian warrior-rock as he watched the ship through binoculars. It was a ridiculous tub, looking like a lowrider cargo hull with four monstrous white boils erupting out of its deck. Tiny men scurried around the top of the huge tanks, cleaning and scrubbing until they gleamed.

He flipped open the phone just before it went to voicemail. It was ancient tech, but it only needed to remember one number and had no GPS tracker. Borden had chosen the take-no-prisoners ringtone because he knew the man on the other end of the call, a medieval son of a bitch with a gold pen and a briefcase. They had met long ago during the heady days of radical action in the West Coast old-growth rainforest, two kindred spirits lurking amongst the hippies. They'd all lived in rusted-out vans, sharing joints and plotting to save the big trees, but both of them had instantly recognized the other wolf in the fold. Borden spent his nights blowing up logging trucks and grapplers while his friend drove ceramic spikes into trees to mess with the fallers' chainsaws, and sometimes the fallers themselves. During daylight hours Borden had slept in the van, staying out of sight. His friend had spent the time talking, telling the hippies what they wanted to hear and learning to work the media.

Fast-forward 30 years or so, and guess which one of them had talked his way into the corner office of a major environ-mental concern.

"I'm here," Borden said into the phone.

"How's she look?" said the voice on the other end, a rich baritone gone a little sandy with the years.

"Like a sitting duck."

"Perfect. God, it's good to be working with you again. I know I've picked the right man for the job. When this is done, you'll be back on top of your world. Instead of - well, you know."

Borden crunched a shell into the sand with the toe of his boot. "You always were a bastard, you know that? I don't need reminding."

His friend oiled the waters, one of the skills that had taken him to the top floor. "I'm excited for you, really I am. This is the chance of a lifetime in your business. After this, any demolition job you want, you can write your own ticket."

The fuck of it was, Borden had no choice and they both knew it. It was either do this job and go down in the industrial espionage book of legends, or live with his current reputation and never get paid to light another fuse.

Still, it was a hell of a thing. "Last chance to call it off. This job won't simply inconvenience a few shareholders. It's going to have repercussions. Think about it, I mean really think about it. They'll run out of body bags. Are you okay with the fallout from this?"

"I am perfectly fine with the repercussions." The baritone got richer. "While this will be a terrible tragedy, we must all understand that the future of the earth itself is at stake. We will learn from an incident of this magnitude. Public opinion must turn against the stupid and harmful exploitation of fossil fuels and convince governments to seriously fund alternative energy sources. We owe it to the world to learn from this and move forward down a new road."

Borden smiled. "Nice speech. Write that yourself?"

He heard a quiet, dry chuckle. "Well, it wouldn't do to have someone else write me a disaster response before the actual disaster, would it? What about you? Are you ready to rock?"

Borden gazed out at the boat executing a lazy turn in the Strait and beamed. "I'm fine with it. Everything's in place to do the job."

"Wonderful. You know the deadline." There was the briefest pause. "You're the best at this, I know it and so do you. Time for you to be king of the hill again." The phone clicked. Borden folded it and put it back in his pocket.

The LNG tanker was swinging around with all the grace of a pregnant water buffalo, leaving behind a wide, sweeping wake. The boat looked as ridiculous now as it had in the photograph, months ago on a café table in Saskatoon.

He'd been limping then, still smarting from a botched contract. It had been a simple job - bomb an oil refinery into a seven-day shutdown so somebody could profit from the spike in prices - ruined by pure bad luck. His foot had slipped on a patch of oil on some metal stairs and a sharp corner had gone right through his coveralls. Loose oil at a refinery, who'd have expected that? He'd had to abort, bleeding from a deep puncture and leaving a satchel of high explosive to detonate outside the employees' dining hall.

He shook his head in the early morning air. Admit the

truth, he told himself. One bad contract could be rotten luck. The oil refinery had been his third failure in a row. In the industrial espionage world, that meant only one thing - forced retirement for the old guy.

The invitation had been phrased as a chance for old friends to reconnect, but Borden knew different the moment the photo landed on the table between them. It was a breathtaking statement. It was radical action all over again. It was redemption.

"You'll have whatever you need," his friend had said.

Now here he was, once again standing on the battlefield. The target floated out there and soon it would come sailing right to him. All the supplies sat in a warehouse on the North Shore.

He turned away from the water and trudged back over the sand towards the trees. The beach was almost deserted this early in the morning, but one beach hippie who'd obviously spent the night in the woods was now at the water's edge over by the rocks saying good morning to the world. He looked the part, with long, shaggy blond hair and smooth muscles without a scrap of fat. Wreck Beach was a nudie place and Borden could see, even at this distance, that the boy had an impressive package.

The beach bum stopped whatever sun-welcoming thing he was doing and swiveled his head to look at Borden. He couldn't even see the colour of the kid's eyes, but felt the intensity of the stare.

It took an effort to turn back to the trees and start walking again. Curiosity will get you killed, kid, he thought as he climbed the stairs to the city. I hope you get caught in the blast zone.

Chapter 2

"This is just a formality," Emma Jacobs found herself saying, "something I do when my care aides experience their first loss." It wasn't a formality, it was an uncomfortable obligation she ordered herself to perform with all her new staff, but Wendy Corbett emanated such calm composure that Emma almost felt apologetic for the interview. Wendy was a nurse, an old pro like Emma had been before she started the Arbutus Home Care Agency. Emma was lucky to have her while Wendy's American credentials made their way through the Canadian system.

"I understand," said the big woman, sitting on the edge of a visitor chair as if she might break it. "You have to know what your girls are made of." She lifted her hands off the lap of a plain blue dress and gave herself a little top-to-bottom wave, from the nurse's cap pinned to her black hair to a pair of new, nonslip, waffle-tread sneakers. "How do I measure up?"

Emma smiled and relaxed a little. She'd arranged the office decor to put visitors at ease. Her business was all about helping families through a rough time in their lives, and the room helped them feel reassured. A handful of comfortable chairs in velvet the colour of old port clustered loosely around the front of the desk. A vase of roses and lavender perfumed the space and accented the warm, peach walls and cream carpet. Emma drew her own comfort from the massive oak desk across which she and Wendy were talking, and the two

20-inch curved screen monitors off to one side. The expanse between them held only a green blotter, a wire tray full of files and a small, brass abacus. "I can see I won't need to worry about you at all. Now, to the details." She spun to face the large monitors and swept her fingers over the recessed ergonomic keyboard. The left screen blossomed into a photo of breakers rolling onto a silver beach, and the right one opened onto her master spreadsheet. With two clicks she replaced the screensaver with a report. "You took care of Mrs. Shrop for almost," she consulted the spreadsheet, "three weeks. The doctor's report says she died of sudden liver failure, no other complications besides long-term alcoholism. Please give me your observations."

Wendy's cap nodded as she thought. "The old dear did love her Scotch. I performed my 6 a.m. check and she'd passed. I'm afraid there's nothing much more to say, all else was routine." She paused. "You're admirably thorough. Do you keep records like this on all your clients?"

Emma watched the screen as she tapped in the new information. "My clients, my aides, everything. Statistics don't lie. I catch problems, make improvements, keep my costs down, all thanks to good records." She gestured at the wire tray, stacked high with file folders. "It's one reason we're so popular. I have a waiting list. Frankly, I could use three more of you." Emma flipped over to a charts page and zoomed into one of them, filling the screen with a long series of horizontal bars moving across a timeline. She glanced at Wendy. "I know you're experienced enough to take this in stride, but I feel like I should apologize. Three weeks is a short time to be with a client. I try to give my new staff an easy entrance to the business. I thought Mrs. Shrop had more time than she did."

Wendy laughed, a low, rumbling thing as big as the rest of her. "You don't have to worry your head about that, I'm sure," she said, the words rolling out with a hint of a Maritime burr. "You're a nurse, too, am I right?" She pointed at Emma's diploma on the wall. "We're tough old birds. I'm certain we've both handled a few pucker-up moments. Why, not long ago I was working in surgical recovery and we got an old biker fresh from a bowel resection. Tattoos like you've never seen, in the most unlikely places! That man must have had some impressive meds tolerance, because he popped out of his anesthetic and announced to one and all that he was going home. If he'd stood up I swear his insides would have hit the floor. I had to put my hand on his chest." She placed one palm on the corner of the desk and pushed, and it actually sank into the carpet.

Emma felt a smile take over her face. She'd retired from nursing to start the Arbutus Home Care Agency. Numbers were better than people any day, but she realized she missed the banter. "I'll bet that stopped him. I once had this tiny woman in Colonoscopy with the strongest cheeks ..." They spent a few minutes sharing stories and laughing.

Wendy rolled off the last chuckle with a sigh and said, "My, this has been delightful, but I'm sure you have other things to attend to. There's no need to concern yourself about my welfare. In fact," she leaned forward, eyes bright with an idea, "why don't you save your younger care aides a bit of grief? Give me the hard ones, dear. The ones that might not have much time left. I'll see them through their final days."

Before Emma could answer, Ruth knocked and stuck her angel-of-mercy face in from Reception. "I'm so sorry to interrupt, Ms. Jacobs, but I have three callers waiting and you're five minutes late for your next appointment. They're out here." Another distraught family needing help for their housebound elder. The Agency had a growing reputation in a growth industry.

"Thank you, Ruth, please tell them I'll be right out." She turned back to Wendy. "You know what? I'm going to take you up on that. Every year I lose care aides because they get too attached to their patients." She pulled up the spreadsheet again, clicking over to a sheet of client names, and studied it. "I'm going to give you Mrs. Creehy. She's not near dying yet, but she's a handful. Let me know how it goes."

Wendy enveloped Emma's hand in hers and stood. Before she let go Emma added, "You know that a nursing cap isn't part of the uniform, right? In fact, I don't think it's used anywhere these days."

The starched, white wings of the cap peeked around the edges of the woman's dark hair. She touched it and said, "This? Oh, I've worn it for so long it's like a part of me. If you don't really mind too much?" She put on what Emma recognized as Nursing Smile Number 3, the one that said the question you'd heard was not really negotiable. Emma let the matter go.

Wendy left and the room was quiet. Emma clicked the abacus, enjoying a breath of empty space and quiet before the next interview. Then she opened the door to Reception.

By now the morning pill was a long-established reflex. Jackson had the cap off, the wad of cotton out and the thing down before he was even fully awake. He stayed in bed a minute longer and watched the slim edge of the sun's first rays glance around the corner of his bedroom window.

His eyelids felt sticky with sleep. This was the third lousy night since getting the call about Emily Shrop's passing. As much as he hated the sickness inside his head, he'd learned over the past three years to give it a grudging, guarded trust. It might dazzle and distract him, and once it had made him a danger to himself and others, but his condition didn't lie, not exactly. It had never shown him things that weren't really there. In Emily Shrop's place he'd sensed - what? A coldness.

At least his condition hadn't embarrassed him. Not this time. In recent months a few home visit patients had noticed him staring at things - a grandfather clock with a swinging pendulum, the pseudo-random flames in an electric fireplace, the splashes in a small water sculpture. He'd been drawn to the tinkling waterfall, even stuck his fingers in the water, so fascinated he hadn't heard his patient asking what the hell.

The sliver of sunshine touched the floor. He swung out of bed to grab a t-shirt and shorts out of the dresser. A framed photo sat on top, showing a woman with the plumpness of a country baker standing next to a straight young man with a world of confidence in his eyes, both of them wearing swim suits and smiles. A dark swath of mountain lake lay behind them, with a wall of trees rising up out of sight beyond the water. Her ice-blue eyes drooped at the corners, a little more careworn than the young man's, and he was two hands taller, but their facefuls of freckles over high cheekbones and identical riots of red curls - his trimmed close and hers bouncing to her shoulders - confirmed the family connection. "Hi, Ma," he said to the photo. It had been taken four summers ago. Before the troubles.

His mirror was to the right of the picture. Same close-cropped red curls, same freckles. Same massage therapist's chiseled shoulders. No paunch yet at 24, and his bicycle was going to keep it that way. The eyes staring back at him looked a little older, though. More like his mother's.

Time for the test. He went over to the window and looked towards Burrard Inlet, the wide swath of ocean between the

North Shore mountains and Point Grey, the rocky thumb with
the neighbourhoods of Kitsilano, Dunbar, West Point Grey and
the University of British Columbia on top and Wreck Beach at
its tip. He could see a fair patch of water from his vantage
point at the base of the thumb, next to Kits Beach. A
freshening breeze blew against the incoming tide and rippled
the water into small whitecaps, tipping each one with a sparkle
from the morning sun. Half a dozen container ships swung
around their anchors in deep water waiting their turn at the
docks, with a big, empty space among them waiting for the
Northern Sea Otter, the LNG tanker everyone was talking
about.

He watched. The sparkles on each wave cast bright, needle-
thin spears of light to the cardinal points of the compass for a
millisecond and then winked out, a thousand of them every
second. The waves rolled in regiments towards the land, visible
evidence of the deep tide underneath pushing in towards the
shore with a thousand miles of quiet strength. The effect was
mesmerizing. The condition within Jackson's head loved what
it was seeing. It wanted him to stay there and gaze.

He closed his eyes and turned away. The pill did its work.
When he opened his eyes again he was standing in a normal
room staring at a normal wall.

He could turn away. He was okay to leave the house.

First impressions were everything. Wendy stood erect and
immaculate on the front doorstep in a crisp, new Arbutus
Home Care dress shirt and the stiff nursing cap with its single
black band pinned to her hair. She'd honed her presentation

over the years to project the image of a solid wall of competence coming through the door. She set her overnight bag down and knocked.

Sue Creehy was the daughter, and Wendy could see at once that she was tight as an anchor chain on a windy day. "You must be the new home care," Sue began, the words scarcely getting out around the tension in her throat.

"Nurse Wendy. Oh, my dear girl." She stepped through and took the surprised woman into her arms, an embrace Sue resisted for the barest moment, then fell into. Wendy stood solid and warm and let her uniform soak up the tears. They would wash out.

"That's all right, Sue, I'm here now. Why don't you set about telling me what you need to?"

They sat in the musty living room. Wendy could sense the sick woman in the bedroom next door, but her patient could wait. The family always needed to tell you all the special tips they thought you didn't know. At length Sue ran out of words. "Remember, black tea in the morning. And turn her pillow every few hours, that settles her down." She took a deep breath, coming back from the world of details into the close, dark present. "You know the hardest part? Mum's like an old battleaxe, tough as nails. She can hardly get out of bed without her canes anymore, but the doctor says she's got plenty of time left. A year, maybe. That's why I called the agency. I need the help, you know? I can't watch her for that long." She realized where she was and gasped, almost embarrassed. "Oh! I'm sitting in Mum's chair. She won't like that."

The tears threatened again. "She won't be hearing of it from me," Wendy said. "Now, Sue, I'm here for the night, why don't you head on home to bed? Have a glass of wine. You've done a good job here, now you need your rest."

"Okay." All she'd needed was the excuse. They both rose

and Sue headed for the door. "I'll be here at eight," she said.

"And so will the care aide on the day shift. Get some rest."

Sue paused once more at the open door. "Don't worry," Wendy cut her off, and placed her hand down onto Sue's shoulder. "It's all fine." She turned the woman around and closed the door behind her.

Time to visit the real patient. This was marvellous good fortune. First Mrs. Shrop, then this one, and every prospect of many more to come now that she'd made the arrangements. In this simple care aide's job she had stumbled upon a whole population that needed her special talents more than any other. Here in private homes, alone with her charges in the night, Wendy could give them what they and their families so desperately called out for. It was utterly perfect.

A low moan came from the other room. "I'm coming, Mrs. Creehy." On her way through the living room she paused. The place was filled with the detritus of a long life and it needed adjusting. She took Mrs. Creehy's chair and turned it away from the fireplace to face the front door. A bust of Napoleon, of all things, occupied center stage on the fireplace mantel. She took it down, replacing it with a candle positioned off to the left. Napoleon was relegated to a corner shelf, turned to face a window. Half a dozen other changes came to Wendy's practised eye, then she surveyed the room. She felt the difference with pride. The room fairly whooshed you towards the exits now. That felt right.

The moan sounded again. Mrs. Creehy was glaring at her from the pillow as Wendy rounded the corner, hair still black and eyes still hard as flint in a face like a crumpled grocery sack. Old-fashioned pancake makeup tried to fill in the cracks but kept falling out. "Didn't know they made nurses in extra-large. At least you look the part. What took you so long? My pain pills are over there." She waved a hand at the dresser, and let out another moan for emphasis. An old battleaxe, for sure.

"And a fine hello to you, too, Mrs. Creehy. Now you relax, we both know that's only the pain talking. My name is Nurse Wendy, and while I'm here you've got nothing to worry about." She popped the proper dosage of Naproxen into Mrs. Creehy's outstretched hand and took the woman's vitals. Heart strong as an ox, but the breathing was off. Shallow, like - a picture on the dresser confirmed it. Mr. and Mrs. Creehy in younger days at a fancy dress ball, both with cigarettes in their hands. No cigarettes or ashtrays sullied the bedroom now, no smell of smoke. Was it any wonder the woman was crabby.

Mrs. Creehy was examining Wendy with those flinty eyes. "Nothing to worry about, eh?" she concluded. "Not so sure about that." She puckered into a sourfaced frown and the makeup radiated spiderwebs out to her hairline with an almost-audible crack. When Wendy lifted her shoulders up to reposition the pillows, the frown squeezed into a grimace.

"It's your back, isn't it?" Wendy could see it. The way Mrs. Creehy twisted, the way her right leg curled over the left, the signs were all there. "Here, let me - " She grabbed a small throw pillow off a chair in the corner, hiked up her patient's right butt cheek enough to slip it under, and let the old woman settle back into the new position. The sour expression unpuckered a little.

"Maybe you know what you're doing," Mrs. Creehy allowed.

"Yes, maybe." The bedroom was none too neat. Wendy picked up the clothes, stacked the bodice ripper novels, and tilted the ballroom picture so it faced the window. She moved the corner chair a little down one wall and aimed it into not quite anywhere in particular. She dusted the heavy, bevelled mirror hanging above it, nudging the frame a hair to the right. The room felt better at once. It felt like a long-held sigh was leaving the place at last.

"Hey! Quit messing with my things. Turn that picture back, I can't see my Jim." Without a word Wendy turned the photograph almost back to where it was. A small concession. The room continued its long breath outward, and Mrs. Creehy was asleep a minute later.

So it was to be the lungs, then. Wendy had a superfine needle in her private tool collection that would do the trick nicely. It would be invisible. It would appear natural. From the sound of her patient's shallow snores, it would be quick.

The warrior woman figurine was a pewter masterpiece, only seven inches tall but with a fine chain-mail skirt over her muscular legs and a splendid double-curved axe slung over her shoulder. Wendy placed it in the bedroom on a bookshelf weighed down with Churchill's complete memoirs, high enough so it could see everything.

"What's that? Bring it over, let me see." Mrs. Creehy was awake. Four days into this new assignment and it seemed like she was always awake. Wendy hesitated, but Mrs. Creehy had the right. She retrieved the figurine and handed it over.

Mrs. Creehy took it, staring hard at the detailing. "That's me, isn't it?" she said. Wendy nodded. "Yeah, Sue always calls me an old battleaxe. Don't think she even remembers that was my Jim's term for me. My old battleaxe, he used to say. Romantic cuss, right to the end." She handed it back. "Don't imagine I'll think any better of you for bringing that in. I've still got my eye on you." She gave Wendy another glare. "I don't trust you."

"My, but you've got no problem speaking your mind," replied

Wendy, replacing the angel on the shelf. "What a fine thing to be remembered for."

Chapter 3

Jackson pulled up to Elora Creehy's place, a vine-covered brick bungalow in Little Italy with a postage stamp front yard that perfumed the entire neighbourhood with lavender. The old lady's lower back had jammed up and thrown her into bed for a week, but that was bread and butter work for a massage therapist. She'd be up on her canes again and bossing the care aides around in no time.

"Hey, Florita," he greeted the young woman who answered his knock, "beautiful day."

Florita was tall and South Seas-dark and serious and still took everything he said literally. She leaned out the door to examine the sky and came back with, "Yes, it is. Mrs. Creehy is ready for you."

"That's great, has there been any improvement?" He got three steps into the living room before the room itself actually pushed him backwards. Jackson retreated a step and almost collided with her. "Oh, sorry, my mistake," he fumbled an apology as he reversed to the doorway and tried not to show the trickle of icewater that was running down his spine.

"She has not improved, no. What is it?" Florita was standing in the center of the living room like nothing was wrong. She didn't feel it.

Don't be doing this, he scolded himself, but it was no good. Even from the foyer he could feel something like a chilly wind blowing against him from the living room door. Except there was no wind, not a breath of one. Only his imagination insisting that he go no further.

Florita peered at him, getting ready to inquire after his health some more, or maybe his stability. The cold non-wind pushed its invisible hand against his chest. This is not happening, he told himself, and strode back into the room.

Mrs. Creehy's living room was pure French colonial, whitewashed walls with oak trim over a plank floor waxed to golden perfection. Spindle-legged end tables and an oak mantle supported leatherbound volumes bookended with marble busts under stained-glass wall sconces. Everything had settled into its natural place years before.

The room was dominated by a dark leather easy chair in front of the fireplace. The chair flickered a sickly green on the edge of Jackson's vision, somehow part of whatever wasn't right. This is a bad idea, he told himself. Then he closed his eyes, cracked open the door to his condition and opened them again.

It was like someone had stretched the cords of the room's web of comfort and order, leaving a misshapen malevolence in its place. The angles of the walls and the strong presence of the fireplace were unchanged, but the rest of the room had been twisted somehow. The result was repellent and vaguely nauseating.

"What is it?" Florita asked again, and Jackson realized he'd ignored her.

"Nothing, I - have you done any rearranging in here?"

Filipinos would be polite to an armed robber, but that just about found Florita's limit. Her perpetual seriousness took on a touch of ice. "We do not touch the client's things," she said.

"No, of course not, sorry. There's a few things out of place," he said as he waded into the living room. Mrs. Creehy's chair was out of its divots in the thick carpet; with a push he put it back, and the legs suddenly matched up with the fireplace and the 45-degree angle shooting from the far corner. The onyx bust of Napoleon, Mrs. Creehy's pride and joy, was somehow over on a shelf and turned into the wall; he replaced it on the mantel where it immediately pulled much of the room back from the brink. A bookshelf had three books pulled half-out; he knocked them back in, and somehow that made a difference. The cold wind eased, then it was gone.

Florita was shocked. "We do not touch the client's things," she repeated, then, "but that does look better. How did that get out of place?" She was looking at the bust. Jackson shrugged, and moved past into the bedroom.

"Can't you ever get those red curls under control? About time you showed your face, my back is killing me," said Mrs. Creehy from her bed. "What kept you?"

He followed the fine curve that arced between the dresser and the card table over to the side of the bed. Mrs. Creehy's squat body was subtly twisted under the sheets. Her own hair was a mass of black wool, and her thick makeup showed a patchwork of hairline fractures that radiated out from her pursed lips in a fascinating and intricate design. He shut his lids tight and said, Go away. He'd said it twice already between the living room and here. This time he bit down hard on the inside of his lower lip and squeezed his eyes around the starburst of pain. When he opened his eyes the lines were gone. The cage door was shut.

"Keeping the devil from the door, Mrs. Creehy, you know how it is." He could still see how twisted she was under the sheets, keeping the pressure off her lower back. She had a jammed facet joint in the lumbar spine, held out of place by a mess of spasmed paraspinal muscles. He could do some good here. Jackson stepped up to the bed, making way for his

appointment book on the shelf by moving aside a medieval
warrior woman figurine.

"You Irishmen, you're all alike," she said. "Get to work,
then."

As he did his job, Jackson checked his patient over very
carefully. So far as he could tell Mrs. Creehy was nowhere close
to dying.

"Excuse me, dear, but - did you do any rearranging in here
today?" Wendy kept the bolt of fear that shot through her from
showing as she went through the handoff routine with Florita.
The skinny, serious girl with the deadpan face clouded up at
the suggestion.

"We do not touch the client's things," she said. Then she
added, "You are the second person to ask me that today. The
massage man, he wanted to know it, too."

The living room had been undone. Wendy struggled for
nonchalance. "Ah. So he was the one?"

Florita bobbed her head once as she handed over Mrs.
Creehy's chart. "He touched things. Like that." She gestured
over her shoulder at Napoleon. "He is strange like that
sometimes. But he does good work." That was about as solid an
endorsement as Florita ever gave. Wendy let the girl go, eager
to be alone with her patient. She needed to think. She needed
to put things to rights.

This had never happened before. Almost every special
adjustment she'd made to the living room was put back.
Somehow, the massage boy had seen her work. Nobody had
ever seen the work before, not since her own mother who'd

taught her. At least the angel in the bedroom was untouched.

Mrs. Creehy's back pain seemed to be better. She spent the evening complaining about the crepes, the pillows, and the evening news. At 11 p.m. Wendy put her to bed and retired to the little care aide's room, leaving the light off.

At one with the night, she ran through her liturgy.

The First Rule was Ease The Suffering. Elora Creehy was getting better, another day or two and she'd be back in her chair. But what then? She was too infirm on her canes to go anywhere unassisted, she pined for cigarettes she could no longer have, and her Jim had gone on before, leaving her to make the family miserable with her pain. Yes, she decided.

The Second Rule was Don't Harm The Healthy. Elora Creehy was in bed and in pain.

The answer was yes.

The Third Rule was When They Suspect, Move West. Far too early for anything like that, she'd only just arrived. Besides, it wasn't a concern now that she'd set things up so marvellously with Emma Jacobs ˗ although she'd have to remember the woman's love of statistics.

The answer was yes.

She waited, sitting on the edge of the guest bed. When the bedside clock read three in the morning she lifted the syringe off the night stand and pulled back the plunger.

A superfine needle, properly handled, left no mark. A syringeful of air injected into a major vein traveled swiftly through the heart, into the arterial circulation and from there either to the lungs or the brain, where it would get caught in the forest of smaller arterioles and cause an immediate and catastrophic backlog, and that would be that. A moment's surprise, a second's sensation of dizziness or crushing weight, and Mrs. Creehy would be free.

The bedroom was dark, but Wendy knew the way. She was

almost to the bed, needle out and poised, when she saw the two tiny, diamond-hard pinpoints of light. "Told you I had my eye on you," Mrs. Creehy growled.

A smart blast behind her left ear exploded stars inside Wendy's skull. She staggered back as the cane whistled through the air again, then the old woman was out of bed and howling. Wendy gasped as three clawed fingernails sailed out of the black and scrabbled over her cheek and neck. Mrs. Creehy was fighting with everything she had. Wendy threw herself back at the old lady and the two of them landed on the bed, Mrs. Creehy yowling and thrashing underneath her.

It had been years since anyone fought back like this. Wendy was a big woman, and now she used her size. She spidered herself over the bed, careful not to put so much weight on the old lady that she'd break bones. Mrs. Creehy let out a grunt and a wheeze, but she was controlled. Wendy fumbled for the needle. Find a vein and the struggle would be done.

The yowling was over. She was running out of wind, poor dear. Then came the brilliant idea. Wendy laid the needle aside and gently, with the greatest of love, put a little more of her weight onto the bed. Break no bones, leave no marks. Just press.

She could feel the old lady underneath her, still trying to kick and move. This was so personal, so truly magnificent, the heat of Wendy's compassion rose through her like a wave. She really was the most perfect person for such a difficult and special calling, even her body was built for it. Over the course of a couple of minutes, the thrashing slowed. Then it stopped.

Another minute for good measure and it was done. Wendy pushed up, switched on the bedside lamp and gazed down at her handiwork, and gasped again as a drop of brilliant red splashed down by three other drops on Mrs. Creehy's right cheek. Wendy's neck was bleeding. She was leaving a mark.

Five minutes in the bathroom stopped the bleeding from the one deeper scratch. Wendy spent the time she needed to clean up the bedroom and scrub underneath the old lady's nails. As the new sun was beginning its rise she went hunting for Mrs. Creehy's pancake makeup before making the morning call.

Kitsilano Beach was why Jackson willingly paid Mrs. Castelli's outlandish rents. Her three-storey brownstone apartment building fronted onto Balsam Street on the last sloping block before it joined Cornwall. Across Cornwall Street the grass and huge trees of Kits Beach Park softened the city's edges, and beyond that a wide crescent of fine sand washed up by Burrard Inlet and dotted with huge driftwood logs. It was Jackson's backyard, his exercise ground and meditation spot. Every time he stepped off the sidewalk and onto the grass he felt the city slip into the background.

The day had fulfilled its promise of sunshine and heat and Vancouverites were making the most of it. A few people splashed about in the early June water. A quartet of male models lobbed a volleyball on the grass over the heads of strollers and dog-walkers. Jackson ducked through a couple of frisbee flightpaths on his way to a prime bit of real estate in the lee of a huge cedar log, cleared the sand of shells and trash, and snapped open a red-checked cloth from his picnic basket. He was the first one here for the weekly potluck. A plateful of triple-garlic pistachio hummus and veggie dippers stayed in the basket with a cooler pack as he waited for the others.

Charles and Georgia waved from the bus stop and made their way across the grass. Charles was coming off a shift in the emergency room at St. Paul's Hospital downtown, and Jackson could tell from the way he carried his six-foot-two on the balls of his feet, practically fast-forwarding through the trees, that it had been a hectic day. Georgia was holding him down with one arm linked around his and the other holding a shopping bag and sandals, her bare feet on the grass moving like she and the earth owned each other. Georgia was the Kitsilano version of old money and spent her days charming cash out of Vancouver's elite for various charities and worthy causes. They were the West Side's own Clark Kent and Grace Kelly.

Charles stripped down to his swim trunks without breaking stride as he stepped up to the log, finishing the job of shaking off the day and saying in a deep baritone, "That feels better! Tried the water yet?" Georgia leaned over to hand Jackson their goodies and smiled through the falling locks of her off-blonde pageboy, then slipped the dress off her one-piece suit and got comfortable on the sand. Jackson moved over to make room for them and added their contributions to his in the cooled hamper - a wheel of Brie and a jar of rosemary fig sauce, water crackers, and a chilly bottle that was not the apple juice it claimed to be.

"Not yet," he replied, "I was waiting for -" and both Georgia and Charles looked up over his right shoulder and waved.

"Hey," came a slow voice from above and behind him, "looks like the party's started already." Leaf kicked off a pair of leather sandals and handed Jackson a tray of hand-rolled sushi. He wore his usual rainbow surfer shorts and nothing else, and already sported a deep tan that highlighted long, blond curls. A few others on the sand called out hellos and he waved back, connecting with each of them.

Georgia gave him a hug. "Great to see you. How's life on the beach?"

He spread his arms and turned in a circle, taking in the whole city. "Perfect days, you know? The tide comes in, the tide goes out, and I'm here to watch it all."

"The tide's pretty high now," Jackson observed. "Last one in!" With a whoop and a holler all four of them jumped up and ran for the ocean. Ten steps in from the seaweed line had them waist-deep and diving. The icy water gave Jackson a full-body slap as he sliced through an incoming wave and surfaced with a gasp.

He dove again. The water was clear and crisp, chilled by the open ocean rolling in to the shore. His skin tingled but he stayed down, hovering above the sand. The pulse of the tide ran over and through him, rippling the sand with its passing. It was a sensation he could never get enough of, and never quite give himself over to. At last his air ran low. He reached for the surface and did a whale-breach backflop, complete with blowhole splutter, getting three good laughs for his efforts.

Leaf was bobbing a few feet away, crouched down in the chest-deep water. "Hey Jackson, hang for a sec. Do you feel it?"

Jackson stilled and took up Leaf's stance. "Feel what?"

Leaf was looking at the waves. "Any second now. And ... there."

He felt it. One moment the rolling waves subtly pushed him towards shore, and the next the pushing had ceased. It was an infinitesimal change, but clear to Jackson's sense.

"Slack tide!" they both yelled. The water was as high as it was going to get. The muscles of the ocean would rest for half an hour before inexorably pulling the tide back to Japan. Leaf threw an arm over his shoulder and they waded back to supper.

The food was delicious. People occupied every corner of the park, soaking up the sun and moving languidly through the gathering evening in that fabulous Brownian motion that was a hundred different patterns all happening at once. The

volleyball guys were still at it on the grass, forcing occasional
walkers to dodge and curse. Jackson munched brie and
crackers, leaning into the log and listening to Georgia tell
fundraising stories. Charles was rapt, eyes on his wife. He and
Charles enjoyed a solid friendship that went back a long ways;
Jackson had walked him down the aisle to join hands with a
radiant Georgia nearly seven years ago. Leaf, reaching for
more veggies, was absorbing Georgia's words but looking
everywhere, taking in everything. They'd known Leaf for a few
summers, ever since he had walked up to one of their potlucks
with chocolate-dipped strawberries and rounded out the tight-
knit foursome. Jackson loved them all. Years into their shared
friendship, the connections between them practically
glimmered in the air.

Georgia was telling tales from a recent party, a fundraiser
for a care home that specialized in dementia patients. "I
slapped tags on them with exotic names from around the
world, and labelled all the appetizers with nonsense words.
After ten minutes I took the tags away. If they couldn't name
who they were talking to, they had to stay quiet. If they
couldn't ask for a food by its new name, they went hungry."

"With that crowd?" said Charles. "They must have gone
nuts."

"They found out how much dementia takes from you. They
were - generous." She sipped her apple juice to a round of
applause.

A freshening breeze blew in from the water and wafted a
strand of hair across her face. Jackson's eyes followed the
movement. The puff of wind flipped up a corner of the
tablecloth, riffled a sunbather's towel farther up the sand, then
rose to play among the chestnut trees. Rank after rank of
translucent spring leaves responded to the breeze in a smooth,
coordinated wave, rolling into a sinuous dance that was the

very wind made visible. With a last tug at the topmost leaf the breeze was gone and the trees stilled. He kept looking, longing to see it again.

Georgia was on to the next story, a new venture with a group building micro-housing for the homeless. Jackson snapped his eyelids closed and didn't open them again until he was once again looking at her. She nodded a welcome-back without breaking stride, saying, "So their target demographic is younger people, the ones who need a little help to get off the streets. It's an honour to be fundraising for them. With a roof over their heads these young people can accomplish anything."

Charles had his doctor gaze on and was staring directly at Jackson. It was the first time in three years he'd seen that professionally-blank, appraising look. Stop it, Jackson thought, keeping his own eyes on Georgia. You don't need to do that.

Leaf was pulling together a small pile of sand and giving Georgia a thousand-watt grin, wise to her latest attempt to help him out. "Thanks but no, sister," he said, his hands forming the sandpile into a little box. "I'm doing all right." It was his standard response to her concerns and usually the end of the conversation.

This time Georgia persisted. "Are you really? We love you, you know that, but all I ever see you with is pretty much the clothes on your back. We don't even know where you go at night." She had a point there; even Jackson had no idea where Leaf's crib was.

Leaf picked up a second handful of sand and plopped it on top of the first, shaping it into a rough pyramid. He poked a hole in one side as a door. "Georgia, really, you don't need to worry about me. This beach? This city? Those mountains?" He waved a hand over his shoulder at the sloping neighbourhoods of West Vancouver climbing up from the water. "That's my home. I have more beds than I need, all over the place. And yeah, one of them is under a roof with proper sheets and everything." He gestured at the little sand house. "But right now, on a warm June night, I'll take this one." He leaned over, squishing the house with one knee, and gave Georgia a hug. "Thanks for asking, though."

"Whoa, heads up!" came a call from the grass. Jackson saw a phosphorescent red streak, rocket-fast, blur out of nowhere across his vision and heard a thoing!, and then Leaf's arms were stretched out behind Georgia's head with a volleyball between his hands. "Nice one," yelled the beach buff, "toss it over here."

Charles was on his feet and snatched the ball from Leaf. "Catch!" he said, and the ball went thoing! again, this time off the beefcake's forehead. The guy went down and his three buddies stepped over him, forming a waxed-pec skirmish line.

A surge of adrenalin lifted Jackson to his feet. The world snapped into bright relief. The three guys in front of them had paused, maybe to see if this was really going to happen, maybe to measure their opponents, but the hesitation wouldn't last. Red Speedo, on the left, was tensing his left leg and inching his shoulders off-balance to his right, aiming for a dodge to their flank. Pec Junior, the smallest of the three but wider and made of iron, seemed to be ballooning himself up in preparation for a bowling-ball rush. Nipple Rings on the right was gathering his courage; Charles could take care of him, no problem.

Jackson could see that Pec Junior was going to move first. The guy screwed his back foot into the sand and an almost-visible disturbance shot through the air to a point halfway between Jackson and Charles. He was aiming to take them both on. Keeping his own feet where they were, Jackson shifted his stance to the right, breaking the line.

Pec Junior stopped, his plan wrecked before it had begun.

A flash on the left told him Red Speedo was making his

move, a wide arc of shimmering air telegraphing the sidestepping dodge as plain as day. Jackson spread his arm out and shifted one foot to the left, cutting off the arc. Red Speedo stumbled, a look of confusion wiping the fight off his face.

"Hey boys." Leaf flowed to his feet, one hand clamping onto Jackson's shoulder and sending out what felt like a palpable wall of force that pushed him aside. The skirmish line broke like waves on rock, Pec Junior taking a step back.

"Uh, hey, Leaf. Didn't see you there," he mumbled, unclenching his hands. "These friends of yours?" He picked up the ball while Red Speedo and Nipple Rings held back their fuming friend, now bleeding from the nose. Red Speedo was still staring at Jackson, looking confused and nervous. "Listen, we're really sorry. We'll be more careful." Without wasting time about it they grabbed their gear and left.

Charles, still vibrating, turned back to Georgia. "You all right?" She said yes and he turned to Leaf. "Thanks. That was kind of impressive. You know those monkeys?"

Leaf was sitting again, reaching for sushi. "Yeah, we've met. Monkeys, that's a little reductive but kind of accurate."

Charles reached for his cup and took a drink. "Well, they sure knew you. What the hell happened there?"

"Nothing really. Just the law." Leaf pointed his chopsticks towards the forest of Stanley Park, over on the edge of downtown. "If you live with Nature for awhile you get to know Her laws, right? They're simple enough. If you want to stop a monkey, be a lion. Works every time."

They wrapped up the potluck in relative quiet, Jackson finishing the hummus so he wouldn't have leftovers. Charles kept stealing glances at him, that doctor gaze coming out again. "What?" he finally asked.

"You were stopping them," Charles said.

"It was amazing," added Georgia. "You freaked them out.

The one in the red speedo went from hard-on to pimple in about half a second."

The visual put a hitch in Charles' stride, but he rallied. "Amazing. That's one word for it."

"All I was doing was being your friend." He kept his eyes on the hummus.

"It's been years since I've seen that look, that's all." Charles turned towards the ocean and the pressure relented. "Thanks for standing up, by the way. It means a lot."

"Don't mention it."

Charles stared out at the big LNG tanker, slowly turning on its anchor chain. The tide had started its long ebb, leaving behind a new line of seaweed and shells.

"Water's nice," Leaf said. They headed for the waves again, all of them glad to leave the conversation behind. Jackson felt the current on his limbs as he dove, pulling with a thousand miles of strength that thrilled him to the core. Go away, he told his condition. You've done enough damage for one night.

The ringing cell phone in his beach bag went to voicemail as he unlocked the apartment door, hung his towel in the bathroom and laid out the picnic dishes by the kitchen sink. Sue Creehy's message took his rotten little evening and pulled the bottom out from under it.

The message was short, conveying the usual information he'd come to expect from years of working with old people - your services will no longer be needed, please send your bill, Mom passed away peacefully in the night. Sue added the bit about his work being a godsend to her mother and how much she appreciated his help, which was nice. Under the words was the complex emotional subtext he always heard in these calls - sadness at the loss, relief that the family could move on, and always a tinge of the big question - why death, why now? Jackson hit erase and killed the call. Mind on fire, he crossed Mrs. Creehy off next week's calendar.

Why death? Why now? He knew why, and the answer spooked him so badly he was suddenly seeing his living room through the wrong end of a telescope and had to grab the wall for support.

Elora Creehy died for the same reason as Emily Shrop. Because her house felt bad.

It made no sense. Even allowing the thought was a step towards crazy, but he'd checked, and there had been no cause for concern. You simply didn't expire from a tweaked back. The only thing wrong had been that cold wind blowing the life out the front door of her house.

He started in on the dishes, letting the hot, soapy water on his hands bring him back down to earth. Two patients were gone, that was a fact. He'd felt something weird in each house the day before they died. That was a fact, too, as irrefutable as the feeling of the hot dishcloth in his hand.

He was the only one who felt it. He remembered Florita standing in the middle of Mrs. Creehy's repulsive living room, oblivious and unconcerned. Mrs. Shrop and Mrs. Creehy hadn't been bothered by what he felt. Except they were dead, of course.

"When you see things that affect your feelings and behavior, but don't seem to affect the others around you, we should talk." Dr. Parma's last words as he'd left the hospital three years ago still rang in his mind. For a heartbeat he was back on the edge of the Lions Gate Bridge, and instead of a sinkful of soap bubbles he was staring wide-eyed at the glittering waves far below, the boats with their wakes, the clouds and the seabirds and the cars at his back all moving together in an achingly complex and beautiful pattern he was reaching to comprehend. Charles was somewhere behind him, talking him back from the edge.

Flashes and glimpses. That was all he ever got from those hours on the bridge. He remembered looking up, straight into the light of the sun. It was the last sunshine he would see for three long months.

He did a long, slow blink and jammed his hand hard against the edge of the counter, the pain snapping him back to the present. The hummus bowl was still full of wash water.

He rinsed and dried the bowl and put it on the second shelf. The hour was late, almost time for another pill. A small, satisfied warmth ran through him as the dish reached its proper place. He grabbed it back and moved it one shelf down among the coffee mugs. A squonk of disapproval went through his guts. He forced himself to leave it there. It was a bowl among cups. It crowded the space. It was as plainly wrong as it could get. He moved it back to its rightful place and the warmth returned.

Like it or not, accept it or not, his condition was still showing him the truth.

He fetched the pills from the bathroom medicine cabinet and let his hands do their thing with the bottlecap and cotton. He grunted into the night with a wry amusement, remembering Sue Creehy's message. Passed away peacefully in the night? If Jackson knew anything about Elora Creehy, Death would have had to fight her tooth and nail.

Maybe it's done, he said to himself in the bathroom mirror. Weird shit had struck twice. Surely that would be the end of it? The freckled forehead beneath his red curls was scrunched into a frown. The mirror's blue eyes scowled back with skepticism and said, you've got to be kidding. He went to bed with ice in his spine. Sleep did not come easy

Chapter 4

Tower Beach was deserted at six o'clock on Sunday morning. Jackson took one more look around to be sure before returning his attention to the small pile of rocks on the sand. Then he lit a match.

The thin line of black powder carried a tiny ball of fire fizzing and crackling over the sand to the foot-high pyramid of beach rocks. The spark disappeared inside, then came a pop. Pebbles tumbled outward. The small stone on top, translucent green and round as a marble, shot off into the air. Jackson watched, holding his breath. It sailed through a perfect parabola, five feet high and eight feet away, and beaned the tower of rocks he'd stacked on the sand.

Bullseye! They fell over in a heap, and he got up to reassemble the target and start again.

Today the game was artillery. Sometimes it was move the big rock, other days it was storm the fortress or blow the wall or dig a hole. Tower Beach was the best place, where high tide would eliminate the evidence and he seldom got any onlookers. He kept it small, fighting the perennial pyromaniac's urge for the big bang. Instead he focused on shaping his charges to get the most from every explosion. That was the real game.

It was always about the angles. He'd judged it right this time, balancing the weight of the pebble with the distance to be covered and setting the trajectory well. He'd even accounted for the loss of force through the sides of his launcher. That was the tricky part. There had to be some way to keep the force of the explosion in. Maybe if he surrounded the pile with sand, built it up like a volcano –

"Looks like fun." The voice came from behind him and disconcertingly near. Jackson spun, and there was a complete stranger not more than ten feet away. He suppressed a flash of irritation at the intrusion, and at himself for letting somebody sneak up on him.

Minimal politeness usually gave people the message. "Yeah," he replied, and turned again to his work, grabbing a handful of sand as he scrunched down to rebuild the launcher.

"Use the wet sand," the stranger said. "If you want it to work."

Really. "Why's that?"

"Because that's what the pros use." The guy had his hands in the pockets of a beige windbreaker, and gave him a knowing wink. "Trust me."

Jackson was intrigued despite himself. "That's what the pros use, eh? Well, who am I to argue." He dropped his dry sand and reached for some damp stuff nearby. It was heavier. After another minute of silence he relented. "Care to lend a hand?" It was all the excuse the man needed. Soon they were both wordlessly stacking rocks and tamping them down.

Jackson kept an eye on the target as he worked. He knuckled out a small concavity in the sand. When a three-deep ring of rocks surrounded it he took a tin of reloader smokeless gunpowder and tapped a little into the opening. Then he dribbled another thin line out the side of the launcher. Once that was done, he took a metal straw and stuck it into the powder.

Which line to take? This launcher was going to be stronger than the last, no doubt. There would be more propulsion behind the pebble. Jackson took the green stone out of his pocket, tossed it up and down to set its weight in his palm, and felt his way into the situation. Same charge. Same rock. Same target. More power. When he knew all the parameters he moved the straw up, and waited, and looked. Not far enough. He moved it again, a little more vertical, and waited, and looked. A wavery phosphorescent line, almost invisible in the deepening morning sun, arced high up and directly down onto the stacked target. A tiny, warm tingle delighted his fingers and he pushed the straw deep into the sand.

"Okay, that's it. Don't move the straw even a little."

"Wouldn't dream of it," said the stranger.

They built, and Jackson stole sidelong glances at his new companion. He was tallish, dressed for a beach walk in jeans and white t-shirt under his windbreaker, but obviously slumming it. Why slumming it? The hair, he decided. Immaculate executive cut, in place like it didn't know any other way, the smallest dusting of grey showing through the sandy brown. Narrow face, no extra meat on his bones but flexible and strong. The guy helped out with a deft touch, not nudging the straw. He didn't mind getting his hands dirty.

The launcher was ready. Jackson lifted out the guide straw, leaving a small hole down to the powder. Then he took the green pebble out of his pocket and placed it over the hole. Another few taps of the powder tin and the line of grainy black extended ten feet away.

The other guy was right beside him. He was at ease, hands back in his pockets, but his eyes gleamed. "So you like this, too?" Jackson asked.

The guy's smile gleamed, too, turning it into a wolfish thing. "Maybe. How do you know it's going to work?"

"I just do." He struck the match. Fizz, and the spark flew into the side of the launcher. Instead of a pop, this time there was a small pow! The launcher didn't so much as quiver. The pebble flew up into the air, way beyond the planned trajectory. It landed with a clatter among the boulders three feet the other side of the target. A cloud of sulphur vapour enveloped them, and both Jackson and the stranger breathed deep.

"That's why the pros use wet sand," said the stranger. "Good shot, your line was bang on. Fix the range and you're in business."

"Yeah." He was already excited for the next launch. Jackson checked the perimeter. Another walker was rounding the bend in the beach and the tide was coming in. Two motorboats were pulling up alongside the Northern Sea Otter, the white lettering on one saying Harbour Patrol and on the other saying Vancouver Police. The LNG ship was getting a visit from the harbourmaster and the cops. No doubt preparing for the looming protest storm, or maybe making a last-ditch effort to talk the company out of their media stunt. Either way, setting off gunpowder on the beach was no longer a good idea.

He gathered up his things and kicked the rocks around. "Coffee?" offered the stranger.

"Jackson," he answered, sticking out his hand. "Borden," said the man. They shook and headed for the parking lot. "So, tell me about how the pros do it," said Jackson.

Borden was a storyteller. They found a table at a cafe on Alma despite the Sunday morning lineup. "Nice job on the beach," he began as the macchiatos steamed, "reminds me of the time I needed to launch a man over a wall. I had one day to build the launcher, in secret, in the woods, on an old farm cart we could wheel into place. Fifteen feet up and fifteen feet over, a hundred and seventy pounds, and have him land on the other side in one piece. Well, I can tell you, that one had me sweating. I ended up doing pretty much what you did this morning, except we used mud instead of sand. Dried hard as concrete, and did the trick."

"Gunpowder?" asked Jackson.

"Used up all we had. You understand how powder works, right? Burns fast, makes lots of gas, and the expanding gas is what does the work? I added some dry mud to slow down the burn a little and sat the man inside a 45-gallon drum inside the mud tube so he wouldn't fry. The human bullet, we called him. No time to test it out. We wheeled the thing out, pointed, and lit the fuse." He sipped his coffee.

"Did it work?"

Borden showed another display of perfect teeth. "The mud held together. Everything was aimed right. The fuse burned, the charge went off, there was a big bang, and our man went nowhere." Borden sat back, daring him to figure it out.

He could see it. A slow burning charge would weaken the force of the blast but it would still look and sound like an explosion. The huge ball of smoke and gas would push outward, looking for release. The man in the barrel was the obvious escape route, but he hadn't moved. Jackson got it. "The farm cart gave. You blew the bottom out."

Borden nodded, impressed. "Sure warmed up the drum, though. Our human bullet came out of there red as a hot poker. Under his own steam, you could say."

Jackson laughed, thrilled at finding someone who knew. "So, where was this? Why not go through the front door?"

Borden demurred with a sly glance. "Well, let's just say that my plan was the most workable one we had. And I told you, we were in the woods. How did you get interested in all this?" He leaned forward, ready to listen.

So Jackson talked. About the primal thrill of striking wooden matches when he was four years old, staring intently as each molecule of the pretty blue clump on the head of the match sparked into bright flame. About starting his first fire, a neat little grass affair at the base of a big pine tree. About watching the dried resin on the trunk practically reach for the flame and carry it thirty feet up in the blink of an eye, and watching the fire department save the rest of the forest.

"I got smart after that and kept it small. I learned what burns and what doesn't, and always kept some water handy. Over time I moved into gunpowder, and I've stayed there ever since."

Borden stared at him, fascinated. "It's the targeting, isn't it? The puzzle? That's what turns your crank."

Jackson nodded. "It's everything about the burst – how much force will move how much weight, in which direction, what will happen if you change the parameters a little. Explosions are an art form, I guess you could say. There's no end to exploring them."

Borden was delighted. "I know exactly what you mean!" he exclaimed. "I feel it, too. Except I don't always keep things small." He winked, and then rapped the table with his hand. "This has been a remarkable start to my day. It's been a pleasure and an honour to meet you this morning, Jackson." He stood to go. "Until we meet again, I have a challenge for you." He grabbed a napkin and started sketching. It was simple enough, a stick with a box on top of it, and some criss-crossed lines spreading out to either side. He spun it around with the flick of a finger.

"I'm going to introduce you to some of the finer points of the craft here. This is a chain-link fence, standard construction, your usual steel poles holding it up. Here's the challenge. Figure out a way to blast through the base of that pole without spilling the cup of coffee that's balanced on top. We'll meet back at the beach in a few days to see what you've got. What do you say?" His long index finger held the napkin down. His look dared Jackson to take it.

A few ideas for how to shape the blast had already crowded into his head. He tugged the paper over to his side of the table. "All right, you're on. How about Wednesday, Tower Beach, six a.m.?"

Borden tilted his head in farewell. "Have fun with that." Then he was gone, his perfect haircut bobbing away over the thickening Sunday coffee crush. Jackson hogged the table for five more minutes, poring over the diagram and jotting down ideas.

Borden picked up his tail again at the bus stop on Broadway. He tsked as he filed back past the cripple seats with the rest of the crowd. Canadian cops used to be some of the best anywhere, but this was the third time he'd spotted the one with the heavy eyebrows and the turned-out left leg. The tail's hair was blond today, in marked contrast to those eyebrows, and he was dressed up like a businessman instead of yesterday's jock. How comprehensive.

The blond spoke into his cuff mike and sauntered over to the bus stop. Borden had to resist the urge to look straight at him. All in all, the cop was doing a tremendous job of being a bumbling idiot.

He forgot about the tail and smiled. Fortune really did favour the prepared. After the meeting in Saskatoon he'd spent three months getting ready for the job. Month one was spent on market research. He never traveled with munitions, not when there were plenty of businesses who would order in anything you needed · mining companies, pipeline builders, demolition companies, defense contractors, even film studios kept warehouses full of things that went boom. Breaking into an army base was a little beyond even Borden's skill set, but North Shore Marine Demolitions could order in what he needed and had manageable security.

The second month was spent setting up the order. They'd never heard of anyone finding a three-foot-thick reinforced concrete bomb shelter on their property, much less wanting to blow it to kingdom come just for giggles. That was what eccentric millionaire recluses with private islands did, he informed them, so cut the bullshit and let's have a blast. He discussed options with their demolition expert and slowly led him around to ordering exactly what Borden wanted. It came with an unbelievably hefty price tag, but Borden's old friend fronted the payment without a second's hesitation.

The third month was spent covering the details. North Shore Marine Demolitions ran out of a warehouse lot that backed onto some scrub forest next to a creek, perfect for an unobtrusive infiltration. To be sure, he'd done a second run past the place on his arrival in town. Basic cameras, occasional site visits by a roving patroller at night. Still delightfully inadequate, except for the shiny new chainlink with the badge by the gate that said Tremblor Dynamics. They'd used his money to upgrade to a motion-sensitive goddamn fence.

His smile widened, encouraging the old hag on the seat beside him to wrinkle up one of her own. That fence had almost caused him to break a sweat. Bullshit, he allowed, he'd been seriously worried trying to figure out a way through it. Then he'd yielded to a wild urge for a walk on the beach this morning, and voila! a natural talent. This Jackson kid might prove to be a diamond in the rough.

The bus did its starting and stopping thing. Blondie was stuck at the front, occasionally checking the reflection in the windshield to make sure Borden was still close by the rear doors. It was pathetic, really. The fact that he had a tail at all, only days after arriving in-theater, was considerably less pathetic. It meant three things. One: because of his recent failures all the police databases now had his biometrics; only to be expected. Two: chances were highly likely the cops had fired up their facial recognition AI and trained it on the public camera systems, picking him out almost the moment he came to town; dirty pool, shame on them. And three: he was going to have to bring his A game to the party. Not a problem.

They crossed Cambie Street and pulled up to a multi-bay stop so the bus could do a big changeover of passengers. A dozen unwashed masses pushed past Borden to get through the rear doors, and more funnelled in through the front. Blondie was tense as a sprinter before the gun, watching in the glass. Borden waited until the last passenger was off and the tail started to relax. When the rear doors let out their pneumatic hush and began swinging closed he stepped down and squeezed through. Blondie took off with the bus, spitting all over his cuff.

The secondary tail was a Nissan sedan with that discreet antenna that let everybody know it was a prowl car, and the two joes in the front seats were looking everywhere but at him. He speedwalked up the hill towards 12th Avenue and cut right into the entrance of the Cambie Street Mall. The secondary tails would take ten seconds to push through traffic to the sidewalk, and wait another couple of seconds to not appear obvious. They could afford the lag, because he assumed they had direct feeds to the mall's security cameras.

Ten seconds took him down the side hall. In two more seconds he was through the door of the men's room. The one place where the general public actively scanned for, and would not tolerate, cameras.

Wasting no time he lifted the bag out of the trash can and retrieved a tight bundle from the space underneath. On went the baseball cap with the fringe of black hair attached and a set of bushy black eyebrows. Cotton wedges changed the profile of his cheeks. Snap-on lifts gave his shoes two-inch platform soles, one of them sanded to a diagonal to alter his gait. He reversed his jacket with a twitch and sauntered back out the door.

The Wreck Beach dude with the intense gaze, now revealed as a set of startling blue eyes, was heading down the hall towards him, dressed now but wearing his shaggy curls like a hippie flag. Borden leaned into his disguise, rolling hard off his canted heel and rummaging in one pocket for car keys, keeping his own eyes straight ahead. He was almost to the mall's center court and turning for the parkade stairs when he heard the boy's footsteps stop and turn. Across the way the two secondary tails shouldered in through the street entrance.

Nothing to do but stick to the plan. He went through the parkade door, sneaking a peek back at the cops, who were holding up their phones and looking confused.

The Accord was where he'd left it, with the brown wig and tweed blazer in the passenger footwell. Wearing his third look in five minutes he pulled out from under the mall and relaxed. Fake tail shaken, real tail dodged. A glance right past a meter maid writing a ticket showed no traffic coming. A glance left brought him eye to eye with the beach bum, standing on the sidewalk. Waiting for him. As he gunned the Accord onto the street the boy stared at him with those icy blues and gave him a slow, single nod of the head.

Experiencing a crawly feeling that he'd just been out-hunted, he headed west and wrestled his mind back onto business. Next task was a walk over the Lions Gate Bridge.

Marilyn finished writing the Tesla's parking ticket, crumpled the paper into a pocket and scratched at the ill-fitting meter reader's uniform. "South observation post," she reported in a quiet mumble to the bone-conduction mic tucked under her hairline. "Target Accord exited and turned west. Out of sight now."

Ahmed's voice came back over her earpiece on their dedicated link. "Understood. Team leader says the job's done. Back to your regular uni and regular duties. I'll see you at the car in ten minutes."

So much for the day's excitement. For the rest of the shift she and her senior partner, Ahmed, would be attending to routine calls and paperwork. Still, getting tagged to be the backup's backup on a one hour surveillance gig was a step up, even if she had no idea who the professor-type in the car was. And she'd had an opportunity to see one of the real undercovers at work.

"Copy that, ten minutes. Hey Ahmed, did you see the undercover? Pretty smooth, how he showed up out of nowhere and gave the target the eye. Great hippie look, too. The target was pretty spooked by it."

There was nothing from Ahmed for a moment, then he came back with an edge. "Team leader says there's no hippie undercover, and we're running a strict no-contact protocol. Is he still around?"

Holstering her ticket book, she scanned the block, legs tensed and ready for a run. No shaggy curls, no hoodie in sight. "Negative, he's gone. Whoever he is, the guy moves like water."

Wendy ducked on the way from her small kitchen to the cramped living room. Snatches of singsong Mandarin drifted down from the family living their lives upstairs. It was an old house in the middle of Chinatown and might have been built for diminutive Asians, if you judged by the doorways. But the basement suite was cheap, and it was invisible.

The living room was dark. She'd pulled the drapes over the small, rectangular windows set high on the walls. She flipped on the light and took in the thrift store sofa, end tables and lamps. She'd added new shelves from Ikea to accommodate the angels. She headed over to the empty spot by the bathroom door.

From her home-visit bag she pulled the pewter warrior-woman doll. The thing wasn't actually very pretty; it had been made with a dour expression, a puckered scowl with huge, protruding lips, but that didn't count. The eyes counted. Round black glass, deeply set, they carried a gleam that gazed right through Wendy as she gazed back. They were Mrs. Creehy's eyes. You did it, they said. You helped me win the battle. Thank you.

She kissed the newest angel, then set it in the empty space. Walking back to the kitchen doorway, Wendy laid her right hand on top of the first angel on the left. "Mr. Conrad. You're welcome." The head of the little porcelain man had the paint rubbed off his scalp, and she was careful. Then the next, a classic cherub complete with wings. "Mrs. Barss, I did right by you." Then on to the next.

It took most of an hour, every day, the praying. But she never failed.

Chapter 5

Ferguson Road was awash in drifting fog so thick that it kicked
up in swirls with the passing of every jet. The commuter rush
at YVR was in full swing at 7 a.m., but the three miles of road
paralleling the runways was deserted save for the occasional
fuel truck or birdwatcher. It was a perfect place for wind
sprints.

"Ready?" called Charles, dialling his bicycle's derailleur
down as they coasted to a stop on the smooth pavement.

"More ready than you," Jackson answered, easing his grip
on the brakes and pulling level. "Go!"

They shot off into the mist, clicking through the gears as
fast as they could bring up their speed. The workout was
deceptively simple - pedal flat out for two minutes, stop to let
their heart rate and respiration ease back from redline, then do
it again, three miles out and three miles back. Jackson
breathed the cool humidity deep into his lungs. He and Charles
were evenly matched for both strength and wind, and when his
timer chirped in two minutes they stopped together, huffing
into the morning air.

"How was the inquisition?" Charles asked, looking off into
the fog.

The patient with the tinkling waterfall had complained
about Jackson to the College of Massage Therapists. There'd
been two complaints in the past month, actually, and when he'd

gone to discuss the issue with Amanda Crouse, the Ethics and Discipline Director and a former classmate, he'd walked into a meeting that strained to be friendly.

"The CMT thing? It was very polite and formal. The Director and I graduated from the same class. She called me weird and told me to behave myself." A jet roaring onto the runway drowned out Charles' reply. He gripped his handlebars and said, "Go!"

For the next two minutes the pavement hummed by under their tires. Charles kept pace, studiously focused on the road ahead. Jackson could practically feel him not looking over and voicing his brotherly concern. When they stopped, their breaths added their own fog to the morning. "It was a gentle reminder. Nothing to worry about."

"Didn't say it was," Charles said.

Two minutes more, shifting and gliding along the smooth blacktop. Jackson could smell the ocean with every breath, lapping against the shore somewhere off to the right and washing up on Iona Beach another mile ahead. Vancouver International Airport was built on Lulu Island, the whole thing only a few feet above sea level. The air was thick and rich, the temperature cool, with no noise save for the passing jets and an occasional seagull and the muted bass note of the city off in the distance.

Jackson was breathing hard now, his heart pounding. Charles was right alongside, puffing breathy mushrooms into the mist. "You've been · good for a long while now," he said, looking over to where the sea was hiding.

"I still am," Jackson replied. "Go!"

The next two minutes seemed a little longer, and Jackson caught himself glancing at his trip timer. When it went off Charles was a few feet ahead of him, and Jackson coasted up until they were level again.

Charles was concentrating on a speck of brown stuff on his front tire. "I saw a look on your face at the potluck the other night. When that breeze pulled you, and with those bozos. Like a part of you had left the stadium for a second. And the College of Massage Therapists has you on their radar for being weird." He swivelled in his seat and faced Jackson. "Are you slipping?"

Jackson glared back. "Go!"

They hadn't cooled down yet. The start took Charles by surprise, but he soon caught up. The fog thickened, sealing them off from the rest of the world. They traveled in a moving pocket of road, defined by the edges of asphalt on either side and the white line pulling them forward. The rush of jets came less often as the control tower shifted to low visibility operations. It was a long time until the beeper went, and Jackson had to remind himself to put on the brakes and bring the moving pocket to a stop.

Charles coasted up this time. They spent a minute breathing hard, then he said, "I'm your friend. You asked me to keep an eye on you, remember? That day on the bridge?"

He couldn't remember. Most of that day, three years ago, was burned forever into his mind, but he only had choppy and incomplete bits from the hours on the bridge. Flashes and glimpses, that's all he could ever get. When a typical morning had exploded into a kaleidoscope of webs and connections and patterns everywhere, accompanied by an overwhelming longing to follow them all, he'd been pulled through the heart of the city on invisible strings of amazement and wonder. He remembered stepping, awestruck, past the twin concrete lions and onto the Lions Gate Bridge, and then only tiny scraps. The myriad webs of boats and harbour and uncountable life dazzling him speechless. The sunshine. The cars at his back. All the rest of the day had come to him second hand. News reports of police sealing off the bridge to talk a jumper back from the edge. Charles telling him about being called from the St. Paul's Hospital ER to help his friend, talking with him for an hour and then guiding him into the back of a cruiser. His memory flared back with the sight of a distraught Charles waving goodbye in the hospital corridor and the sound of thunking magnetic locks as the doors closed on the restricted-access psych ward.

He remembered the locks. He'd not seen freedom for three long months.

"You say I asked you to help me out a little."

"That's right. I got you off the bridge. When you left the hospital you asked me to keep an eye on you. To question you sometimes, if I thought it was warranted. Those were your exact words."

"So you think it's warranted, do you?"

He was looking for the water again. They could hear it, but the ocean was hidden by the fog. "Don't you?"

"Go!"

It took almost no time for Jackson's heart rate to jump and his breaths to come fast. He strained at the pedals, slamming each one to the ground as it topped its arc. He had no right to be angry at Charles, he knew that. By the time he heard the chirp his anger was gone. So was his wind. Charles caught up a second later and they both stood there, panting.

"I'm not slipping," he said at last. "Nothing to write home about, at least. Thanks for asking."

Charles patted the fog between them, looking for peace. "Okay, okay. That thing on the beach - I'm only asking, that's all. Anybody can have a bad day." The hand dropped. "One."

"Go!" Jackson jumped again into the fog, leaping for the far end of the pavement, standing on the pedals. Running as fast as he could.

The heat of the morning was lifting the night fog from Chinatown, cooking together the aromas of back alley, barbecued duck, gourmet coffee and delivery truck exhaust into a unique and exotic smell Wendy had never encountered before. Street markets spilled bins of oranges, kitchenwares and unidentifiable vegetables onto the sidewalks, grudgingly sharing the block with electronics stores and a shiny cafe, so new to the neighbourhood their awnings weren't yet moldy. People hustled and strolled around her, and she was enchanted by it all.

Mrs. Creehy was gone. Wendy had been given Arbutus Home Care's silly day off between assignments to recover from the shock. Two short-term postings in two weeks had come and gone. Now she'd been given another real job, taking care of the ailing Mr. Lowe. A familiar sadness bloomed in her breast thinking of how the strong old man's body had betrayed him. Stuck to his bed and chair by a congested heart and no longer able to manage the basement stairs to finish the carvings she had discovered there, all Mr. Lowe could look forward to was a long, painful decline, staring out from a useless body at all the things he could no longer do.

She'd been doing her best for him. Mr. Lowe loved to eat, but the orders from the doctor were written like a felony judgement on the refrigerator door: no salt. No fatty foods. No butter. No bacon. No cream. No alcohol. Who wouldn't be crotchety and sore, denied all the things they loved? It was criminal. So she was out shopping. Some meat, that was what he needed. And some good, dark beer to wash it down. She had a small box of kosher salt in her canvas shopping bag, and some skim milk for Mr. Lowe's coffee in the morning. He needed to live a little. She chuckled into the morning air at that thought, causing a few nervous glances from the shoppers around her.

Sometimes, for the sake of appearances, she had to let one go. Mr. Lowe was grumpy and sore, poor man, but he needed to serve out his sentence on this earth. Wendy kept quite close tabs on the scuttlebutt and whispers after a passing, when any question or suspicion would come out like a bad smell. She had heard nothing, and the two postings in between Mrs. Creehy and now had created a comfortable buffer. Still, she'd had such wonderful opportunities to ply her trade it would get noticed if she didn't slow down. She had to let Mr. Lowe live with his terribly bad heart. All she could do was feed him well and make his remaining time as enjoyable as possible.

She stopped in the middle of the sidewalk, thunderstruck by a way of caring so incredible, so impossible to trace, she wondered that it had never occurred to her before. It was perfect.

She rushed into a produce store, found a stack of strawberries and shovelled some into a bag. Back in the coolers she found a carton of whipping cream, the old-fashioned kind you had to practically squeeze out of the spout. She grabbed some bacon on the way to the till.

Mr. Lowe was going to eat very, very well indeed. Wendy hugged the bacon to her heart. He'd be needing an angel.

Herbert Lowe relaxed in the warm, comfortable glow of a breakfast well done and waited for the massage guy. Sausages! Strawberries with cream! Not since his Molly kicked off had

Herbert eaten so well. He reached down and gave his belly a pat under the flannel PJ's. If he wasn't careful somebody would have to buy him a new pair.

Which stopped his good mood like a runaway bus. Damn useless heart had taken him off his pins, pinched his circulation so bad that his legs had withered up, and now he was next to useless. The care aides always tried to cheer him up, when he was damn well good and cheery already. Always cooking him what the doctor ordered, too, bland mush that made him wish his reunion with Molly would hurry up and get here. Oh, those nurses had their uses, he supposed. Some of them were even a little cute, and Molly wouldn't begrudge him that. Still, he'd rather be able to do without them.

Then the big one had come along. Nurse Wendy, working the night shifts. An old-fashioned kind of nurse if ever there was one, built like a bull mastiff, wore that stiff white cap and took her job seriously. Always here early, always staying a bit late, making good reports to the day girls so they knew what was going on. And strong! She could pick him up with one hand without breaking a sweat. When she wasn't taking care of him she was dusting, cleaning, rearranging stuff, doing all the things he couldn't.

And she didn't pay attention to the doctor's orders. The first time she laid out a meal of bacon-wrapped steak with mushroom sauce and an honest-to-goodness frosted glass of stout, he practically proposed to her right then and there. He'd have some explaining to do to Molly about that one. Nurse Wendy had just smiled and told him to eat up, said that seeing him eat made her happy. Well, he was only too willing to oblige.

Every supper and every breakfast was better than the last. Before she'd left this morning he let slip a little mention of eggs Benedict. She'd winked, and now he couldn't wait until tomorrow.

But first there was the massage guy. This day kept getting

better and better. Jackson was another one who took his job seriously. After each session Herbert could use his legs a little, even walk a few steps. They felt more alive, not like two sticks weighing him down. Worth it by a long shot.

"Jackson! Good to see you, boy. Come on in." If he ever let that mass of red on his head grow out it would be a disaster. Dressed in shorts and shirt, as always. Herbert looked closer. The boy didn't look well.

"Hang on there. You got anything?"

"What?" Jackson paused in the bedroom doorway, where he'd been peering around like he didn't know the place. "Uh, no, I'm fine. Who gave you that?"

The kid was pointing off in the corner. On top of his dresser next to the silver teapot and cup was a doll, for Hell's sake. It was a strange-looking thing, some kind of dark red plastic. It was a happy, big-bellied guy holding his arms up to the sky and laughing his fool head off. Skinny little legs, only standing because he was anchored to a post.

"Dunno. Never seen it before. You sure you're feeling okay? If you're sick, I don't want to see you." The Reaper could drop by anytime, but Herbert didn't want to go out puking.

Jackson seemed to pull himself together. "Nah, perfectly fine, Mr. Lowe. How about you?"

"Great! Feel like a million bucks, except my legs won't move. I think life is agreeing with me."

"And if it won't agree with you, then it can go to Hell, right? I've seen your kind before." The boy was over by his bed now. "Hang out there a minute, let me look at you."

Herbert watched closely. This was the part that always impressed him. Jackson took half a step back, and his eyes changed. It wasn't like they lost their focus, but like they switched over to focusing on something else. Herbert had the sensation – creepy the first time, but not now – that the boy was looking right through him. X-ray eyes, maybe.

"You've been putting on weight," he commented, scanning Herbert from top to bottom. "Not bad. Not, maybe, good either ..." He drifted off. "Nothing much new. Looks like your legs are holding their own."

"Thanks to you, or they'd be holding nothing at all by now. Okay, kid, do your magic."

Jackson grinned, and reached for his oil bottle. "You got it. One circulation boost coming right up."

Herbert leaned back. This was going to be good. And it was. But he peeked partway through the rub and Jackson was looking around again. He was staring at that doll thing. And not happy about it.

Whatever, thought Herbert. His legs were tingling back to life. That was what counted.

The storage space under the front stairs had nail-ends sticking into it. Wendy could smell mouse droppings and her body was cramping from the confinement. But her outrage kept her hunched inside, peering out the cracked doorway at the wreckage of Herbert Lowe's living room.

She'd had to be sure, so she had hidden after Dahlia came to take over the day shift. Now she knew. Jackson Teague could see her work. She'd watched with her own eyes as he stopped dead in his tracks in the middle of the doorway. He could feel the tension and worry leaving the house with a cool rush, she saw it in his face. A wild hope had touched her heart. Maybe, just possibly, she'd found a kindred spirit. After twenty years and a lonely trail that led all the way back to the Maine coast, maybe she had found somebody she could talk to.

Then he'd grabbed the easy chair and twisted it to face the fireplace again. He poked about with the heavy, old chisels Mr. Lowe had been sharpening on the workbench and destroyed all of Wendy's careful geometry. She watched from her tiny hiding place, feeling her hope crumbling and helpless to stop the desecration. Then he tromped on the braided rug by the mantel, the fine little touch that took all the room's energy and funnelled it out the front door, and pushed its edge back up against the wall. Useless, destructive, and plain wrong.

She had almost let her anger take her. One dash for the big chisel, one plunge into the boy's chest was all it would take. The Second Rule quashed that thought, and rightly so. She did not harm the healthy. Dahlia had called him away. Now Teague was doing whatever he did with Mr. Lowe and Wendy was left here to fume and cramp.

She could hear Dahlia humming to herself in the back room. It was time to sneak out and go, but Wendy couldn't leave the house like this. She had to take the risk and put things back where they belonged.

Then she would run, of course. When They Suspect, Move West. She would run like never before, away from something far worse than mere suspicion. She was seen. Of course actually going west was out of the question, her back was against the Pacific. Would she run north again, into the small communities, unprepared and without the papers to work in this country? It was too soon. She squirmed around inside the rough space, desperate to stave off an impending cramp, desperate to get away. Her home-visit bag was against her feet. A nail jabbed her in the shoulder.

There was the small, dark perfume vial tucked deep inside her bag. Without daring to think it over she pushed open the closet door.

Dahlia was singing in the back room; good, Wendy could

keep tabs on her.

The trap had to be one that only the boy would find. Wendy pulled the chair back into its proper alignment to face the door, feeling the room's energy sigh once again and start to drift away. Jackson would come into the living room, be startled to see the change and use the chair's right arm to yank it back. He would use his left hand as he passed, wrapping his fingers an inch back from the handrest.

In the drawer of a small desk she found a roll of scotch tape. She stuck a doubled-over loop of it underneath the armrest. A wine glass from a collection by the table got wrapped in her coat and fell victim to her heel, providing needle-sharp glass shards. These she gingerly stuck to the tape, leaving the rest of the mess inside the storage space under the stairs. Then, with the greatest of care, she painted the shards with a tiny brush from the perfume vial, coating them with a thick liquid.

Wendy didn't much approve of Botox, but she'd had her frown lines done once to give her access to the doctor's office and a box full of the tubes of powdered toxin. Botox powder itself was ridiculously diluted, and doctors watered it down even more with saline for their injections. But Wendy was patient, and she knew how to study, and she knew her chemistry. Days of cautious distillation with the surprisingly delicate bacteria had yielded half a gram of reasonably instant death. It wasn't pure botulinum toxin, not by any means - a gram of the pure thing could kill a sizeable portion of North America - but good enough to keep on hand.

On her way back to the storage space she grabbed a walnut-handled lathe chisel off the workbench.

This was not going to happen again. Jackson fought a mounting sense of anxiety as he worked some blood back into Herbert Lowe's stringy legs. Against all odds he was back in a bad house. There was no way it was costing him another patient.

Like there was a fat lot he could do about it. He kept his hands doing calm, relaxing things while his thoughts rode a frantic tide and struggled to sort it all out. He was getting a handle on the bad-energy thing. Someone was moving items around in the houses. There always seemed to be a doll involved. Whoever was doing this could see what he saw, but they had it all wrong. With a few rearrangements they managed to kill a lifetime of established patterns in each house. Then, the very next night, the owner of the house was dead. What could he do against a force like that? And what was up with the dolls?

Jackson was trying really hard not to get spooked by it all, and he was failing.

Do whatever he could, was the answer. At least Lowe's living room was fixed. He'd managed to shuffle it back to a semblance of normalcy before Dahlia spotted him. It might make a difference.

He scowled over at the laughing Buddha on the dresser, big belly exposed and arms stretched to the sky. You were supposed to rub his belly for good luck. Right. Dolls didn't materialize out of nowhere. Who the hell was doing all this, anyway?

Three different homes. Who else had been to all three? The home care girls, which in all three places had been either Dahlia or Florita. There was Dr. Dick, semi-retired and so fiercely dedicated to his long-term patients that he was seeing them all out even though he was over seventy himself. Jackson had picked up all three jobs on Dr. Dick's recommendation. Was there anybody else? He didn't think so.

"There! That should hold you for a week," he said to Herbert as he finished up.

"Good, feels better already. Where's that Filipino girl, it's almost time for my mush - I mean, my lunch." Lowe winked at him. This old boy had life left.

His hand was moving the moment the idea came to him. "I'll put this in the living room see you next week," he said and snatched the Buddha doll off the dresser. Holding the thing away from him he left the bedroom.

"Not mine anyway," came Lowe's words after him.

Jackson almost dropped the doll on the carpet as he rounded the corner into the living room. It was back. The house felt terrible again. Anger overcame his revulsion and he stepped into the room. This narrowed the field of suspects. A lot.

He set the Buddha down in the middle of the workbench where anybody could see it. It hit the bench with an echoing clap, the sharp plastic ting somehow magnified off the stairs behind him. Dahlia would see it and flinch, or stare, or look at Jackson, and that would be the final answer. Jackson wasn't sure what he'd do then, but at least he would know.

She was doing the laundry; he had a minute. Jackson let himself relax, then let himself look. The web of angles and lines that joined everything in the room to everything else was barely visible, a shimmer at the edge of his vision, but it was there. Most of the room was actually still together. The dull, grey wisps that curled like smoke across the floor and out the front door came from the easy chair. It was in exactly the wrong place again.

One quick grab of the armrest would fix it, just like before. Jackson switched his appointment book over to his right hand and bent over to wrap his left hand over the old leather. Dahlia's footsteps in the doorway snapped him up again. He leaned into the quick movement and knocked his knee against the side of the chair, plopping the legs into the deep divots in the carpet they had occupied for years. The room felt better.

"Dr. Jackson, you are finished?" Dahlia was folding a tea towel as she walked, smiling and happy. He watched her with his perceptions still open and saw the firm, grounded contact her feet made with the floor, the mesmerizing precision with which she made her folds. Stop it, he told himself.

"Yes, um, I'm looking ... " He left the sentence deliberately unfinished, casting his eyes about the room and down at the chair.

She followed his glances. He watched. She looked over the chair, around the room, directly at the Buddha at least twice, and her smile never wavered. There was no flicker. Not even a momentary dent in her fundamental happiness. "Looking for what?"

He was improvising here, and he improvised some more. Lifting up his right hand with the appointment book he said, "Found it." Laughing, Dahlia wished him goodbye and went back to the kitchen.

She couldn't be that good. Jackson was nonplussed. He turned back to give the living room one more look; some angle somewhere still wasn't right. He was almost to it when Dahlia's voice spun him around again. A glint flashed from the storage closet door underneath the stairs, light on the steel catch maybe, as Dahlia announced, "Cookies, Dr. Jackson! Please take them. I made them before I remembered Mr. Lowe's diet, and it will be very bad if he smells them. Here."

You couldn't suck all the energy out of a room and then make cookies. That just wasn't possible. Was it? Feeling hopelessly at sea, Jackson took the bagful of chocolate chip specials and went to his next appointment.

Five minutes later, seeing the room in watercolour through tears of frustration, Wendy emerged and replaced the chisel. She flicked a lighter under the glass shards on the armrest, incinerating the poison, and left the house. There was shopping to do for Herbert Lowe's last supper.

Tonight it was blessed lasagne, thick with cream sauce and glued together with three different kinds of cheese. "I think I've died and gone to Heaven," he exclaimed as Nurse Wendy wheeled him over to the table. A glass of red wine and a slab of garlic bread lay next to the plate.

"Not quite, Mr. Lowe, not quite." Wendy smiled. There was a plate for her, too, and they ate together. She was sitting in Molly's chair. Not in Molly's spot, Herbert saw, somebody must have moved things around a bit. He tucked in and enjoyed every bite, right through the ice cream for dessert.

Afterwards the nurse moved him to the living room, picking him up and dropping him light as a feather into his recliner. The living room looked different as well, not quite like he remembered, though he couldn't put his finger on it. Somebody had been messing with his chisels, he could see that.

"Great!" he said. "I gotta thank you, Wendy, those are some fantastic meals. They could keep me going for years."

"You know, Mr. Lowe, I'm starting to think you're right," she answered, but the sound was all wrong. He swivelled his head over to where Nurse Wendy was sitting, beside him and a little behind, where he didn't remember ever placing a chair. "And that's terrible. I may be doing you a great disservice." She was clearly upset, dark even. Something was up her skirt.

"What? How's that?"

She was looking down at her hands folded in her lap. They were huge, like the rest of her, and thick from years of work. "I care about you, Mr. Lowe. I know how upset you are at the way life has turned out. I've heard you talk about it."

"Now, don't let the ramblings of an old fool get under your skin, girl. I know I'm a grouch, but it's not all that bad."

She was staring down and it unnerved him, she was so intense about it. Her voice got lower. "But you can't fool me, you know. I hear it in your voice. You can't walk. Your legs hurt all the time. You sharpen your chisels, then you can't get downstairs to do any woodwork. You are so upset with all this waiting about. I hear how sad you are when you say these things."

She lifted her gaze to him, and for the first time since the war Herbert Lowe felt afraid. "Hey, lady, I don't – " but she was going on.

"I'm feeding you all the worst things, Mr. Lowe, but they're not helping. You look like you're getting stronger, for mercy's sake. That's not right. So now," she rose slowly to her feet, and God wasn't she tall and broad and strong as a bloody ox, "it looks like I have to do it differently."

She had those meathook hands of hers out front, and Herbert was stuck in his easy chair, he couldn't get away because of his damn useless legs. He scrambled to the back corner of his chair and hated himself for doing it, but the nurse was looking all black and intense and absolutely like she was going to go completely around the bend and do it, and her hands were all he could see now as she got closer. He opened his mouth to scream, shout, get some attention, and the pain in his chest nailed his throat shut. He only knew in hindsight that he had already taken his last breath. Damn fucking nurse, he thought his last thought at her, thanks for the great lasagne.

The nurse's eyes were over him, looking down, breaking in on what was supposed to be a private moment. Stealing even that, the bitch. She looked pleased. "So that's all it took," he heard her say.

Then there was his Molly, and everything got better.

Wendy was delighted, mostly. The scare had worked like a charm, a wonderful technique she would remember for the future. Even Teague's repositioning of the angel was perfect. There it was, still in the living room on the workbench, watching over the place of Mr. Lowe's passing with a laughing relief.

Something still needed to be done about that. A flush of shame touched her face as she remembered the botox trap and the feel of the chisel. Don't Harm The Healthy, that was the Second Rule. The boy was young and alive, he had years ahead of him. The situation needed a fix, but not that.

She went about the living room examining each detail before the morning call. She peeled the remains of the poison trap off the bottom of the armrest. She picked up the angel, gazing at it with love. Before placing it inside her home-visit bag she gave the little Buddha's belly a rub for luck.

Teague had brought it out to the living room and drawn Dahlia's attention to it. She thought about that. He didn't know who to mistrust. She could misdirect him. A trap could take many forms. Wendy gave the little angel another rub for luck and thanks, and tucked him into her bag.

Chapter 6

A steady drizzle hissed off the tires of the departing bus as Jackson popped open his umbrella for the short walk to the Clinton Park Community Centre. His stomach crimped five steps from the door but he pushed it open, wading through a cross-current of figure skaters on his way to the changing rooms.

Why was he still coming to Aikido when it made him so nervous, and had for weeks now?

The answer, like always, waited for him in the changing room. As he took off his street clothes the day dropped away. As he slipped on the age-softened cotton dogi and folded the belt into a tight knot at his waist the simple, familiar movements sidestepped him into a quieter place. He took a deep breath - his first of the day, he realized - and headed for the dojo.

A dozen other students warmed up on the mats. The Sensei, Toshiko, was a small-boned and quiet knot of focus in kneeling seiza against the far wall. Jackson was just in time. With a sharp clap of her hands Toshiko bounced to her feet, took position at the front of the class, and knelt again in seiza, feet tucked behind her, as the students knelt in a line. They bowed to the portrait of Aikido's founder, Ueshiba-sensei, hanging on the wall, then Toshiko-sensei pivoted and they bowed to each other. "Onegai shimasu!" she gave the traditional greeting and the class responded, setting the tone for mutual respect and cooperation.

The warm-up routine went from hand and foot stretches to full spine twists to tuck rolls across the mats. Each progression eased Jackson further into a kind of moving meditation. Tonight the synchronized movements of the warm-up also called to his condition. He found himself wishing each exercise would keep on going, extending the dance forever. Shut it down, he told his head, and sweat began to dampen his hairline.

"Okay, Katatori Ikkyo," called Toshiko-sensei, demonstrating one of Aikido's foundational techniques on a senior student. The class paired off and Jackson found himself facing Johnny, a square block of a man easily twenty years his senior who moved like a dancer. They bowed, then took turns trying to grab each other.

Johnny latched onto the lapel of his dogi. The hand was not a weapon; it was a lever, an extension of the other person's energy. Jackson stepped to the left, out of the way of the oncoming force, and swept his hand down Johnny's arm, pulling him off-center. When his hand reached Johnny's he was in perfect position to grasp. Then, in the essential, spiral magic of aikido, he pivoted around to the outside, rolled Johnny's elbow up and over and stepped through. The combined wrist lock and elbow control bent Johnny to the floor. Jackson had him pinned, chest to the mat.

"Good!" Johnny said, rising. "Nothing I could do about that one."

"Okay, now you – " Jackson stopped as he felt a light tap on his shoulder. Toshiko-sensei was standing behind him. He and Johnny bowed to each other, then he turned and repeated the honour with her.

"Ikkyo," she said, and indicated her lapel. He grabbed for her and a wash of force sent him spinning to the floor. Toshiko was a fourth-degree black belt; Jackson hadn't felt her touch.

She held his lapel in turn. She was smaller than him, lighter by a good twenty pounds, but he knew better than to go soft on the technique. He turned, stepped, and pivoted, giving it all he had. Toshiko-sensei went to the mat but got up frowning.

"That was muscle," she said. "Not what this is about, Jackson. You know this. Again."

She had another fistful of gi before he could register the grab. Again, he stepped, swept along her arm, pivoted, and she went down. Then up. "Again."

Another grab, another step and pivot. But this time she didn't move. He had the proper grip on her hand, he'd pivoted and had control of her elbow to direct her down, but nothing was happening. Toshiko was standing there, her small hand still full of his shirt, her eyes glittering a hard look of challenge.

"Not muscle," she said, and waited for him to do something about it.

He pivoted again. Nothing. He tried stepping back and pulling her off balance and almost undressed himself. Some of the students nearby had stopped their practice to watch. Jackson pivoted once more. It was like hitting a tree limb.

"Stop." She still held him in her unbreakable grip. "Relax, Jackson. Don't try. Relax."

Was he tense? The sweat was making his dogi droop. The simple movements of Ikkyo followed the beautiful spiral that was the heart of Aikido. His condition strained to fall into the technique with a dangerous abandon and he was holding himself back by main force. Loosen up, he told himself. Just a little. He closed his eyes and cracked open the inner door.

He became aware of a massive force. It was right in front of him. It had hold of his lapel. He saw the straight solidity of the force, immovable in its line. He saw, with complete clarity, how unstable it was from the side. He could work with this force. He could redirect it.

He would need to apply a touch here, like this. He would need to urge that force along a line it wasn't expecting, like this. Then one more gentle touch here, and –

"Good. Very good." The sensei's voice came from below. Jackson looked, and Toshiko was on the mat. He let go, and she sprang up. "How did that feel?" she asked.

"Easy," he answered. "Like there was nothing to it. It felt good."

"Remember that." Toshiko turned to the class, who by now were all watching. "Use these moves to feel for the opening. Learn what aikido feels like. Then you will no longer need the moves. No matter what comes at you, you will know what to do." She bowed, and moved on. Jackson was back with Johnny.

He spent the rest of the class fighting to close the door in his head. By the end of practice the sweat was dripping down his back.

The call from Herbert Lowe's son caught Jackson as he was stirring fresh thyme into a bubbling lamb tagine. A low, grey overcast had erased the North Shore mountains and was washing Vancouver, so tonight's potluck was a house party at his place. He turned the heat down on the stew, threw his cell phone across the apartment onto the sofa and smacked the countertop. Herbert Lowe was gone. He hadn't stopped a damn thing.

The buzzing intercom from the apartment building's front

door took him down the hall. "Hey man," Leaf's voice crackled through the lousy speaker, "it's beautiful out here but I sure hope you have a spare towel." A minute later he was dripping on Jackson's hall floor, black t-shirt stuck to his magazine abs and sun-blond curls hanging straight down to his shoulders. Leaf didn't do umbrellas.

"You okay, Jackson?" Leaf glanced out from under the towel. "You look like someone walked over your grave."

"Fine. Grab a spare shirt out of the second drawer," Jackson told him, "I'll see you in the kitchen." By the time he'd set Leaf's cheese scones on the table Leaf was back and strapping on an apron. "Roasted baby potatoes and carrots," he said, pointing to a pile of vegetables next to some olive oil and rosemary. Leaf accepted the end of conversation, pulled a chef's knife out of the block and went to work.

Leaf knew how to move around the small kitchen without upsetting Jackson's rhythm. He diced the vegetables with a rapidfire flurry and had them oiled, salted and spiced in short order. Jackson swung open the oven door as he passed by and Leaf slid in the pan.

They tried out the stew. "More cinnamon," suggested Leaf, and Jackson made the adjustment. Then there was nothing much to do as everything simmered.

"You're good with a knife," he said as they moved to the living room with mugs of tea to watch the rain.

"You hang around awhile, you pick up some skills," Leaf laughed, his grin a flash of white against his tan as he relaxed into the cushions. "On Saturday mornings I teach whittling classes for the kids in Stanley Park. In the afternoons I take a few teenagers aside for throwing practice."

"That must be a pretty short walk to work," Jackson replied, fighting to keep a straight face. Leaf, no fool and wise to Jackson's ways, let a corner of his mouth twitch as he deadpanned his reply.

"Oh, a hop, skip and a jump, you know. But it's not work. It's a volunteer gig. I do lots of them - whittling, juggling, survival skills, forest walks, lot of things, all over the place."

"No paycheque, then. I guess money's not your thing."

Leaf shook his head around a sip of tea. "No, don't ever say that. You've got to have respect for the currency, man. Money is energy, as much a force of Nature as the rain out there. It has to flow through your life like everything else. I don't need to put much attention on it, that's all."

Jackson leaned forward, pushing a little. "So you've watched and learned, and once in awhile you show some kids a few tricks. Ever thought of doing more? There aren't very many old beach bums, you know."

Leaf gazed out the window and shook his head. "Nah, man, I leave the work for other people. I spend my time in school." He pointed outdoors where the shower had intensified into a downpour, heavy drops bouncing off the parked cars with a steady drumming. "There's my classroom. You want to know how to stand tall? Head over to Stanley Park and hang with the trees. You want to learn how to fight? Watch a cat, or a crab. You want to live in the moment? Spend some time with a dog. It's all out there, my man." He pointed his teacup out the window. "The rain knows what I'm talking about. When it's not ready it stays in the clouds. When it gathers enough weight it falls down, no fuss, no question. Nature is run by laws. I spend my time studying them."

Life and death had laws, too, Jackson thought, remembering Herbert Lowe's laugh. He saw the hole in Leaf's philosophy. "So tell me this, friend. What happens to the rain when it hits the ground?"

That one caught Leaf. "It bounces?"

"It changes direction. Nature's laws tell it where to go." He pointed to a photo on the wall by the kitchen pass-through, a deep forest canyon with a creek carving through the bottom. Jackson had taken the shot himself. Both he and Leaf knew the spot well. "It's only when the rain changes direction that Nature can put it to work."

Leaf was silent. They finished their cups to the sound of the downpour. "Stew smells good," Leaf said at last. Right on cue the intercom buzzed and in a minute Charles and Georgia dripped in the hallway, handing off their contributions.

Standing with them was a courier guy pulling his electronic scanner out of a big, waterproof pouch. "You're Jackson Teague? Sign here please." Jackson signed and received an envelope bearing the logo of the College of Massage Therapists in the upper left-hand corner. The courier nodded, dripping rainwater off the bill of his ball cap, and was gone.

"You two have been busy," Charles sniffed appreciatively as he made his way down the corridor. His right hand reached up as he passed the tiny hall shelf where Jackson kept a notepad and pencil handy. He flicked the pencil, knocking it into a crazy angle against the pad, and strode into the living room.

He'd done that move on each visit for the past three years. The neat squares and parallels of pad, pencil, shelf and wall disappeared with a psychic gronk. The discord itched. Which, of course, was the point.

Jackson passed the test. He tucked the letter under the notepad but left the pencil alone and kept going. Georgia's pomegranate sorbet was warming in his hands and needed to find the freezer.

The crew got settled as Leaf passed around cups of steaming tea. Georgia checked out Jackson's bookshelves for new arrivals (the usual mix of medical texts and popular novels, heavy on the Dan Kalla and Robin Cook) while Charles and Leaf set the table. Jackson busied himself in the kitchen.

Dinner was fabulous, and the stew disappeared quickly.

From far off in the darkening night a ship's foghorn moaned, and Georgia frowned over her spoon. "There's the sound of trouble," she said.

"The Northern Sea Otter?" asked Leaf. "That's going to be a party. Everybody will be down on the waterfront to hoot and holler at them."

"That's just it," she said. "Everybody. I can't believe the natural gas companies thought this was a good idea. Sure, to them it looks like a nice, quiet sail into the harbour, look at how safe and clean we are, but they're giving all the protesters in town the biggest focus they've had in a generation. And some of them won't be there to sing songs and wave signs." She stabbed a carrot and pointed it at Leaf. "I won't be anywhere near the Vancouver waterfront that day, and I don't want you there, either. That's one party you're not going to." She swallowed and jabbed the empty fork again. "Promise me."

Surprised, Leaf hemmed. "Well, every party needs a juggler. Besides, it's a boat, what can a bunch of people on shore do? We'll be there to make sure the powers hear us, and you do that with your voice."

"Promise me. You'll be nowhere near the Vancouver waterfront. Say it." Georgia was serious. Jackson could see her sincerity register on Leaf's face.

"All right, sister. Sure. I promise." To seal the deal, he handed out the pomegranate sorbet. They moved over to the comfy seats in the living room and Jackson lit some candles to accent the gathering night.

"What about you?" Jackson asked. "You've got the voice of the people in your bones."

"Oh, I didn't say I wouldn't get involved. I'm headed across the bridge to the North Vancouver waterfront, that's all. It'll still be jammed, but less so. I think the real action will be on this side of the harbour."

He turned to Charles. "So you're headed to the North Shore, too?"

Charles shook his head. "I'll be pulling an extra shift at the hospital. The word's gone out to all the staff. There's a lot of planning and preparing going on behind the scenes for this one. Whatever it looks like, we'll be ready."

Jackson hadn't thought about it. The day of the big sail was a regular day on his schedule, but the work of a traveling massage therapist depended on manageable traffic. He might have to reconsider.

They spent a quiet minute enjoying the melting sorbet and listening to the falling rain.

"I ran into a bad seed the other day," Leaf commented, "over by Cambie Street. Crossed paths with him a couple times, actually."

Charles took the bait. "Okay. So what made him so bad?"

Leaf smiled, easing back into the sofa. "Well, part of it was the disguise. Bad hair, distorted cheeks, he even gave himself a limp. Part of it was the cops trying to chase him through the mall. But mostly it was the eyes." He paused for sorbet. "The guy had the eyes of a hyena. No doubt, no question, tearing things to pieces is all he knows."

Jackson remembered his dance with the volleyball goons on the beach, the look of consternation on Red Speedo's face. "I bet I'd have spotted him," he said.

"No, you wouldn't." Leaf shook his head. "You've got some mad skills, my man, but what you see is disturbances in the patterns. The best predators have the best camouflage. They know how to look like nothing special. This one is completely smooth, he doesn't make any disturbance at all." He licked his spoon. "I've been to Nature school. When I see that kind of smooth, I know what I'm looking at."

Georgia shivered, pulling Charles' arm over her shoulders.

"Did you tell the police?"

"Didn't need to, one was standing right there. They let him go." Leaf put on a smile Jackson hadn't seen before. "No problem, they'll get another chance. I'm tracking him."

"What!?" The three of them said at once. "Why the hell would you do that?" Charles demanded.

Leaf gave another shrug. "Somebody needs to. The police didn't see him and I did, and he's a dark soul. The guy might be a hyena, but he's in my forest now."

That stopped the conversation for awhile, and they listened to the rain pattering on the empty streets. "Okay, out with it," said Georgia into the quiet. Jackson looked up from his half-full dish and everybody was staring at him. "You've been moping around ever since we got here. What's up?"

Moping? He'd been a little subdued, maybe. "I lost another one," he heard himself say, and in four words managed to say far too much.

"Another what?"

Well, what the hell, he thought. These are my friends. "Another patient. Herbert Lowe died last night." He gave them a brief rundown of the old guy with a penchant for carving. "A heart attack over dinner, apparently."

There was a chorus of awws. Charles said, "Not a bad way to go, all things considered. It happens to all of us sooner or later."

"Not like that it doesn't." Shut up, Jackson told himself.

"Actually, pretty much exactly like that," Charles answered, puzzled. "A good meal to stress the heart, an influx of fats and cholesterol into the bloodstream, and bob's your uncle. Unless there was something more." The hiss of the rain lent a soft blanket of sound to the room.

Shit, thought Jackson. "His house killed him. No, that's not what I mean. Well, sort of. It's like this." In bits and pieces, as best he could, he laid it out for them - a home's natural geometry, the cold molasses feel of Herbert Lowe's house, his efforts to handle it, and the inevitable phone call. Feeling every moment like he was swimming into deep water and losing sight of shore, he kept going till the story was done. Charles' face clouded from puzzlement to professional concern.

He paused for breath and Georgia asked the obvious question. "What did you mean, another one?"

Go ahead, Jackson told himself. Swim out a little farther. Some small part of him was glad to have it out at last. "There was Mrs. Creehy. And Mrs. Shrop last month. None of them were ready to die." He went over it all. The chill, dead feeling in every house. The dolls. The deaths, always natural but always a surprise. "It wasn't the right time for any of them," he finished. "You know, Charles, death from old age announces itself. A fall, an illness, somehow their health gets worse before the end. They don't simply pop off. Usually. You asked." He took a deep breath and drank the last of the melted sorbet in one long swallow.

"Wow, that is some story," said Georgia, "but you look a little better for the telling." He caught the note of seriousness in her voice. Of belief.

"Yeah, man, what a tough run," said Leaf. "I knew you were down, but that's really wild."

"Did anybody else feel anything strange in these places?" asked Charles.

"Nobody else noticed a thing. Just that some stuff had been moved around."

"You see things other people don't, " said Georgia. "That's your gift."

"Yeah, right." Most gifts don't get you locked away. He kept his mouth closed to avoid embarrassing himself any more, and there didn't seem to be much else for anyone to say. Before too long Leaf and Georgia got up to tackle the kitchen.

"Show me the letter," said Charles, putting his wine glass down on the table and standing.

Jackson stood, too. "What letter?"

Charles was already on his way down the hall. "The one from the CMT," he called over his shoulder. Before Jackson could get to him Charles had it in hand. He held it out. "Open it."

The logo of the College of Massage Therapists was both fancy and formal. The script below the return address said Office of Ethics And Discipline. Confidential was stamped in red along the bottom. "You're going to read it anyway," Jackson muttered. "You do it."

The letter from the Ethics Director was one page. Charles read it, then passed it over.

To: Jackson Teague, RMT, reg. #6541684

Re: Complaint from D. Pearson, Patient, and other complaints on file

Dear Mr. Teague: This office has received a complaint of unprofessional conduct from one of your home-visit patients (encl.) detailing unusual behaviour you exhibited at her residence that led to her loss of confidence in your reliability.

This is not the first complaint our office has received about you. While 'strange behaviour' is not, strictly speaking, a punishable offence, you are reminded that our profession demands a high degree of decorum and responsibility from its members. Home-visit sessions even more so. Given your medical history and ongoing treatment for mental issues, we are concerned.

This office hereby places you on probation. One more complaint of any kind about your conduct will result in your massage therapy registration being suspended. You will have the opportunity to appeal this decision if it is made.

Yours in health,

Amanda Crouse

Director, Ethics and Discipline

"The galley's shipshape," called Georgia as she rounded the corner from the kitchen, "and it's time we were on our way." She paused for half a step as she caught sight of the two of them in the hallway, the letter still in Jackson's hand. "Definitely time. Come along, husband, your friend needs his beauty sleep."

That broke the spell. Georgia gave Jackson a solid hug on the way out the door, whispering into his ear, "You're doing all right, you know." Then she grabbed Charles by the elbow and they left.

Leaf handed back his t-shirt and said, "I know what'll heal your soul. Lynn will be calmed down soon. Want to set a date?" It was a great idea, and they pencilled Lynn on his fridge calendar for a couple of weeks away. Leaf added, "Thanks for the words today, Jackson my man. You got me thinking."

The letter still burned in his hand as the door closed. "At least I'm good for something."

Then he was alone in the hall with the faces of three dead patients crowding his mind and his profession hanging by a thread. "Yeah, right," he said to the darkness. On his way back to the living room he reached over and straightened the pencil.

Stanley Park smelled of deep earth and rich, damp life. Wendy stepped carefully along the black path, breathing it all in and letting her night vision open wide. The huge forest canopy had absorbed the day's rainfall, and now in the starlit hours after midnight there was a distinct chill in the air. No matter. Her inner fire was glowing hot.

Only in the last few years had she given herself these little treats, and only very seldom. Her harvest walks weren't a necessary part of the work, but it was always worth reminding herself what a dangerous place the world could be for a woman walking at night alone.

The tree trunks were as wide as six of her and towered up into the blackness on either side of the path. There would be no wild animals to worry about - Stanley Park was a scrap of temperate rainforest on a spur of land with the city behind it and the water before it, only the slim ribbon of the Lions Gate Bridge connecting it to the North Shore mountains and real wilderness - but she still felt a tickle of primal night wariness electrify her spine.

She smelled him first. A puff of sweat and hormones sailed to her on the soft air currents eddying through the underbrush and then there he was, a deeper shadow next to the rough bark of a tree. "Out pretty late," came the words, soft and low and stinking of bad teeth.

There it was, the jolt of current that ran from her toes right through to the top of her head, the fear so close to excitement it was impossible to tell the difference. She stopped and took a nervous step back, practically shivering, her eyes straining to see more than just dark on dark. "It's likely past your bedtime, too," she said, the tension making her voice rise. The more she helped him talk, the more she could be sure. And she had to be sure.

"Night's my time," he answered. "This is my path." Now he moved away from the tree and onto the strip of bare earth and she could see him. Taller than her, thin beneath a black cloth coat, face obscured by an unkept beard. A flash of silver down by his right side. "I live here."

The flash of silver had disappeared, which was bad. If she couldn't see the knife it might come dancing out of anywhere. She stepped to the left, to the center of the path, hoping the man would do the same and be revealed. "I don't think the forest belongs to anyone," she said.

"Nope, more like everybody," said the voice out of the dark, calm but tinged with an edge. "Means you gotta be careful. Don't know who you'll meet." He stayed inside the edges of the dark.

Wendy felt the flood of adrenalin ebb away. She made the decision her body had already embraced and stood easy. "I'm not here to hurt you," she told the man.

He let that sink in, then stepped to the center of the path. "You walk like you're here to hurt someone, I'll bet on that. Don't worry, lady. There's a few of us who bed down in the trees and we keep an eye on things. This is my path." A glint of silver flashed again in the slender light. An old flask materialized in the man's hand. "Drink?"

She took the offering. "Why, thank you." It was rum, dark like her father had liked. She stepped to a massive tree trunk and hunkered down. "So, what's a nice man like you doing in a place like this?"

Chapter 7

Tower Beach was deserted and the tide was out across the sandbar. Borden jammed a length of steel fencepole two feet into the sand, watching how gingerly Jackson handled the backpack he was carrying. Interesting. The boy also looked pleased with himself. Even better.

"So, how did you do with my little challenge?" he asked. "I suspect you came up with something impressive."

Jackson gave the pole an appraising ting with a pebble. "Maybe," he said, "although I don't know. It's pretty far from what I usually do." He knelt down, dug into the pack, and produced a metal can with a tight screw-on lid and - of all things - a package of sparklers. When Jackson took the lid off the can and started piling a ring of speckled grey-brown dust around the base of the post, Borden whistled low. Damn it, the boy might have the answer.

"Thermite is pretty simple," Jackson explained as he worked, "it took me no time at all to study up on it. Basically it's a mixture of powdered aluminum and ground-up rust. Gives a hot enough burn to melt through metal, but it isn't an explosion, so it doesn't rock things. Ignites with a sparkler, which makes a handy fuse." He stuck a sparkler deep enough into the sand so it touched the charge, then stood. "What do you think? Will it work?"

An idiot savant, thought Borden. Fortune had favoured

him again. "You get an A for effort regardless. One small adjustment." He bent down and spread some sand over top of the thermite mix. "Don't want a stray spark lighting this up before we're ready. Okay, do it." He slid back a pace while Jackson knelt to light the sparkler. Unpredictable stuff, thermite. But the sparkler sputtered and burst into bright life without incident and they both ran back to a safe distance. "Don't look at the reaction," he warned, and they ducked down and turned their backs to the pole.

The sparkler's crackle graduated to a throaty yowl and the beach lit up with blue-white arc welder flashes. As the glow was dying down they both heard the dull thump of a pole falling onto sand.

"There goes the cup of coffee," muttered Jackson.

"Nonsense!" Borden exclaimed as they trotted over, "fabulous work."

There was an inch of burned and blackened slag sticking out of the ground. He could melt one fencepole, snip a few links, and be in and out of the North Shore Marine Demolitions yard with his packages before the gendarmes even heard about the light show. Then he could get on with the real job.

Time to go. The police might be underfunded bumblers but they weren't completely blind, and he was exposed here. "Good!" he slapped Jackson on the back. "You pass, with flying colours. Listen, I have to run. Bury all this and get the hell out of here. I'll be in touch."

As he speedwalked up the beach he heard what sounded like a hippopotamus crashing through the brush covering the steep hillside. The stupid cops didn't even know the paths. Chalk up yet another one for the industrial saboteur. This city didn't stand a chance.

Jackson stared after Borden as the man disappeared up Trail 3. Bury it and get the hell out of here? No way was he about to leave a jagged iron slug under the sand for someone's bare feet to find. Borden's weird departure left him feeling off balance. He'd been hoping for another coffee and maybe some shop talk.

He began scooping up the cooled bits of hardened metal lying on the beach. As he worked a man came struggling out from the wooded slopes a few hundred yards away. Investigating the burn, maybe. Jackson pretended not to notice him as the man stared hard in his direction, looked around a bit, then walked down the beach, rubbing the corner of his mouth with his shirt cuff.

Balsam Elder Care was a delightful place to work. Tooly Carleton had discovered Jackson's traveling massage therapy service and instructed him to attend the upper-crust assisted living care home, and when he succeeded in freeing her stuck neck she'd introduced him to her friends, Sherry Howe and Delores Kilborn. The place provided well-heeled seniors with private two-room apartments, exercise and entertainment facilities, a real chef in the kitchen, and care aides to supervise the tricky bits.

Jackson could make an entire practice out of this place if he chose to. Tooly wielded influence at the Balsam and made no secret of how much she valued Jackson's ministrations. The head nurse, Olivia, had approached him once with an offer to spend more time here. Jackson had declined, preferring more variety to his work.

Tooly's treatments were easy. Once he had loosened up her cervical fascia and vertebrae as far as her arthritis would allow – which gave her about a 30 percent increase in range, enough to check over her shoulder and see who she was cutting off with her wheelchair – his work with her consisted of keeping the gain from backsliding. Sherry Howe was another easy session. When her impressive girth – you couldn't really call it a waistline anymore – became too much for her knees to bear, she'd landed with a thump in a wheelchair and liked the fit. Jackson's work with her was more active than passive, consisting of range of motion, resisted movement exercises and circulatory work. He kept in touch with Cathy, the Balsam's rehab assistant, who was now able to help Sherry walk a hallway a day.

Then there was Delores Kilborn. Jackson had come to the Balsam one day to find Sherry and Tooly both in the lobby waiting for him. "You will be seeing someone new today," Tooly announced. Delores was her oldest friend, and Tooly had pulled more than a few strings to get her into Balsam Elder Care. He suspected Tooly was paying the woman's bills, too. By rights, Delores Kilborn belonged in a whole different class of facility.

The first time he'd visited her, he had openly gasped. Then he had bent down, taken the frail, silver-haired woman in his arms as gently as he could, and hugged. Delores returned the hug with one arm fluttered onto his shoulder and said, "Good man. I don't expect you can help much."

Every joint in her body was larger than it was supposed to be. Her shoulders knobbed under her dress. Her knuckles stretched their skin to a smooth whiteness. Her knees were flesh-coloured softballs.

When Jackson looked at her he saw stars. Each joint in

Delores' body was producing bright, shooting sparks of pain. The woman was being eaten from within by inflammatory arthritis and putting a brave face on it. Strong medications made the pain bearable.

"Let's see what we can do," he'd told her. And they had begun.

For the first time in his professional career Jackson had started with energy work. The heat from each joint was so fierce he could feel them as they passed under his palms. He simply moved his hands an inch away from Delores' body, thinking cooling thoughts. It had helped, a little. He progressed through the gentlest of touches, then gentle joint movements, hardly more than a whisper. Now, three months down the road, Delores was cautiously optimistic. She felt better. Neither of them had any illusions, of course. Time would do its marching, and damage done was damage done. But, at this stage of the game, any improvement was more than welcome.

This morning was as delightful as usual. Olivia waved to him from the nursing station as he came through the front doors of the Balsam. Tooly kept him entertained with a story about a new resident, an eligible and distinguished bachelor who found himself landed in a house full of old hens and was valiantly trying to fight them off. "I will have him over for tea by the end of the week," she announced. "Before that Colleen in 312 gets her claws into him."

"Happy hunting," Jackson replied, and made his way onwards.

Sherry was coming along, pushing back against his exercises with all the gusto she could muster. "Did you – umph - see the new man in town?" she asked, grunting into a leg push. "He's a looker, no doubt. I have to get in shape." Jackson grinned, and said no more.

He stepped into Delores' living room and stopped, a pain

beginning behind his eyes. Just when he'd almost managed to forget what it felt like.

There was so little in this room, how could it have changed so badly? There was the beige carpeting, running smoothly from the hallway to the far wall of the sitting room. Delores' Oriental rug, with its intricate pattern of peacocks and fans, sat in the middle. Her recliner was in its usual place on the right, next to the small bookcase and an end table. The only other furniture in the room was the television by the doorway to the bedroom.

Jackson willed himself to let go. He didn't want to, knowing what would be waiting for him. But he had to do it, if only to prove he wasn't imagining things.

Delores' room was askew. Her recliner had been moved so that it faced the TV at an odd angle. The doily on the back of it could have been accidentally twisted off-center, but Jackson knew better. The books had been moved to give the illusion that the bookcase was top-heavy and about to fall over. A small, posable artist's figurine with wooden limbs and a blank face tucked into a corner of the books was twisted wrong somehow, into some subtly impossible stance. It was like looking at the room through a funhouse mirror. He felt like he was about to fall over.

He closed his eyes and told his condition to knock it off, but the weirdness remained. He was spooked all over again.

"That you, Jackson? I'm ready," came Delores' thin voice from the bedroom.

"Coming, one second," he called. He straightened the doily, swung the chair the fraction of an inch necessary to make it feel right. He straightened the doll to simple attention. Nothing he could do about the books. "Let's see what we can do today," he said as he went into the bedroom.

Who was doing it? As he walked down the long hallway

towards the lobby afterwards, he tried to logic it out. It had to
be someone who'd been at every place, which left Dr. Dick or
the Filipino girls as the only candidates. But the Balsam had
its own care staff, and Dr. Dick didn't work here. Logic had no
answers.

His feet took him towards the nursing station.

"Hi Olivia," he said before he could catch himself, "can we
talk privately?"

Olivia had been there. She'd worked the wards, the OR, the
private hospitals. She'd taken the university courses, and
taught a few of them. She had the grey hairs, the level gaze,
the unflappable demeanour and the private office. She lifted
her head from her paperwork, instantly alert, and said, "Sure,
Jackson." They both stepped over to the glass office.

It was used more as a paper storage place than a sanctum;
she preferred to be out in the open. But the room had a desk
and chairs and the door closed. She shut it, sat down, and said,
"What's on your mind?"

What the hell to say about all of this. Jackson forced
himself to measure his words. "How's Delores Kilborn doing
these days?"

He could see the files being opened behind her eyes.
"Nothing unusual, so I'm aware. She's improved somewhat
since moving here, thanks in part to the food, in part to having
company close to hand, and in part, so I'm told, to your work.
Why?"

God, this was tricky. He concentrated hard, then found a
way. "Um, Olivia, you're a nurse. Do nurses – I mean, do you –
ever go on intuition?" Intuition, that was it. The great feminine
sense. He would be safe with that one.

Olivia nodded. "Of course. We pay great attention to it.
Why?"

"Well. I guess, I mean, I have a bad feeling about Delores.

It's not based on anything, like I've seen anything wrong, but it's like something's not right, you know? So I was wondering if there was any way you could, -"

"Keep an eye on her? That's what you're suggesting, right? Of course. I will leave a note for the staff to do some extra checks on Delores, day and night." Olivia shifted back in her chair. "You're a professional, Jackson. I trust your judgement. Thank you for bringing this to me." They stood, and Olivia laid a warm hand on his shoulder as they went back outside. She has the touch, he noted, probably gives great massages.

"Thanks, Olivia. I'm sure it's nothing." He headed across the lobby.

The others had had nurses and home care. They'd been protected. They were dead. He found himself detouring past the door and back to Tooly's room. He found her sitting up, watching soap operas.

Care home night shifts were easy but necessary work, consisting mostly of sitting in the nursing station with one eye on the bank of panic lights and doing the occasional meds run. Every once in awhile someone might need help getting off the potty, but mostly you read magazines and chatted with the other nurses to keep yourself awake.

"So you've been all over? This job is a great one for traveling, I want to go to Toronto, you know, work in the Children's Hospital there, it's the best. Never thought about going to another country though, pain about the paperwork, eh? Gets you stuck doing the night shift in places like this, and doing care aide shifts! Ugh, give me a busy OR or Emerg any day. We're supposed to keep an eye on Mrs. Kilborn tonight, room 114, no other notations in her chart, don't know what we're supposed to be looking for. I want to see Europe, too, don't know if I'd like nursing there, probably have to learn another language, but maybe as a tourist. Switzerland has world-class biking trails, a friend was telling me about them, amazing verticals. Toronto first, though."

Thank God Sandy wasn't snapping gum in between sentences, or Wendy might have to smack her. As it was, the girl was only being twenty. A year out of nursing school and fit as a skateboard model, she was still young enough to think that screaming down a mud path with nothing but a helmet between you and an old-growth cedar was somehow a sensible thing to do. But her attention was always on the panic lights and her charting was precise and prompt. She was going to make a good nurse.

"There goes Mr. Jolson, he's got a bad prostate keeps him on the john forever and then he gets stuck. I'll get it," Sandy flipped off the blipping red light and stood to go in one motion, then Wendy was alone.

She breathed in the mingled office and medicine aromas of the deserted nursing station. It was delightful to be working in an institution again. Emma Jacobs at the Arbutus Care Agency was thrilled to have someone who could fill in at places like this. Wendy was glad for another chance to exercise her mercy in a familiar setting.

The note about Delores Kilborn was a possible concern, but it actually made Wendy's task easier. Now she had an excuse to enter the poor woman's room and ease her terrible suffering.

"I'm back," announced Sandy ten minutes later, "all handled."

"I'm going on a round," said Wendy. "I'll look in on 114 along the way."

She went straight there. Mrs. Kilborn's closed door looked like every other door spaced down the hallway, but behind this one it was going to be a special night. She'd made the adjustments the night before. The angel was in there, watching over Mrs. Kilborn's last hours, the little posable artist's model suspended on thin wire with all its beautiful, perfect articulations. Everything was ready. Whether she knew it or not, Delores Kilborn was ready.

Wendy pulled the finger-thick syringe out of her skirt pocket and tucked it inside her right hand. The plunger was already drawn back, the syringe loaded with 200 mg of succinylcholine. One quick shot into the fold of the buttock, where a single small puncture would never be seen. 30 mg of the powerful paralytic and a physician could stick a tube down someone's throat without inducing so much as a shiver. This dose would disconnect all the muscles in the poor woman's body in a very few seconds. Including, and most especially, her diaphragm. There would be no sound, no breath. Nothing but the blessed peace and Delores' trip into the final quiet.

The door slid open and Wendy stepped inside. She closed it again without a click, then turned into the darkness, the familiar compassion starting its slow fire.

Something wasn't right. She stood, reluctant to try a light, feeling into the space. It smelled like any other patient room, old perfume and old body fighting it out over the background of institutional carpet and drywall. What she could see appeared normal. The feel of the room was nothing special.

It felt empty. Like there was nobody here.

Fighting a growing confusion, she placed the syringe back into her skirt and slapped on the lights. Her adjustments had been undone. The bed was made. Delores Kilborn was already gone.

And she'd taken her pillow with her.

"Mrs. Kilborn is not in her room," she announced a minute later at the nursing station. That brought Sandy up out of the pages of Freewheel Monthly in a hurry.

"What?"

It took them three minutes to find the sticky note, on Tooly Carleton's file and not Delores'. 'Mrs. Carleton will be having a sleepover tonight with Mrs. Kilborn and Mrs. Howe.' "Whew!" said Sandy, "thought we had a runner there for a minute. Not that I'd ever expect 114 to run anywhere."

"Hmm." Wendy was already past the crisis, her nose deep into the back pages of Delores Kilborn's chart. There it was, plain as day. She had a massage therapist.

The heat of her compassion settled into a slow, deep burn.

A mountain creek gurgled in its bed to Borden's right as he strolled up the parkway path swinging a black nylon bag. It was well past midnight. The North Vancouver air reeked of green things and the damp, brown dirt left behind when they died. The white marker rock was still in place, practically glowing against the dark soil. Borden checked across the creek rocks and up and down the trail, making certain he was alone. Then he breathed deeply of the night and sidestepped into the thick salal.

North Shore Marine Demolitions was a halfhearted affair on a fenced lot, tucked between the blank industrial warehouses that lined the creek. A prefabricated double-wide by the street entrance served as the public face of the company, but the building's back wall showed chipped paint and streaks of the creeping mildew that was everywhere in this town. A

Quonset hut to the left held three utility trucks and a couple of zodiacs on a trailer. Close to the creek end of the lot was a pile of old drill bits and rusting machinery leaching heavy metals into the earth. Behind the Quonset but well away from the chain link perimeter fence was a cinderblock square with a pitched metal roof squatting on a thick concrete pad.

There was no sign saying 'Explosives - Keep Out', but to anyone in the industry the storage building said, 'Things That Go Boom - Come On In.' They'd gotten some things right, he'd give them that much. The bunker had a decent setback from the Quonset and the office. The foundation, walls and roof were no doubt fire and bullet proof, fully up to code. The problem lay with the man door beside the reinforced loading ramp entrance, and he'd spotted it at once on his first driveby. It was a solid wood door set in a steel frame with thick hinges and an ordinary shopping mall handle, an oversized padlock above the handle securing a beefy hasp for insurance.

A poorly-run business with an oversized explosives shed secured by locks that would cost him all of thirty seconds. The setup was perfect. Except for the fence.

His arrogance had betrayed him, no question. The story about finding an old concrete bomb shelter and wanting it gone had found a willing listener in the cordite-sniffing freak who answered the Demolitions telephone. Cost be damned, he'd told the man, and why don't we have a little fun while we're at it? They discussed penetration and blast patterns for a pleasant half hour, Borden walking the conversation around till the guy suggested exactly the ordnance he was looking for. Then, as he'd hit Enter on the extortionate deposit, he'd slipped. "Your facility is secure, right? Don't want this falling into the wrong hands." There was simply no excuse for it.

So they'd spent his deposit, and now he found himself staring down a chain link fence with some fancy little balls atop each post and a network of thin, grey wires threaded through odd links from the dirt to the concertina wire. Fencepost tremblors and cut sensors, paid for with his money to keep operators like him out. The tremblors would call for help if they detected any impact larger than a stiff breeze. The cut sensors covered all the links from a foot either side of each post. Only an excess-of-caution recon had saved him from blowing up what was left of his career. Only by going directly through a post could he hope to access the facility.

Then he'd gone for a walk on a beach. Now, courtesy of the kid, he was going to defeat the system. The night was quiet. He tucked himself in by the fence, reached into the bag and pulled out a set of geared bolt cutters, strong enough to manage tempered lifting chains and smooth as butter with fence links. He pulled a dental mirror from his pocket and slipped it through a link at the bottom of the fence. The back side of the link was clear of the thin cut sensor. He snipped it and moved up one, angling the mirror to see. In six minutes he had a crick in his neck and a rectangle of cuts almost three feet high and two wide, with a fencepost right in the middle.

He pulled a plastic can out of the bag and eased the lid off, mounding the powdered thermite around the base of the pole. He produced three flat, asbestos oven liners that he stuck into the ground in a semicircle around the thermite. They would hide at least a little of the reaction's glare. Lastly he placed a sparkler into the mix and covered the mound with dirt.

Even the most meticulous plans hinged on a little slice of luck. "Here goes nothing," he muttered, sparked the fuse and hustled back into the salal.

The glow lit up the surrounding warehouse walls like a klieg-lit crime scene. Borden's body tensed and his heels dug in at the magnitude of it, a classic startle response, but nobody came running. The creek burbled, the thermite gave an occasional crackle, and nothing else stirred. The reaction took forty-five agonizing seconds to burn itself out. He waited in the bushes for another six minutes. Then he levered himself up and went over for a look.

The bottom half of the post was gone. The section of cut fence hung by the few links he'd left for the purpose. A puddle of slag lay on the ground beneath the remainder of the post, which was suspended on the fence and still smoking with an arc welder tang. He wriggled through the snipped section of fence, careful not to disturb the tremblor still in place on top.

The locks on the bunker door gave him no trouble. He stepped into the explosives shed, closed the door behind him and hit the lights.

The thick plastic shelves along both walls were loaded, charges on the left and detonators on the right in neat sections. He could see crates of dynamite and Semtex and some spools of detonation cord in the back. The Marine Demolitions character was a kindred spirit, no question of that. The smell was heavenly, and he took a moment to breathe it in.

In the middle of the floor was a three foot tall pine box with military stencilling. After the inventory numbers was the label Chg, Demo Shaped - 40 lb M3A1 - Comp B. He felt a warm glow start up in his midsection imagining the sweet piece of ordnance inside. He found a pry bar and got to work.

The dark green cone looked like the nose off a man-sized model rocket. The bottom was deeply inverted, painted green but made of pure copper. The 25 pounds of Comp B plastic explosive inside the thing would turn that copper inside out, into a superheated bolt of plasma as brilliant as a solar flare. The molten arrow was strong enough to punch through 60 inches of reinforced concrete. It was just the thing for opening up an old bomb shelter. And more than enough for the real job.

The M3A1 had all the right military markings. He plucked

it from the packing foam and it had the right weight. He lifted it up and took a long sniff, then grinned into the night. They hadn't thought about the smell. This metal had never been near explosives.

They kept underestimating him. An order like this would naturally trigger some interest from the authorities, and of course they'd match the timing with current events and try some stunt. That was why he'd been watching the lot since late afternoon. He was confident the police weren't watching the bunker. They'd placed all their bets on him falling for a dummy device.

He set it aside and rummaged around some more. By the loading dock he found yesterday's shipment, a wooden crate with Alford stamped in flat grey ink on top. The side label said Rebar Cutter, 25 Count, Unloaded, but it lied. He'd stolen this crate from the Alford plant five weeks ago, packed it carefully and shipped it himself. Inside, sealed in a vinyl bag, was a stack of plastic-wrapped bricks labelled Comp B, all emanating that wonderful RDX aroma.

The M3A1 and the bricks of Comp B made his bag almost 65 pounds. He'd spent the last month training for this and shouldered the load easily. In a side pouch he placed a handful of electric detonators from the right-hand wall.

He turned out the lights and waited by the door a full minute for his night vision to return. No one was waiting outside, he was certain of that. Still, fortune favoured the prepared. He danced around a little to settle the load on his back, pulled a Ruger American from a clamshell holster tucked into his pants and wiped some moisture off his forehead.

He went through the door and dodged three crouching steps to the right, gun forward and eyes scanning for movement. There was none. No shots. No running footsteps or shouted orders. Borden backed his finger off the Ruger's trigger and stood up in the empty yard, allowing himself a deep breath. Okay then.

Halfway back through the hole in the fence he was at maximum crouch, both hands working the chain link and his Ruger stowed away. A metallic snick-snick out of the salal froze him in mid-wriggle for a split moment, then he scrabbled to get free of the wire. His head labelled the sound - not racking slide but clicking phone camera - as a white face zoomed out of the dark almost to spitting range.

The fucking beach freak. The one who'd recognized him at the mall and had the nerve to stalk him. Here he was again, now in black from head to toe, his shaggy mop tucked into a watch cap.

The shock and confusion at seeing such an impossible thing would have paralyzed a lesser man. Borden had trained for this. He knew better than to let his head get in the way of threat assessment and radical action. Still halfway through the fence, he twisted the hip with the gun towards his diving fingers, actually touching the grips, when the hippie lifted a black cell phone.

"Gotcha," he said in a soft singsong, and blasted the camera flash through Borden's dilated irises and right into the back of his skull.

Borden heard the asshole run away as he thrashed out of the fence and toward the sound of the creek, finding the path with his feet while searing, white balls of light bounced off the inside of his head. It took three minutes for his sight to clear. No way was he going to find the guy in all these woods now.

Settling the duffel on its straps again he turned right on the creek path, breaking into a light jog and refusing to feel weirded out. His future was waiting. And if his future involved another encounter with that hippie, the hippie wouldn't have one. Of that he was damn certain.

"Inspector, are you sure about this?" The RCMP sergeant frowned down the length of the surveillance van at Simon Takeda. Takeda felt his jaw muscles ratchet up another notch as the target jogged off the screens of three treetop cams covering the creekside trail. "I mean, it's your show," the sergeant continued, waving at the screens. "I'm only here as the North Van jurisdictional rep, but we got the guy dead to rights. He tripped every alarm the company has."

"Breaking and entering, destruction of property and stealing a worthless hunk of metal." Takeda hated saying the words, like he hated everything about this op, but the orders had come straight from the top. "They want the brass ring on this one, not a string of small charges. We have to stop him in the act of rigging the device. The second we can prove he's a terrorist and not just an ordinary idiot, then we move. Not before. Speaking of idiots," he added, catching movement on another monitor and reaching for the van's door handle, "I'll be back in five."

Takeda slipped into the dark, glad to be doing something. He stretched his legs into a fast high-step through the bush and came out onto the creek path 20 feet ahead of the flasher. Point one for the young man - he stopped for a moment then resumed walking forward, unafraid.

"What the fuck was that all about?" Takeda demanded, keeping his voice quiet. He flicked the beam of a small penlight over his VPD badge, then over the subject. Six feet even, standing loose and quiet like a big cat. Black yoga tights, black long-sleeved tee, black cap. No place to hide a weapon, other than his phone tucked into a shirtsleeve. Blond curls sticking out from the cap here and there and his face was too white, but overall not bad. "Vancouver Police. Identification." He thrust out a hand.

The kid - early twenties maybe - slipped a card holder from his waistband and produced a driver's license. Takeda looked it over and recognized the name. His flashlight moved back up to study the kid's face.

"You look more like your mother. Okay, answer the question." He handed the license back.

The young guy spoke in a soft countertenor, slow and easy, never taking his eyes off Takeda. "It's simple enough. That guy's a predator and he's stalking around in my back yard. I'm watching him. Because until a minute ago, I thought you weren't."

"Predator. Huh." The kid wasn't wrong there. Takeda reached for the mic clipped to his shoulder. "Team One, break cover." With hardly a rustle three of his best men rose from the bushes and strode onto the path, two behind them and one down the creek a ways. The kid jumped, surprised and then impressed.

"So you saw some guy that looked dangerous and you decided to follow him. That's a whole bunch of not very smart. Ever think of calling us?" He tapped his badge.

"You were already watching him. Um, not too well, sorry. So I figured I had to."

Takeda took that all in and chewed on it, found some gristle. "You're telling me you watched him all the way to here? It's the middle of nowhere in the middle of the night. What did you do, watch him from inside his trunk?"

He gave Takeda a flash of teeth. "Almost." He made a move for the cell phone, paused to let Takeda nod, then pulled it out and swiped to a screen. It was a map of local streets. On it was a blue dot, moving out of range over the Second Narrows

Bridge. "GPS tracker under the trunk. Once I saw he was headed for the warehouses, I knew what he was after. So do you, I'm guessing."

Takeda might almost be starting to like this guy. "I see. I can tell you two things. First, you're making things worse not better. Our surveillance is the kind neither you nor he will ever see, but if your prank has scared him into some evasive maneuvers we might lose him. Second, he's above your pay grade. Stay far away from him and let us do our work. I trust you can find your way home."

The boy recognized the dismissal. "Yes, sir." He started up the path, away from the parking lot and deeper into the night. He was as silent as Takeda's team, a fading blotch in the dark. Big cat moves.

"Wait. One more thing." The boy's face turned into view again. Takeda said, "If you ever feel the need to make a mark in life, consider applying. I think you'd like it." He pointed a finger towards the curls. "You'd have to lose those."

The boy grinned. "Good night, officer. Thanks for the words. Happy hunting." He melted back into the night. Gesturing for his men to follow, Takeda did the same.

Chapter 8

When Jackson's phone buzzed first thing Wednesday, the call display said Balsam Elder Care. "Could you come by my office this morning?" The gravity underneath Olivia's few words dragged at his heart.

Olivia led him to the office, closed the door and sat down. "I saw you come back in after our discussion the other day," she said without preamble. "What did you do?"

"What happened?" Jackson wasn't sitting yet. He'd known since the call, but still he had to hear it.

Olivia was silent for a moment. "Mrs. Kilborn passed away last night. Now my question."

Jackson sat down before he fell down. "I asked Tooly to have her friends sleep over."

"Why?"

"Did she? Did Delores spend the night over there?"

Olivia was unused to having her questions answered with questions. She pursed her lips, restraining her irritation, and said, "Yes. Mrs. Carleton asked, and the logistics were manageable, so I agreed. I hear she even bribed the kitchen to supply popcorn. Now answer. Why?"

A hot flush started below his collarbones and galloped up his face. He dropped his eyes down to the papers on Olivia's desk. "I wanted her to be safe. Around other people."

"That much is obvious. Again, why?"

"So she wouldn't die."

Olivia stared at him for five more seconds while his insides rolled. He'd seen it, he'd fixed it, and still he'd made no difference.

At last she blinked and sank back in her chair. "So you know when the end is near. Okay, I've heard of that. Tell me about it."

"You haven't heard of this." Fighting another furious blush, he told her. The rearranged homes, the chilly wind, the dolls. Of course that movable wooden thing in Delores' sitting room had been a doll, he'd been stupid not to see it. The telling brought with it a sort of embarrassed relief, like putting down a loaded pack after a long hike. He kept his voice level and kept talking. He told Olivia about his condition.

"Then they all died. Every single one of them, the very next day. It's like I can't do a thing to stop it."

Silence settled into the office for a long breath, save for hushed murmurs from the nursing station outside. Olivia stirred at last and fingered a file loose from the pile on her desk. "That is some story. In case you're wondering, Jackson, I already knew about your OCD. Did you know you have a certain way of walking in here? You don't cut across the lobby from the front door to the hallways like everyone else. You follow the design in the carpet, into the lobby then veering right. If someone's in your way, you keep as close to the line as you can.

"About all this sneaking around. I believed you when you came to me the other day. I took steps based on your intuition. That should have been enough for you." She lifted her hand from the file and wagged a finger. "Don't go behind my back like that, Jackson. Don't sneak. It's not respectful, and it's not dignified."

He nodded. "Didn't even work," he said.

Olivia hefted the folder, a patient file with the letters KIL in colourful tags down the flap. "Which brings us to the rest of this. I trusted your concern. Enough so that, when Mrs. Kilborn passed yesterday, I asked the doctor to give her a closer look. Do you know what he found?"

Jackson rocked forward, clenched. "What?"

"Nothing. Delores Kilborn simply stopped breathing during the night." She flipped open the file and read from it. "There were no signs of foul play or suspicious activity." Olivia moved forward herself, the ghost of a smile reaching up her face and the corners of her eyes reaching down. "Sometimes these things happen, Jackson. It's good that you have your eyes open, and that you trust what you see. I'm flattered that you trusted me enough to tell me about it. But we both have to trust the evidence, too." She closed the chart. "That's all."

He made sure not to follow the carpet on his way out.

By the time he got the door unlocked and was standing alone in his quiet apartment the weight of Delores Kilborn's absence from the world dragged at his heart. One more face to add to the growing carousel of the recently departed that whirled on the edge of his mind.

He needed some big medicine. It was time for lasagne. He set some noodle water on the stove and got out a tub of ricotta cheese, thumbing the TV remote onto the news channel for background noise.

Good sauce started with the big three -garlic, roma tomatoes and oregano. The kitchen rhythm soon lulled him into the peaceful trance of slice and stir. It wasn't till the announcer mentioned explosives that he paid attention to the newscast.

"The thief failed to gain entry to the explosives bunker," the woman was saying, "managing only to melt his way through the fence before running away from the police, who were alerted to his presence." The camera panned over the back side of a commercial lot, then focused in on a section of wire fence. The links had been cut to make a neat flap, attached at the top to a pole that was charred black and ended in a nubbled stub three feet above the ground.

"Ass. Hole." He stared at the TV as the lasagne noodles bubbled behind him. Borden had taken his little solution and used it. He'd been successful, too, whatever the anchorwoman was saying. As the camera held still on the ravaged fence he could see two sets of footprints in the deep earth underneath. The set coming out was much more indented. Borden had been loaded down.

He'd found what he was looking for. He'd found a lot of it. And he'd used thermite to get it.

Layering the noodles with sauce and cheese got him back into the kitchen zone. There was no need to call anyone. Whatever Borden was up to, no doubt the cops knew way more about it than Jackson did. The whole thing was more than he wanted to think about when he had enough troubles of his own.

They were done, of course. Jackson wished Borden the very worst of luck with whatever the hell he was up to and resolved to forget the whole thing. Chalk it up to a lesson learned. He layered the last few noodles with sauce and dusted the top with parm and some extra oregano, then popped it in the oven and turned up the heat.

'Hoo, hoo hoo!' Wendy laughed in delight as the model train's shiny locomotive sounded its horn from the eaves of the living room. Samuel Long, onetime CP Rail signalman and more recent widower and invalid, lived in a virtual train museum. Every inch of his small house was filled with whistles, lanterns, framed schedules, posters and all things train. His couch had been lifted from an observation car. The breakfast nook in the kitchen was a leather and brass Pullman reproduction. Mr. Long's pet retirement project had been to install a model train track along the high ceilings of his living room. He insisted on falling asleep each night to the sound of its clacking wheels and tinny electric hooter.

She stepped back through the hall to the bedroom and looked in on her charge, feeling the old, familiar sadness bloom again. A stroke had robbed him of one leg, one arm, and half his face, transforming him in a blink from scrappy independence to a wheelchair and assisted living. All he could do was sit and stare at his little train. It was no way to finish a life.

She listened to Sam Long's leaky-tire snores and retreated to her cup of tea in the kitchen. This was why she'd been given her calling. She was the only one strong enough for what needed to be done. It was as clear to her now as when her mother had been lying under three blankets in the ancient Queen Anne bed and her father, such a big man with so few words, stared into the knotted wood of the kitchen table with his heart breaking and said, "Care for her, Wendy. Care for her."

Burrard Inlet sparkled beyond the kitchen window in the cool glow of a full moon, the sight filling her with an old love. She had grown up by a different ocean. The water of her childhood was harder, saltier, greyer than this ocean here, and it scraped up against a rugged and windblown land where

Vancouver's magnificent firs and cedars wouldn't have lasted a day. None of that seemed to matter, though. The compass in her soul said she'd found home.

The Maine of her childhood was strong in her mind, as she supposed everybody's childhood stood out in bright relief. There was the ocean rubbing the granite boulders into sand; there was the village, and the bus rides to school with the twenty-odd kids from her county. There was her father, large and solid and quiet in the morning on his way out to fix lobster traps, mend nets and layer fibreglass on the curvy Cape Island boats, large and solid and tired when he came home at night. He always made the time to play with her, and sometimes made her things, so many games and so many toys she'd forgotten most of them. He seldom spoke much, so few words on so few occasions that she was sure she remembered every one.

Always strong in these childhood memories was her mother, Hilda Corbett. Not big — Wendy inherited her bulk from her dad — but strong in other ways.

Wendy's mother was the village witch. Not so you would notice if you saw her walking down the street, but all the locals knew it. Hilda was who the women invited over when they were having trouble with their children, or their man, or their garden patch, or if they just wanted to talk. She would sit in their kitchens in her thrift-store dresses and listen to each woman's story. They would tell her their fears of a husband's infidelities. They would tell her of longing for a child, or about their sick relatives, or the knotgrass in their garden, or their money problems. Hilda sat there and listened to it all. Sometimes Wendy went along with her, when the conversation wasn't going to be about other children or about sex, and sit in the corner with a comic book or a doll and munch cookies and take it all in. Wendy learned a great deal about life when the adults' backs were turned. She was certain, with the hindsight of years, that it had been part of her mother's plan for her from the very beginning.

Sometimes, if the problem was a simple one, Hilda would pull some yarn from the huge bag she always carried and knit a scarf, the long thing materializing as the conversation went on. When the woman had talked herself out Hilda would give her the scarf. "Now, Melinda, you says you wants your Mike to stop going out at night, but what you really want is for him to pay more attention to you, right? So you take this here scarf, it's loose at the bottom. You pull the string, and the knot'll come undone, see, like this. These knots have your problems in 'em, right? Now, every knot that comes undone, you pause and say to yourself, 'I love my Mike and he loves me.' Don't you raise your brows up, that's what you're telling me you really want. You do this. Every knot, you say that to yourself. I expect this scarf to be gone in two days. And he'll stay home. Knot magic, you can trust it. You watch."

For the harder problems, sometimes Wendy and her mother would take the woman for a walk on the beach on the other side of Watcher's Point. Hilda would talk low to the woman so Wendy couldn't hear. Then they would spend time arranging driftwood on the beach, or drawing words or pictures in the sand. Hilda always got the other woman to do the work. Then they would stand there, sometimes for hours, until the incoming tide had taken it all away.

Her mother helped in more direct ways, too. Sometimes she just walked through the village to another woman's house and had a quiet talk; 'balancing things out,' she called it. Or she would leave presents for people. Often she left dolls.

Hilda made wonderful dolls. Each child in the village owned one, and Wendy herself had three. Hilda would carve them out of driftwood, or sew them from old socks or bits of bright cloth she brought home, or bits of sail her husband brought home. They were always fun and attractive, although seldom what you would call pretty. The kid who got a Hilda doll held onto it for life.

The other thing her mother did, in every house, was move things around. Hilda would walk into a woman's kitchen, look around, and spin a toaster on the counter so it faced the other way, or move a pitcher of water farther from the door, or nonchalantly turn the kitchen table around 'so's I can sit behind it.' The changes always seemed to put the other woman more at ease.

For Wendy, the changes were thunderously loud. It was like, in moving one thing, her mother was taking the whole house in her two small hands and shaking it like a snow globe. One time Hilda repositioned some books on a shelf and saw the look of shocked surprise on Wendy's face. "Ah, so you see it, too," she'd whispered. That was all she ever said on the matter.

The village was a quiet place, and largely peaceful. Wendy was sure her mother had a lot to do with that.

The change came on Wendy's fourteenth birthday. "Think I'll rest some today," her mother said, and went to the couch and stayed there. She missed the small party with Wendy's friends. It was no big deal. But it was.

In a matter of days her father noticed, then a very few days after the entire village knew something was up. The doctor from Bangor was called, the word nobody wanted to hear was said, and Mr. and Mrs. Corbett started driving into the city for treatments.

Wendy stayed home. She told her dad there was nothing to do in the city, but the truth was she needed to be home. While her mother and father were gone, Wendy prowled the house and rearranged.

She sat on the kitchen floor and searched, straining hard, for the thing that would make the difference. No improvement showed itself to her; the frying pan on the wall, the magazine rack in the corner, the chairs around the table, were all in their proper place. Of course, why would it be else, her mind said. Think of who put them there.

But there had to be something. Day after day, while her mother and father spent their time in the city hospital, Wendy roamed the house and searched.

Before they came home, in desperation, Wendy would choose an item and move it. A picture, the living room couch where her mother collapsed when they came home, the big, enamel breadbox on the kitchen counter. Then she'd look for her mother's expression. Hilda caught the change within minutes of coming through the door. Sometimes she'd smile, a small, sad flicker of a thing. Then she'd fall asleep, and Wendy, trying not to cry with frustration, would move the thing back again.

Her mother lost weight. She lost colour. She lost life. It was almost as if Wendy could see it leaving her, a thin stream that fled under the doorsill and vanished.

The day came when her mother didn't notice. It was the day her father had to help her in from the car. "That was the last visit," her father told Wendy in the kitchen that night, after Hilda was fast asleep upstairs. "No more of that, thank Christ. Now we get to care for her." He looked her straight in the eye then, a thing he rarely did, and she felt the force of it like a December gale. "Care for her, Wendy. I'm about played out. Care for her."

It was his pain that did it. There was so much of it, rushing through that single stare and simple plea, the first thing her father had ever asked of her. With a crack that shook the world down to bedrock a space opened inside and Wendy could see it all. The whole house throbbed with pain and she knew how to get rid of it.

She stood up from the kitchen table, went to the counter and pushed the breadbox over by the back door. It made no difference whatever to the breadbox or the room. But the huge charge of pain in the kitchen started ebbing away under the door.

"Think I'll go to bed now," her father said.

Her mother was too weak to come downstairs the next morning. Hilda had seemed to shrink in the night. "Something's wrong, Wendy," she murmured up from her pillow. Then she thought about that a moment and gave a wry grimace. "I mean, more than this little thing. In the house. Will you look around for me? You know what I mean."

Wendy laid her hand on her mother's head and said with pride, "I have, Mumma. Nothing's wrong, I've set it all right."

Her mother frowned but had no strength to argue. "That's okay, then. I guess I need to sleep." She closed her eyes.

Wendy spent an hour at her mother's bedside. Hilda Corbett's time to walk in the sun or dance her toes out of reach of the waves or even eat a meal in the kitchen was done. Her time with Wendy was done, and Wendy spent the hour sobbing out her goodbyes. Then she spent another hour playing with things in the bedroom. She shifted the dresser, but that didn't seem right. Then she rearranged the things on top of it, mostly pill bottles now. She closed the window, opened the closet door, took a picture of the ocean off the wall. At last, when every detail of her new vision had been fulfilled, the room felt perfect.

She went back to the bed and gently shook her mother awake. "I've done it, Mumma. I know now. See."

Hilda lifted her head from the pillow's deep indent, looked at the closet to the left, then swept her gaze around. She took it all in. Wendy watched, her heart glowing with pride, as her mother's remaining days drained away like an ebbing tide and that sad, beautiful face flashed through confusion into a black horror.

"Oh no," whispered Hilda Corbett, one hand to her chest and her eyes fixed on her daughter, "oh no." Then she sighed back into the pillow and was gone.

Wendy didn't cry at death, not then, not ever after. She fairly split open with the huge feeling inside. Her great gift had brought peace.

In Samuel Long's kitchen she finished her tea and rummaged through her night shift bag. She laid a syringe on the kitchen table alongside a package of RapidKlot, then rose to get a glass of water. Sterile saline would be better, but it didn't really matter. She tore open the gauze pad – for emergency external use only, said the big, red warning – and dissolved the grey powder into the water with a few stirs.

This was going to be different. She paused, running over it again. It wasn't cheating, really, but insurance. There had been a fair number of deaths since her arrival. One more with her at the bedside might draw attention. A single regret flashed by for the difficulty it would cause Jackson Teague, but that was for the best. He needed a new direction for his career, too. One that would take him far away from her.

She filled the syringe, washed out the glass and headed back into Mr. Long's bedroom. The slim shape under the covers rippled as he rolled over in his sleep and from the door she could see the unconscious grimace as his left leg stayed where it was, cocked at a difficult angle. She stepped over and moved the leg over one-handed. There was no danger of waking the old man with the touch. "Like an old log," he'd proclaimed on their first evening together, prodding it with his dinner fork. "Can't feel a thing."

She lifted the sheet and exposed his skinny, atrophied calf.

Chapter 9

Jackson felt like a kid on his first train ride whenever he visited Sam Long's place. Settled on a large lot behind a tall cedar hedge that bordered the Arbutus rails-to-trails corridor, the white Cape Cod spoke of old Vancouver as much as the long-retired train signalman himself. A shiny green door with a brass knocker shaped like a cowcatcher let into a living room that was a monument to train memorabilia, from the old conductor's cap hanging in the corner to the HO scale model on tracks near the ceiling.

He scrolled through his mental notes on Long as he headed up the flagstone path. "Tough old bird," Dr. Dick had commented when he phoned the referral in to Jackson, "but sooner or later everybody's goose is cooked, eh? Advanced emphysema, complicated by hemiplegia from an ischemic CVA. Do what you can for him." Bad lungs and a stroke, in other words. Dr. Dick usually gave Jackson open-ended referrals and Jackson appreciated the inherent trust in his skills.

For Sam Long, what he could do was joint motion and circulatory work. To everyone's surprise his smoker's emphysema hadn't been what threw him into bed; he was perfectly fine trundling about his house and yard, dragging oxygen along and pausing to chug for breath like an old engine. Then he'd woken up in the hospital one day with a leg and arm that wouldn't move. His kids had done the usual putting down of foot and insisting on a nursing home, and Long had done the usual setting of jaw and insisting on staying in his house, and the care aides had moved in as the normal compromise. Not long after, Jackson appeared on the scene. He visited Sam Long each week to massage life back into his legs and take the stroked one – "my deadwood," Long called it – through some basic range of motion to keep it healthy and pliable. Long had no feeling whatsoever in the thing, but the rest of his body noticed when his leg felt better.

"Hello, Jackson," said Florita as she opened the door, "Mr. Long is ready for you."

Jackson was five steps into the living room before he slowed to a stop and said, "Oh no."

"What is it?" asked Florita, standing by the conductor's cap.

The first thing your eyes landed on when confronted with Sam Long's living room was the bullseye lanterns mounted on the far wall. Then maybe you saw the dark wood panelling, or the plush carpets, or the gleaming brass accents and tasselled chairs. The coffee table was a polished steel train wheel that must have weighed a ton. By the time you took it all in you expected the scenery outside the windows to be moving.

Nothing was moving now. The room was dead. Again. He stood in the center of it feeling a chilly wind blow along the floor and raise goosebumps on his ankles, his heart sinking and a spooky weirdness crawling up the back of his spine. What had changed?

"Have you rearranged in here?" he demanded. He didn't realize how sharp his voice was until he saw Florita's eyes flash at him.

"No, I have not. I do not touch the client's things, remember, except maybe to dust and clean sometimes. No rearranging. Stop asking that, please."

"Sorry, Florita, I didn't mean to bark. But somebody's

moved things here." One change was obvious; he strode over to the far wall and yanked a tack out from behind the right-hand lantern. It fell back against the wall, maybe half an inch, and again its huge lens pointed straight ahead. That helped a bit. It also brought a gasp from Florita. A big wooden train whistle lay across the coffee table, a long, square block that would play four deep notes at once when you blew through it. He lined it up lengthwise to the room instead of crossways. It didn't seem to help, so he spun it back again.

What else? One of the plush chairs was moved off its place, he could see divots in the carpet where it had been. He moved it back, and the energy in the place picked up a little more. "I did not do that, – " started Florita.

"It's okay, see, it belongs here." That wasn't all, not even close. The room felt dizzying. In a weird illusion, like standing still after moving fast, Jackson felt like the room was sliding backwards.

He couldn't fix it. Florita was watching him, concerned and suspicious, and he could not afford to be noticed in that way. Jackson pushed through into the hallway and down to the bedroom.

Sam Long was in bed, all ninety-eight pounds of him, grinning and waving. "Hey, kid," he sucked a breath through the thin plastic cannula hissing oxygen under his nose, "thought you'd never get here. Gotta keep," suck, "good time." He gestured to the big train-station clock mounted above the dresser, its black arms sweeping through five minutes past the hour. A trainman to the last.

"You old coot," Jackson laughed, "still puffing along, I see. How you been?"

"Out of sorts today," he wheezed. "Nothing" – suck – "specific, just kind of draggy. Rust on the tracks, you know. Except" – suck – "for the old wooden leg here." He thumped his left leg, the stroked one. "Might as well cut it off for all the good it does. Probably" - wheeze - "kill me dead, though, eh?"

"Your body would miss it. Let's perk it up a bit."

The massage for Sam Long was deceptively simple. The first part of the session was circulatory work to flush new blood through tired tissues – out with the bad blood, in with the good, so to speak. Then came range of motion, with Jackson lifting and rotating Sam's hips, knees, ankles and feet through all the ways they could move. This boosted circulation some more, freshened up the cartilage and fired the nerve endings that reminded his nervous system the leg was still there. Some detailed point-pressure massage for the soles of his feet was a massive stimulation for Sam's balance centers and basic body awareness, and some general massage finished things off.

Behind this fundamental work was Jackson's constant attention and assessment. For all Sam Long's brash talk, he'd lost his wind and was now as brittle as an old stick. There was only so much massage his system could take and Jackson kept an eye on Sam's face and an ear on his breathing to make sure he wasn't pushing things. Elder massage was always and forever a balancing act. Do what good you can without overtaxing the system.

He pulled back the sheet. Sam's skinny legs were the same as ever, wiry and hard-muscled and uniformly chilly. They would be nice and warm after he'd finished. "Looks the same as always," he mumbled to himself, and reached for his oil bottle.

Sam Long dozed off within a minute. The room grew quiet except for the sound of his even breathing and the steady hiss of the cannula. Jackson finished the massage on Sam's good leg and switched over to the left one. He started at the cool foot and worked his way up.

'Whoo! Whoo!' He almost jumped, then grinned as the little train in the living room repeated its tinny hoot. Florita had succumbed to temptation and thrown the switch on the wall. He could hear the tiny clacking as the train ran about its track.

Sam's eyes popped open at the sound of the whistle and he broke into a smile. He laid back to listen and his grin turned into a puzzled grimace.

Something was missing from the room's soundscape. The oxygen machine was purring on, but Sam's breathing wasn't. His face beeted up and he flapped his hand at Jackson, alarm rising to panic in his eyes. Jackson stopped massaging Sam's calf and jumped for the door. "Florita!" he yelled. "Ambulance, now! Call 911!"

Sam's breathing wasn't happening. Jackson ran back to the bed. The old man was scarlet now, hands clutching his upper chest. Jackson knew first aid, of course, but this was beyond him. He placed his own hands over Sam's, feeling the awful stillness of the ribs.

"Breathe, Sam!" He tried squeezing the brittle ribcage, forcing some air out so more air could come in. What came out was Sam's eyes, bugging so far they almost popped. He shook his head in two rapid jerks and grabbed Jackson's hands. Jackson stopped. It was all he could think of.

The realization came to them both at the same time. Sam Long, still holding Jackson's hands, dropped his panic like an old habit and stopped straining. He gave Jackson a slow nod. One corner of his lips jerked up in a wry half-grin, he held Jackson's eye for a last moment. Then everything relaxed. His face started a long, slow fade into blue.

Jackson placed the old man's hands back onto his unmoving chest. The oxygen machine still purred, the cannula under Sam's nose still hissed, but Jackson didn't move to take it off. It seemed rude, somehow.

"The ambulance is – Jackson?" The room dimmed, and he felt slim arms under him. Then he was sitting in a chair and that felt better.

The ambulance came. He remembered the blue-jacketed paramedics, remembered one of them crouching down to speak to him. He remembered saying something back. Then Dr. Dick was there. He remembered Dr. Dick lifting him onto his feet, a strong move for such an old man, and passing him off to Florita, saying, "Tea. Black, sweet, and strong."

Then he was in the kitchen, drinking tea, and he came back to himself. The house was quiet. The train was off, the ambulance people were gone. So was Sam Long.

Dr. Dick came striding into the kitchen, a squat mound of a man with a volcano of white hair and too much vitality for his seventy-plus years. Florita handed him a steaming mug. "That did it," he assessed, looking Jackson over. "Back with us, are you? Now tell me what happened."

Jackson took sips of the thick tea and told him. Not about the things in the living room, nor about the feeling he'd had. Just about the death. The stopping of breath, the look, the nod. He was back now, and knew what not to say.

Dr. Dick leaned his chair on its hind legs, sipping his own tea, and considered. "Pretty much to be expected, all in all. Pulmonary embolism from the sounds of it. My guess is you ran over a clot, it traveled up, found a new home in his lungs, and end of story. It happens." He sipped and glanced over the table. "That will be my report to your college."

Jackson woke up a little more. "Report?"

"Hah! Thought that might shake out the last of the shock. Standard procedure, my boy. Chiropractor, physiotherapist, massage therapist, whatever. If there's a death during treatment, the governing body gets notified. Don't worry. I'm convinced there's nothing you could have done to avoid it. Of course you checked for the signs." He sipped.

Jackson felt his own face flush. "Of course. No redness, no

swelling, no unexplained hot spots. No new bruises. There was no indication of any problem whatever. I looked. Mr. Long reported a vague uneasiness, that was all. It could have been anything. It could have been a cold, for God's – "

"My boy!" Dr. Dick's voice cracked at him. "Nobody's blaming you, get a grip! Yes you checked, you did everything right, there was no sign to find, and still it happened. Shit happens, Jackson, and today it happened to you. Well, Sam Long, actually. You're still damn close to being in shock. Take the rest of the day off. Have a glass of wine. Relax." He snapped his fingers and jabbed one of them into Jackson's chest. "Hey. Get yourself a massage."

That got them all laughing, which loosened everything up. "Excuse me," said Jackson, and went to find the bathroom.

As he passed down the hall he scanned the small guest room reserved for the care aides. The one missing piece was there, lying half under the foot of the bed. Two steps and the sock puppet was in his hand.

It was the doll, crude and childish but here. There was an engineer's cap on its head. There was a long, thick needle sticking out of its calf.

The shock butterflied his knees and threatened to derail him again. The connections flashed through his head in a series of images. Sam Long, dying as soon as Jackson touched his calf. Voodoo queens from black and white movies cackling as they stabbed needles into wax figurines and watched their victims dance. Old beliefs, island rituals. South Seas magic.

He headed back towards the kitchen, holding the crippled doll. The red waves inside his skull ebbed enough for one rational thought. Jackson tucked the doll behind his back as he stuck his head around the corner and said, "Florita! What religion are you?"

Florita jumped at his volume and said, "Roman Catholic.

The Philippines are a Catholic country." She cracked a rare smile. "Why, do you wish to give a confession?"

If she only knew the sins he'd been contemplating. "No, just wondering. I'm opting for the wine, Dr. Dick. See you both later."

Jackson left, dragging weirdness along with him in the form of a homemade doll. The world looked too bright, like a cartoon, and was full of lines. On the way home he threw the clumsy and obvious trap in a dumpster.

As he arrived home an incoming text from Charles lit up his cell phone: "We'll be over at 6." Jackson was too spooked and exhausted to wonder what the hell. He had barely enough wherewithal to call up his clients, apologize to those he'd missed and cancel the ones he was going to miss, take a hot shower and collapse into bed.

The building's front door intercom woke him up. Before he could get to it the whole gang was knocking on his apartment door, Charles and Leaf loaded down with takeout bags. They piled into the hallway and enveloped him in a massive, multi-armed hug. It felt wonderful, and he let it in.

About ten seconds was all he could stand. He shook himself free, stepped back, and said, "How? I mean, you don't know – "

"Word gets around," Charles said. "Somebody dies during a massage, it gets talked about in the ER. When it's a home visit – well, there just aren't that many of you. We figured you might be having a bad day." He extended his carton, which said Vij's and smelled of heavenly curry. Leaf, back in his beach clothes, was carrying a bottle of amber mead. "Tough break, man.

Thirsty?"

Everyone loaded up a plate. He told Sam Long's story again, dropping the words into a roomful of silent respect. The mead was tangy and fresh, and he felt himself finally relax. At last he ran out of story and they all sat with it, sipping mead.

"And then there was the house," he heard himself say into the quiet. The words escaped before he could bite them back.

Georgia nodded. "Thought so. More weirdness, right?"

Why not, he said to himself. They're your friends.

"Yeah. It happened again. The moment I stepped through the door. It was like somebody had pulled a plug and drained the place. This time I found some of it. He had lanterns on the far wall, one of them had been shifted. And a chair had been moved, you could see the marks in the carpet. It was real."

The silence in the room grew a little stiff. Charles stepped into it. "Did you do anything?"

"Yeah, I moved the things back again."

"Hmm," was all he said.

"Did it help?" asked Leaf.

"Maybe, a bit. I'm sure there was more, but I didn't have time to find it all. The place felt a little better, but – not much, really. It still felt pretty bad."

The room fell silent for another stretch. Charles broke it. "Well, our friend here has had a tough day. Let's clean this mess up and get out of here." They all got busy.

Charles hung back when Leaf and Georgia departed. "I'll see you at home," Georgia said, giving Charles a short squeeze. She hugged Jackson for a long time, warm and solid. "You did fine today," she whispered into his ear. Then she was gone, and he and Charles were alone.

"You've got to stop talking like this." Charles was on him, so close and tense that Jackson took a step back. "Quit doing this to yourself. At the very least, don't tell other people. You're making it stronger, don't you see that?" He turned away and strode back into the living room.

Did it matter that Charles was right? Jackson followed, the pit of his stomach in knots. "You think I don't know how crazy it sounds? I'm not about to tell anybody. Only my circle, okay? Maybe even my best friend. Okay?"

Charles got the hint and his shoulders deflated. "Sorry, that was a little heavy maybe. It's just - in the wrong ears all this could come back to bite you. Listen, it's been a tough day. You sure you're okay?"

How soon was he going to regret asking Charles to ask that? "Yes. I'm fine."

Charles gave a sideways wave towards the hall shelf. "I tweaked the pencil when I came in."

That caught him by surprise. "I didn't notice."

"Yes you did. It took you about three seconds to set it right. And in the living room you sat us all down in a neat, six-pointed star. Nobody said a word because we all know what kind of day it's been. You going to sleep tonight?"

He'd done all that? "We'll see." He folded Charles' fingers back over the sleeping pill in his friend's palm. "Maybe Sam and I will talk." He laughed as Charles' look of concern shaded towards alarm. "I'm joking! Now get going."

He did sleep, long and hard. Sam Long didn't show up in his dreams, because he didn't have any.

Chapter 10

Ruth clicked off the phone's headset and pulled a tissue out of the box on her desk. Florita had put the client's daughter, Matilda Long, on the line. That always did her in. She wiped her eyes and stood tall before knocking on the door to Ms. Jacobs' office. Her boss was a saint for putting up with her sensitivity nonsense. No tears, she told herself. You have news to give, and you also have a seed to plant. Be strong.

She knocked and went in. "Mr. Long passed away this morning."

Ms. Jacobs looked up from her paperwork. "Emphysema? Loves trains? Who was the nurse on duty?"

"Florita. She says it happened while he was getting his massage."

Ms. Jacobs absorbed that. "How's the therapist? What does Florita think?"

"Just the questions I asked. She says the therapist knows what he's doing. Says he's pretty shaken up by it."

"I expect Florita's a little shaken up, too. Well, make all the usual arrangements." Ms. Jacobs pushed a finger to her glasses and bent down to her paperwork again.

Ruth stayed put in the doorway, like she'd planned. "Yes," said Ms. Jacobs without looking up.

"Do you want me to reassign Florita right away, or give her some time off?"

That brought her head up, and the tiniest trace of a frown. "The usual arrangements include a one-day quiet time before any new assignment. You know that."

"Yes, of course. And what about Wendy, the night nurse?"

Ms. Jacobs paused, and there! The seed was planted. "I said the usual arrangements. She was his care aide too, so she gets a day as well."

"Yes, of course. I'll let them know." Ruth closed the office door and went back to her desk.

As Ruth snicked the door shut, Emma Jacobs placed both elbows on her desk and thought about Wendy Corbett.

Nine patients since she'd arrived, and four of them had died on her watch. Now this one, Mr. Long, passing only a few hours after the night shift. Wendy was definitely bucking the odds.

Emma pulled up the five patient files and arranged them over her two oversized monitors. She reviewed each patient's history. The causes of death all matched the patients' underlying conditions, or near enough. None of the incidents had triggered surprise or suspicion in either the families or the physicians.

And each death had been different.

That clinched it. Emma knew all about death angels, every nurse did. Nurses with murderous hearts had plagued the profession since the dawn of time. Technique was their fatal flaw - most death angels found one method that worked and stuck with it. Their method was what revealed them, that and the sheer numbers. Death angels sometimes racked up impressive statistics before they were caught.

Five deaths, all different. All within a short time of Wendy Corbett's arrival. All expected, more or less. Emma shook her head and closed out the files, adding her final notes to the Sam Long page. Even nurses had runs of bad luck. The schedule for the next month needed to be redone. She opened the spreadsheet onto her clean monitors and got to work.

Jackson woke up, took the morning pill and shoved Sam Long to the back of his mind so he could get on with the day. First up was Russell Smith, a computer games programmer in the Yaletown tech hub who'd been unplugged by a fine case of coder's shoulder. Towards the end of the session, as he was unwinding Russell's fascia with the slow traction-and-twist that would give it enough room to heal itself, a young woman came in carrying a bundled baby in the crook of her arm.

"Hey, Jackson, meet my wife and daughter. Susan and Chloe, meet Jackson. He's reverse-engineering my shoulder."

"Shut up and let the man work," Susan said. "And if he tells you to sit up straight and take lots of breaks, you listen."

"Sit up straight and take lots of breaks," said Jackson, easing a thumb into Russell's armpit for emphasis. Right on cue, the baby-sized bundle laughed.

"Been like that since day one," said Russell as Susan pulled back the blanket to reveal a happy, ten-month old Chloe blowing a spit bubble. "She's a real doll."

A vision of Sam Long's empty bedroom flashbulbed onto his mind. He hadn't seen the doll. Only the fake one, the old wool sock with stuffing held in by thick, boxy yarn. Cross-stitch eyes, for hell's sake. Ridiculous, and tailored to catch him at his most spooked and steer him towards the care aide. It had very nearly worked.

But not the real one. He was a little ahead of schedule and the croostown traffic was relatively light. Sam Long's place was on the way to his next appointment, kind of. He had to be sure.

Wendy paced down the alley again, pausing at the spot where she could see the Long house between two hedges. Everything was all wrong. The family's three cars still filled the street. No way could she get in to retrieve Mr. Long's angel.

She should never have let Samuel Long go to his peace without her being there. It was like cheating, somehow. She'd had no control over the death. Did it go well? There was no way to know. She had sat up all yesterday morning on the edge of her bed, anxious about it. She hadn't even felt the moment. No warm glow of satisfaction at a job well done. Wendy only found out when Ruth from the office called to give her the news and her silly time off. All she was left with was a void.

Now she was here to pick up the angel, but the place was full of relatives setting up the little cry-fest that made the family feel better. They should be dancing for joy, was Wendy's opinion. They were inside, and the angel was stuck inside with them. She had to get it.

Once more around the block. This time Wendy went two blocks, intending to come up on the house from the front side so as not to make anybody suspicious of her constant alley pacing. The detour took about five minutes.

Good. Most of the cars had gone, only the eldest daughter's still at the curb. Wendy had met Matilda before; she could talk her way in now.

Another car pulled up outside. Teague Mobile Massage Therapy, the side window said. How could that be? Wendy held back, trying to make sense of it. He must have been suspended by now. He'd killed a patient, then blamed it on the little Filipino girls with a twisted story about black voodoo and evil spells. She knew it, she'd made it happen. By rights Teague should be locked up. What was he doing here?

Jackson knocked on the door before he could second-guess himself and a sixtyish woman, so thin and sharp she couldn't be anyone else than Sam Long's daughter, pulled it open. "Yes?" she asked.

He smiled, putting on polite and a little apologetic. "Uh, hi, my name is Jackson. I'm – I was Mr. Long's massage therapist. I think I might have left my appointment book here yesterday, and I'm really lost without it. May I come in to check?"

Of course she would know he'd been the one to kill her father. Realizing only now how very bad this could get, Jackson braced himself for the worst when she got all soft and said, "You must be so shaken up. Dad liked you, you know. Come in, I'm Matilda." She opened the door and he stepped inside.

What a strange feeling. The wrongness was still trying to push him back out the door. Now, in addition to that, there was an emptiness to the place, like it had stopped being a home and was simply a house. A more lawful, natural emptiness, but sad for all that.

"Dad said you kept his wheels greased," Matilda said, looking not at him but at the living room. The Pullman at rest. "That was high praise coming from him. I'm so sorry you had to experience that yesterday, but those things happen, I guess."

"It was a first for me," he said, his eyes flicking about the room. "I'm sorry for your loss, too. My kind of work gets me close to people, and Sam was quality. I looked forward to my visits with him."

Matilda nodded. "Thank you. We'll miss him, but it was time, I think. Well, obviously it was time. I haven't seen any appointment book here, but feel free to check around."

"Thanks."

Jackson went to the bedroom, now empty of pills and oxygen machine and Sam, and looked hard. He let the inner door slip open. He saw how the bed was askew from the ambulance attendants making easy access, saw the organic arrangement of dresser and night table in the corners. Nothing was wrong in this room, and of course there was no appointment book.

Matilda was in the back of the house somewhere. He speedwalked to the living room and tried again to see why it felt so wrong. He couldn't.

She was behind him. "It really is a museum, isn't it?" she said. "He collected these things over years and years, shined them all up, restored them to their glory days. He even made himself a model train. Have you seen it run?" Before he could answer that yes, he'd seen it often, Matilda walked over to the wall and threw the big knife switch.

Jackson's mind yelled. The train lit its front light, gave a tinny hoot, and started chugging around the track. Backwards. Sitting on the locomotive, giving a sunny smile and a denim-shirted wave at the retreating world, was a train conductor doll.

"Hmm, that's weird," murmured Matilda, and switched the awful thing off.

"I wonder," Jackson heard himself say, "I gave Sam that doll up there a few weeks ago, I wonder if I could have him back, you know, as a keepsake, sort of." He held his breath, trying to stanch the furious blush that threatened to erupt from his shirt collar.

Matilda waved at the train. "Of course, go right ahead. Here, stand on this, your bones are younger than mine." She offered him a wooden conductor's step. Jackson reached up and grabbed the cloth and porcelain engineer. It felt perfectly normal in his hands. Immediately and powerfully, the room felt better.

In as few words as possible he made his escape.

Wendy sat on the park bench across from Mr. Long's house and twisted her hands over and over inside each other. Tears leaked from her eyes at the awful realization of what she was seeing. Of what a horrible mistake she had made.

Teague was leaving, and in his hand he clutched Samuel Long's angel. He shouldn't have come back. There was nothing for him here, why had he come back? How had he spotted the angel, and why in Heaven did he decide to take it? The thing was so impossible she couldn't wrap her mind around it.

She forced her hands apart and slapped them hard against the rough bark of a towering fir tree next to the bench. The sudden sting was no more than she deserved for her awful transgression. She'd created a passing and not been there to witness it. Her punishment for this mistake was the loss of an angel.

The boy opened the car door and threw the little engineer doll onto the passenger seat. Wendy felt outrage in her bones at his cavalier treatment. It was a desecration.

She could not allow this.

Teague Mobile Massage Therapy, said the side of the car

window. It gave a phone number and a website. She wrote it on her palm as the car rattled past. Then she rose, took a last look at Mr. Long's house and strode the three blocks to the nearest bus stop.

The drive to his next appointment was tough. Not because of the doll, now an innocuous, well-made, elegant figurine lying on his passenger seat. The problem was all the other things he was seeing.

Jackson had let down his guard at Sam Long's place. Now his condition was on him, strong and pervasive. He saw tracers and hints everywhere. The complex rhythm of the busy streets was a massive and beautiful flow all around him. His own car carried a wave of almost-visible intention in front of it, a suggestion of phosphorescence that responded to each flex and twist of his hands on the wheel. A champagne-coloured Mercedes nosed out too far at an intersection ahead and he saw it as a flash of red at the edge of his vision. Two lanes of cars bowed and bent in an intricate calculus to make room for the driver's mistake. His hands moved and so did his car, swerving in time with the traffic.

It was lovely. Irresistible.

He gritted his teeth, gripped the wheel. "Knock it off," he muttered to no one, and stared straight ahead.

He made it to the next session, made it through without embarrassing himself, then went straight home. The first thing he did when he walked in the door was go to the bathroom, pop the top off his meds and down a pill. The little engineer doll he placed on an alcove shelf by the kitchen. By the time he had to leave for his afternoon schedule the door inside his head was closed and locked again, with his condition on the other side.

It was simple to find the boy's address. Eight minutes at a library computer gave it right to her. Jackson Teague, RMT, living close to the beaches at the bottom end of Balsam Street. Wendy even had his apartment number.

She sat back in the squeaky library chair and tried to calm down, but it was useless. The boy had stolen a treasure that by rights belonged only to her. She would have the angel of Mr. Long back, and that was the whole of it.

The bus dropped her off at the beach a block away from his house.

Wendy spent half an hour wandering through the neighbourhood where Teague lived. His building was easy to spot, a three-storey brick affair half a block up from the beach. She even picked out his apartment by looking through the curly-barred windows at street level as she walked past. It was easy – his was the one with the little engineer doll in plain view on a shelf.

In plain view. It trivialized Samuel Long's soul and horrified Wendy beyond all measure. The boy's car was nowhere to be seen. The entire building was quiet. Waiting and pacing was done. She walked up to the front door.

It was white-painted wood and thick, bevelled glass. The usual call panel with buttons and names told her nothing more than she knew already. How to get in? She'd given it no thought, trusting to her anger to get her through. But breaking this door would be loud, messy, and very public.

She tried the loopy brass handle. To her astonishment, the door pulled open. She looked and saw the latch covered over with a length of duct tape. Someone must have moved out, taped the door open during the move and neglected to lock it again. So much for building security.

She stepped inside. The hallway was long and dark with wainscoting below and some godawful 1940's corrugated wallpaper above. It had a dogleg halfway down its length. Beyond the bend was the door to 104.

Teague's door was locked. The dogleg hid her from view of the front entrance. She placed a hand on the door and gave it a push. The wood, much less sturdy than the front door, gave a little.

She'd read somewhere that Bruce Lee could exert an unbelievable amount of force by simply flexing his muscles all at once. Her hand covered the deadbolt lock. She stepped back, leaned in with her weight for a little more oomph and ground her right foot into the carpet. She relaxed. Then, all at once, she tensed.

The door bowed under the push and sprang her backward across the hall. She recovered her balance and burned. That didn't work. The angel was still on the other side of that flimsy little door. Still in the hands of that flimsy little massage therapist. She stepped back against the far wall and ran, leading with her shoulder.

It didn't stand a chance. One too-loud crack and she stumbled into Jackson Teague's apartment, breathing hard. She turned, glanced each way down the hall and saw nobody. Then she eased the broken door shut.

The place was neat as a pin. Everything in it was well-chosen, tasteful, and in the wrong place. The books in the bookcase went from large to small. The three high stools by the kitchen counter all shared the same angle, with one leg poking out. She knew without needing to look that the line made by the legs matched the left edge of the refrigerator on the other side of the kitchen. Everything in the apartment was aligned with everything else.

The boy was deranged. She'd had no idea his awareness of spaces went this deep. It must be to the point of acute pain for him.

She lifted Samuel Long's angel from its prison. Her heart was tripping like a hummingbird and a thrill of fear sang in her ears. The boy could be back any second. Anybody in the building could be coming down to investigate that crash. She needed to leave.

The sofa met the corner walls at exactly 45 degrees. An art deco floor lamp hung its stained glass shade over the center of the center cushion. The small, walnut coffee table looked to be nowhere in particular, until Wendy saw that it was equidistant from the sofa, the easy chair, and the small alcove built into the front window. The apartment's overall effect was repugnant enough to make her want to vomit.

Wendy had never conceived that anyone could see the world the way she saw it and get it all so wrong. The boy was seriously ill. Being in his lair was like standing at an accident scene; she had to look around.

The living room was a geometrically perfect nightmare. The bedroom was soul-suckingly sterile. She forced herself to reconnoitre in the bathroom. Front and center in the cabinet stood the medications she'd expected.

On her way out of the bathroom, struck by a delightful inspiration, Wendy bent over and spent a minute mucking about in the tub.

It really was time to go. On her way past the kitchen she spotted his fridge calendar, a big whiteboard with squares for each day. Teague had pencilled in a date with Lynn. She knew that name. In her short time here she'd discovered Lynn, too.

She tucked the tiny engineer doll inside her shirt, whispering an apology to Mr. Long's soul for the impertinence. With a brief glance out the door to be sure no one was looking she left the apartment. Once she was outside she took in a big breath of fresh air.

Things weren't right, but they were a little bit better.

It was a rewarding afternoon's work. Jackson went to see young Garth Finch and helped the ten-year-old to breathe again after a minor car accident had thrown him against the seat belt and spasmed his diaphragm. He spent an hour easing off the tension in Catherine Jaston's scoliosis, her muscles and fascia still trying to torque her spine even after implanted Harrington rods had straightened her up and saved her life.

Halfway home Jackson's eye was drawn by a young executive standing at a Broadway bus stop. Close-cropped blond hair, shoulders filling out a tungsten-grey business suit, crossed hands holding a black padfolio in one hand, he stood at ease and emanated confidence. Jackson saw passers-by alter course a little to swing closer to the young man who was so obviously going places.

The executive looked around, saw Jackson and broke into Leaf's familiar, slow smile. Jackson blinked twice, to be sure. Then he swerved to the sidewalk, ignoring a transit bus, and threw open the passenger door.

"Thanks, man," Leaf said as he got in, "I'm headed for the Skytrain station. Making my way to New Westminster for an appointment."

Jackson laughed, trying to split his attention between the traffic and this friend in a stranger's clothing sitting in his car. "Must be some appointment! This is - well, it's a new look for you. Where are you going?"

Leaf held out the padfolio. Jackson caught a glimpse of a fancy crest embossed on the cover with a wreath of maple leaves, a crown on top and Servamus written in a big curve inside. Underneath, in gold lettering, was Justice Institute of BC - Vancouver Police Department Information Session. Leaf explained, his voice animated and almost fast. "I heard you at the party, my man, loud and clear. Your words gave me a nudge, you know? Got me moving. Then I got another nudge, gave me a direction, and here I go. I'm being put to work."

"Wow." Jackson thought about it some more as he got closer to the Cambie Skytrain station, then repeated, "Wow. I mean, there's changing direction, then there's changing planets. The VPD? Really?"

Leaf shifted the folio from hand to hand, actually excited. "Why did you choose massage therapy? Because you played to your strengths, right? You see how people are built. Well, I've spent all my time learning the laws. The real laws. I live within them, because I know what happens if you don't. Everybody loses. So," he waved the padfolio, then winked. "Besides, I don't think the fitness test will be much hassle."

Jackson pulled over at the Cambie station. As Leaf got out he said, "You've twisted my day right around, man, thanks. Go for it, I'm happy for you!"

Leaf waved and strode into the crowd, showing off his suit's impeccable tailoring.

A tailored suit? Leaf? Where the hell did he hang it?

His good mood and a sense of fraternal pride in Leaf's big move lasted the rest of the drive. On the way into his buidling the weirdness descended again. The doll was waiting for him.

What the hell had he been thinking? He hadn't, of course, just run on impulse again. His impulses were going to get him into trouble someday.

The doll was also evidence.

He snorted at the steering wheel as he levered into a parking spot on Balsam Street. Evidence of what? That he'd accepted a posthumous gift from a dead man who couldn't refute the fact? And who was he going to tell, the police? He could hear the padded doors whoosh shut behind him.

He'd get rid of it. Hand it to a thrift store with his next batch of old clothing. Let a kid find it and give the thing some love. That was good. He would do it tomorrow.

"Jackson! You are home. Call the police!" Mrs. Castelli, down from her penthouse on the third floor, was waiting for him in the hall. That wasn't good. She clutched his hand, making her bangles collection dance, and dragged him from the front door and around the dogleg. When he saw the mess of his apartment door he knew that no kid was ever going to find the little train conductor in a thrift store. It was gone.

Jackson called the police. "No report, no insurance, you call them!" Mrs. Castelli said, and kept at it till he had his cell phone to his ear. Yes, there had been a break-in, with damage. No, he didn't know what was missing yet, he hadn't gone inside. No, he didn't think anybody was still in there. No, nobody had seen anything. The dispatcher announced that somebody would be by soon. He was to catalog the carnage.

Of which there was precisely nil. They hadn't even made an effort to disguise the reason for the break-in. Everything was in perfect order, exactly where he'd left it, except for the vacant shelf. The little engineer was gone.

Jackson found himself on the floor. "Are you okay? I heard a thump!" Mrs. Castelli called from the hallway. He called back, assured her he was fine, but his head was spinning and he stayed down, not altogether sure his feet would hold him. He shook his head to clear the fog. Some nasty things were crawling out from dark corners of his mind. A small parade of facts he'd refused to see was coming into full view and scaring him senseless.

His actions had pissed somebody off. Of course they would know who had taken the doll, and he wasn't that hard to find. Now they had come and crashed through his apartment door. Some person had done that, somebody strong from the look of things, for the express purpose of taking back that doll.

Another ugly fact crawled out from the shadows and leered at him. Some person had purchased that doll. They had placed it on Mr. Long's train. They had made the train run backwards.

Some person with a good sense of energetic geometry had rearranged the lamp in Mr. Long's house.

The ugly thing waved him on. More, it was saying.

That person had moved items around in all the houses. Specifically to drain those homes of life.

The nastiest fact of all strode out from the blackness and stood in the light, proud of itself.

Some person – that person – had engineered those patients' deaths.

The intuitive realization had thrown Jackson to the floor. Now that his rational mind had caught up, the floor was where he stayed. No, he kept saying. No, it couldn't be. That's too much.

The empty shelf told him differently. The broken door, through which Mrs. C was still calling, said an incontrovertible yes.

Somebody had made those people die before their time. Of natural causes that were anything but. That took skill.

That person had come here to get the engineer doll back.

That person had been in his house. Maybe an hour ago.

Jackson was on his feet again, stomping. "Jackson? What is it? Should I come in?" He paced around the place. He wanted to get the vacuum cleaner. He wanted to scrub the whole place down with bleach. He wanted to fucking move, he was so viscerally disgusted. But he couldn't. He'd called the police. They wouldn't like that. That would be tampering with evidence, or something.

"Don't come in," he called out to Mrs. C. "We don't want to mess up the crime scene." Mrs. C had an evening Netflix habit heavy on the true crime shows; she stayed clear.

He stalked through his place to verify for sure that nothing had been touched and to try to walk off his anger. In a short time the front-door intercom buzzed. Mrs. C admitted two VPD officers. When Corporal Uphram, a mid-forties Persian linebacker with a serious face and a black brushcut, and Constable Mathers, a twentyish, ponytailed triathlete who moved like she knew how to handle herself, asked politely for permission to step through the ruined apartment door, he ignored the humour in favour of a growled assent.

They took his attitude in stride. Corporal Uphram spent a minute examining the doorframe while Mathers ventured ahead to calm the waters and ask the questions.

"Bit of a tough day, Mr. Teague. Mind telling me what happened here?"

"Jackson," he growled, then let go of a bit of the gruffness. She was kind of cute, in a gunbelt sort of way. "Looks like I got broken into."

She was busy looking around. "Well, sort of," she said. "Tell me, did you clean up in here before we came?"

"No."

"Hmm. Okay, I'm confused. Somebody definitely did insult to your door. Did they take anything?"

"A doll."

To her credit, Mathers wrote this down before she tilted her eyes up from under her brows and shot it back to him. "A doll?"

Don't say it, thought Jackson. "A doll. A train engineer doll, about eight inches high, good quality. It's evidence in a series of - premature deaths."

That stopped the note-taking, and got Corporal Uphram's attention away from the door and the vociferous Mrs. Castelli. "Would you mind explaining that?" Mathers said. "Start with what you mean by 'premature deaths.' That's a highly unusual turn of phrase."

Last chance. Don't do this, he told himself as sternly as he could. Let it go, apologize, gloss it over, bury the fucking thing. Don't say it, whatever you do, not here, not to these people. "I'm a massage therapist, and recently a number of my elderly clients have died before their time. They weren't accidents, they weren't natural, and they all had dolls." Shit. Feeling distinctly like he was falling off a cliff, Jackson took a deep breath and laid it all out for them.

When he was finished the shadows in the room had moved along a little and he could hear a starling in a tree outside his window. He ought to feel relieved. He ought to feel glad, now that the officials had the file, now that these crimes were going to be investigated. He'd done his part. But the silence in the living room lengthened. Jackson got the feeling the rope he had just tied around his neck was lengthening with it.

Corporal Uphram was busy pecking at his cell phone. Constable Mathers decided to break the silence. "Let me see if I get this right. Some elderly clients of yours – by your own admission, in the last stages of their life – have been passing away. Their deaths, and the manner of them, come as a surprise to nobody but you. You're upset because, in each of these cases, you go into the house a day or two before and feel something strange. Things have been moved around, and they've –" she consulted her notes – "'drained the house of life.' Only you can feel these changes, they don't seem to affect anybody else in the house."

"Except the owner, who dies," said Jackson. He was so screwed.

"Right." She tried not to drawl it out, and mostly succeeded. "And in each of these places you noticed some sort of doll that wasn't there before, and that seemed to be the focal point of all this nasty energy. In the last case, a Mr. Samuel Long ... let me get this straight ... you were there when he died?"

"Yes." His face was beet red now, he could feel it.

"You went back to the house the next day, saw an engineer doll sitting on a toy train, and claimed it as your own. A gift from you to Mr. Long. But you hadn't given it to him?"

"No. And it wasn't in the house before then."

"So you stole a dead man's property. Then you took the doll home and set it on that shelf over there." She pointed, and he nodded. "A good quality doll. You said that. In plain view of anybody looking in from the street. Then somebody breaks your door down, and the only thing they take is that doll." She checked her notes again. "Do I have it all, Mr. Teague?"

"Yes."

Uphram leaned over and showed Constable Mathers his phone screen. Then he levelled a gaze at Jackson.

"Mr. Teague, you're under psychiatric care, am I right? For OCD? You came to our attention a few years ago because of it?"

The padded doors were swinging open. He felt his knees try to go and locked them. "Yes."

"Are you still taking your meds? Still receiving treatment?"

"Yes." A spark rose up. I'm not making this up, he tried to say, but he was finally holding his tongue firmly, painfully, between his teeth.

Uphram paged to a different screen on his phone. "Seems like you've already received some heat from your bosses over this. Okay." Uphram was pissed, it was plain, but he held it in. He rose to his feet and Mathers followed suit. "Mr. Teague, I'm going to play it like this. I am going to record the break-in, so your landlady can access her insurance policy for the door. I am not going to record any of this cockamamie story you've told me, not officially anyway. I'll forget about you being guilty of theft, even. In return for this huge reprieve, I am going to direct, not suggest, that you get in touch with your physician and get your meds adjusted, or whatever it is you need to do to get this under control. I am going to keep an eye on you. If you make a wave, raise a flag, register a complaint, or further this idea of yours in any way, then we are going to get very official, very fast. I believe you've been down that road before, am I right?"

"Yes."

"So we have an understanding. Get yourself some help, Mr. Teague." He left to go, but turned around once more at the door, unable to resist the dig. "Stop playing with dolls."

He left. Mathers turned around at the door as well, giving him some sort of searching look. Then the doorway was empty.

Mrs. Castelli came back downstairs after. "I'll have the door fixed tomorrow, insurance company says okay. You put something to block it tonight, all right?" He smiled at her. She did a double-take, then came over and wrapped a scrawny arm around him. "It will be all right," she said close, wafting capicollo and red wine into his ear. She went away.

Jackson spent a long time on the sofa watching the

sunshine track its way across his floor. Then, about the time the daylight faded out and the streetlights winked on, he headed for the shower. A good dose of heat might blast him into a sleep without dreams. The building had a workhorse of a boiler, designed and built by men fresh off the war effort, and Jackson cut back on the cold a little to fill the bathroom with a satisfying steam. He yanked the shower curtain closed to keep the floor dry as he let the clothes fall off him and positioned a towel by the tub. The shower was hot enough to hurt a little getting in, but it was going to do him good.

He pulled the curtain back and was rewarded with a wall of hot steam that filled his nostrils. It had a sweet scent, vaguely fruity-flowery, that Jackson's tired mind almost puzzled about, almost recognized as he stepped in. Of course, he realized as his right foot hit the enamel and he transferred his weight, smells like my shampoo.

He fell faster than thinking. The slip of his foot on the slick, alkaline slime coating the tub carried with it a blazing-red rush of bright momentum, and then his head exploded like he'd been shot point-blank.

Everything hurt. He was lying full-out in the tub, curtain askew. The ceiling was spinning, and he felt sick, and everything really hurt. The whole place smelled of shampoo. Pieces of his brain slowly settled back into his aching skull from the far corners of wherever, and when the last one clicked into place he came to fully and realized that he didn't just hurt. He was burning.

The tub wouldn't let him go. Jackson churned and flailed in a reflexive flurry of movement to get away from the too-hot rain of water, but succeeded only in coating himself head to toe in lavender and apple blossom slime. Finally he got a knee under, convinced his limbs to move slowly despite the urgency, and crawled out of the tub onto the floor. His stomach retched at the effort and he lay on the bathmat for a minute while the shower continued without him.

Son of a bitch, was his first coherent thought. The pain coalesced into a solid throb at his occiput and dimmed away everywhere else. His insides calmed down. He got himself together enough to take stock and stand up.

He was red from head to foot, but it was mostly a hyperemic blush - a heat reaction, not a burn. He must only have been out for a few seconds. His pupils looked equal and responsive in the mirror and nothing unfortunate was leaking from anywhere. When he touched the back of his head he felt the beginnings of a fine goose-egg.

He was covered in goo. Most of the shampoo was gone from the tub now, but there was the bottle in the far corner, tipped over with the top off. It was a mean trick, nothing short of diabolical. The biggest response an accidental death in the tub would get was a sad tsk tsk. From now on he would look before he leaped.

After dialling the temperature down to chilly and carefully scrubbing the bottom of the tub, he stepped in again and washed off. By rights he should get checked over at a hospital, but he was feeling better, no more nausea, and the day had wrung him out. Two Advil and a gentle towel-off and he was in bed, dead to the world.

Chapter 11

Squadroom Three was almost empty. The big red numbers on the LED wall clock counted out the last seconds of the day shift and Ahmed Uphram swung a well-creased Whitecaps Football Club jacket off the back of his chair. He leaned over the cubicle wall and said, "You coming?"

Marilyn Mathers glanced up from her desk, where she'd been stuck with her chin on her hand for the last half hour. She had that look, like she saw a dark shape from miles away and wasn't sure what it was. "What? Oh, no, you go on. I'll see you tomorrow."

The Whitecaps were hosting the Houston Dynamo tonight and Houston was starting their new young forward. Ahmed really wanted to see what the kid had. But the game didn't start till 7:30, and what kind of training partner was he, anyway? The jacket went back over his chair. "Okay, we caught eight cases today. Which one is it?"

Marilyn kept a tidy workstation. Her monitor was open to the daily reports screen, and a daybook sat in formation at her left elbow. A few reminder stickies and memos were pinned to her cubicle wall along with two photos: a high-school photo of a freckle-faced young man that looked as goofy as all high-school photos, and a blow-up of the Vancouver Police Emergency Response Team promo shot - three officers in full tactical gear, the middle one staring at the camera. Ahmed was pretty sure that Marilyn wasn't going to be his partner for long. Better get his training in while he could.

She waved a hand at the screen. "It's the therapist. The OCD guy who thinks somebody is killing his clients. It won't let me go."

Ahmed sighed. "Apparently. You know why?"

"Uh huh." Her hand went up to the picture of the young man with freckles. "He even sort of looks like Andrew."

"Kudos for honesty, but no, he doesn't. Look closer. Teague and your brother have different height, weight, facial features. The only look they share is a faceful of freckles. You know why he really reminds you of your brother."

Marilyn thought. "Same kind of crazy."

Ahmed wiggled a finger at her. "Actually different kinds of crazy, and we call it mental illness around here, but yeah. So he sparked a memory of your late brother. That's still not the reason why you can't let it go." He leaned forward. "You know why?"

She was dialled in now, focused on the problem. After a moment of scrunched eyebrows she admitted defeat. "No, I don't."

"Good. That's the right answer, and an excellent place to start. The case won't leave you alone, you don't know why, and you have to do something about it. What do you have so far?"

"You don't think I'm nuts?"

He laughed. "Not even close. But the case has you hooked. My official job as your superior partner – " he ignored her fist slamming into his thigh – "is to beat all that curiosity out of you. Privately, and I'll deny it if you tell anyone, sometimes intuition pays off."

She brightened. "So you think there's something there, too!"

"No, I don't." He retrieved his jacket. "I think he's off his meds, which he as much as admitted to us, and he's seeing things. But it won't let you alone until you chase it down, and you may as well not sleep here as not sleep at home. Good thing you're still unattached. Want some sage advice from an old hand?"

"Of course."

He slapped her on the back. "Figure out what you know. Then pick the next logical thing you need to find out and find it out. Almost always that next thing proves it's all hooey and you can get some rest." He headed for the door of the now-empty squadroom.

"What if it doesn't?" she called.

"Then we'll talk about it tomorrow."

Ahmed was pure gold. He was sharp, intelligent, and he was teaching Marilyn street-level police work. She watched him leave and then turned back to her desk. Of course, class learning had its place. One thing class had taught her was the clarity to be gained from writing things down.

She turned to a fresh page in her daybook. Jackson Teague, Registered Massage Therapist, OCD. Hospitalized for it three years ago, spent three months in close supervision - read, enforced confinement. He must have been pretty far gone, those beds were hard to come by. Currently on probation in his professional life for letting it get out of hand again. Worked in homes, often on old people. Lately had five of them die, one during the session. That must have been tough, she thought, and wrote that down next to the facts – tough.

He'd felt like something wasn't right in each person's house the day before they died. Dolls started showing up. He'd developed this theory that someone was messing with the homes, putting these dolls there, killing the patient and making it look like natural causes. Almost a voodoo thing, she thought. She wrote that down, too – voodoo.

In the last place he didn't see the doll at first, went back after thinking about it, spotted a new doll and took it home with him. Then someone had broken in and stolen it.

Those were the facts as she knew them. Marilyn leaned the office chair back on its springs and stretched, thinking of the General Tso noodle bowl waiting in her fridge. Ahmed was right. The therapist was nuts. Cute, if you liked the red hair and freckles thing, and now that Ahmed mentioned it not at all like her brother. But nuts. Still, this wouldn't leave her alone.

Find out the next thing and that will prove it false. Good advice. She could have used it thirteen years ago when she'd been twelve and her brother Andrew a gangly seventeen. Andrew had taken her aside one day early that summer and told her about the men in the alley. They were outside right now, he'd said, waiting for their chance. She remembered the raw fear in Andrew's face, the smell of it in his room. She remembered catching it like a virulent flu, feeling afraid all the time and doing everything Andrew told her to do to stay safe. She kept her curtains drawn. She sometimes left the house through the dining room window.

"Trust me," he'd whispered into her ear.

She had done everything except look down the alley, where there were no men.

The main thing to know about delusion was Ahmed's point - it didn't stand up to scrutiny. Go one layer deeper and it fell apart. Once Andrew had been taken away her parents, as gently as they could, opened Marilyn's curtains and pointed down the alley. Then they sat her down and explained his illness. Ahmed was reminding her of what she'd already learned.

Teague's condition was a known. She'd pulled his police file from the day he'd been talked off the Lions Gate Bridge. A Dr. Parma described Jackson as suffering from pattern-fascination OCD. Everything had to line up, be in its right place, that kind of thing.

The deaths were real, verified through a simple records check. She could order up the physician reports or call the families and ask unsettling questions about the deaths, but that kind of official inquiry would put a spotlight on Teague. She'd probably cost him his job right there.

So, where to stick a probe into this investigation without making waves? The doctors and the families were out. She glanced back down at her notes. All the deceased had employed home care. That might be a way in. Care aides were observers, they saw things others missed.

A quick search showed a hefty handful of nursing agencies in Greater Vancouver. Not unmanageable, though. She glanced at her watch; some of them might still be answering calls. She picked up the headset on her desk phone.

"Mathers, Marilyn! You here?" The question cannoned through the empty squadroom at parade-ground volume. She leapt to attention as a tingle of excitement shot through her. The headset clattered to the desk.

"Inspector Takeda! Here, sir!" Takeda was standing in the doorway like he owned the room. He zeroed his gaze on her and frowned.

"You're at the end of your day," he said, glaring at her. "You must be tired. Want to go home?"

As if. "No, sir!"

The frown lifted and his face cracked into a wide grin. "Then drop what you're doing and get down to Briefing C.

You're seconded to Operation Padlock, observer trainee status."
He executed a quarter turn then looked back. She was right
behind him, her office chair spinning at the desk.

Briefing Room C was now set up like a war room. Marilyn saw
open laptops and wall maps through the glass wall and at least
ten people milling about inside. The ERT squad had
established a beachhead in one corner and she made for it.

"Where is he now?" A detective was leaning over one of the
techs and staring at the screen. Dovinder, she pulled his name
from memory, fairly high up the food chain.

"Just used the Cambie Mall dodge again," the tech was
saying, "left Williams behind in the food court." He pointed to
his screen. "Here's the parkade cam, there's his Corolla pulling
out into traffic. Here," he pressed a few keys and pointed again,
"the GPS on his car is back online. Turning left on Heather
Street. My guess is he's on his way home for the night."

"Hey, fresh blood. Welcome to Operation Padlock." One of
the men from ERT stood and shook her hand, a slim Tom
Cruise lookalike who didn't quite reach her five foot nine and
had Jukes on his nametag. He nodded towards the tech. "We're
doing a Keystone Cops on the target. He thinks he keeps
shaking our very obvious tails, when in fact we've got him
pegged six ways from Sunday. Guy's dumb as a post."

"I played meter maid at the Cambie Mall the other day,
kind of a redundant backup I suppose, but I wasn't in the need-
to-know loop. Who is he?"

Jukes led her into the knot of ERT members. "Calls himself
Borden, at least while he's in Vancouver. He's a contractor, a

professional bad guy for hire. Advertises himself as an industrial saboteur with a specialty in blowing things up. You remember the slaughterhouse fire back east, about a year ago?"

"The Barbecue? Everybody remembers that." A bomb had been rigged to the underside of a diesel tanker scheduled to refuel one of the largest abattoirs in the country. Something had gone wrong with the timing and the truck exploded in the stockyard. No damage to the factory, but around 300 fenced cattle met their end in a sea of burning fuel. The smell, from all reports, reached into the next county.

Jukes said, "And how about the Halifax Explosion?"

She narrowed her eyes and gave him are-you-kidding. "December, 1917? Troop carrier versus munitions ship, took out half the city?"

He laughed. "You paid attention in history class. I'm talking about the one two years ago in the railway switching yard, off the container docks. Ten pounds of TNT buried under the lines. The button was pushed when a trainful of anhydrous ammonia went over it."

That brought her eyebrows up. "No! I never heard, and I have friends in Halifax!"

"Yeah, turns out Borden planted the bomb on a side track. Dented one car as it passed by, that was all. The guy's past his prime. This time, though, he's playing on our turf and he's playing for keeps. Facial recognition spotted him on the waterfront cams a week ago. You've got three guesses why he's in town. The first two don't count."

Marilyn felt her heart thump a little harder. "The Northern Sea Otter." The huge liquefied natural gas tanker had been prettying herself up in Burrard Inlet in preparation for a spectacular exhibition run under the Lions Gate Bridge and into the harbour. The idea was to firm up popular opinion and political will for the construction of LNG plants along the BC coast. If the oil companies proved that a massive tanker could safely navigate the wrinkled coastline, much of the environmental complaining might go away.

Jukes nodded, his face a dark mask. "Yeah. There's industrial sabotage. Then there's losing the downtown. We don't look too kindly on that."

She absorbed the implications and frowned. "But the Sea Otter's not carrying, it's a publicity thing. Surely he can't pack that much explosive."

Detective Dovinder chimed in. "Eyes over here," he called out to her and pointed a green laser dot at a diagram on the wall. "Here's the Lions Gate Bridge." It was an engineer's drawing from side-on, showing the water and the bridge deck and the long, steel support cables suspended between two massive uprights. A draftsman's mark with an arrow at each end went from the waterline to the center of the bridge deck, with '61 metres' pencilled in the middle. "Here's the Northern Sea Otter." He moved the laser dot to another, more amateur sketch that was recognizably a boat hull with a long, straight deck ahead of a huge aft superstructure. Four white spheres bulged above the deck like giant, albino peas in a pod. In real life those were cryogenic storage tanks, insulated nickel-steel spheres each with capacity for 27,000 cubic metres of liquefied natural gas. More drafting marks and figures filled in the space beside the drawing. 'Keel to masthead 70 metres', said one. 'Empty draft 7.1 metres', said another, pointing to the area below the waterline. 'Heavy draft 10.4 metres', said a third.

"Oh my God," Marilyn said, doing the math. "They're bringing it in loaded."

Dovinder's green laser dot bounced from ship to bridge. "The only way they can do it, even at low water," he said. "The vent stacks on top of the superstructure will have about three metres clearance, but the bunting poles and their antenna array will clear the bridge deck by maybe one. It's a special trip for public relations. Nobody is supposed to know. But, obviously, someone does."

Marilyn mulled it over. "So the bridge is Borden's launch point, then. But so what? He can stand on the bridge and shoot holes in those tanks all day, they still won't explode. It takes a lot more than that to get liquefied natural gas excited."

Jukes piped up from beside her. "North Shore Marine Demolitions."

"He nabbed a shaped charge," said Dovinder, "strong enough to punch a 4000-degree flaming arrow into the heart of one of those tanks. Or he thinks he did. We slipped him a dud."

"Soon enough he'll make a run onto the bridge to set it up," said Jukes.

Marilyn's grin was practically hurting her cheeks. She could hear her pulse pick up. "And?"

Jukes and the four other Emergency Response guys shared a laugh. "Look at the brand new trainee, all ready to rock," said Jukes. "We're going to let him waltz right up there and do it. Then we'll take him down. You - " he jabbed a finger into her chest, "are going to stand back and watch."

Chapter 12

"You're a big one. I bet the customers don't give you much trouble, do they?"

Wendy beamed as she stepped through the door and Mr. Knowles tottered back on his two canes and slippered feet. The old fellow's sparse hair framed a thin face graced with a natural expression that rested somewhere between surprise and delight. He was tall and undernourished, with matchstick arms and legs. The addition of the canes gave him the appearance of a daddy-long-legs. "Oh, I'd say it's been a long time since anybody's given me problems," she said. "Is my patient at home?"

A quick laugh burst from his chest like it had been waiting for the chance. "Hah! Not much other place for her to be. Upstairs and downstairs are about her range these days, same as me. Elizabeth's in the bedroom." He waggled a cane towards the center of the house and began a slow topple. Wendy, startled, almost lunged to catch him, but he landed the cane and straightened up. "She'll wait. Come in, I'll show you around."

He turned and four-posted into the main room. "We have a spot all set up for you girls. Pretty much a routine now, been doing the home care thing almost two years. I keep telling them I can handle it all, but they don't seem to believe me." He tossed the smallest of glances over his shoulder.

Wendy laughed, charmed. She wouldn't be needing the room for long. Two patients had come under her care since the trainman and they both still inhabited the earth. Her mercies hadn't been needed - one job had been for a young man needing short-term help after surgery, and the other job was filling in for a few days as another care aide tended to a sick child. She'd found herself hoping that the next posting would need her special skills. Now here she was in a new home, and the sweet smell of impending death was everywhere.

The main room was typical, a testament to the years this couple had spent in it. Family pictures, shelves full of books, comfortable chairs. No TV in this room, there must be a separate den. An ornate rug and some fine brass urns bespoke a long-ago trip to the Orient.

Wendy looked around for the special thing and wasn't long in finding it. The paintings on the walls were spectacular.

Mr. Knowles reached the far end of the living room, turned on his canes and waited. Wendy stopped in the middle of the room to stare. The right-hand wall was full of portraits, spanning the range from newborns to centenarians. Each one was alive. The faces in the paintings carried their owners with them, capturing in look and shading and eyes whatever made each person unique. The end wall was landscapes. They showed mostly flat prairie, but painted so that Wendy suddenly understood the allure – she could see the wind in the grasses, the wide expanse of sky that made you want to jump up and never come down. The left-hand wall was still lifes, both intricate oils and sweeping watercolours. The artist had exceptional range. They had all been done by the same hand, of that she was certain.

Wendy found herself drawn to a painting on the far wall, an anomaly at the edge of the prairie shots. It was the Atlantic. The painting was waves on rocks on a blustery day, nothing more, but it was the Atlantic, she was sure. She had jumped about on these very rocks as a child, crackling the dry seaweed under her shoes. The iron-hard water, caught in mid-curl just before landfall, was the same as she'd seen out her kitchen window. She even knew it was November, the month when sky and water were the same colour and people took to lighting candles in the daytime for a reminder of light and warmth. She stood in front of the painting, from so many miles and years away, and felt a tear leap off her lashes.

"Ah, we have an Easterner," Mr. Knowles said softly. "Liza is always interested in who looks at what. She painted this one over Maine way, oh, about forty years ago. I'll tell her you liked it."

The woman was an artist. With a shuddering wash of inspiration and gladness, Wendy knew what her angel would be.

Elizabeth Knowles was slow and calm and relaxed in her bed as only a person on major painkillers could be. "Hello, dear," she called from her pillow, "so you're the new night nurse. I like the cap, it adds a touch of class. Looks like I'm in competent hands."

Wendy smiled her greeting and stepped across the spacious bedroom straight to the pill table, pushing aside the chair with the white doctor's coat draped over it. All the heavy hitters were in evidence: Naproxen, Flexoril, an old prescription for Percocet shoved off to the side, and a nice neat row of oxycodone bottles right up front. Other assorted prescriptions littered up the place, but these ones told the story. Elizabeth Knowles was crippled with perhaps the worst case of osteoarthritis Wendy had ever seen, and she was getting the best help modern medicine could give her. Which, of course, was hopelessly inadequate.

So it was to be pills, then. She had just the ticket.

She attended the bedside. Fluff up the pillows, that was always the first thing. Lifting and positioning with a gentle show of strength and finesse, she said, "Lord, yes, Mrs. Knowles, I'll take care of you. Peaceful nights, that's what I'm all about. You'll see."

The old lady was instantly at ease; one master didn't take long to recognize another. She closed her eyes and sighed back into the pillow. "A top massage man, and now a top nurse. I could get used to the good life. Thank you."

"You're welcome, dearie." Elizabeth Knowles was asleep.

Wendy held back her frustration until she was out of the bedroom, then slammed a fist hard into her thigh. Why hadn't it worked? Teague had killed a patient. Somehow, against all the odds, he hadn't been drummed out of his profession for it. The boy must have horseshoes.

He wasn't even injured. She settled her night bag in the care aide's quarters and stalked through the house, nudging things here and there. That trap in his bathroom was a regrettable lapse. It had been reckless and foolish, and it ran against her code. Don't Harm The Healthy, that was the Second Rule. Her trick had been born of plain vindictiveness and spite, and she was glad it had come to nought.

The kitchen needed arranging. As she worked the Third Rule began to hum again at the back of her mind. When They Suspect, Move West. The boy suspected, in a way that no one had ever done before. He didn't know who to suspect, thank Heaven. Otherwise she'd be out the back door and running, not repositioning a ceramic cookie jar to the top shelf.

Teague saw. In all the long miles and years between her mother and now, he was the only one. A second tear splashed onto Wendy's bosom. The fact that he got it backwards was a problem, of course. She snapped a square of paper towel off the roll to blow her nose and almost laughed through her tears at the understatement. It was more like a colossal cosmic joke than a problem. It was like finding your kindred spirit after a lifetime of searching and discovering he was a moron.

Running was getting so old. So was she, if she were being honest about it. The very thought of packing up her angels and moving somewhere new made her bones ache and added a sense of crushing futility to the mix. Vancouver was a wonderful city full of life and opportunity, and she wanted to stay here. Some part of her had already made up its mind about the matter.

There it was, then. The table needed moving, and she lifted it off the floor to make no noise. The exertion felt good. If she wasn't about to go, then the massage therapist would have to. He needed another push - nothing hurtful, the Second Rule and a growing respect and kinship for the boy prohibited that - a push that would move him out of her way forever. For both their sakes.

The sock doll at Mr. Long's place had been amateur and silly. He saw what she did and she needed to respect Teague's gift. Still, the principle was sound. And there was the doctor's coat in Elizabeth Knowles' room. In a minute she had the plan.

Mr. Knowles tapped down the hall and into view at the kitchen door. "You've been busy in here," he commented, and she watched him take a long look around. The animated sparkle in his eyes dimmed even as he scanned. "Looks off, somehow," he said, half an octave lower and ten decibels softer. "Well, I'm tired. Going to bed." The canes tapped away and she heard the quiet buzz of the lift chair carrying him upstairs.

Five days after the tub incident the bump was almost gone and the last blotches of red had faded from his chest. Outside his curtains June was putting on the big show that was summertime in Vancouver, the sun rising early and strong with the promise of heat. Jackson woke up whistling and kept it going on his way to work.

Mrs. Knowles was first on his schedule this morning. He'd seen her twice before, an overweight matron laid low by a vicious and prolonged run of osteoarthritis. The wandering Irish tune he was whistling slowed and then stopped as he approached the Knowles place on West 18th. Dr. Dick's immaculate, silver Miata convertible was parked outside. He pulled his Subaru in behind the Miata, remembering the last time he and the doctor had met at a patient's house and wondering what he was going to find inside.

The Miata's top was down, paying homage to the bright sunshine. A brand-new bobblehead Einstein was stuck to the beige dashboard. Dr. Dick wasn't normally into sticking things onto his collector-clean car, but the wild-haired, lab-coated figure did bear a striking resemblance to the old guy.

"Come on in," bellowed Mr. Knowles, another old coot not so far from home care himself. He was in his armchair, waving his hands and yelling at Dr. Dick, who stood like a squat, snowcapped miniature mountain in front of him and argued back. Dahlia was nowhere in evidence, probably hiding in the kitchen.

"No you may not give her pills whenever she damn well needs them, that's what the home care girls are trained to do. They're not candy, George," Dr. Dick was saying. He turned when Jackson came into the room and grabbed the opportunity to change the subject. "Jackson! Good to see you, maybe you can help out Elizabeth today, she's been feeling poorly. About to go see her myself, let's go." He stumped up the stairs over Mr.

Knowles' blustering.

"Be right there," Jackson called after him. Then he gritted his teeth and forced himself into the living room through an almost-visible gale of graveyard chill. It was awful, like one long howl scratching at his nerves. He'd never felt it this strong.

Mr. Knowles was sitting in his chair, canting his head around so he could watch Jackson enter. His chair normally faced the door. "What's wrong, boy? You look like you've seen a -"

"Nothing, I wanted to look is all," he stammered. He didn't have to look hard. The living room was an energetic disaster. Every painting was crooked by a fraction of an inch. Some left and some right, not even any pattern in the disorder. It was a masterpiece of geometry gone bad.

Dr. Dick was waiting for him upstairs. Jackson speedwalked from the entrance to the old guy's recliner, gave one solid hip check that knocked the chair back into its depressions, exited and headed upstairs. Mr. Knowles growled at him from the living room.

It wasn't enough. Even if he fixed the whole house, it still wouldn't be enough. Even if he somehow spirited Elizabeth Knowles out of here for a night, or two or three, it still would not be enough. He'd already done all that, and they were all dead.

Dr. Dick was at the top of the stairs listening to the tirade coming from below. He clapped a hand on Jackson's arm. "Glad to get out of that. He wants to help his wife but there's only so many of those painkillers she can take. I can't blame him, but he'll follow my orders or Elizabeth is going to the hospital and that's that. Maybe you can help a bit, you always seem to." He turned left into the bedroom and Jackson followed.

Mrs. Knowles smiled when she saw them enter. "My two knights errant, saw your way past the dragon again. It's good to see you, Darius."

"And you, Elizabeth, how's it going?"

Jackson made himself small against the wall and watched. Even from there he could see the pain Elizabeth was trying to hide. He could see in the curve of Dr. Dick's spine and the tight, green knot between his shoulders that he knew it. And the doctor knew, with the long practice of someone who'd been there a hundred times, how little he could do about it. Between her words Mrs. Knowles smiled her understanding. It was beautiful, and heartrending.

"I've got to go," Dr. Dick was saying, "but you're in good hands with my man Jackson here. Good hands, get it?" He reached over and gave Jackson a solid slap on the arm. "See you again soon, Elizabeth. Remember, take everything the nurses give you and nothing your husband does."

"My husband hasn't had much to give for quite awhile now, Darius. Oh, take your doctor coat this time, you forgot it the other day." She gestured with a twisted hand at a white lab coat draped over a chair.

"Say, that's where it got to. Forget my own head if it wasn't fastened on." Dr. Dick snatched the coat off the chair and threw it on. Giving the chair a sidewise look, he moved it a few degrees to the right so that it precisely lined up with a Georgia O'Keeffe self-portrait print propped against the wall. "Well, the coat's mine, but this isn't." He pulled a flash of brilliant pink out of his oversized white pocket, slapped the thing down on the dresser and announced loudly, "See you again soon, my love." He grinned and disappeared into the teeth of a roar from downstairs. A naked, three-inch troll doll was left staring into the bedroom.

Elizabeth was laughing, and Jackson forced himself to turn away from the doll and smile down at her. "They have the highest respect for each other. Yelling and growling is their way of keeping the juices flowing, I suppose. Good to see you, Jackson," she sighed, and seemed to deflate a little before his eyes as she dropped the façade. "Today's not so good a day, tell the truth. I wonder if there's much you can do."

"Always," he said. "Let's see what we've got." He pulled back the sheet and blanket and let his sight widen, loosen, wander. Elizabeth was an amazing sight to be sure. She had eyes that saw the artist's truth, and a narrow, even face that grew wrinkles like unironed silk. Below her neck things billowed out. Overweight mainly from years at the easel and more years in bed, but that wasn't the thing. She was twisted, there was no other word for it. At shoulders, hands, hips, knees, feet, and pretty much everywhere else that two bones met, a thickened and distorted mess of calcified build-ups pushed the joints out of alignment and ruined the geometry. Articular calcification was the body's last-ditch effort to support a destroyed joint, but it didn't work. To Jackson's eyes it looked like Elizabeth Knowles was burdened with thick, grey rocks.

Today every joint was bathed in a dull, red glow. His condition was actually showing him the inflammation at work. He took a breath when the full impact hit him. No wonder Mr. Knowles wanted to boost her painkillers; the woman was suffering terribly.

You can see it, can't you," she murmured. "Literally see it, right? It's your gift." She sighed again. "Fortunately for me, your gifts don't stop at your eyes. Have at it, young man."

Jackson hesitated. She wouldn't tolerate any intensive work or range of motion today; a soothing, gentle massage was the best approach. Twenty minutes later the red glow had faded and she was asleep.

The troll doll's eyes burned beady little holes into the back of his head. An animal part of him wanted to be spooked, outraged at the implication. Which wasn't a possibility, of course. He'd worked on Dr. Dick's patients for two years now. The old guy was fiercely dedicated to his remaining clientele, staying on well past retirement so none of his patients - his friends, many of them in his practice for decades - would have to switch doctors in their final days. Jackson had the highest respect for Dr. Dick and was honoured to work with him. No way was he responsible for all this.

Doctors must know a hundred ways to hasten a natural death. Dr. Dick would know each patient's precise weak spot. There was the Einstein bobblehead, and now this troll doll. Exactly where it needed to be for - well, for whatever Dr. Dick had planned next.

Jackson gave his head a shake, trying not to let any of this nonsense filter down his hands into the treatment. No matter how much Dr. Dick might be looking forward to Arizona golf courses and being done with work, he wouldn't commit a heresy. He wore his ethics like a silver suit. No way would he knock off a single patient for his own convenience, let alone a slew of them. Jackson was at Elizabeth's ankle now, almost finished. Elizabeth moved in her light sleep. She probably never slept well anymore.

He might do it for their convenience. For their suffering. And what about the chair? Dr. Dick knew how to line things up. To some extent he could see the geometry of a place, too.

When he was done Jackson debated with himself for a moment, then murmured, "Elizabeth?"

"Yes?" She was awake at once.

"I have something to tell you. It's going to sound a little weird." As carefully as he could, and not mentioning Dr. Dick at all, he told her that her life was in danger. He told her everything. "I'm already in trouble for talking about this," he ended. "I just don't know what else to do. I'm worried for you."

She considered it all for about a minute, then laid a knobbed hand over top of his on the bedspread. "That is quite a tale, no question of it. But I believe you. I've known since our first visit that you see the world differently. I know how that difference can sometimes bring misunderstanding and difficulty, can't it?" He nodded, and she patted his hand. "Well, we artists have to stick together and support each other. I believe you, Jackson. Thank you for telling me."

He squashed the bedspread under his hand, letting his frustration show. "I've tried anything to keep my patients safe. I don't know what else to do."

"Safe?" Her eyebrows arched together over those level eyes, and she smiled. "Safe from what? From death? In that case, my boy, you think too much of your talents." That brought a laugh. At the end of it she winced a little. "Listen to me. There is only so much you can do. Life will find a way to do what it will, so if you've done all you can about it, then stop fretting. You'll only give yourself wrinkles."

His smile was short-lived. She saw his frustration returning and spoke again. "Enough of this now. You've told me, and I thank you for it. Now whatever is going to happen will happen, and you are not to take it personally. I'll see you next week, Jackson." She patted his hand once more.

On his way out the door she said, "One thing, though. Before you go, could you set those paintings to rights?"

Elizabeth was awake at 3 a.m. when the nurse came in. The oxycodone only muted the pain now, so she hardly ever slept. George had taken to sleeping in the guest room so she didn't keep him awake, too, and that was all right. Their love could see through walls.

"Is it time?" she asked, and she could see that Nurse Wendy was startled to find her up. The nurse was superbly silent for such an ox of a woman. The peaked white cap pinned to Wendy's hair looked old-fashioned and dowdy, but Elizabeth could see clear through to the heart of the woman and she knew. The uniform was her disguise.

"Why, hello," said Wendy in that soothing contralto. "Yes, it's time for your medications again. I'm expecting you'll be wanting them by now. I know how much it hurts."

They both knew medication time wasn't for another two hours. Like she had time for lies at this point in her life. "You have poor Jackson in a frazzle, you know." She fixed the nurse with The Stare.

Wendy tried for one more second to maintain the disguise. Then, like on that computer morphing program her grandson had shown her, she watched the girl's syrupy-sweet facade melt into honesty. Such little changes - a more relaxed curve to the lips, a dropping of the eyes, the way she held herself - and Elizabeth was looking into the face of Death. Tonight Death looked filled with sadness, and a more real caring, and calm confidence. That was a face she could deal with.

The nurse sat down on the edge of the bed, careful not to nudge Elizabeth's aching bones. "The massage therapist, yes. I'm so worried about him. He's had such a hard time of it lately, and I'm afraid he sees far too much."

Elizabeth freed her left hand from the covers and brought her knuckles down in a sharp rap on Wendy's hand. The nurse had the good grace to look shocked instead of amused. "You leave him alone," she ordered. "He's a good man. If you and he cannot work it out, then it's too bad for you. Leave him be." Her hand was throbbing and the outburst took the last of what

strength she had. So much of her life was swallowed up by the
pain now. She sighed back into the pillow.

Wendy looked abashed, thoughtful. Then, after a minute,
she got up and started fussing about at the medicine table.

"Is it time?" Elizabeth asked again.

"Yes, it's time," Wendy said, coming over with a glass of
water.

Elizabeth sighed. "I presume you know what you're doing."

The nurse interpreted the question correctly and held out
her hand. "I do. You're going to have a good sleep at last."

Elizabeth took a look; her usual three oxycodone and three
new, small, white ones with Soma stamped on them.

"It's about time," she said.

Chapter 13

"She passed in her sleep," Florita's voice told him. "Mr. Knowles wanted me to tell you he is grateful for your help." There was an empty space, then she added, "It looked very peaceful, Jackson. Nothing to worry about. I will see you at the next one."

He let the cell phone die in his hand. He wanted to smash it against the wall. There would be a next one, and another after that.

Elizabeth Knowles had called him an artist. That was a memory worth holding onto, at least.

There was work to be done, but his concentration was shot. While his hands took care of a sheet-music crick in the neck of a professional cellist, his mind was full of Elizabeth and her paintings. Some exacting jaw work on a Coal Harbour stockbroker with tinnitus managed to focus his attention for awhile, but the man had a beautiful condo, appointed with a European flair and an eye to elegant simplicity, everything in its proper place. By the end of the treatment the condo itself had distracted him, pulling his head into thoughts of who else he knew with a sensitivity for spaces.

The same person, he realized on the way back to his car, who'd recently stuck a bobblehead doll on the dash of his car.

He dropped his massage table to the sidewalk, punching the numbers on his cell phone before he could think himself out of it.

"Hello?" The voice was gravelly and busy chewing. Belatedly, Jackson realized it must be suppertime.

"Hi, Dr. Dick? It's Jackson Teague calling."

"Jackson! Always a pleasure. What can I do for you?"

"It's about Mrs. Knowles. I – "

"You're wondering about her death? I just got the post-mortem results back, was going to look at them in a few minutes. You want to talk. Sure, come on over. You know where my office is. Half an hour?"

"Uh. Okay, that would be good."

"Fabulous! Looking forward to it."

Dr. Dick's office was a suite of rooms at the front of his house in West Point Grey, grandfathered in from before there were bylaws about home offices in zillion-dollar neighbourhoods. It was a bit of a bike ride up the hill from Kitsilano, but traffic was light. Jackson spent most of the ride trying to ignore the pleasing, repetitive symmetry of the passing cars.

Light shone through the bevelled oval of glass above Dr. Dick's porch door. Jackson took the three wide steps to the left of the wheelchair ramp and the brass knob turned before he was finished knocking. Dr. Dick stood in the entryway, a checkered napkin tucked into a pressed white shirt that matched his hair. "Almost finished my ribs, come on in. Shoes off."

Jackson had been to Dr. Dick's office a few times before. They stepped from the entry into a waiting room done in shades of coffee and cream, with comfy chairs to the right and a small desk to the left. He knew the door behind the desk led to a Norman Rockwell treatment room, white tile and steel sink and enamelled trays and all. Now Dr. Dick led him through the other door, deeper into the house, over thick, quiet carpeting that led past an oak staircase and prodigious bookshelves into the dining room, where a basket of Tony Roma's finest lay half-demolished next to a snifter of red wine.

The place was immaculate. Of course it would be. Not a crumb or a speck of dust, not a book out of place. The house rang with perfect placement. It was the logical extension of the revealing moment Jackson had seen in Elizabeth Knowles' bedroom. Dr. Dick saw.

"Don't have much company for dinner since Mallory died. My grandkids keep expecting me to hook up with some hot young thing from the assisted-living home. Bound to disappoint them, though. So what's on your mind, Jackson? Elizabeth?" The old man grabbed his wine and tossed his napkin over the ribs, leading him to two leather chairs in the corner. The chairs had been angled a little shy of ninety degrees - perfectly placed for two men to have a conversation, so they could talk closely without staring each other down. A small end table was tucked between them, and on it lay several unlabelled manila folders. Dr. Dick reached for the top one.

Jackson stopped him. "Why'd you do that? Why order an autopsy?"

Dr. Dick got a sour look on his face. "Autopsy? I ordered nothing of the sort. There's no reason whatsoever to have Elizabeth's mortal shell cut and sawed into pieces. Couldn't countenance such a thing. She's been a friend of mine for over thirty years. I ordered a post-mortem, just a thorough once-over to see if anything was wrong."

Jackson conceded the point, not taking his eyes off the doctor. "Okay, a post-mortem then. Why?"

"For one reason and one reason only, to get a blood test

done. I wanted a count of the opioids in her system at time of death. That damn fool George, I wouldn't put it past him to hand Elizabeth the whole bottle just so she wouldn't hurt. I needed to see if that was what happened."

"And if it was?"

Here the old stump of a man seemed to shrink a little, and his voice got quiet. "Damned if I know. Nothing, probably wouldn't even call him on it. He's been through enough already. They both have. Now at least one of them's got some peace."

Quiet settled between them for a minute. The smells of leather upholstery and old books mingled well with the tangy barbecue sauce still coming off the ribs. A clock ticked somewhere out of sight. "So?" Jackson said at last.

"Hmm?" Dr. Dick picked up the folder and opened it to the single page inside. "So nothing. Levels of oxy consistent with the prescribed dosage. No other sign of trauma or problem. George didn't do anything. She died, Jackson. That's all."

Jackson realized he was tense, and tried to dial it down a notch. "Nice place you've got here. You know how to arrange things very well."

Dr. Dick lifted out of his reverie to look around. "This old place? Thanks. I guess I've moved a thing or two around since Mallory passed, but mostly it's still her doing."

Jackson was almost there, but he had to be sure. "I'm going to try a little thing here. Excuse me," and he got up and started moving about the room.

The changes were simple once you'd seen them a few times. Jackson studied the room and its spare lines. Then, giving his perceptions a twist that was distressingly easy to pull off, he saw how to make it all go south. One hard yank on a corner of the carpet pulled it a degree out of alignment. That skewed the table and chairs, but not enough. Jackson nudged the table a little the other way. Then he moved down the bookshelf on the far wall, pulling out the odd book just enough to upset the smooth line. Lastly, he took the plate of unfinished ribs and slid it to the right and out of reach of the chair. The solid, slow-moving river of energy that had coursed through the place for years shuddered, curdled in on itself, and started to spin down an invisible drain.

Dr. Dick was watching, a growing amazement on his face. "My God, you know how to wreck a place quick! Never seen anything like it. Now put it all back."

Jackson stood an arm's length away by the table and said, "No. What does it feel like?"

The old guy was getting irritated, jerking around in his chair. "Feel like? It feels like you touched my dinner. Mallory and I brought that carpet back -"

"Feels unpleasant, doesn't it?" Jackson was watching closely. Almost sure.

"Damn straight it does, now -"

"Would you spend any time in a room that felt like this?"

"All I want you to do is put things right again. I don't feel -" This time it was Dr. Dick that ran out of words.

"You don't know whether to get angry or cry or get up and leave, right?"

"All of those, but more and more I'm feeling like boxing you about the ears. Now fix it!"

That was enough. In less than a minute Jackson had everything back to its former place and the geometry of the house resumed its lean perfection. It shocked him how easy that had been. He took a deep breath, asking himself once, is this a good idea? Nothing better occurred to him, so he sat back down and said, "Let me tell you a story." He laid it all out. The disturbances, the deaths. The dolls and the traps. He told Dr. Dick a bit about how he saw the world, and that was the hardest part of all.

"Those people still had life left. They weren't supposed to die." He kept a firm grip on the leather arms of the chair. "I had my hands on those people. There's a – a rhythm to dying, a pattern to it. If you don't get hit by a bus, then you can kind of see it coming. With Mrs. Knowles? With the rest of them? Death wasn't supposed to happen, not right then." He was out of breath, so he pushed himself back into the chair and stopped.

Dr. Dick didn't say anything at first. He sipped his wine. Then he took up Elizabeth Knowles' report again and read the page. Finally he put it back down and turned himself to face Jackson. "You know how long it's been since anybody told me a story like that? Never, that's how long. If you hadn't done that little dance around my place earlier, I'd have thrown you out on your ear for it, too. But now?" He smoothed down his hair and looked like the earth had jiggled a little under him. "Now I think I might just believe you.

"Not that I think all these people are being killed," he added, holding up his hand. "Remember, I'm the doctor here, and not a half-bad one. I know what you mean about the timing of these things, but Death keeps its own schedule. I examined everyone except your Mrs. Kilborn and I certified them all as natural causes. Because they were." He thumbed the report. "Including Elizabeth, rest her soul."

"I - you said you believed me."

Dr. Dick waved a hand around. "I believe you saw what you did. That you're not simply making it all up or delusional. You showed me how somebody could deliberately make a place feel terrible, and let me tell you you're good at it. But when I went to those patients' homes, you know what I saw? The usual mess that happens when someone is nearing the end and the rest of the family stops caring about housekeeping. It's one of the things home care is for. The day nurse, or sometimes the night nurse, tidies up and does the dusting. I thought they were slacking off. I didn't feel any of what you're talking about, Jackson. All I saw was a mess."

This was exasperating. "Of course you know what I'm talking about. You see it, too. Everything in your house is in its proper place. You feel it like I do." Jackson was edging close to a whine, and again he snapped his mouth shut.

Dr. Dick was looking around. "Thanks, I guess. I've always known you see things a bit differently. All your patients commented on it. Pretty unique, they said, x-ray eyes and such. Can't lay claim to anything like that myself. You know what skill I do have?" His eyes were back on Jackson.

"What?"

He smiled. "I'm a neat freak. It's a job hazard, maybe a requirement, most doctors have some version of it." He finished his wine and stood. "I appreciate you bringing your concerns to me, Jackson, and thank you very much for that demonstration. That's something I won't soon forget. As for the rest of it, my advice is to calm down. You've had a bad run of it lately, enough to unsettle anybody. But take it from me, there's nothing wrong. It's just life."

Jackson let his handlebars find their way home as he rode back down the Point Grey hill with his mind spinning as fast as his gears. Dr. Dick had given him the answer. It was so obvious, he should have seen it long ago.

They'd all had a night nurse. He didn't have a name yet, but he would.

Jackson jumped into the morning with a rush of purpose and

excitement, his pill down and breakfast done before the sheets
cooled. He was going to wrap this mess up today. He needed
the name. No way to ask Dahlia or Florita who the night nurse
was, because he had no idea where they were working now. He
would have to go to the agency.

The Arbutus Home Care Agency was located, appropriately,
off 38th and Arbutus, on the upper floor of a demure, two-
storey brick and glass affair that spanned half the block. The
street level shops were a demographic snapshot of the city's
moneyed southwest corner - a custom dress shop, a financial
management agency, a coffee boutique, and an eyeglass store
where a set of frames would cost you as much as laser eye
surgery. He knew the block, had even visited the agency's
second floor office a few times on business. Ruth the
receptionist he remembered as friendly and professional, but
he couldn't just stomp up the stairs and ask her to show him
the staff files. He walked right past the glass entry door and
ended up in Caffe Fantastico, fuming over a tiny cappuccino
and a cranberry orange muffin the size of a hubcap.

This was irritating. The name of the night nurse was up
there in their files, on their computer screens. He couldn't bluff
his way to the data; he had plenty of strengths, but subterfuge
wasn't one of them. He did have clarity of purpose, a pressing
need to know and the drive to find out. Wasn't that supposed to
be enough? It was a cosmic principle or something. Well, it
wasn't working.

The coffee was excellent, the muffin big enough to be
second breakfast. He polished them off and then, still feeling
lost and more than a little awkward, exited through the back of
the cafe into the alley.

Arbutus alleys were as immaculate as Dr. Dick's living
room, not so much as a stray coffee cup or oil stain to disturb
the order. Towards the end of the block Jackson saw a young

woman come through a steel security door, white trash bag in one hand, and stand at the railing on the three-step concrete landing. She gave the bag an expert lob and it arced into a nearby dumpster without spilling so much as a Post-It note. No doubt if it had, the girl would have rushed to pick it up. She gave her accomplishment a sweet smile then disappeared back inside.

No one who visited the Arbutus Home Care Agency ever forgot Ruth's smile. He sent up a word of thanks to the cosmos and swerved for the dumpster.

Back at home he put down a dropcloth and spread out the office garbage. It took seconds to find the crumpled-up schedule with a full printout of each care aide's postings for the entire month. Wendy Corbett was a busy woman. That name was on plenty of night shifts, including the last night slot before Mrs. Elizabeth Knowles disappeared from the schedule. Today she was off to start with somebody else.

The real gold was down at the bottom of the bag, shredded into small pieces that took him over an hour to reconstruct - employee tax forms. Including one that gave Wendy Corbett's address in Chinatown.

Marilyn twitched the edge of the tactical vest away from her thigh and settled into a deeper crouch behind the steel girder, beginning to sweat under the balaclava and the flak helmet. The stubby, black Heckler & Koch MP5 felt heavy but comfortable in her gloved hands. This was the picture she'd stared at for so long at her desk back in Squadroom Three. She was actually here.

She glanced over at Corporal Jukes and whispered, "You guys always dress like this for parties?"

Amusement mixed with consternation crinkled his eyes as he tapped his left ear, where the com unit nestled under the balaclava. Just like hers. "Cut the radio chatter," came Inspector Takeda's terse command. "Remember your approach pattern. We go in five - four - three - two - now!"

She gripped the rifle and focused on the solitary figure leaning over a railing at the top of the bridge's curving deck. The quiet scene was shattered with noise, light and motion as the six ERT members broke cover, snapped bright LED spots on the target, and yelled for him to stop and drop. Following her assigned trainee pattern Marilyn kept to the back of the team, scanning the edges for interference and problems.

The target whirled around. He was tall and sandy-haired, his face a study in fear and intent. He spun back to face the edge of the bridge, placed a hand on the railing and made a leap for certain death to the water below.

Sergeant Orson on the left flank was ready. He pulled his weapon and, with a crack, two leads flew from his taser to the suspect's disappearing back. The wires tightened as Orson pulled the trigger and shouted, "Zap!" Then they went slack.

"Too late!" Takeda flipped the big sodium lights back on in the warehouse roof and stomped over to the mock-up of the Lions Gate Bridge deck. "He's over and gone, and all his intel with him. We run it again in three minutes!"

This was the tenth training simulation they'd practised today. Marilyn removed her helmet and balaclava for a sip of water and a breather. Jukes joined her. "So, let's see. We've done straight takedown twice, resisted takedown three times, unexpected ordnance twice, attempted suicide twice, and that one with the hidden accomplice. You bored with ERT yet?"

The shine in her eyes was answer enough. She gestured

towards a tight knot of about a dozen recruits in street clothes keeping close to the warehouse wall and watching the drills. They were all young, fit, and intensely interested. "One of those things is not like the others," she said.

Jukes agreed. "Yeah, I noticed." The difference was subtle at first glance, but as the day had worn on the tall, chiseled one with the deep tan and blond brush cut had been the only recruit not drawn into a side conversation. He never took his eyes off the drills. As far as Marilyn could tell he'd never even moved from his stand-easy pose. Jukes slipped his balaclava back on, gesturing for Marilyn to do the same. "Takeda has his eye on that one. Same as he did for you. Come on, next drill's about to start."

"Debrief," called Takeda, and they all gathered around the base of the bridge. It was a hundred-foot section of makeshift girders, cables and sidewalk done out of plywood and painted bridge green and pavement black, enough to give a good approximation of the difficult job ahead of them. "It's a high-visibility situation with multiple variables and constant civilian traffic," Takeda began the litany, when the radio at his hip squawked an all-squads bulletin.

"Alert, units in the vicinity of Duchess and Prior Street, possible 928 in progress, high priority, please respond." The dispatcher gave the street coordinates of a suspected sexual predator in a playground.

"That's four blocks away," said Takeda. He pointed at Marilyn. "Trainee, you came in a cruiser. Jukes, go with her." He flashed his teeth. "Keep your rifles. Scare the son of a bitch to death."

He had her address. She might be able to stay invisible on the job, but Wendy Corbett's home would be full of rock-solid proof. Jackson was going to find it and give it to the police.

The repair job on his apartment door was a fresh, unpainted scar on the frame. He grinned and went to rummage under his bed, coming out with a smallish package he stuffed into a pocket. This was a perfect time for the Open Sesame. He owed her that.

The section of Strathcona where the nurse lived, a couple of streets back from Chinatown's shops, was what the real estate agents called a mixed neighbourhood. 1940's-era wood frame homes, some in good repair and some most definitely not, shared street space with ambitious row houses and a small condo complex. The colour scheme ran the gamut from gunmetal grey to red brick to honest-to-God hippie rainbow. It was a neighbourhood on the move, but anybody's guess in which direction.

The address on the shredded form was for a stucco bungalow, but Jackson could see on his first walk-by that a young and active Asian family lived there. A tall woman busied herself with a vacuum cleaner in the living room, looking frequently out the big picture window at the street. That stymied him. He checked the address again. It was correct.

He kept on going and turned the corner. The block was a planned mini-neighbourhood, a ring of newer houses with a pocket park in the middle. He turned in along a slim pathway between two houses for a look. The fenced back yards all fed onto a rectangular, paved walking track. A hump of grassy earth with some playground equipment at the top occupied the center of the park.

Two grade-school girls played with diggers in a sandpile by the hilltop's log and rope jungle gym. He walked up the hill, stood by the empty slide and spotted the six concrete steps going down from ground level to a half-sunken door in the bungalow's foundations. Wendy Corbett lived in a basement suite.

The evidence of her crimes was in there, he could feel it. Jackson peered more closely at the basement door, fingering the stiff slips of folded paper in his pocket.

Gunpowder was such a useful tool. He'd wondered a few years back how he might open a door if he needed to, and Open Sesame was the end product. Two thick ribbons of cardstock, folded over, held a respectable layer of smokeless powder glued inside. They were thin enough to slide between any wooden door and its jamb, one above the lock and one below. Two fuses trailed out and wove together into one.

The trick was the fuses. Wood was resilient. Hit it above and below a lock simultaneously and the door would flex like a tree in a windstorm. So Jackson had staggered the fuses by the tiniest bit. The two packages blew with a fraction of a second's delay between the top and bottom. The combined shock and twist made the most of the small charges and neatly cracked open all the doors he'd tried it on.

The Asian woman was in the back of her house now, running the vacuum some more and keeping an eye on the kids in the playground. Small as the Open Sesame was, she was going to hear it. He would have five minutes, tops, to find the evidence before the police arrived. He could feel himself vibrating with excitement, his eyes everywhere, seeing everything. Five minutes would be plenty of time.

He brought his excitement into focus by concentrating on the target. The top half of Wendy Corbett's apartment door was visible above the concrete steps, white wood surrounding a small window covered by a frilly yellow curtain. He ran the faces of the nurse's victims through his mind, lingered on each to build his resolve. When the moment came he wrapped one hand around the Open Sesame in his pocket, stepped out from behind the slide and stormed down the hill toward the concrete steps.

His feet diverted him onto the walking track and back towards the pathway to the street even as he registered what he'd seen. The Asian woman standing in her kitchen window with a deep scowl and a phone to her ear, looking right at him. The frilly yellow curtain in the basement window moving half an inch as a finger pushed its corner.

His resolve drowned under a wave of pure fear. Never trust a schedule you find in the garbage, he scolded himself. Wendy Corbett was home. And she'd seen him.

"Halt! Police, don't move!"

Fear exploded into dread and Jackson stopped, hands flying into the air. The policewoman's voice came from behind him. A spot between his shoulder blades broke into a furious itch as he imagined the pistol she had trained on his back.

"Teague? Jackson Teague?" It couldn't be. He dared to swivel his head around and his knees practically buckled at the sight of a helmeted nightmare in full jackboot riot gear painting his chest with a red laser dot from a full-on fucking machine gun. Deep inside his ribcage absolutely nothing happened for a full two seconds. At about the time his heart started beating again, strong hands clamped onto his shoulders from behind and another huge voice said, "Down! On the ground!"

He was going down by the feet of a second stormtrooper when that first voice - it had to be Constable Mathers - said, "Wait. Let's walk him." One hand from each of them hoisted him up and mashed his biceps. He was frog-marched off the playground as the Asian woman ran from her house and herded the two schoolgirls off the swings and inside.

They threw him into the back of a waiting police cruiser. It was as full of unforgiving lines as a cage and smelled like a queer mix of plastic, gasoline and bad body. The last time he'd been in one of these he hadn't seen freedom for three months. And now he had a pocketful of explosives.

They had their helmets off. The driver was definitely Constable Mathers, but the guy wasn't her partner. He was short and lean and looked like a young Tom Cruise on a mean day, except that Tom Cruise would have been acting. Right now the guy was keeping one eye on him as he cast looks at Mathers. She was the one in charge here. Right now she was scowling at him, trying to put pieces together.

"I can explain," he started.

"Oh, I can't wait."

The best way into icy waters was fast. "I found out who's killing all those patients. She lives - "

"Wait, what?" Mathers was immediately unhappy and edging her way towards steamed. "This is that doll thing, isn't it? You're still on about this? Except now you've got - " She spun around in her seat to face him fully. "Teague, were you about to do a B&E? A frigging daylight burglary, off an occupied playground! Tell me you're not that stupid."

"I'm not that stupid." The spinning wheels in his head found some traction. "I was just looking, that's all. The nurse lives in the basement suite. I was going to walk past, look in the windows, and if I saw anything I was going to call you. I still have your card."

She was silent. The other guy was watching, interested but obviously not involved. Then Mathers focused a hard gaze on his face. "Let's be clear on this. Jackson, were you about to break into that lady's house?"

He focused on the memory of the tall woman in her kitchen, phone to her ear. "No," he said.

"You were going to walk by the house and call me if you

saw anything."

"I was going to walk past the house, look in the windows, and if I saw anything suspicious I was going to call you. That was all. A little foolish, now that I think about it. But that was all."

"Walking past a woman's lawn when she's in the window staring at you? Foolish doesn't do it justice. And what did you hope to find in your look through the windows?"

He could answer this one honestly. "I don't know. It was a long shot." He left it at that.

"Just for the record, Jackson, did you have any interest in those girls on the playground?"

"Oh, come on."

The other guy tossed in his two bits. "Sounds like trespassing to me. Sounds like it's not worth our time. Like, we have bigger fish to fry, and the frymaster's waiting for us." He tapped a finger to his ear.

Mathers took one more second to mull it over. Then she said, "Okay. You are one lucky son of a bitch, Jackson Teague. This is another note in your file, and I'm going to write it in red. Again I won't take it any farther, but this is it. You drop this nonsense, effective immediately. No more visits to Chinatown, you're not to come within three blocks of this place. Are we clear?"

Jackson gave several quick, sharp nods. "Yes, absolutely."

Mathers got out and opened the back door for him. "Get lost."

He was three steps away and almost into a run when Mather's voice stopped him in mid-exit. "Jackson. Did you lose any more?"

She'd seen him after Sam Long. "Elizabeth Knowles."

She said nothing else. Jackson got the hell out of there.

"You know why I'm on the SWAT team?" Jukes said to Marilyn as they drove back to the warehouse.

"Why?"

"Because I'd have just swatted him." He settled into the passenger seat, eyes front. "You beat cops have a lot more patience than me."

Jackson held it together through his afternoon appointments then rushed back to the apartment, looking in his mirrors for police cars. Once inside he bolted the new lock and closed the blinds, pulled his knees into the corner of the sofa and stared at the door. Constable Mathers was going to come to her senses any time now and break it down to arrest him.

Maybe he needed to get locked up again, if today was the best he could do. The depth of his stupidity was astonishing. What did he have? An unreliable address from papers he'd found in the trash and a story so weird even he had trouble believing it. He'd been ready to go rogue on a complete stranger's door over that. Really, a trip back to the ward was what he deserved. He didn't even know what the nurse looked like. She could walk right up to him on the street and he wouldn't know until it was all over.

Tonight was potluck night. He hauled himself off the sofa and spent an hour tidying up his apartment before the beach party. When the last dish was straight on its shelf he was surprised to find himself a little out of breath, a shine of sweat on his face.

The North Shore mountains still carried patches of late-Spring snow and a thick offshore fog bank had erased the Gulf Islands from the horizon, but the air coming off the water was warm and redolent with the smells of ocean and forest. He laid out the red-checked tablecloth by the big cedar log, placed his edamame succotash and fresh rolls on the center squares and waved as Charles and Georgia stepped off the bus.

Errant breezes played with the leaves overhead, trying to distract him. Charles and Georgia carried their basket between them again, Georgia kicking off her sandals the second they reached the grass. Charles must have saved somebody in the ER today. He was doing the full Superman, head up and shoulders back, striding forward with his eyes locked on Jackson and waves of confidence rolling off in all directions. Georgia was being his lightning rod, grounding him through the picnic basket from a half-step behind, waving at friends and casting eddies around them that washed away Charles' speed. For the first time Jackson saw how hard she had to work at it. He stood as they came close.

"Hey," came Leaf's voice from over his right shoulder.

"Whoa!" said Charles, and Georgia's face dropped into a picture of dumbfounded shock. Jackson spun around, delighted.

"You made it!" He thumped Leaf hard on the back. "I wasn't sure if you'd be, you know, employed." Georgia ran a hand over the pale fuzz on Leaf's head and laughed.

"Not quite yet, man. I passed the first level, we'll see about the rest." He filled everyone in on his decision to try for the Vancouver Police, the involved recruitment process and his tour around the departments. "It's about time I got put to use," he finished, with a sidelong smile for Jackson. Then he gestured towards the tablecloth. "Nice spread," he said, a different tone in his voice.

Everybody looked down. "Yes, very pretty," Georgia remarked, and they all stood there. Jackson saw his succotash hogging the center and got the message.

"Oh, here," he said, pulling it off to one side to make room. That seemed to break a spell. They sat down and handed him their contributions. He put Charles' pate and veggies, Georgia's cabbage rolls, and Leaf's almond cookies where they belonged and everyone spent another moment staring at the spread. "Dig in," he encouraged them, breaking the spell again, and the party was on.

Leaf dished out the meal as Georgia poured the apple juice. Charles regaled them with a story about trying to de-splinter a ticklish boy's foot, an athletic operation that eventually involved two orderlies and a security guard. Jackson tried to pay attention, but Wendy Corbett's basement door and frilly curtains kept filling his mind. Behind those curtains, caught in dim glimpses, was a horrifyingly blank face.

The party had grown quiet. Charles spoke up. "Okay, Jackson, out with it. Tell us what's going on."

"What?"

"Look down." He had that irritating non-judgemental voice on again. Jackson looked down.

He was sitting at the comfortable point where a 45-degree line bisecting the north corner of the red-checked cloth passed right through his navel. The sand in the 270 degrees of arm's reach around him had been tidied of cigarette butts, seaweed and broken shells. The remaining bits and driftwood had been arranged in neat geometrical patterns, triangles intersecting squares merging with hexagons, all the way around him. A few unbroken shells varied the pattern with their whorls and rays, causing pleasing waves amongst the straight lines. It was beautiful. Zen garden beautiful. Simply looking at it made Jackson feel better. Each pattern lined up perfectly with the thin, phosphorescent grid that projected from the red-checked tablecloth.

"Oh." Then, for emphasis, "Shit."

"Your picnic spread was very nice," Georgia commented, "we all saw it when we got here. A work of art." She gestured at the sand. "This is a little much. What's up?"

"I lost another one." Holding his tongue never did any good anyway, and these were his friends. "That makes six, in less than two months. I'm pretty sure I know who's behind it all. But I can't get near her." He told them about Elizabeth Knowles. He told them about his conversation with Dr. Dick, and his visit to Arbutus Street, and his aborted visit to Chinatown, including his close shave with the police.

"I'm a little stressed. I guess it shows," he concluded.

"It does sound pretty scary," said Georgia. "People are dying. Your place got broken into. No matter who did it, that has to be upsetting."

Leaf's eyes gleamed. "I was at an Emergency Response Team practice today. I saw those two get called out to arrest you. That must have been a real underwear moment." He ran a hand over the stubble on his head. "Tough breaks, man, more than I knew. I've met some of the cops on the force. They know their job. If you've laid it all out for them and they say it's nothing, well - maybe it's just weird. Like rolling snake-eyes six times in a row. It's weird, but it does happen." His hand reached over and squeezed Jackson's knee. "Maybe you shouldn't sweat it."

Jackson tugged a wrinkle out of the tablecloth, then caught himself and laughed. It came out sounding higher than usual. "Yeah, it's a tangle, all right."

"Is there anything more you can do?" asked Georgia. "Talk

to somebody, or – "

"Like Dr. Parma," announced Charles, with enough volume to silence his wife. He continued, dialling it down a notch. "The situation might be messed up, but what really matters is what it's done to you. Every doctor knows what it's like to box a patient. We're trained to handle it. Somehow I don't think that's covered in massage school."

He picked up a carrot stick and waved it around. "This is big, Jackson. This – " he waved at the beach artwork – "says that you've let it get under your skin. You've built up stories around it. Somebody breaks into your place and instantly it's connected to the conspiracy. You tried busting in on someone else. The police are watching you." That last sounded like a condemnation.

"She's out there," Jackson said, feeling a flush violent enough to roast his ears. "She killed those people - "

"In ways nobody else can see." Charles was speaking soft but intense, staring into him. "Listen, Jackson. Three years ago, when you got out and got settled, you asked me to keep an eye on you. You said you trusted me. Well, trust me now. I'm your friend, and I'm telling you this is over the edge. Seriously over. If you want to rearrange things, if your OCD grips you hard and you have to move things around, that's one thing. But conspiracy theories? Ones that lead you to take action, make big mistakes that cost you? That's a whole different kettle of fish."

"Charles," said Georgia.

He turned to face her. "I know it's hard to see when you're close to someone, but this is a textbook case. I run across it downtown almost daily." He turned back to Jackson, soft again. "You know, too, don't you?"

Jackson picked up the corner of the tablecloth and tried to mess it up. The pattern shifted, barely-visible lines rearranging themselves around the new geometry, and the wrinkle turned into the dash of imperfection that enhanced the beauty of everything else. It was wonderful. He was screwed.

"Those people weren't meant to die. Their houses had been changed." It was almost a whisper.

The group was silent, letting the declaration hang in the air. Movement intruded on his peripheral vision. Charles, handing him a phone. "Take it," he said. Jackson did.

"Now. I'm your friend, and I'm your failsafe. You're going to call Dr. Parma, at his home, right now, and make an appointment to see him tomorrow. Or I'm taking my phone back and calling 911."

Nobody spoke. Silence gives assent and his friends sat there saying nothing, waiting for him to make the call. A muscle began to uncramp deep inside his head. Maybe he could use a little help. "I don't know his home number."

"Already keyed in," Charles said. Of course.

His thumb hovered over the Call icon. It's all real, his head wailed at him, they're dying and she's doing it and she's moving things around and she knows who you are. The phone was waiting.

He reached around and swept a hand over the sand, ruining the sticks and sending a tiny shriek through his mind. "Fuck it," he said, and pushed the button.

Chapter 14

The bus from Kits Beach to 3rd and Trimble was one of the new models, smooth and hushed, half-empty in the late evening. Charles spent the quiet trip peering into a dense fog that had rolled in and turned all the porch lights into halos, thinking about his job on the beach. Nobody had said much after Jackson finally made the call, and he was all right with that. It was the same in the hospital. There wasn't much to be said after you'd made the hard decisions.

Tonight had been tough on Jackson. Letting him continue down his rabbit hole would have been worse. Charles knew he had some repair work to do on their friendship, but maybe in a month or so — no, it would take longer than that for Jackson to forgive him. A month from now he might understand how close to the edge he'd come. Charles snorted. Close, hell. Jackson had escaped jail because a cop was too busy to book him. This affair was one step away from hitting the papers.

Georgia sat beside him, her nose in a book. He could feel the sun's warmth radiating off her skin scant inches from his arm, tempered by a touch of silent frost. He sighed and turned back to the window. He guessed he had some repair work to do there, too.

The bus dropped them at their stop. He slowed to match Georgia's pace as they walked to the brown, clapboard two-storey with the stone porch that had been in her family for three generations. Jackson was in good hands, at least. Pranjit Parma was one of the best OCD men in the country and dedicated as hell. He'd appreciated Charles' warm-up call and been more than willing to say yes to a Saturday appointment when Jackson rang from the beach.

They entered the house and Georgia took off for the kitchen. Before he had stowed away the beach basket he could smell hot chocolate. Oh. In the unspoken code of their relationship, hot chocolate meant conversation. He was being called to the kitchen for a conference.

Two pillars of steam rose from the mugs in the nook. Georgia was seated on the left-hand bench. He slid into the other one and they spent some time looking out the windows at the gathering night in the back yard. Charles knew better than to speak first, so he waited and sipped.

"Jackson's going through a rough patch," she said.

"Yes."

"He needs his friends behind him right now."

"Yes. I think he got that tonight."

"You think?" She looked up at him now, and the expression on her face wasn't warm. It was appraising. "I don't think you were very much of a friend to him at all."

That set him back against the nook's slanting wood. He forgot the mug. "Hey, that's not fair. That was hard, what I did tonight. Harder than it ever is in the hospital."

"Oh, I'm sure it was." There was still no warmth in her voice. "I'm sure it was terribly hard for you. I'm sure you're still all broken up about it. Maybe you won't even sleep tonight."

He wasn't at all sure where this was going. "Come on, Georgia. You think Jackson's going to have a harder night tonight than he's had for the past couple of weeks? You saw the guy, he's a wreck. All I did was help him make a decision he should have made long ago. Now that the appointment's set, I bet he sleeps like a log."

She took a drink of her hot chocolate. The mug was a little too wide for her mouth and left two tiny upcurls of rich foam at the corners of her lips. "Maybe you're right. Maybe he will sleep better tonight. He'll sleep better because, before this, he didn't know what to do. Now he's had somebody he respects tell him what to do and scare him into doing it."

"But?" There was concession in her words, but none whatever in her voice.

She gazed at him again. "But it wasn't a very nice thing you did."

So that was it. "So what? It was necessary. You saw that thing with the sand. Jackson knew this might happen three years ago when he was released from the hospital. He asked me to keep an eye on him, remember? He said, when the time came, I had to do precisely what I did tonight."

"Scare the bejesus out of him? Threaten him with the thing he fears most, going back to the hospital against his will?" The steel was in her voice now.

"Yes! If that's what it took to get him to make that call, then yes. Don't you see? I had no choice. You saw the mess he was in. Would you want him like that, on the street, thinking and doing God knows what? I mean, he already tried to break into some nurse's home. What next?"

Georgia took another sip and considered. "Okay, point taken. He went overboard there, no doubt. He's not seeing clearly. But neither are you."

Charles leaned forward. "So out with it already. What am I not seeing clearly here? What should I have done differently?"

The steel was gone, leaving Charles feeling overbalanced, like he'd tried to punch a cloud. Georgia's brown eyes let him fall. "You could have tried believing him. You could have tried being a friend instead of a doctor. You were the only one tonight

who never for a moment considered that Jackson might be
telling the truth. Sure, he was upset. Sure, his gift was getting
the better of him. He's had some hard times lately. But you
never considered that your poor, stressed-out friend might have
wanted reassurance that he wasn't crazy. Instead you told him
in no uncertain terms that he was. And threatened him with
his own personal version of Hell if he didn't do something about
it." She drained her cup and stood. "I don't think you showed
much friendship tonight, that's all."

Charles spent a long time in the nook after Georgia was in
bed, feeling the heat leave his mug.

Marilyn eased her gloved hand around the edge of the steel I-
beam and held her index and middle finger pointed down in the
man-walking signal. Then she snapped it into a fist with the
index finger curled up, the question signal. She'd only learned
the first few tactical hand gestures that afternoon, but it was a
simple question. Are you sure he's going to show?

From the other side of the Lions Gate Bridge upright Jukes
extended his own hand, then flipped it palm up. Loosely
translated the sign meant, how the hell do I know? Marilyn
cracked a smile behind her balaclava and tried to peer deeper
into the fog. The dense mist, combined with the moonless black
of 2 a.m., made it hard even to see the occasional passing car.

A tone from the bottom key on the world's biggest pipe
organ shook the fog and rattled the deck under her feet for a
long, three-second blast. The Northern Sea Otter had an
impressive horn, and had been using it every minute for the
past hour.

Borden had capitalized on the foggiest night in months for his rigging run. Surveillance had caught him leaving home with the bomb in a large backpack, then lost him. He'd out-driven both the fake tail and then the real one, then dumped the car with the GPS tracker in a mall parking lot. Takeda had scrambled the entire team to their ready positions.

Now they covered the center third of the bridge, tucked behind the two massive support pillars and folded into faded green utility boxes installed for the occasion, waiting and staring into a swirling wall of mist. Borden could pass within five feet of Marilyn's position and she'd never know unless he was wearing cologne. Even their night vision gear was doing them little good. She moved her MP5 a little farther away from the steel pillar and stared into the swirls.

"Heads up." The whisper from southern point, closest to the Stanley Park approach, stopped her thoughts with a jolt as she felt Jukes settle into readiness. Borden was stepping onto the bridge.

Marilyn, as an observer trainee, was stuck with Jukes at northern point, six hundred feet past the center of the span. The least likely place for anything to happen. She'd be lucky to observe any part of the takedown with this weather. The bridge deck's apex was only visible in jagged glimpses as the fog rolled.

A ghost of a breeze stirred the mist and there he was. Tall, angular, pulling something large and conical out of a duffel bag. "He's reached center point, starting his run," came Takeda's mutter over the com. "Takedown on my go."

Marilyn strained to see what she could through the fog. The breeze made another pass over the bridge and separated the thick haze for a moment into lacy tendrils. Borden was fiddling with the top of the cone now. Rigging it, with amazing speed. Then she saw a shred of fog coalesce into a solid shape.

"Third party," she whispered hard into the mic, "third party at center point."

Wendy was in Heaven. This was a genuine pea-souper like she hadn't seen since the mists of her childhood, when the back yard disappeared from the kitchen window and her father refused to allow her outside. Moving through a fog like this was a miraculous thing. She was in her own little pocket of the night, and as she moved, a tiny bit of the world came in to greet her and the tiny bit she'd occupied slid behind into nothing. The sounds of the invisible city were muted to an undifferentiated whisper. The rich moisture filled her nostrils with the scent of the sea.

She was far from tired even though she'd been walking for hours, doing the long loop through the city, over the Second Narrows Bridge and along the North Vancouver waterfront. The long sweep of the Lions Gate Bridge would take her back towards Chinatown and home in time for the first glimmer of dawn. The mist got thicker as she walked up onto the span, so that even the occasional car passing by to her right was only a flicker of headlight and then gone. She would have the apex of the sidewalk to herself for one last, long gaze at the fog.

A swirl in the mist revealed a slim man at the railing when she was thirty feet away. "Now, girl, it's not like you own the night," she muttered to herself as a wave of disappointment came and went. He was welcome to stare into the fog as much as she. He wasn't exactly standing still, though. As the distance between them closed she saw he was wrestling with some ropes and what looked like a big, metal light fixture.

"Lovely evening," she said from a dozen feet away so as not to startle him. The man jumped like he'd been bit, then stepped in front of his metal thing before giving her a nod and a smile. He squeezed over to the rail to let her pass.

It was the smile that stopped her. Thin and cold as a needle in the night, it was the smile that said, 'I know you're going to die soon.' She was familiar with that smile. She turned to face him.

"The fog always makes for a lovely walk, don't you say? What's this then?" She swung a foot and tapped the cone-shaped metal thing with her toe. The contact made a dull thunk, not a clang, so it wasn't empty. The man jumped higher this time and the grin fell off his face.

"Careful, lady. Have a nice walk." Fear-sweat popped out on his forehead and he reached down to pick the thing up. Whatever it was, it had some weight to it.

The LNG boat exercised her foghorn again, the deep kettle-drum roar that had pulled Wendy out of her house and accompanied her all through this wonderful night. Now it was close enough to shake the bridge itself, a truly impressive and primal instrument. No doubt the captain would be blasting it during the big parade into the inner harbour. Wendy wanted to be here for that, right on this very spot where the big ship would pass only a few feet beneath her.

Which was all the hint she needed, really, to see what this fellow was up to. He clutched that big metal thing like it was precious and delicate, and sweating like he couldn't wait to be rid of it. Malicious death rolled off him like a bad smell. A length of fishing line trailed out of the cone and ended in a loop, just the thing to catch a passing ship's protrusions. At the moment when all the world was watching, this little man would turn the Northern Sea Otter into a bomb.

He gave her that needle-thin smile again, trying to get her

to leave. "Oh, for Mercy's sakes," she said. As the poor man shifted the cone thing to reach for his gun she flipped him and his device over the rail. The rope and the fishing line whipped after him.

Three steps into the continuation of her walk an explosion thunderclapped her eardrums as the fog strobed with a sizzling yellow flash more brilliant than the sun. Something clanged the underside of the bridge deck like a gong, the concussion almost lifting her off her feet. That will bring some attention, Wendy thought. She vaulted the sidewalk railing, slipped through the fog to the other side of the bridge and speedwalked the downslope towards home.

Behind her the bridge erupted into shouts and running feet and a blaze of lights.

Chapter 15

Saturday morning dawned clear and cool, the world bedecked in jewels of dew from the receding fog. Jackson was wide awake to see it. He'd come home after making the call to Dr. Parma and fallen asleep like falling into a grave. Now he was up, staring out the window at the first sparkles on the water, wondering what the day would bring.

His appointment with Parma was for 9 a.m. He tried not to think about how easy it had been to set up a Saturday morning visit. About how Parma had answered on the first ring, completely unruffled. Like he'd been expecting the call.

The 5 a.m. sunlight was tinged with dusty rose. Hardly any sounds drifted in through the window. The city was as quiet as it ever got. This was the time he'd ventured outdoors, those first tentative days when he'd left the hospital, when there was no traffic or wind or people and he could safely practice locking away his new condition. That had been a raw time, working his way back into the world. Now he felt raw again, like the whole situation had rubbed off his protection and his nerves lay exposed to the air. It stung.

He was so tired of this. Maybe a visit with Parma was a good idea.

By 8:30 the day was brilliant and the cycle out to UBC peaceful and unhurried. The fresh air helped to quell his nerves. Dr. Parma wasn't a bad man, he knew that, but his limbic system remembered when the small Indian doctor led him through the locking doors and signed the admission papers. He couldn't get past the wall of suspicion he felt every time he went to Dr. Parma's office to get his prescription renewed. He'd give the doctor the least information needed to get the job done and get out of there. He clicked into a lower gear and pushed on the pedals to get up the Point Grey hill, past Dr. Dick's neighbourhood to the UBC campus that occupied the seaward edge of Point Grey, to the Medical Sciences Building.

Parma was standing by the glass doors as he crossed the parking lot. "Jackson!" he called, "great to see you!" The little man showed every sign of actually meaning it. "Be with you in a minute."

A smallish, 50-something woman in a green calico dress and sandals clutched a black purse in one hand and Dr. Parma's forearm with the other, hard enough to crease both. Her shoulder-length brown hair showed the dull frizz of long-term stress. Even from across the lot Jackson could see her entire body shimmer with tension. She desperately needed a massage. "But Dr. Parma," she was saying, "it's right over there." She nodded her head in the direction of Wreck Beach at the tip of the point.

Parma gently unwrapped her from his arm. "Yes it is, Syren, that is where the ocean is supposed to be. Now, do what we talked about and go look at it each day. Take a Seabus ride each week and keep up with your medicine. One step at a time, that's how we do it. We'll talk again soon." She sucked up what confidence she could from his steady gaze and passed Jackson on the balls of her feet.

So he wasn't the doctor's first patient this morning.

Parma's office was on the third floor and they rode up together. "I followed your advice, Jackson, and I've taken up ocean swimming," Dr. Parma announced, pleased with himself, in a light baritone accented with plenty of Harvard ivy and a touch of southwest Mumbai. "I go over to West Vancouver where the water is a bit cleaner and jump right in. You were right, floating with the waves is quite soothing. Although I'd never tell my last patient that." The doctor chuckled at the thought. Jackson gave a weak smile and tried to remain calm.

Parma's place was a marvel of contrasts. The wide oak desk said business. The white lab coat hanging by the wall of medical texts said doctor's office. The other wall of family photos and the glassed-in bronze Ganesh spoke of dedicated family man. The rich, quiet carpeting and muted halogen lighting brought it all together and gave the room a warm, inviting softness. Dr. Parma himself suited the room. Dark like the wood, slightly plump like an archetypical happy dad, with clear, penetrating eyes and a ready flash of a smile, everything about him said relax and be okay.

As always, Jackson clenched his suspicion tight to his chest. It was too easy to let his guard down here.

"You've been having a rough time of it, Jackson, or so I'm told," Parma said with concern. "Have a seat and tell me about it."

The overstuffed armchair was built to bear-hug you. Jackson chose the straight-backed wooden school chair next to the desk and sat. "Nothing much to tell, really," he began, and then his eyes fell on the doctor's desk.

Three papers sat on it, carelessly jumbled together. The heading on one said Balsam Elder Care. Another said VPD Theft Report. The third bore the crest of the College of Massage Therapists.

Parma knew it all. "Well, maybe there is," he revised. When he opened his mouth again it all fell out. It took about fifteen minutes. Even now, despite everything, it felt like he was correcting all the half-truths in the paperwork and telling Parma what had really happened. His brainstem yelled at him the whole time but he refused to leave anything out.

The room was quiet for a minute after he finished with the beach party, the sand and the phone call. Dr. Parma had perched his butt on the corner of the desk and stayed there, listening intently. Now he nodded. "That is definitely a rough time of it," he said. "So, what do you think?"

That was it? "What do I think? You're the doctor. I think I'm here because everyone says I'm not thinking straight anymore."

Parma slid down into the overstuffed chair and crossed his legs, on the same side of the desk as Jackson. "We've known each other for, what, almost four years now? Yes? You've learned a great deal about how your condition presents itself. You're not deluded right now. You are seeing me today on your own – regardless of your friend's coercion, you are here on your own – and so you are uniquely positioned to have an opinion on the matter. So, yes, I ask it. What do you think we should do about all this?"

This was a different session than he'd expected, and it took Jackson back. Then the answer came to him. "I want it all gone," he said, with a force that burst out of somewhere deep. "I want to be done with all this! I want the impossible. That's what I think. For what it's worth."

Dr. Parma rose, walked around the office, grabbed a book off a shelf and settled in behind his desk. He opened the book and read a few words. Then he flipped open a hidden laptop and started typing and mousing. "I'll be a minute," he muttered, and went back to it. He reached whatever screen he wanted, leaned back in his chair and considered. Then he clapped his hands together, giving Jackson a brief namaste.

"I think we may be able to do some good here."

A clinical trial had just finished up, he said, with startlingly positive results. There was a new medication, not on the market yet, but with some stores still available from the study. He said a few things about Jackson fitting the parameters. He spread his arms wide in a theatrical embrace. "For once, I may be able to grant someone's wishes. That would be nice, yes?" He closed his laptop and looked a question at Jackson. "Is this what you really want?"

Jackson knew the truth of the old saying that nothing comes without a price. "New drug, eh? New enough that you don't know the side effects yet?"

Dr. Parma laughed and slapped the desk. "Nothing gets past you, does it? Side effects! Of course you would ask." Then he got serious. "In fact, this particular compound seems to have remarkably few. Some possible disorientation at first, maybe the occasional upset tummy. That seems to be about it."

He started gesturing with his hands, going into lecture mode. "This drug, unlike most, is water-based. Very simple compound, easily absorbed, easily eliminated. You know how your current medication works, it builds up in your system to a certain level, then the pills you take maintain that level, yes? Well, this one works like an on-off switch. Quite amazing. Minutes after you take it the full force of the medication is working in your system. When it wears off, it totally wears off. Gone, history, square one. It is fascinating, from a pharmacological point of view."

That didn't sound so bad. "So, what does it do?"

Parma stabbed the air between them with a finger. "Right to the main point, you are so direct." He was delighted. "What does this little thing do? I could go on about normalizing neurotransmitter function in the caudate nucleus and axonal pathways around the basal ganglia, but the only important word in all of that is normalize. I believe this little baby will remove your condition. We've had consistent results in over 50 test subjects. Although your particular presentation is somewhat unique, I think it will work. It will, as you asked, make you normal. Just like that."

"Let's do it."

Dr. Parma restarted his computer. "Another person added to the study. I will have some papers for you to sign, one minute please."

It turned out to be five minutes of almost steady printer whirring and a stack of legalese an inch high. When the last paper was turned over Jackson set the pen down and said, "Now what?"

Dr. Parma gave him a largeish bottle of standard-looking pink pills. "Now you switch meds. One of these every eight hours. Here is the thing, Jackson, that you have to remember. Here is the big thing, yes." He got serious again and leaned close. "I told you that these are like an on-off switch, right? There's no grace period here. Taking one every eight hours gives you a comfortable overlap and a seamless experience, but if you forget, or if you end up far away from your pills for even a bit too long – bam! Your condition will be on you, maximum intensity, in a very short time. Here." He handed Jackson a plastic meds travel case large enough for six pills. "Load this up and keep it with you at all times. All times, yes. I think you remember what happens when your OCD gets the better of you. I think you don't want us to go there again, am I right?"

Jackson bobbed his head once. He didn't even want to speak about it.

Dr. Parma was all smiles again. "Okay! Off you go. See me in three weeks. If you need anything before then, here are my numbers." He handed Jackson a card with business, home and cell numbers on it.

He popped the top off the bottle, placed six of the pills into the little carrier, then took one and flicked it down the hatch. Normal. It sounded really, really good.

Jackson spun down 10th Avenue from UBC, reveling in the rush of air against his face. Saturday morning traffic had started to pick up. 10th was West Point Grey's commercial strip, two lanes each way with sidewalk parking to serve the shops. Vehicles in both of his lanes were slowing for the Sasamat Street red light, but there was plenty of room between the moving cars and the line of parked vehicles tucked against the sidewalk. Keeping his senses tuned for door prizes he zipped into the slot, barely touching his brakes.

The girl and her mother popped out between two parked pickup trucks without so much as a flicker of warning, their appearance flashing an iridescent red bar across his vision. They were looking away from him, down the block at the red light, wondering if it was safe to try a quick jaywalk, completely blocking his path. Much worse than a door prize. A yellow blaze streaked through the left edge of his vision and he grabbed for his rear brake and skidded into the only possible save, pulling a wicked left power turn between an Audi and an old Mercedes. His shoulder actually brushed the Audi's hood as he leaned into his tires' sidewalls. The oncoming lanes were still clear. He shot across the street as the Audi gave him a horn blast. The girl next to her mom said a big-eyed "Whoa!" and he made it to the opposite sidewalk.

A day in the life of a Vancouver cyclist. Still, it might be time to get off the main drag. He turned down Sasamat to the 8th Avenue bicycle route.

8th Avenue was lined with parked cars but quiet, a much easier trip. He let his hands and feet do their thing. Would Charles be surprised at the outcome of his appointment? Surely he hadn't known about the clinical study or he would have mentioned it to Jackson long before this. Would he be surprised to see Jackson still breathing free air? That darkened his thoughts for a few blocks. If Charles so much as raised his eyebrows the next time they met, their friendship might take a hit. So might Charles, for that matter.

The growing brilliance of the day soon burned the darkness out of him. Macdonald Street was coming up, two south lanes and one north lane busy with Vancouverites rushing through their Saturday chores, separated by a concrete island with small gaps for bikes to cross. 8th Avenue had stop signs on either side of the approach to Macdonald, but they were for pussies without any sense of timing. There was always a gap. He picked up his peripheral vision as the intersection came close.

A fair number of cars accelerated along the two lanes closest to him to catch the next light. The opposite lane was mostly empty. A young couple were approaching on the sidewalk. He looked. He blinked and looked again. He didn't see the gap.

Five feet from the white stop line he yarded both brakes to the handlebars, popping into a front wheelstand to avoid hitting the couple. The girl flinched, the guy flipped him a finger and said, "Asshole!" and he crashed over sideways onto the pavement. Feeling foolish and confused, he dragged his bike over to the patch of grass by the stop sign and wondered what the hell had just happened.

Dr. Parma had said to expect disorientation. Could this be the pills? With a sudden surmise, Jackson drew an arm through the air in front of his face.

No shimmer followed the movement. It was an arm moving through the air. He turned, and the cars on Macdonald were only cars. No flashes told him where they'd been or where they were going. Taking it a step further, he cracked open the inner door and let the pattern of the traffic wash through him.

There was no pattern. Nothing pulled at him. The inner door had opened onto an empty room.

He jumped into the air and let out a whoop. From fifty paces down the sidewalk the guy yelled back, "Asshole," but Jackson couldn't care less. He was better! A four year nightmare was finally over. Dr. Parma was going to get flowers for this.

He walked his bike the rest of the way home. Once inside he stowed his old pills in a back corner of the medicine cabinet and put the new ones, the ones that worked, front and center.

Chapter 16

Nurses were just like other people. They got sick, they had family emergencies, they died. Wendy was filling in on Vancouver General's Neurology ward for an older nurse – only a bit older than Wendy herself – who had gone to sleep and not woken up. The hospital was already too short-staffed to comfortably fill the gap, so they'd called around and Emma Jacobs had arranged for Wendy to fill in.

It took the usual hour to satisfy her coworkers that she knew her job. Then she was mated with Nurse Gifford for the rest of the shift.

"That's done, then. Time for reports," said Nurse Gifford ‐ Rose ‐ once they'd made the rounds. They sat down at a monitor and keyboard behind the nursing station.

Rose had her own passcode to get into the computer and she was lousy at hiding it. Wendy memorized it on the fly as a matter of habit. Rose toured her through the new patient filing system. Each patient's history and treatment was marvellously recorded and interlinked. The charting took no time at all.

"Excuse me," said a deep voice behind them. A man in a shirt and tie, stethoscope around his neck and acting like he didn't really see them, was looking at the computer. Rose stepped back and motioned for Wendy to do the same. She obeyed, keeping her mouth shut. Imperious doctors were never her favourite people, but this wasn't her hospital. Not yet.

They stood back while the doctor worked the keys. He flipped over to another part of the system labelled Alerts and Warnings and exercised the same lack of caution with his passcode. Then he pulled up a screen, typed in a patient's name, and a more comprehensive version of their medical history and charting came up. The doctor typed in Alert - Suicide Risk into an empty line near the top and hit enter. Wendy watched, fascinated. A box flashed up on the screen. It said, Alert: Hospital, Health Region, Fire, Ambulance, Police, All? and had check boxes by each. The doctor clicked Hospital, Health Region, and Ambulance, and closed the box. Alert Registered, said the screen.

Then the doctor signed out. "Thank you," he said, and left the station without looking at them.

"Dr. Crummins," said Rose. "He's old school. We stay out of his way." Wendy stepped back and they moved on to restocking meds carts.

An idea had come to Wendy, bright as a new sun. She watched and waited for her time to put it to use. Near the end of the shift she found five minutes alone at the nursing station. More than enough.

The doctor's passcode got her to the restricted screen. The massage therapist was the only Jackson Teague in the system. She opened his chart. It confirmed what she already pretty much knew – OCD, pattern-fascination type, admitted three years ago, stable since.

Wendy found the blank Alerts space near the top of the form. She typed in, Alert –Psychotic Break, Danger To Self And Others. Apprehend And Admit. She hit Enter and the box came up.

Alert: Hospital, Health Region, Fire, Ambulance, Police, All? No question. She hit All and every check box lit up with a mark. Wendy closed down the computer with a warm sense of a job well done. This little stroke might get him out of her way for a very long time. In any case, it would get the poor boy the help he so desperately needed.

The rest of Saturday was a voyage of rediscovery. Jackson spent most of it wandering the city. He walked through Yaletown and up Robson Street, crossed with the lights and watched the cars and bicycles dodge and weave. He strolled through the Pacific Centre mall from one end to the other, immersing himself in the weekend shopping crush. Nothing caught at his mind. No pattern anywhere jumped out and threatened to pull him under. Even a trip down to watch the Skytrains blasting into the station with their electric yowl and rush of tunnel air elicited nothing.

By the time he got to the evening Aikido class his cheeks hurt from the constant grin.

"Someone's feeling chipper tonight," murmured Johnny during the warm-up. "Win the lottery or what?"

"One of those days, you know," Jackson whispered back. "Everything's going right." He'd never told anyone in class about his little problem and wasn't about to start now.

"Sounds great. Let's pair up, maybe some of it will rub off."

Toshiko-sensei ran the class through the basics - Ikkyo, Nikyo, Sankyo and their variations. He and Johnny squared off and practiced taking each other to the mat. At first he found himself guarding against the seductive rhythm of the techniques. Old news, he told himself, relax. The rhythm intensified with the speed of the practice - left side, right side, forward, back, attack, defend. He relaxed more, feeling the grin return, and gave himself over to the practice like he hadn't done in years. The room grew warm with the collective effort of the class.

Johnny got quiet, looking curiously at him as they sparred. A mischievous smile flickered across his face and he did something as Jackson went to grab him for the next move. Instead of getting a handful of Johnny's dogi Jackson mashed his fingers into the big man's chest. "Sorry," Johnny rumbled. Two moves later he stepped wide when Jackson should have been guiding him to the floor and Jackson ended up off balance and on his back. On the very next move, a hand feint to the face in advance of a Sankyo wrist hold, Johnny moved a little too close and they cracked forearms. Jackson called a pause to rub away the sting.

"You're practicing like you read it in a book," Johnny mused. "Your moves are all good but there's a piece missing. Your timing is off. Like you're sparring with yourself and I'm along for the ride." He wasn't upset · the dojo showed up the best and worst in everybody, and patience with your partner was considered a virtue · but he was interested. "You sure you're having a good day?"

"Best day in years," Jackson came back, bowing. "Onegai-shimasu. Dare you to try that again."

Johnny did, a few times, and Jackson never caught on. It didn't matter and Jackson paid it no mind. He walked out of the community centre into the heart of a city downshifting into its night groove and felt no dangerous pull whatever. Today was a watershed day in his life. No awkward Aikido was going to put a damper on his relief.

'Curl your fingers back, dear. Remember what Mumma taught you.' Wendy guided the flat of the chef's knife with her knuckles as she sliced the potato into neat cubes, then slid the cubes onto the blade and dropped them into the pot on the stove, trying to pull calmness from the simple act. The haddock chowder was beginning to defeat the Asian cooking smells that permeated the bones of the house. The thick, tangy aroma mixed with the smell of biscuits just coming due in the little oven and she breathed it all in, imagining for a moment that the scene outside her window reflected Elizabeth Knowles' painting.

Comfort food was the medicine she needed. Mrs. Knowles was gone to her peace with no chance of it coming back to Wendy, but everything else was as wrong as it could be. Her sweet little plan to point the massage therapist at the old doctor and get him suspended hadn't worked. Instead he had come to her door. Her door! No one had ever come that close before. The Third Rule had never permitted it. If it weren't for her overprotective landlady calling the honest-to-goodness riot police down on the boy's head, he'd have come right into her very apartment. The whole event had left her shaking.

She dipped a spoon into the creamy chowder, blew on it, then sampled. A dash of salt and a pinch of dill, she decided, and made the necessary adjustments. Her suitcases sat on the bed in the next room waiting to be packed. When They Suspect, Move West. The boxes and wrappings for her angels waited, too. It would be the work of about two hours to tuck them all away. Then she'd be off.

The biscuits smelled ready. She took a mitt off its hook on the wall, opened the oven door and pulled out the pan. Without any rush she laid it on a cooling rack and stood in front of the stove, letting the warmth and the rich smell wash over her.

The alarm bells in her head screamed at her to hurry up

and be gone, so loudly she could barely think, yet here she was, setting a fine table and smiling at nothing. It made no sense at all.

Of course it does, you silly horse, said another part of her, shocking the alarms into silence. You're tired of all this gallivanting about. You're by the ocean again, since goodness knows how long. And you've got the most wonderful job you've had in years. Stop fooling around with suitcases and boxes. Start getting on with what needs to be done.

'What you do matters more than what you think.' Her Mumma used to say that, too. What was the Third Rule, after all, but something she'd made up in her head? The plain fact of it was she didn't feel like running away. The chunks of haddock were thick and flaky. The biscuits warmed her to the core and settled the world slowly back into order. As the fear in her head subsided it was replaced by a deep warmth, one that surprised her by its strength and grew to fill her from fingers to toes.

No more running away. The sound of those words was like parole from jail. Wendy gave a start when she felt a hot tear scroll down her cheek.

The chowder was gone. She reached for a small pot warming on the stove and poured hot rum sauce over a bowl of ginger cake, the smell completing the little kitchen's transformation. 'No prize comes without its price.' If Wendy wanted to stay, she had some things to do.

The boy had an impetuous streak, that was plain. But he'd also had the very life scared out of him by the police. He wouldn't try visiting here again. Still, he knew things he shouldn't and he was impulsive, reckless. He needed to be scared some more.

How to manage it? The answer raced in almost faster than the question, like her subconscious had been holding the information in reserve. It was a name, printed in an over-careful hand on the refrigerator in Jackson Teague's kitchen. He was going to see Lynn on Monday morning.

Well, she thought, scraping the bowl clean of rum sauce with a finger. She would have to join him.

Remembering Dr. Parma's admonishments about how quickly the new meds wore off, Jackson made sure to put the pill bottle on his bedside table where he'd find it first thing Sunday morning. He thumbed the cap off and downed a pill, then went over to the window to look at the water. Burrard Inlet was still there. The waves still sparkled in the fresh sunlight. Nothing more than that. It was a completely normal June morning in Vancouver.

Traveling massage therapists tended to be in demand on weekends. Today's work schedule had three names on it. Ten o'clock saw him downtown at a suite in the Hotel Georgia, de-stressing a tightly-wound young diva in town to play the lead in Carmen and so stressed about her debut that the muscle tension had pinched her voice. Noon took him to a condo in Southlands to help an executive banker whose sacroiliac joint was killing his squash game. The one-thirty appointment was a new mother in a basement apartment who propped a bassinet under the head of the massage table so she could play with the baby while he worked on her bad case of nursing shoulder. None of them booked a next appointment, which was a little unusual, but in general it was a typical day.

By three-fifteen he was home, swim trunks on and towel in hand, headed for the beach.

What would it be like? The ocean was still a little crisp for mid-June but he pushed himself into deeper water. Once he was over his head he grabbed a deep breath and dove for the bottom.

The sand was riffling into tiny peaks and valleys with the push of the tide. Each wave overhead brushed a few more grains off the peaks on its way into shore, and piled them back up on the outward trip. He watched the dance for a moment, then closed his eyes and floated in the middle of the water column.

His skin registered the tiniest increase and diminishment of pressure as the waves passed. That was all. Without his eyes on the sand he couldn't tell if they were shorebound or headed out. As for the deeper thrust of the current, he had no inkling if the tide was pushing in against the mountains or heading back towards Japan. The ocean could be making a right turn for Alaska for all he could tell.

He broke the surface and grabbed a breath. So that was what a normal swim used to feel like. He pulled for the beach and his towel. Somehow he didn't remember the ocean being quite so underwhelming.

The sand and the grass had filled with bodies soaking up the afternoon heat. He dried and dressed, then went for a walk around the park, enjoying the view. A large knot of people over by the big chestnuts was gathered around some entertainment. He strolled over to check it out.

Leaf was slacklining. He had a neon-purple three inch ribbon ratcheted tight between a couple of trees and was performing for the crowd. He was down to his surfer shorts again, and the stark lines of his new haircut only seemed to accent his abs all the more. Leaf caught sight of Jackson from his vantage point two feet above the spectators. He grinned and waved Jackson over, then went into a tree pose, maintaining his balance on one foot and touching the other to his knee without even seeming to notice. The crowd applauded, of course.

"Hey!" he called when Jackson got closer. "C'mon over, man, show them how easy it is!"

This would be good medicine for his dampened mood. The bystanders made a path. Leaf had taught him to slackline last summer, and turned out walking the ribbon was easy once you got it. This was going to be fun.

Leaf's webbing was ratcheted tight between two thick trees twenty feet apart, far enough off the ground to be impressive but not quite enough to ballsack you if you slipped. It still swayed, though, which was the whole point. Slacklining was a dance, moving to the music of your own balance with gravity as the conductor.

Leaf jumped down. "Hey, man, it's been a couple days," he murmured. "Doing okay?"

"Yeah, pretty good."

Leaf nodded and waved him to the line. He picked up the volume, ever the showman. "Give it a go," he said, and held out a hand.

The hand was to steady Jackson as he got on and did the walk. It was a beginner's aid, and he waved it off. "I remember how." First one foot, curl your toes and find the balance, feel the natural sway of the line, then up with the other.

The line dipped and Jackson's feet landed back on the ground. "Rusty," he muttered, and got up again. Feel the sway, anticipate it, let your leg do the work, then up with the other one. He was up, both feet on the line.

Then he was down. The slackline thwapped between his legs, stinging his thighs. "Damn," he laughed, "really rusty."

Leaf held out his hand again and this time Jackson took it. Up, both feet on the line. It was tough to get his balance. Maybe you did have to learn it over again. He took a step and found himself gripping hard on Leaf's hand. The cords in Leaf's shoulder stood out, but he held Jackson firm.

Two steps, then three. The line was a strange thing, moving unpredictably. He couldn't catch up with it. One step closer to the middle and the largest amplitude of the rope's sway, and he was off again. This time he stumbled, and Leaf caught him. "Man, looks like I forgot it all," he panted when they'd untangled.

"No, you didn't forget it," Leaf said, but nothing more. They went back to the beginning and started again.

By the time Jackson tried the line six more times, most of the crowd had dispersed. Leaf made no move to jump back up and resume entertaining. He held Jackson's hand over and over, encouraging and praising each successful step. But the fall always came. Jackson never found the balance. He never so much as made it halfway.

After the seventh attempt he'd had enough. The initial rush was gone. He was back in his head, and it was a black place. "I'm done," he announced, and headed for the beach, away from the trees and the line. Leaf kept pace with him, leaving his kit behind.

A day that had started so well was turning into a complete waste. He was going to keep on walking until his mood changed or his feet fell off. If Leaf wanted to tag along, well, he wasn't going to be very good company.

Fifty yards down Kits Beach he was surprised to find himself changing course. Leaf's shoulder was pushing on his with the perfect amount of unobtrusive force to trigger his move-over reflex. They were heading for the water, now only ten feet away. He was being herded. It irritated him, and he pushed back.

It was like pushing a loaded spring. Leaf pulled a hard left, his shoulder still matched with Jackson's, and they both hit the water at almost a run. "Hey!" Jackson tried, but Leaf kept him off-balance and pushed him further and further into Burrard Inlet until they were practically tits deep. Then, with no warning, Leaf brought up both hands and slammed Jackson in the chest.

Salt water got everywhere faster than Jackson could spit it out. His back found sand. He thrashed around until he got his feet under him again and rocketed up, spluttering and ready to fight.

Leaf was right there. He looked Jackson over with an appraising eye, said, "No," and rammed his hands into Jackson's chest again. A foot was behind Jackson's knees and he went back to the bottom.

It was cold, and all his clothes were wet, and his frigging towel was still under his arm, and his wallet was in his pocket, and he was royally pissed. Jackson shot to the surface again, not spluttering this time, but ready for a deep breath and a roar. "No," Leaf said again, and there was nothing Jackson could do. He went down for the third time.

It was cold, and wet, and buoyant. Jackson touched bottom. It was quiet, the buzz of the city replaced by bubbles and the swish of current on sand. Leaf's legs stood in front of him. Jackson got his feet on the sand, grabbed Leaf's ankles and gave an almighty shove.

He found air when his head broke the surface and enjoyed the sight of Leaf flying over backwards and smacking the water. It was Leaf's turn to come up spluttering, and he stood three feet away and gave Jackson another searching look. "Better," he laughed. He was right.

They waded back to shore. Leaf gestured eastward. "Want to speedwalk some more?" he offered.

"Nah," said Jackson, and that was all. They dripped back to the slackline.

Jackson sat on the grass while Leaf took the line down. There was still a dark, whirling mess in the center of his head, but the dip had disconnected him from it somehow. "Thanks," he said at last, "glad you didn't break any ribs."

Leaf sat down beside him, concern on his face. "That was first aid, man. You need more than that. People don't forget how to slackline. I'm serious, you're missing something. You've lost your balance. What happened?"

"What happened is, I'm cured. I'm all better." He ran through the session with Dr. Parma. "So all it takes is this pill, three a day, and I'm good. Normal. Let me tell you, Leaf, it's been a long time since I could say that."

They were quiet for awhile as Leaf rolled his line. "No," Leaf said again. He lifted the bundle of webbing. "Normal? Let me tell you, man, normal people can do this. I know, I've taught them." He was silent for a beat, then added, "Whatever you're missing, Jackson, I think you need it back."

"Whatever." The day had drained him. Jackson couldn't think about all this now. He pointed down the street towards the food shops. "Pizza?"

Leaf gazed at him sideways for a minute, then grinned and shook his head. "No, I got places to go. Thanks, though." They stood up.

"Where do you go at night, anyway?" Jackson asked. "You could have a tent in the woods or a Yaletown condo for all any of us know."

Leaf smiled again, and there was a distance to it. "Yeah, something like that," he said. He turned and gave Jackson a hug. "Tomorrow morning, remember. Lynn."

"Oh, yeah!" He had forgotten. It had been more than a week since he'd checked his fridge calendar. Perfect timing, Lynn always helped his moods. "10 a.m. at the parking lot. See you there!"

He had just enough energy left for pizza and the walk home. Sleep hit him like an anvil and he was done with the day.

Chapter 17

Monday morning was another gift from the weather gods. Jackson whistled Irish pub songs at the traffic as he drove over the Second Narrows Bridge to Lynn Creek. It was going to be a hot day - perfect for a dip into some very cold water.

Leaf was perched on a rock in the small parking lot on the east side of the creek, where the stream left the steep walls of Lynn Canyon and meandered through the coastal flats before dumping into the inlet. They shouldered their packs and headed up the trail to where it entered the woods of the canyon. A quiet pool a few paces inside the woods was the perfect spot for them to squeeze into their wetsuits and go creekwalking.

Jackson had laughed when Leaf first suggested it years before, but creekwalking turned out to be a wonderful adventure. The streams of the North Shore mountains were wild, boisterous affairs, tumbling down from the peaks through narrow, ragged ravines that were mostly inaccessible. Unless you walked, waded, and swam straight up them.

The air above the pool was rich with the smells of forest and water. Ten steps upstream the rock walls narrowed into the start of the canyon and the water rushed over the first of many rapids. The Spring melt was done; the rapids could be walked for the first time this season. "Okay, let's do it," said Jackson. Full wetsuit, hood, face mask, gloves, and diver's hiking boots. A power bar tucked up under the body zipper. They wouldn't need to carry any water, of course. In minutes, they'd stashed their packs in the bushes.

It was a hell of a workout, but so much more than that. To Leaf and Jackson it was church. Lynn Creek was a long, frigid baptism where city life fell away and you were reborn. Jackson gasped at the first rush of icewater redemption into the neoprene of his wetsuit, then they started the climb.

Wendy breathed the damp, mossy air deep into her breast and started up the thin trail on the west side of the canyon. Lynn Creek chuckled to itself down below and the two boys, dressed head to toe in rubber, had slid into the water. It was working out.

She felt strange, proceeding like this without a clear plan. Wendy knew about Lynn Creek. The big guess had been where the two would go – the lower canyon? The upper canyon beyond the big waterfall? The high reaches of Lynn Headwaters, where it carved a rough course down from the mountains? She'd chosen the first one, arrived early and felt a rush of warm fate when they came straight to her. Now that they were all here the only thought in her mind was to follow, keep them in sight and see what opportunities turned up.

The only sure thing was the outcome. Wendy huffed up a muddy incline and into the woods. Jackson Teague would tremble at the thought of her by the end of the day.

He tested the mask seal and found it good. Lynn Creek was elementally cold and clear as a command from on high. Sunlight arced through to the bottom of the pool. Jackson kicked off and followed it down.

Sizeable rocks littered the creek bed, forming small caves and hiding places where they tumbled against each other. Brought down from the cliff sides by wind and weather and moved around by the current, they created a different landscape each year. Jackson stuck his nose into as many of them as his first breath would allow, then rose, buoyed by the suit.

Leaf surfaced with a blow ten feet away, signalling all was well. They turned as one and began swimming upstream. They found more pools. They splashed through rapids and waterfalls, explored sunken trees and discovered quiet amidst the rush. Their hike had a hard limit at the big waterfall halfway up the canyon, the one with the suspension bridge, and would also be limited by their cold tolerance. Until then, there was the water. He followed Leaf up the first knee-deep rapids and dove into the next pool, exploring the deep quiet amidst the current's rustle. Rapids, pool, rapids. They walked and swam, stopping to check out nooks and crannies, swimming alongside small fish fry gamely trying to repopulate the city stream. People somewhere up on the trails grabbed a moment of peace and trees and water before heading back to their lives, but Jackson made a point of never looking up to see if anybody was watching. This was a private time for him and Leaf, and he didn't want to share it.

Salal bushes grabbed for her ankles and the branches of small trees tried to dissuade her. This side of the creek was seldom traveled, which had its pluses and minuses for sure. At least nobody would see what she did today.

Amidst the hard job of putting one foot in front of the other and keeping up with the boys she almost missed the dark edge of that thought. What was she going to do, exactly? Teague needed to be scared off and threats hadn't done the trick. Whatever opportunity eventually presented itself, she was fairly certain it would give the poor boy some physical discomfort. She was glad, she realized, that no one was here to bear witness to her breaking the Second Rule.

Don't Harm The Healthy. Jackson Teague stood between her and everybody else she was meant to help. Was that enough?

A renewed flood of certainty powered her up and over a tangle of roots. Don't be bothering yourself with silly questions, she told herself, focus on the task at hand. That decision's been and long gone.

She could see them down below, scampering and splashing in the water like two frolicking birds. Get tired already, she thought down to them. I can't hit a moving target.

They didn't make it to the big waterfall today. At one deep, secluded pool, by mutual unspoken consent, they pulled themselves onto a rock ledge and had lunch. The chill of the creek was reaching them and they would both be shivering by the time they got back to their packs. This would be good for now.

The sun was perfect, straight overhead, threading its way

through overhanging cedar branches to the water. The warmth on their faces was lovely. The pool was wide enough here that the current was abated and languorous. After their meal he and Leaf returned to the water, turned onto their backs and grasped a piece of the rock ledge to anchor themselves. It was time for The Float.

Nothing washes away time and trouble like the gentle lift and fall of tiny waves, the sound of water shooshing past hooded ears, the pleasant tang of creek water seeping into your suit. Jackson needed this. He laid back fully into the stream and let himself go, allowing only the one anchor of his hand on the rock. He fell into the meditative state of a deep reset and let the world go on without him.

The tiniest of extra splashes told him that Leaf was moving about. He peeked. Leaf was out further in the pool, not quite as tucked into the ledge as Jackson, and his eyes were open, staring up to the cliff top. He lifted one hand out of the water in an almost-wave, but tentative. Jackson got the impression that Leaf was deciding something. Then Leaf's wave turned into a pointing finger. "You're her," he said.

Then he was moving. Like a water snake, going from horizontal to vertical and zero to lightning-fast in a heartbeat, straight at Jackson. His hands slammed into Jackson's chest again. Hard, insanely hard. Jackson was lifted bodily out of the water and he felt a rib yelp as he slammed into a corner of rough stone behind the ledge. His breath left him in a whoosh.

Not fair! There was a humongous splash in the pool, waves all over the place, spray obscuring his vision. Leaf was moving. He was going to come again. That was rude, catching him with his guard down. Jackson wasn't even doing anything stupid. He certainly didn't deserve the look of set, hard determination he'd seen on Leaf's face, an expression so dark it lingered in Jackson's mind as he tried to regain his breath. Jackson

readied himself to dodge, fight back. He'd slam Leaf back, if
that was what it took, then find out what the hell was going on.

Nothing hit him. The pool grew quiet. Leaf was nowhere to
be seen. Jackson had his breath back, and he used it. "What
the fuck?!" he yelled. "Leaf! Explain that!" No answer came.
The creek resumed its soft murmur.

Five seconds went by, and they were long ones. Suddenly
filled with apprehension, Jackson grabbed his face mask and
upended, hurtling down to the bottom of the pool. He saw
rocks, and the grey trunk of an old fir, and the sun rippling
down. He saw a thin, translucent ribbon of red streaming by in
front of his nose.

He spun left, upstream, following the red. Leaf was against
the ledge and his suit was bearing him back up towards the
surface. Leaf wasn't helping. Leaf wasn't doing anything. The
red was coming from where his neoprene hood met his right
cheek. The hood had a funny shape to it. His eyes were closed.

Jackson was at the surface. Leaf was in his arms. He was
making for the rapids and the trail through the woods, and he
was screaming.

It was the North Shore Search and Rescue guys, or the fire
department, or some bunch of people in heavy gear with a big-
wheeled stretcher who came and threw blankets around them.
It was they who cut Leaf's wetsuit off as Jackson, cracked rib
and all, struggled out of his. Someone turned Jackson aside
before they got to Leaf's hood. Jackson heard a hushed silence
and then a bunch of terse orders while the someone started
asking him details, like who he was and who the injured

person was. "Leaf," was all he could say, "he's Leaf."

In the ambulance a young woman – he was seeing faces now, and hers was full of quiet concern – wrapped him in an electric blanket, and until that time he hadn't known he'd been shivering. "How's Leaf?" he asked once, and nobody answered him.

He was coming down by the time an emergency room nurse rounded on him with a clipboard and asked for ID. Leaf was on a gurney now, being swarmed by people behind a curtain. He gave his particulars, but couldn't say anything more about his friend. "He's Leaf, that's all we know him by." He gave them Charles' phone number as a contact person.

The nurse laid her clipboard down by the computer workstation in the middle of the ward and started hitting keys. "My God, that's Colin," came a woman's voice from behind the curtain.

The nurse at the keyboard paused. "You know him?" she called.

"Colin Palmerston. We all do." Another moment of hushed silence. Then, "Call his parents," ordered somebody. The nurse abandoned her computer and headed for a phone across the nurse's station.

Jackson watched her stride to the phone. Her left foot's slight pronation gave an added hitch to her hip as she went. Her course was straight as an arrow and solid as a painted line.

The wall clock confirmed his fear. He should have been back home by now. His pill was wearing off. What was it Dr. Parma had said? Like throwing a switch. On, or completely off. Which was why he was always to carry an emergency stash with him. The little plastic container currently in his pack under a bush five miles away.

The clock clicked off perfect seconds in a beautiful symmetry. Oh dear.

The desk nurse hurried back towards Leaf. Or Colin. "Nurse?" he flagged her down, and she slowed. "I need to speak to a doctor. Right away."

She gave him a half-second look up and down. "As soon as we're able," she said, and disappeared behind the curtain, which lit up with the movement.

He was going to have to ride this one out. A thrill of joy filled him at the prospect and he squashed it as firmly as he could, gritting his teeth. He knew the chaos that joy could bring. He knew it was a very short walk from this ward to the wing with the locked doors.

Thinking of Leaf would help take his mind off it. Colin Palmerston, wow. Palmerston Investments handled all the nine-figure bank accounts west of the Lions Gate Bridge. The Palmerston Building had held sway over the West Vancouver shoreline for three generations. Four floors above the emergency ward, housing the Lion's Gate Hospital's oncology department, was the Palmerston Wing. Leaf was West Vancouver royalty, for hell's sake.

Jackson had pestered Leaf for years about where he slept. The highest he'd aimed was a Yaletown condo. Pretty short of the mark there.

The door from the waiting room swung open and an orderly led a woman and her young son, maybe eight years old, over to another curtained bed. The boy was ashen-faced and holding onto his right elbow. His whole arm lit up to Jackson's eye. Humerus out from the body, elbow held at 45 degrees, the forearm's radius and ulna frozen in a position that kept the boy's hand upturned to the sky. Classic least-painful position for a swollen joint, and Jackson could practically - no, he could - see the growing knob on the outside of the elbow. The boy had pulled the head of the radius out from the joint. Probably grabbed a branch falling out of a tree and pop! Off to the emergency ward. It was clear as a bell.

The nurse at the station appraised the boy with a glance, grabbed the intake forms from the orderly and started tapping on the keyboard, entering data into the system. She hadn't gotten around to Jackson's paperwork, but it was only a matter of time. He knew what she would see when she pulled his history. She would read, and take a second look at his bed. Then the questions would come. The look into his eyes.

A doctor flipped open the boy's brand new chart and headed from the nursing station to the curtains, a matter of only a few steps. Everything was close to hand in this place, carts full of bandages and scanners and who knew what else within easy reach and the nursing station placed where it could rule the room. The ward was so tight it sang.

Knock it off, Jackson yelled at the inside of his head. He'd never had it come on him this fast.

The lights sparkled. Curtains parted across the way and four people wheeled Leaf out of the corner. Jackson caught a glimpse of white bandages around his head before they all disappeared through a swinging door, deeper into the hospital. He'd looked angel-pale.

The other door banged open and three people bustled through it, sending angry red swirls of motion into the room. First through was a tall, rugby-built man in the full prime of his fifties and a power to his stride that bent the entire room to him. He was flanked by an equally tall woman with fear radiating from her and eyes everywhere, searching. "Where's the doctor?" shouted the man. "Where's Colin?" called the woman.

Third through the door, beelining for Jackson's bed and a sight for sore eyes, was Charles. "Hi, I heard," he said. "Here." He shoved a box into Jackson's hand. Then he took a closer look at Jackson's eyes. "Just in time, I think."

It was a plastic pill six-pack. Jackson flipped it open. His new meds, not his old ones. He hadn't told Charles about the switch; these pills were a clinical trial, unavailable in the system. The man was a magician and a good friend. He popped one and gritted a swig of water past the pain in his chest. "Thanks," he managed.

"No sweat. Now tell me what happened." Charles sat down on the edge of the hospital bed and Jackson told him.

He sat there in silence for a minute after Jackson was done. "So you guys were floating, and Leaf looked up and waved?"

"Yeah. More like he pointed."

"Any idea who he was waving at?"

"No. I think Leaf knew, though. He said, 'You're her.'"

"Some hiker, I guess."

"Yeah. Then all hell broke loose."

"Okay." Charles got distant, wrapped up inside himself. Over in the corner the Palmerstons tried to get through the door Leaf had exited by, and were being blocked by two nurses who struggled to keep them calm. The word surgery was mentioned.

Charles was looking moist-eyed. "Here, let me look at that rib." They were both glad for something to do, and Charles spent five minutes in a detailed and careful examination. He had sensitive hands and didn't hurt more than he had to.

"You'll heal," he said at last. "You've got a nice laceration on your back from the rock and your rib is cracked in two places. We don't even tape them anymore, those bones are completely wrapped in muscle and fascia. All it needs is time. No lifting, no heavy breathing for two weeks."

"And my work?"

"Oh, yeah." Charles gave it some thought. "A few days off, and find a luggage carrier for your table. Forget about the shoulder strap."

The Palmerstons stood by Jackson's bedside. He hadn't seen them coming. The meds were back on again. "Harold Palmerston," said the man, hand outstretched. Jackson grasped it gingerly, hoping the reverberations wouldn't reach his rib, but Palmerston only squeezed, then let go. "Tell me."

Jackson went over it all again. He wasn't sure what he expected from these two, but he was tense when he finished. Neither Harold nor his wife – Louise – had even the faintest ounce of hippie tree-hugger in them. He carried himself like he went from mansion to Mercedes to office to gym to lounge, and she looked buffed and polished, like her office was a day spa. He expected recriminations. What he got was another hand on his knee and a face of infinite grief. The man was shattered.

Louise broke the silence. "He spoke of you often. And you're Charles, right? He spoke of all of you. The Beach Party, he called you. He has groups of people he meets, from all over. But yours is the one he feels he belongs to. I'm happy to meet you at last."

Jackson had to ask. "We never knew who he was. Well, he's Leaf, of course, but you know. Are you – um, sorry – are you okay with him wandering the beaches? With the life he lives?"

Palmerston sighed. "You know Colin. It didn't matter how we felt. He's been a nature boy since the day he was born. We couldn't keep clothes on him till he was almost five. No, it was either accept him or lose him."

"Now he's chosen a career," Louise added. "I understand we have you to thank for that."

"Any word on how he is?" Charles asked.

"Not yet," Louise said. "The rock caught him in the side of the head, from a long ways up. He's in surgery now. We know the neurosurgeon, he's the best in Vancouver."

"They tell me you have a broken rib," Palmerston said.

"Leaf pushed me out of the way," Jackson answered. "He saw the rock, I didn't."

The big man sighed. "That's Colin. That's him."

After some more silence Palmerston rose. "I'll let you get your rest. I need to talk to the hospital administrator." Leaf's parents left.

Charles left, too, and was back in a minute. "I talked to the ER doc and he says you're free to go. There's nothing more we can do here. Come on."

The Seabus bobbed and wallowed its way out of the North Shore dock and set course across the harbour for downtown Vancouver. Wendy sat in the last row of seats and trembled.

What had she done? The opportunity to give the boy a scare had seemed so perfect, so simple from thirty feet up on the cliff's edge. Then Teague's friend had seen her. And instead of bending the Second Rule for an extraordinary circumstance she had broken it to bits.

The ferry rocked back and forth as it caught some chop from the wake of a passing container ship. Her attention was caught by the only other occupant this far back in the boat, a terribly jittery stick of a woman clutching herself a few rows away and muttering something about the ocean. The electricity coming off the troubled soul was impossible to ignore. "You could take a bus over the bridge, dear," she offered.

The woman was on some horrible edge, her eyes staring over the cliff. "I hate the ocean," she breathed. "It eats people and you never see them again. You fall in, or it reaches up with one big wave to grab you and then your eyeballs are crab food.

Did you know that, they go for the eyeballs first? I read that somewhere. The ocean is full of crabs. But my boy Joe moved to Nanaimo, over on Vancouver Island, you know? Someday he'll get hurt or married or who knows what and I'll have to take the ferry. The big one, out over deep water. My doctor said take the Seabus, get used to it, you know? Baby steps." She gave out a laugh that made nobody happy and twiddled a thin hand in the air. "Syren," she introduced herself. "Funny, right? Water goddess, lures sailors to their death? Funny." Wendy doubted the lady even knew who she was talking to, and didn't bother introducing herself back. The poor woman curled up, strangling her handbag and staring at the abyss.

"There's always somebody in worse pain than you," her Mumma had said often enough. Well, wasn't that the truth, and the proof of it right here. Wendy sank back into her own long-distance stare. Not that it excused anything. When at last the boys had stopped for lunch they were thirty feet below her, more than enough. A one pound stone from that height would take almost a second and a half to fall and leave a bruise Teague would remember for a week. She dug around at the cliff edge, found the rock and settled down to wait.

They'd floated, two rubber-coated human stars bobbing on the water, the other boy, Leaf, farther out in the pool. She'd leaned out with the small stone in her hands.

Then Leaf had opened his eyes.

She saw the spark of blue from thirty feet up. She saw his hand wave, then the impossible recognition, the pointing finger. She'd heard his words. You're her, he said, clear as a bell. In a flash of pure fright she'd left the stone and yanked a ten pound rock from the muck. The crunch and the splash came with a terrible rush of inner heat that weakened her knees and left her breathless. Then she'd heard the wail. Jackson Teague's voice, uttering the ancient cry that hadn't changed from the first day death had touched the world. Then, as Wendy ran back down the path, he'd started calling for help.

Wendy had almost cried out herself then, stumbling down the path in a cloud of shock and shame. She'd hit the wrong boy. In her arrogance she'd used a sledgehammer where she needed a scalpel and now an innocent was suffering. She had been willing to stray from the code in service to the greater good, but not this.

The Seabus bumped into its Vancouver dock and the poor, mad Syren was pawing at the doors before the boat even stopped rocking. Wendy took her time on the long walk up to the street and the bus ride home. Maybe it was enough. Maybe this near-miss with his friend would convince Jackson to live and let live. She could hope for that little bit of good to come out of the mess.

Because she dreaded the thought of what she'd do if he didn't.

The orderly was 6 foot 2 and maybe 19, with the bland face and almond eyes that said southern Asia, a nametag that said Marko and a tongue that spoke purebred Saskatchewan. Marko stopped pushing the wheelchair just shy of the hospital's doors and said, "You sure about this, Mr. Rogers? The doc said you got another three days here to heal that shoulder up, you want."

Borden had taken the Fred Rogers wallet on the night of his bridge work · the one with a Victoria address on the ID and pictures of him wearing a grey cardigan and an insipid smile, although nobody got the joke · and that was what the hospital staff had found in his pocket when he'd somehow dragged his singed and sorry ass to the front doors of the emergency room. They'd done a passable job of putting his left shoulder back in its socket, reinflating his lung and calming down some of the bruising on his ribs and face, and he had spent the past two days being all soft and apologetic and nice to everybody at the Lions Gate Hospital. But now it was time to take his leave. He braced his good arm on the chair and twisted around to look Marko full in the face. "Fuck off," he said.

A gratifying shock flashed over the kid's mug before he closed it down. "Well, that's the way you want it," he muttered. "There's the door. Have a nice day."

Outside in the fresh air Borden squinted at the sunshine and tried to get his bearings. Marko had shown him to a side door of the hospital. The grounds, full of grass and huge trees and pathways, stretched out to a road. Beside the door was some kind of air conditioning plant, a mass of piping and condensers that kicked on as he stood there. It was afternoon and the shadows reached to the right; okay, he was facing north.

Which didn't matter one good goddamn. There was nowhere he could go. Right now the police and his old friend both thought he'd been blown into fish food. Once the Sea Otter sailed into Vancouver harbour unmolested and intact, he might as well stay dead.

He sank onto one of the benches that lined the approach to the hospital. His career was ashes. The bridge run had been a perfect plan, the fog a nice added security blanket. He'd done the cratering charge up to look like an extra bridge light hanging from a stout line below the deck, with an invisible loop of fluorocarbon fishing line attached to the detonator, ready to snag the bunting pole on top of the first cryogenic sphere as it skimmed under the bridge and loose hell upon the town. 25

seconds to rig the support line under the edge of the sidewalk, another 15 seconds to carefully attach and lower the bomb into place, and exit stage left into his spot in the history books.

Except he'd stood up after attaching the support line and found himself facing a fullback in a dark grey dress not six inches away. She'd taken one look at the repainted M3A1 in his arms and one other look right through his eyes into the back of his skull. She'd said, "For Mercy's sakes," and thrown him over the side. God help him and all his training, a woman had thrown him like a ragdoll.

His first reflex had been to let go of the high explosive. He'd been setting up for his second reflex - screaming like a girl all the way to the waterline - when the support line snagged his left arm and whiplashed him into the girders under the bridge deck. His shoulder joint had separated with a champagne-cork pop, most of the stuff holding his arm onto his chest had shredded, and his lung had deflated by the time his good arm found the fog-slick underside of the bridge. That was the memory he was left with - pop, rip, whoosh.

And then flash, as the M3A1 reached the end of the support line with a jolt and did what it was born to do. The world lit up as the hand of God lifted Borden face-first into the underside of the bridge deck. Something clanged and reverberated off the big steel close by his head. That was all he remembered until falling off the last girder practically by the North Shore bridge control centre and stumbling into the shoreline brush. He remembered staring at the red and blue circus lighting up the fog on the bridge, then wheezing up to the hospital doors, then nothing for half a day.

The damn evil bitch had saved his ass. The police had been all over him and all over the Lions Gate Bridge. If she hadn't tossed him bodily over the rail, he'd have been face down on the pavement with a knee in his back. He owed her his freedom.

Big deal. There was a gaping, empty hole inside where his reputation used to be and nothing but the certain knowledge of his own incompetence to fill it with. He was the demolitions guy who couldn't make an entire boatload of natural gas go boom. He was done in the industrial demolitions business.

Maybe his accumulated savings would last a few years in some place where you didn't have to pay for central heating. Like Paraguay.

People passed by in front of him, their oh-I'm-sick whines and complaints an added irritation. A breeze picked up and threw the tree branches around. Then a voice caught his ear. He glanced left and experienced a small-world moment - the whiz kid, Jackson whatever, strolling out of the hospital doors with some other guy who actually resembled Clark Kent. Jackson was walking like he'd gone three rounds with a body-puncher. Borden turned away and pretended to stare at the rhododendrons as the kid walked right past him.

"I still can't believe how fast he moved. I'll be feeling this for days," Jackson moaned to his friend. "Get me home, I'm going straight to bed." They were past him and gone.

Borden shook his head. The boy would never know how close he'd come to notoriety. "I met the guy who did it. I actually had coffee with him, and we talked explosives! If I'd only known." The kid had been a useful tool, giving Borden that thermite trick. And he had quite the way with angles and trajectories.

The breeze became a wind, throwing the willows and maples into a fit. The condensers against the hospital wall kicked back into life, sucking the hot, diseased air out of the hospital and shoving good air back in. One willow thrashed about in the wind, tossing its branches in a long arc practically onto the air conditioner's piping. They should knock the thing down before it caused a problem.

He stretched out on the bench in the warm June sun and smiled for the first time in days. Paraguay was too hot this time of year. He was too smart, too goddamned young, to slink off and hide for the rest of his life. He had knowledge. He had one good arm. He had the boy's crazy talent. He still had a few days, for chrissake. Worlds had been destroyed with less.

He would need a new place. Then, with the kid's help, he would make a new plan. Borden rose and gave his body a little test shake. The pain pill was doing its work. Time for him to get on with his.

Chapter 18

Marilyn could close her eyes and still see the flash, feel the fog concuss her face as the lightning bolt of superheated plasma cracked open the night and boiled the water of the First Narrows. Operation Padlock had ended in an unintended blaze of glory, leaving behind it one second of stunned silence and then a chaos of reports and commands in her com unit. "Man over! Man over!" "Bomb!" "Secure the scene!" And Takeda's voice over all, "Get that woman!" It was no use, though - big as she was, in the three seconds it took them to mobilize she had vanished into the night.

"Trainee." Takeda had called her in to his office as the sun was burning off the last of the fog. His face had changed overnight from wood to stone as he prepared for the storm that was coming his way. They'd let a known saboteur walk around with live ordnance. They'd lost their surveillance. They'd let a complete stranger walk into an op and vaporize their subject. She didn't envy him the day he was about to have.

"I've spoken to your unit chief. Two days off, effective immediately. Then back to your desk. You had no real part in this, there's no reason for you to get burned. Your interest in ERT is on record. There will come a time." He flicked his eyes down to the papers on his desk and that had been that.

Now she was once more at her cubicle in Community Policing. "Hey, soldier. Back from the wars, I see." Ahmed was at the side of her desk. "So spill it already. Official word from Public Affairs is that an ERT training exercise got a little carried away. Word on the street is you guys turned night into day and put a new dent in the bridge." He pulled up a chair and leaned in. "So what happened?"

Takeda had laid out the consequences of varying from the official story. "Only a training exercise," she stared back at Ahmed, slipping her middle finger over her index one on the desk. "It was an anti-terrorist drill and Takeda thought we should work with a real threat. Somebody packed the thing too tight and it made a big noise. That's all."

Ahmed noted her fingers. "That bad, huh? At least there's no body count. Okay. You're mine again, at least for now. So let's get back to work."

Marilyn took a relieved breath and squared her shoulders. "Right. Back to scrubbing the streets and picking up the trash. What've we got?"

Ahmed tapped a finger on the papers on her desk. "For today, reinvolvement. Paperwork. You dropped everything when you moved downstairs, now you get a day to pick it up again. Refamiliarize yourself with the old cases and finish up your files." He rose. "Do it quick, before you get called to the bomb squad." She thumped him on the leg and he went away.

Her desk was untouched, the same clutter she'd left behind. The file on top was the cute, crazy massage therapist. The Chinatown incident report occupied top spot inside the folder, but she remembered doing some other follow-up on his case. She flipped the report up and found the list of local nursing agencies.

Oh yes, phone calls. She put the tip of her pen by the first number and reached for the headset.

The van's tired springs squealed and rocked as Borden jammed an empty pop bottle into a pail full of sand on the floor behind the passenger seat. Traffic sounds filtered down from the Knight Street bridge high overhead, but the rest of Mitchell Island was quiet. The van, an ancient Ford Econoline that had been camperized with a bed and basic kitchen, was so rusted and beat up it looked like it belonged down here among the auto graveyards and metal recyclers. It had been the only accommodation he could find at a moment's notice in this overcrowded excuse for a city and at first he'd been none too happy with the decline in his living standard. But it did have some few advantages. One of which was that he was now completely unfindable.

The plastic bottle, which was nose-down in the sand and had its bottom cut off, was firmly snuggled into the pail. He held a small carpenter's level to all four sides of the bottle, adjusting the set until it was perfectly vertical. He was out of time, and would only get one chance to do this right.

He lifted a ceramic bowl down off the van's tiny kitchen counter, grasped a silicone whisk he'd found in a dollar store and spent five more minutes slowly stirring the thermite powder he'd already spent a half hour mixing. Working seven pounds of aluminum and iron dust into a completely homogeneous powder was a sore workout for his good arm, but there was a world of difference between a good job and an excellent one, and this needed to be his very best work. When the mixture looked as silky as a black sand beach he put it down and moved on to the next task.

The internet was full of simple, easy instructions for mixing thermite with plaster of paris to make cute little thermite bombs. Pour the glop into an ice cube tray, stick a magnesium ribbon into the top to act as a fuse, and amaze your friends by melting holes in the driveway. That was all well and good for the hobbyist, but Borden needed something a little more robust.

He slipped a respirator over his nose and mouth and pulled on rubber kitchen gloves before picking up the can of industrial epoxy resin and checking the instructions for the tenth time. This wasn't his momma's household glue. He'd found it at a marine supply store on the other side of Mitchell Island. This was the stuff that held harbour tugboats together. He poured a precise amount of the resin into a large measuring cup, then exactly the right amount of hardener into another. The fumes from the hardener stung his eyes in the confined space and he reached over the driver's seat to crack open the window. Once he mixed the two there could be no distractions. He would have 17 minutes before the mixture hardened into a compound that was stronger than steel. 17 minutes to mix the epoxy, stir it into the thermite and pour it all into the pop bottle.

He stilled his thoughts, emptied his breath, picked up the hardener and the van filled with Mongolian warrior-rock. Muttering a curse he placed the hardener back down and dug the phone out of its hiding place. "Yeah," he said.

"Well well, you're alive. After that fine display on the bridge last weekend I thought we'd lost you. I was just checking to make sure the phone was dead, too."

"I'm fine, thanks for asking. It was a minor setback, that's all."

The mahogany-rich baritone gave him a soft laugh through the phone. "Minor setback? Hardly, my friend. I don't know what happened up there and I don't want to, but your little stunt did the trick. Have you been listening to the news? The police are calling it a training exercise and nobody's buying it. Hints and suggestions are surfacing all over the popular media that this was a close call, very close indeed. This could be the last nail in LNG's coffin." He put on the laugh again. "Well done, my friend. Mission accomplished."

Borden held the phone away from his ear and frowned at it. The guy was giving him the stage voice. Beyond that, the things he was saying didn't make sense. "What do you mean, mission fucking accomplished? The boat's still out there. Vancouver is still out there. You know what else is still out there? My reputation, that's what. After this I'll never work another day in my life. Nothing's finished until the 6 o'clock news says it is."

The stage voice was gone. "No, you're done. The rest of the payment is already in your account. You've done what we wanted and I'll make sure the world knows about it. Besides, from what I hear about Saturday night I'd say you used up all your materials."

"What, you don't think I'd have a Plan B? You hired a professional, remember? I'm doing this job. As we discussed."

The voice took on a crackly edge. Was that fear coming through the line? "Borden, no. I'm telling you it's done. The media's in an uproar, we've got what we need. There's no call for the rest of it. I'll double your fee." There was some clicking on the other end of the line. "There, done. That's a nice little retirement nest egg, my friend. I know it's not what you were looking for, but call it a day."

Borden glared at his phone again, a wave of unfamiliar emotion tugging at the corners of his eyes. Son of a bitch. One more test, to be sure. "So, it's good. You're happy, we're done, contract complete. With a bonus. Hmm. Maybe I can retire on that. I suppose I could go lay on a beach somewhere."

The relief in his old friend's voice was nauseating. "Yes, good idea! Send me a postcard, I'll drop by for a cerveza."

In the darkness of the van Borden lifted his free hand, sighed, and waved goodbye to one of the only friendships he'd ever had. The emotion pulling at his eyes changed direction and turned them into slits. "Know what I think, Eustace? I think you never meant for this job to go through. You hired me for my reputation. You wanted me to try, and fail, and make a big splash doing it. You'd have your publicity without any of the mess. You've gone soft, Eustace. And you're a bigger asshole than I ever gave you credit for."

Eustace had gone cold. The fear was thick enough to freeze the airwaves. "There's no need for that. Stop this now, before anybody gets hurt. I never had any doubts about your ability to pull this off, old friend, but you don't need to take the risk. Don't risk it. I have my media storm, you have your retirement. Forget about Plan B."

It was Borden's turn to laugh. "Thanks for the reunion, Eustace, it's been fun catching up. Once this is over you'd better hope that I forget where you live. Keep watching the news. And if you have any friends left, tell them to leave Vancouver."

The phone came apart in his hands and he shoved the sim card deep into the thermite mix. He gave himself sixty seconds to curse the end of a friendship and calm his blood pressure. Then he donned the face mask again and carefully, so carefully, poured the hardener into the resin. This really was his last chance. He was going to give it his all.

Emma Jacobs was old school, there was no question of that. Once she'd found the right nursing agency Marilyn had tried to save time and do an interview over the phone, but Jacobs had insisted, with a respectful but unmovable firmness, that any discussion about the home care agency or her care aides be conducted in person.

So here Marilyn was at 38th and Arbutus, being ushered into the back office of the Arbutus Home Care Agency by a trim pixie of a receptionist with a black pageboy and a sweet smile. Emma Jacobs' office was spacious and spotless. Diplomas and an old nursing school grad photo shared wall space with a large Emily Carr print. Soft carpeting, comfortable chairs and a muted garnet colour palette added to the reassuring ambience.

A monolith of an oak desk, straight out of a 1920's newspaper office, formed an impressive barrier between the visitor chairs and Emma Jacobs. Two large monitors positioned off to the left added a palisade. The rest of the desk held one wire filing basket and a small, brass abacus. Jacobs herself, walking across the room with her hand outstretched, was a fortyish off-blonde with a serious face, a bit of mileage weight and a business handshake. "Call me Emma," she said, and waved Marilyn to one of the visitor chairs. "Thank you for coming by. What can I do for you, constable?" She resumed her post behind the desk and crossed her hands atop a green blotter.

"Marilyn, please. This probably won't take up much of your time. I'd like you to look at some of your recent client files and let me know if everything checks out. I know that's a bit vague, but it's just due diligence on a case. I mentioned a couple of names on the phone; here's the full list."

Emma took the list with one hand and began flicking the brass abacus beads with the other. The woman loves numbers, Marilyn decided. More than she likes visitors. As Emma looked over the names the clicking sped up.

"One of these, Mrs. Kilborn, wasn't a client of the agency. The other five are all clients of ours who have recently passed," Emma said after a moment. Marilyn nodded. "This tends to happen in our line of work, there's nothing too mysterious about it. What was it you said you're looking for?"

"Nothing in particular. If you could take a look at the files and let me know if anything jumps out at you, I would really appreciate it." Marilyn dropped her eyes, gave Emma apologetic, and set the hook. "Providing, of course, you keep some kind of statistics."

The clicking stopped and Emma's hand slipped down out of sight. To a keyboard tray, apparently, because the monitors sprang to life. "I do," Emma replied. "All right, let's have a look."

She typed and moused, stared at her screens, then did it again. Marilyn saw an interesting shift in the woman's face as she worked. A subtle relaxation as she laid her hands on the keys and turned to her monitors, one less wrinkle between the eyes and a loosening of the lips. Then the wrinkle and tension returning as Emma dug deeper into whatever was on her screens.

"Did we catch something?" she asked.

Emma stopped typing, laced her fingers together on the blotter and gave Marilyn a creditable poker face. "I'm not at all certain there is a 'we,' Constable Mathers. I have nothing against helping you with your inquiries, but I also have a professional obligation to my clients and my staff. You see the difficulty, I'm sure. I know nothing about your investigation, but I do know that when laymen are introduced to records and statistics they often see connections that don't actually exist. You want whatever information I can provide, but I don't want to bring any unwarranted attention down on my clients or my care aides."

A tingle started at the base of Marilyn's spine. She leaned forward, laced her fingers on the oak and mirrored the poker face. "Emma, I know all about confidentiality and obligation, I deal with it every day. I also know that whatever you saw on those screens made you pause and give that little speech. I can't tell you more about my investigation, that's just how it is, but you can show me what you're looking at, and also tell me how to interpret it." She held the level gaze for one more second, then offered up a half-smile and a twinkle. "Come on, let me in on the secret."

Emma softened up and relented, unable to resist a teaching opportunity. She swivelled one of the big screens. "I've always liked statistics and the things they can tell you. That's why we're one of the biggest agencies in the city, because I run a good ship and know where to steer it. Now, look here." The screen was divided into six partitions, five patient forms and one bar chart. "These are the clients from your list. They've all passed within the last two months. We're used to that around here, the end of life is our stock in trade. Notice this. And this. And this." She used her mouse to highlight the patients' health conditions, then their causes of death as reported by the attending physicians.

The Latin medicalese was all Greek to Marilyn. "What am I looking at?"

"In essence, nothing," replied Emma. "All of these patients died of their conditions, or of something related or expected. Nothing out of the ordinary."

"Okay then." Marilyn pointed. "What's that last screen? The chart?" Multicoloured bars marched from left to right along a timeline, most fairly long and a few making it to the end. There were lots of them.

"This is a record of all our patients for the past year and a half, showing how long they've been under our care. As you can see, some patients only last a few weeks, some for months, and some are truly long-term care. It's quite a varied business. Look here." The mouse waved at some shorter lines towards the bottom.

"More recent clients?"

"Yes. In recent months there has been a trend towards shorter-term clients. Does that pique your interest?" Emma glanced over, waiting for the answer.

Marilyn gave it. "Yes, in fact."

"It shouldn't. This is within the range of normal variability. The 'shit happens' factor, if you will."

"Okay. So if all this is normal, what has you concerned?" She glanced down at the abacus. The clicking of brass beads was filling the room. Emma noticed and pulled her hand away, then swiveled the second screen around. It showed another bar chart, with less bars and a much more striking difference.

"This is my Time Spent chart," Emma explained. "It shows a running average of how much time each of my care aides spends with clients before they're reassigned."

"Reassigned? Because the client dies?"

"That's the usual cause, yes."

"Hmm." Marilyn pointed. "Now you're going to tell me how I'm misinterpreting that." All of the bars made it halfway across the timeline, a good number extending almost all the way across the screen. All except one, which was barely a stub.

"Exactly," Emma said with some emphasis. "That employee is actually a highly skilled nurse, working for us while she's in between jobs. I give her my most challenging clients because I know she can handle it. That skews the statistics." There was certainty in her voice. Of the 'lady doth protest too much, methinks' kind. Marilyn's tingle intensified.

"Are you telling me that this care aide - nurse, pardon me - was present for all five of these deaths?"

"She was engaged with these clients," replied Emma. "But before you jump to conclusions," she added, "I have to tell you that what you're thinking isn't possible."

Marilyn hadn't jumped, not by a long shot. She raised an eyebrow and said, "Please. Educate me."

Emma pointed back to the patient charts. "The deaths are all different."

Nothing more seemed to be forthcoming, so Marilyn prodded. "Educate me a little more than that."

Emma frowned. "You're thinking that these deaths were deliberate. That I have an angel of death on my staff. I'm telling you that's not so, and these stats prove it. Now, I'm not exactly wet behind the ears, constable. I know that these things happen. Goodness knows they make a big enough splash in the news when they're found out. But nurses who kill their patients usually aren't the sharpest knives in the drawer. They figure out one method to do their work, maybe two if they're exceptional, and they stick to it. That's how they get caught. These deaths," she pointed at the screen again, "were all natural. All different, and pretty much the direct result of their underlying conditions." She squared herself to the desk again. "All I'm saying, Marilyn, is please don't think that you can take action based on any of this. Believe me, if I thought there was anything even remotely conclusive here I would have taken action long ago. But there isn't. These charts can simply be flawed by their short timeline. By the clients I'm giving this nurse. Even by a simple run of bad luck."

The room was silent. "I see what you mean," said Marilyn at last, "and thanks for the tutorial. So your skilled and competent nurse could be the unluckiest employee you've ever had. Or she could, just possibly, be that scary good." She sighed. "In my line of work, that means I have more work to do. I notice," she pointed at the Time Spent bar chart, "that you've hidden Column A. Show it, please."

Emma hesitated, long enough that Marilyn started wondering if she'd need a warrant. Then she moved the mouse and clicked. The chart shuffled about, placing names in front of all the bars.

Marilyn pulled a thumb drive from her briefcase. "I'll need copies of those charts, please. And Wendy Corbett's resume and employment records."

She'd taken the next step, and far from settling the matter, it was stirring up more questions. Marilyn felt the beginnings of a headache.

Jackson Teague might, possibly, not be as crazy as he sounded. The poor boy must be tied up in knots, she thought. A flush crept into her cheeks when she remembered how quickly she and Ahmed had shut him down. It had taken guts, telling the police a story like that. And now there was the smallest hint that he could be telling the truth.

Not enough of a hint to call him, not yet. Teague would have to stay in the dark until she checked out a few more things. She hoped the pressure didn't really make him crazy. The thought of another trip to the psych ward must feel like a sword over his head.

She'd gone through the locked doors fifty times to see her brother. She'd seen Andrew have apologetic days when he couldn't stop hugging her, wary and watchful days when he stayed away from the ward's windows, and dull and despondent days as the doctors tried and failed to stabilize his sanity. Her parents had been wise about it and let her go as often as she wanted. Until another patient having a bad day had snapped Andrew's neck in the lunch room. She still remembered how much relief had been mixed in with the sorrow.

Now here it was, the question all over again. If the massage therapist was nuts, then the nuthouse was probably where he belonged. If he was right, then Marilyn Mathers was chasing the tail of an extremely capable killer. For the life of her, she didn't know which one to prefer.

Chapter 19

A fine bruise bloomed over Jackson's ribs. Georgia made it go away with onion and comfrey poultices while he ate painkillers so he could breathe. Charles kept them company when he wasn't visiting Leaf in the hospital.

"He's in a bad way," Charles said the day after the Lynn Creek accident. "The rock only glanced off his skull, but that was enough. They have him stabilized. He's not in a coma, but he hasn't regained consciousness yet. Now we just have to wait." He handed over a copy of the North Shore News, with a picture of Lynn Canyon on the cover. Orange-suited Search And Rescue teams wrestled with a stretcher. "You made the front page," he said. Jackson stared at it and Charles made the paper disappear.

So they waited. Jackson slept and healed and thought about Leaf. Colin Palmerston, of all people. Running from a life of money and influence and falling into the arms of Mother Nature. In the end, it had been Nature that was his enemy. He'd spent his life running towards that rock.

On Wednesday Jackson got up, put the rest of the pain pills at the back of the medicine cabinet and gave Charles a massage. With a few adaptations to his technique, it was possible. Which was good, because his bank account was suffering from the inactivity. He decided he could manage one client, hauled an old luggage carrier out of the closet for his table and headed to Gastown.

The Seymour Gym was the last of its kind. Long ago chased away from Seymour Street by upscale storefronts and sky-high rents, the boxing club had landed against the ropes down by the railway tracks. At the bottom of an unmarked set of stairs was a large room redolent of canvas and old leather. Those who didn't know about the Seymour Gym would never find it; those who knew about it didn't need directions.

Abraham Franklin was the last of his kind, too, a boxer turned promoter turned coach turned gym owner. Everybody who was anybody in the business knew him. When your boxer was at the top of his game you took him down those crumbling concrete stairs to find out what he could really do.

Franklin knew the value of a good massage. He had Jackson down the third Wednesday of each month. He still sparred with the trainees and Jackson loved to work on him. The old man's body was polished ebony topped with a white afro frizz and a bumpy knot of a nose, but working on him was like massaging a teenager. Franklin's muscles were lean, amazingly strong and soft as butter. Judging from his connective tissues he was the healthiest person in Vancouver.

Jackson gave Franklin his best, devoting all his attention to working the old guy over from top to bottom. It was a relief to concentrate on doing his job and let the last few days fade into the background. One by one he found the minor kinks and knots in Franklin's body and worked them out. His rib gave him only minor grief. It felt good to get back into the swing of things.

After it was all over, Franklin got up – no modesty in the gym – and towelled off the oil before stepping into an old pair of grey sweats. "I guess I'm going to have to call you over more often," he remarked, in a voice used to being heard across the gym.

"Really?" Jackson said, breaking his table down.

"Yep. 'Cause it'll take three of those massages to equal what you usually do."

Jackson stopped putting the table away, stunned by the words. Franklin pulled a white t-shirt over his head and then stood there, waiting. Finally Jackson had to say something.

"I didn't think it was noticeable, but I had an accident the other day, and – "

"You hurt your ribs, I know," finished Franklin. "Right side, about halfway down. Saw it before you got down the stairs. Never saw your table on a luggage rack, for starters. But no, that didn't slow you down. What I'm talking about goes way deeper than that." He stopped again, giving Jackson that same solid-wall look, waiting.

Had he really been that distracted? "I had a friend get injured in the same accident, a really good friend, and he's hurt badly. I didn't think I was letting it bother me, but – "

"No, that's not it either." Franklin was scowling now, his eyes boring into Jackson's. "Sorry to hear about it, but that's not what I'm seeing, either. What I'm talking about came through your hands, not your head."

They had set up in Franklin's office and now the old man pointed through the window into the gym. One of the three rings was occupied. A star boxer was sparring with a skilled partner.

"Tell me what you see there," said Franklin, pointing at the pair.

"He's good," Jackson said immediately. "He's got it all over the other guy."

"That's because the other guy is his sparring partner, not an opponent. I said, tell me what you see." There was a whip in the command.

Jackson looked. "His punches come from his whole body, not just his shoulder. See how his hips pivot with every move?

His feet move well, and he knows where to land his punches. He doesn't miss." He turned back to Franklin. "He's a pro, a star. Right?"

The look Franklin gave told Jackson he'd failed a test. "Something missing here," he said, almost to himself. Then Jackson felt a tap on his shoulder, a hard tap that left a sting. Franklin had hit him. Before he had time to react, say quit it, move, Franklin hit him again, an open-handed bitchslap on the side of the head.

"Hey!" he said, moving his head aside far too late. The old man's hands were like lightning, there and gone again before the movement even registered. Franklin's face was still searching, growing more disappointed. Jackson saw his face harden into an implacable fighter's mask an instant before his right side exploded into pain.

"Wh – ow!!" he wheezed, all the air knocked out of him, and he doubled over. Franklin had tapped again, directly on his cracked rib. The pain was amazing. It took him a full minute to recover and stand up straight.

"Wha – what the hell?" he managed. Franklin was still watching him.

"My sentiments exactly. What the hell's happened to you, Jackson? You look at one of the best fighters in the world, with the eyes that I know you have, and you see nothing. Not a word about the dance in his moves or what happens when he takes a swing. You know what I see when he lands a punch? I see the world shake. And you're going to tell me you see nothing?

"I tapped you three times. I telegraphed all of those moves. That last one I did in slow goddamned motion, you'd have to be dead on your feet to miss it. And you missed it. Sorry if I set you back a couple of days, but I tell you, it's no great loss. Whatever's got you, it's got you all the way down."

Jackson couldn't catch his breath enough to answer. Not

that he'd have anything to say. Franklin's words hit harder than the taps.

Franklin sighed and laid a hand on Jackson's shoulder. "I don't know what you're fighting, but you're losing. You're on the ropes. Take some advice from an old pro. On the ropes is the worst place in the whole ring. Whatever you need to do, you do it. Get out there and go toe to toe with whatever this is."

He handed Jackson his fee and made for his desk. "Tell you what. Give me a call when you got your moxie back. Then we'll schedule our next session. Good luck, kid."

That was it. Another client down. More empty space in his schedule and his side hurt like blazes. Jackson slapped his table into the luggage carrier and struggled to get it back up the stairs.

"St. Ignatius, Records." Young, male, bored. Probably pulling him away from Super Mario, Marilyn decided. She kept it brief and formal, stating the name and records she was after and jotting down notes on the sheet of paper in front of her. It was the third sheet. This was the 16th hospital she'd called, working her way back through the nurse's employment history position by position. After the fourth she'd started plotting them on a map of the States. They made a ragged line that stretched, unevenly but unerringly, from her previous job in Eugene, Oregon over to this small hospital outside Boston. Wendy Corbett had nursed her way all across the country.

It took a few minutes for the boy to get back to her. "This is an oldie," he said. "Goes back to before the hospital started keeping employee records on computer." The complaint was implied, the whine almost audible.

"You mean, it's stored with the paper records."

"Yeah, that's right."

"Tell me, where are the hospital's paper records kept?"

A pause. "In the next room." The whine was nearly there.

Marilyn let a bit of her irritation creep in; she'd been making these calls in between other cases for two days. "Please."

The boy gave in and she heard his chair squeak back from the desk. He spared her the hold music and just plunked the phone down. She could follow his progress across a tiled floor until a door opened and closed. Then she was alone, both in Vancouver and Boston.

16 hospitals. In each one Wendy Corbett worked for sometimes less than a year, sometimes more than two, and only ever gave the one previous hospital as a reference. In each one, the records showed diligent work in a variety of disciplines, on a number of floors. Nurse Wendy got around. In each one, no reason had been given for her departure. Sometimes it was listed as none, sometimes personal. Twice, in earlier hospitals, the word 'incompatible' had been written down.

After each call Marilyn checked in with her instincts. And after each one, her itch remained. None of them quelled her feeling that there was something to this that didn't jibe. She wanted to go back further, and further. Now she was at the end of the line.

The phone was picked up. "Okay, got it," the boy droned. She heard a file folder opening. "What do you want to know?"

"Dates and places of work, previous employers, work notes and citations." She had it down by now.

"Okay. She worked at St. Ig for 14 months, on three different wards. Took pretty much every course that came up, looks like.

A citation for quick thinking in emerg, probably saved a kid or something. No previous work experience, just lists her home address." He gave it, a place in Maine Marilyn had never heard of. "No reason given for leaving, but it's labelled DNR."

Marilyn ran hospital terminology through her head. "Do not resuscitate?"

That got a laugh, high and nasal. "Say, that's a good one! No, down here it means, 'Do Not Rehire'. She must have pissed somebody off."

"Oh." Marilyn wrote it down.

"Say, this is weird." More paper shuffling on the other end.

"What?" Marilyn moved forward in her seat.

"A handwritten note here, bottom of the file. Says, 'Any inquiries into this employee should contact Cecilia Cummins, RN.' Gives a phone number. This must be pretty old. You want it?"

"Yes, please." She jotted it down, glad to say goodbye to the young man and let him get back to his game.

The first thing Jackson did was stop into a drugstore and get an instant ice pack, shake it into usefulness and slap it under his shirt. The noise from his rib died down almost at once. The second thing he did was make the short drive through downtown to Sunset Beach.

He needed to sit, listen to waves, be near the water and recover. His anger at the old boxer's harsh treatment, sadness and worry over Leaf and a mounting sense of subterranean frustration were combining to spin his head. He leaned back against an old driftwood log and closed his eyes to the warm sun. Sailboat traffic puttered in and out of False Creek in front of him. An instructor was talking a sand yoga class through Sun Salutations. Behind him, up in a tree, a crow was trying to bash open a mussel.

His side hurt. Each time he took a breath he felt Franklin's hand tap him, probably as lightly as the old fighter knew how. Every stab took him back to Lynn Creek, feeling Leaf's shove, hearing the terrible splash. Seeing the line of red running through the water. It had been a hell of a week.

The sound of the waves and the heat on his eyelids was soporific. A slight breeze played with his hair. The waves were only waves, the breeze just a current. No tracers blazed a path across his mind. At least one thing was right.

A burst of laughter from down the beach made him peek. "Come on, tree pose, you can do it." The yoga instructor was standing on one foot with her other tucked against her knee while the rest of the class fell all over each other trying to find their balance in the sand. "You can do it," she called again. One by one, to varying degrees, all the students managed it.

He smiled as he recalled Leaf and the slackline. The smile faded at the memory of his own failure. Leaf had said he was missing something. How had he put it? "Normal people can do this. I know, I've taught them." It would be a long time before Leaf taught anyone anything again.

The sun delivered a bone-melting warmth. He shifted his butt to make a more comfortable divot in the sand and his rib barked. Damn Franklin. The old boxer had set him back at least a couple of days. And for what? Because Jackson hadn't lived up to the guy's expectations. Because he was having a bad massage day. Because he couldn't see Franklin's fist headed for his ribs.

Or see a rock fall. The thought brought Jackson up straight. He'd seen nothing at Lynn Creek. Not the rock, not Leaf arrowing in to push him out of the way. He'd missed whoever Leaf had pointed at.

The paper said the rock had come loose from the cliff wall. It happened, part of the natural forces always at work in Lynn Canyon. It was gravity.

"You're her." Leaf had said that. Not like he had known the person above them. More like he'd seen pictures of her or heard about her and was only now seeing her in real life. Jackson had avoided replaying that scene but now he went back to the pool in his mind. "You're her." Had there been a dark tone in those few words? That could be all in Jackson's imagination. But the pointing finger wasn't. Leaf had done that. Said those words. Like he was picking somebody out of a lineup.

"Oh!" The cry burst out of him as the realization slammed into his brain, perfect and complete. The nurse had been in his place. She'd seen the date for Lynn Creek written on his calendar. He'd stormed over to her own home and, with that little adventure in Chinatown, practically dared the nurse to try something. He'd drawn her right to the cliff above the pool. She'd followed them up the creek, found a rock and aimed for his head. She'd been right on target, too. Only Leaf's action had saved him. And now Leaf was in the hospital with a broken head instead of Jackson.

The yoga teacher was looking over at him. He raised a sleeve to his face and yelled, "Ah-cha!" Then gave a loud snort as he wiped his nose. She turned back to her class.

Leaf had seen Wendy Corbett. He'd seen the rock sailing for Jackson's head. Had Jackson missed all of that? How was that even possible?

A noonday wind blew in from the inlet, bouncing off the last of the waves and ruffling Jackson's hair on its way further into the city. It smelled of salt and floating diesel fuel. He turned and looked for it, saw the same breeze whiffle around the top leaves of an elm tree on the shore before melding back into the atmosphere. It was delightful. He wanted to see it again.

He was overdue for another pill. On and off, like a frigging switch. Jackson fished out his pill container and popped it open.

Could he have kept the creek from happening? The pill was in his hand. Was there some way he could have stopped the nurse before this? There was simply no way to know.

He laid the pill back down and snapped the container shut. Too many emotions and revelations crowded his skull, it felt like it was about to crack open. He kicked off his shoes and socks. He got up and strode for the water, not stopping when the waves lapped over his feet. Into the water, into the sheen of fuels left by the constant boat traffic, up past his waist when the sand gave out and the bottom dove away and Jackson was under the water. It was cold. It smelled. He held his breath, let his feet leave the earth and let the False Creek water slap him in the head.

The shock was total. His thoughts stopped. He was suspended in icy, stinky water, and for that moment nothing else existed. He floated.

Three seconds was all he could stand. Then he took two powerful and painful strokes backwards, found the bottom and came up blustering. He was 15 feet downstream from where he'd started, taken by the tide. His feet gripped the sand and he stomped, fully-clothed and dripping wet, back to his shoes.

People looked at him funny, but so what. The storm in his head was gone. He had access to a minute or two of clear thought.

He was mad. Furious. His anger was bigger than anything he had ever known. At himself, for sure, but there was no time for that nonsense. He was toweringly angry at the night nurse.

She had to be stopped. She wasn't going to quit, and Jackson couldn't let her pack up and go somewhere else. Still, even now, there was nothing he could prove to anyone.

He needed all of himself in this fight. As much as he might not like it, that included his condition. He needed to be able to see the patterns.

Not all of it, said the voice of reason through the clarity of his dip. That way lie madness and the short path to the padded room. But some of it. Would it work? Could he do that? It was monkeying with his medicine, but he had to give it a try.

He took out one pill, held it between his fingers, and nibbled it in half. Down the hatch, and the other half back into the little box. In twenty minutes he would know if this was going to work.

In twenty minutes he would be on his way back to Lynn Creek. He had to be sure. He had to see.

Harold Palmerston hated this place. He hated the nauseating mix of smells, the endless bleeping machines, the nondescript pastel floors and walls. He hated the doors that blocked you everywhere you turned. But most of all, he hated that his son was here.

Leaf. Colin was his name, but he'd insisted on Leaf for so long that even Louise and he had taken to it. For all Palmerston's influence and mastery of pretty much any situation, he'd found it impossible to understand his own son. From the very start Leaf had run away from the advantages of a privileged life. Instead of university, he'd gone to the beach. Instead of networks and connections among his peers, he'd chosen random groups of friends and the call of Nature.

Then, not three weeks ago, Leaf had announced his intention to join the Vancouver Police. Palmerston had breathed a deep sigh of relief, pulled a string and Leaf was in the door.

Now here he was. A terrible accident, because he'd been crawling around in a creek bed looking for beauty. Beaned by a big fucking rock, and now he was lying in a white bed with bleeping machines, surrounded by pastel walls and the pervasive hospital miasma. It was too much.

"I want him out of here. Home is as good for him as this place. I want it done now."

He'd been saying the same thing, over and over, for almost an hour in the hallway outside Colin's room. Harold Palmerston knew that if you stuck to your guns and loaded them with money you could blast down any opposition. Still, it was taking a long time. First the nurses had shaken their heads, saying nothing in the eloquent way nurses had. Then Theodore Marks - Vancouver's best neurosurgeon and a family acquaintance - listened to Palmerston's demand and said no.

"He still hasn't woken up from the surgery, Harold," he said. "No way is he leaving here, no how." Then the bleeping from Colin's room got loud. The nurses had elbowed him out of the way like he didn't own the place and left him in the cold hallway.

They came out of Colin's room thirty minutes later. Marks was a little less tense and some of the nurses had smiles. "He woke up for a few minutes. Just a bit, enough for some assessment. We have some work to do, and he's not going anywhere, but you can see him now."

Palmerston walked into the most difficult room of his life and stared down at his son. Even through the bedsheet he could see that Leaf was an amazing specimen. The beach lifestyle had given him that, at least. His body was perfect. Except for the big white bandage. Palmerston felt like bawling his eyes out. He felt like tearing a hole in the wall and carrying his son out of here on his back.

Leaf felt the squeeze on his hand. He squeezed back. Then Palmerston saw the flicker of blue and the flicker of white. Leaf had seen him, for a fraction of a second. He had smiled.

"He's going home," Palmerston said to Marks outside the door.

"No, he's not. I'm sorry."

His next talk was with the Administrator, a man Palmerston had helped put there. His talk was full of numbers, both positive and negative. Soon enough, the Administrator had Ted Marks in a corner. Palmerston got ready. He knew there would be one more objection; if he could get past that, then Leaf was home.

Marks stomped back down the ugly hallway, obviously disgruntled. "I won't let your son go without ambulance transport, and 24-hour nursing care. But not just any nursing. He's not entirely stable, it has to be someone who knows when to hustle him back here. Nothing happens without that in place."

"Consider it done." And Palmerston had done it. Three phone calls and the best damn nurse in the region was on the line with the doctor, who peppered her with questions and grew increasingly impressed with whatever he was hearing on the other end. Finally he hung up and turned back to Palmerston.

"We still have tests to run. Tomorrow morning is the earliest I'll allow it." He half-turned to the Administrator. "That's solid, Geoff." Palmerston knew an absolute when he heard it and let it go. Tomorrow would do.

He forgot the doctor. Leaf was going to be in his own bed by tomorrow night. And he would have the best nursing care money could buy.

It was like a sadistic game of daytime-nighttime. The half-pill mostly kept the world normal, but now there were moments when everything was suddenly, breathtakingly connected, there and gone again in the blink of an eye. It rocked him back on his heels each time, left him feeling dazzled and longing to follow and somehow hopeful. His condition flashed into full strength three times during the twenty-minute drive. He barely avoided creating a traffic accident as he made it across the Second Narrows Bridge and up to Lynn Creek.

The less-traveled path on the west side of the creek was hopeless. Thick salal bushes slapped at him, obscuring the rocky bits of trail. Where mud or dirt or pine needles replaced bare rock the trail was such a confusion of footprints and dog tracks it was impossible to isolate anything. Less-traveled, in a metropolis of over two million, was still pretty damn used.

When the trail drew close to the canyon's edge Jackson caught glimpses of where he and Leaf had been. He recognized a rapids, saw a pool where they had found an old truck tire mired at the bottom. Then the path veered away from the cliff and he was walking through forest.

He was in deep woods, at least 30 feet away from the canyon wall, when he knew he must be level with the floating pool. No path broke through the bushes towards the water. No footprints headed away from the trail. He stood still, at a loss.

Then it happened. The wall of tangled salal leaves and brambles stopped being a messed-up barrier and became an electric, living tapestry. Every branch was right, growing exactly where geometry and genetics dictated it should be. Each leaf hung off its bud equidistant from its neighbours, angled to catch whatever sun was filtering down through the trees above.

Except for the tiny disturbance ten feet ahead. The branches in one spot had been pushed aside and were angled slightly awry. The side trail to the creek was obvious. The pull for him to follow was irresistible.

The flash left. Jackson shook off the lingering wisps and headed for the break in the bushes. It took him to a shallow clearing at the edge of the canyon, maybe five feet wide by ten feet long. Below him, still and dark in the early afternoon, lay the floating pool.

The cliff's edge was rotten with gnarled roots and loose clods of dirt. Jackson went down onto his belly to search it safely. After a minute's effort he found a dent scooped out of the ground, smooth and sharp-edged, with recently-vacated worm holes in the dirt beneath. The rock had been pulled from here. He could still see finger gouges around the perimeter. Jackson felt himself grow cold.

One thing left to find, and it didn't take long. In the soft dirt next to the edge, behind the divot, were two footprints, clear as day. Five feet to the left were two more, deeply indented where the person had leaned forward, directly above where Leaf had been struck. The imprints were smallish but deeply set, suggesting a big person with tiny feet. The moist forest-bottom loam revealed a square-mesh block tread crossed by dozens of small sipe marks. A standard, non-slip sneaker tread. Maybe a little lightweight for a city hike over forested ground. But the shoe of choice for long shifts on a hospital ward.

He rocked back on his haunches, making another set of impressions in the soil, and tried to think through the slow, red anger building up behind his eyes. He had sneaker prints, and finger gouges, and wild, unsubstantiated accusations. Nothing that would come even close to convincing anybody else. But enough for him.

He ran all the way back to his car, partly to burn off steam but also to get hustling. He had a date in Chinatown and he didn't want to be late.

Chapter 20

"Hello?" With one word, the voice served Marilyn a heaping bowlful of her grandmother's apple betty with a dollop of whipped cream in an oven-warm kitchen.

"Mrs. Cummins, I got your name from the file of Wendy Corbett at St. Ignatius Hospital." Marilyn gave her credentials. "A note said I should talk to you."

"Well, it's about time. That was years ago, I expected this call long before now. She's been good, I guess."

Marilyn was sitting full upright now, the chair's edge digging into her thighs. "What do you mean, Mrs. Cummins?"

"It's Cecilia, dear, and I'll tell you right out there's no proof of any of this, none whatsoever. If there were I'd have spoken up."

"Yes ma'am, no proof. No proof of what?"

"Of why you're calling me, of course. That nurse, Wendy Corbett. The Death Angel. That's what we used to call her on the recovery floor. Tell me, is she still messing about with the dolls?"

Marilyn felt like she was losing a race. "Dolls? Can you – "

"Yes, Constable Mathers, the dolls. She was discreet, but I caught her at it. She'd sneak a doll into a patient's room just before she killed them. Then she'd take it out again afterwards. Never would have known otherwise. Damn clever, that one."

"Are you saying, Mrs. Cummins, that Wendy Corbett was

murdering patients?"

A hard laugh. "No, girl, no proof of that at all. Every single death Wendy Corbett was present for was above-board. Not exactly expected, mind you, sometimes a complete surprise, but the whole lot were natural causes. Nobody but me suspected a thing. Of course she was murdering them. Like she's been doing, I suspect, all these years, and what you're finally catching up to now. So, is she still doing the dolls?"

"We think so, yes."

"Good, that's one way you can maybe catch her. Tell you what, call her hometown's police chief. I talked to him once and it was quite enlightening. Good luck, Constable. Let me know how it turns out."

Jackson forced himself to wait for a full 10 minutes on the far side of the playground, trying to remain inconspicuous as he surveilled the house and the nurse's basement door. After two flashes of his condition showed him nothing special, he strode through the back gate, across the yard and straight down the concrete stairwell. Nobody was home upstairs. As for whether the nurse was in here somewhere - well, it had been a very long time since he'd plowed somebody in the face.

The brass doorknob turned when he twisted. Okay. He pushed. The door flexed but stayed closed.

There was a deadbolt holding it back, shoulder high. The lock was more old brass, brown with tarnish. Jackson didn't have the Open Sesame with him. One broken jamb deserves another, he thought, and threw his good shoulder into it.

Old growth fir that had been hardening for a century

catapulted him back onto the concrete steps and his rib told him never to do that again. Jackson caught his breath and stood back up. Nobody was running or shouting. The entire neighbourhood must be at work.

The stairwell put his head at ground level. To the right was a scrap of lawn that wrapped around the side of the house. To his left was the first post of the upstairs porch and bare dirt underneath it where the sun didn't reach. The crawl space was littered with a coiled hose, some old cans, and a few rocks. One of the rocks was tucked into the corner between the stairwell and the house. He picked it up, hoping. There was no key underneath.

Well then, a rock for a rock. It was heavy. He turned back to the door, twisted the knob again and slammed the rock against the deadbolt. He heard the frame crack. He did it again, bruising the door and ruining both the lock and the paint around it. On the third try he heard a big crunch and the door was open.

There must be nobody home for a hundred yards, thought Jackson as he stepped into the kitchen of the small apartment. He set the rock down in the middle of the formica table and looked around. The place was neat, tidy, populated with 1960's appliances and 1970's rec-room panelling, and subtly weird in a way he couldn't place. He could feel himself grow tired just looking at it.

A flash came on and Jackson had to overrule his feet to keep from running out. Everything was off. The table angled away from the wall, its corner pointed towards the door. The chairs were askew just enough to set his teeth on edge. The microwave on the tiny counter, the knives in their block, the dish rack, all of it had been placed perfectly wrong. Even the stove had been nudged to make it off-kilter to anything else. Nothing matched up, and it felt like a cold wind was trying to push him back through the door.

The flash was gone. He steadied himself. Evidence, he muttered, you're here to find evidence. You know she did it. Now prove it. Holding his breath, Jackson stepped through the kitchen into the living room.

For a second he couldn't process what he was seeing. Then his breath left him in a dizzying rush. No flash, no flash, please God don't do that to me, he prayed as the full impact of the room hit him.

The entire living area was dolls. They crowded two rows of shelves the nurse had mounted around the room. They covered the TV and a second formica table. The back of the worn sofa was lined with dolls. The visitor's chair was laid three-deep with them. All of them had been carefully placed, organized, and tilted off kilter. There must have been a hundred of them. Maybe two.

They were magnificent. Beautiful porcelain angels with white dresses and halos shared space with stuffed old-granny dolls with dried up apples for faces, next to wood carvings, bronze castings and clay figurines. Every form of doll-making was represented, and they were all exquisite.

They were all people. Jackson tried only to register the bare fact, saving the significance of it all for later. Evidence, he said to himself, find the evidence.

Dolls weren't evidence. They proved nothing.

He tossed the place, as best he knew how. Closet, bed, drawers, shelves. He sifted through the rack of identical nurse's uniforms, a second rack of casual shirts and slacks, and used a tortoiseshell hairbrush to stir through the drawer of oversized panties and bras. He left a mess behind. He rifled through the medicine cabinet, checked under the sinks. He found nothing to prove that Wendy Corbett was what he knew her to be.

Ten minutes, and Jackson's nervousness was starting to trump his fury. He had to leave. But not empty-handed. He ran back to the living room and grabbed three dolls off the shelving: the trainman, Mrs. Shrop's huge Scottish girl and Herbert Lowe's little smiling Buddha. Then he left, striding back across the yard and over the hill to his car. He left the neighbourhood and was gone as the last of his righteousness deserted him. His hands shook on the wheel with leftover nerves all the way to the safety of Kitsilano.

The tide was out at Tower Beach. He walked out as far as he could before burying them. A cool breeze gave him shivers as he dug with a piece of driftwood in the evening's long shadows. What was it the Japanese general said at the end of the Pearl Harbour movie? "I fear all we have done is to awaken a sleeping giant and fill him with a terrible resolve." Jackson had ransacked the nurse's place. He'd broken her door. And had precisely shit to show for it.

The dolls looked good at the bottom of the hole, facing the ocean. Like they were ready for whatever came next.

Wendy rounded the corner of the little path to her basement door and stopped dead at the sight of splintered wood. She'd had a break-in. A wave of sick violation flooded through her, but she told it to get lost. Such a thing was almost to be expected in this neighbourhood. Wendy had nothing of interest to anybody, no cash or electronics, not even a TV. They would have come and left. She moved forward again down the concrete steps.

A current of air a degree or two warmer than it should have

been stopped her again halfway down the stairwell. It was body heat, she knew its character well. The perpetrator had been here, moments before, leaving her apartment.

Or entering. Another feeling washed over her and she placed the grocery bags on the dirt under the back porch. The poor soul might still be inside, rummaging, searching, getting increasingly desperate at finding nothing. He was probably a drug addict looking to prolong his agony; this place was an easy walk from Vancouver's drug central where the pain was palpable on the streets. The poor, misguided soul was probably frantic.

Her compassion filled her with a deep warmth. Whoever he was, he needed help. He needed it now. She rolled her shoulders to loosen them and went in fast.

It took ten seconds of swift motion through the place to determine she was alone. Her frustrated compassion degenerated into a slow burn. The thief had tossed her beautiful, perfect home, destroying the harmony. But he hadn't found anything important. A quick look into the bathroom confirmed that. He'd rifled the vanity cupboard under the sink, but her hiding place was undisturbed.

She went back to the living room to begin the cleanup and saw the three holes. The empty, sobbing places where three precious angels had been deliberately taken. Mr. Long. Mr. Lowe. Mrs. Shrop. Her wordless cry filled the small room.

Then she was at the bedroom closet, grabbing down suitcases and boxes and flinging them onto the bed. Ten minutes to pack, ten more to get all the dolls into boxes, folding and padding be damned. Say another ten to get a taxi to her door. Then she'd be gone. Her legs ached with the urge to get out of here. She had ignored the Third Rule for far too long.

When They Suspect, Move West. To where? She was halfway to the first suitcase with an armful of underwear.

She'd still made no preparations for an exit plan. There was no hospital farther west waiting for her acceptance letter. There was no farther west, except for islands.

Hot tears of frustration blurred the room and the stack of panties in her hands was trembling. She threw them onto the bed, distraught, at a loss. The Rules had kept her safe for so many years. Was this really the time to forsake them?

The nurse took over, solid and practical. Nonsense, girl, she chided herself, speak the truth now. You've made no plans because you've planned not to. You're in a beautiful place. You're at the ocean again, for the first time in dog's years. There are people here who need you. The truth has been plain to see for a good while. So face it. You aren't going anywhere.

The trembling stopped, the tears quit with a last snuffle. The evening's last sunshine was slanting in through the tiny window above her bed, lighting up dust motes in the air above the pile of underthings. Well then. A good nurse - hell, a good Maine girl - knew when the wind had shifted. She got up and started refolding them into their drawer. The movement helped settle her decision.

Jackson Teague was a problem. She finished with the underwear drawer and started putting suitcases back in the closet. The massage boy knew her name. He knew where she lived and had no compunctions about making himself at home. He was set on stopping her. And somehow he knew about her room magic.

Ease Their Suffering was the First Rule, plain as day. Don't Harm The Healthy was the Second Rule. The Third Rule - When They Suspect, Move West - had now been retired. The Rules governed her life. They had kept her safe. But, for the first time ever, Wendy realized they had an order.

And didn't that just nicely clear the path.

A deep, hot bud of sorrow kindled in her heart for the poor

boy. He either needed to stop or be stopped, and the state of Wendy's apartment said he wasn't the kind to give up. Still, it had taken a bit of courage to do what he had done, coming in here like that. Commendable, in its way.

She finished stacking the suitcases back onto her closet shelf. They would gather dust before the next time she ever used them.

Maybe he would try her apartment again. Courage, after all, was close friends with stubbornness. The chance was slight, but it wouldn't hurt to be prepared. Under the kitchen sink she found the perfect item for the occasion. A few minutes in the bedroom made it look right, then she went back to her tidying.

There was the other boy. Leaf, or Colin as the papers were calling him. He'd seen her and recognized her. There was no way to get close to him, tucked away in the hospital on the North Shore. She would have to trust that she'd smashed all memory of herself out of his head and leave it at that.

The groceries still sat on the floor of the living room. Teague had been in here, searched everywhere and left with three angels. She began stowing groceries in her kitchen. He hadn't found Wendy's tool kit, the only thing which could give her real grief. Jackson had blown his roll and come away empty.

Was he done now? Would he leave her alone? She'd give a lot to know the answer to that. It would be so much easier if she were sure that the boy was done with his witch hunt. After all, it was a big city. They didn't need to cross paths. They could work out an arrangement, if only she could be certain he'd stopped struggling against the inevitable.

There was a way to find out. It was risky in its own way, but less dangerous than tearing the boy to pieces in his own apartment. She would know for sure. She and Jackson Teague would be finished. That would leave only the question mark of Colin Palmerston, and nothing to be done about that.

Wendy picked up her phone to make the arrangements and it rang in her hand. Only the agency had this number. She answered the call and Emma Jacobs said, "Wendy? I might have a job for you, one more suited to your skill level. There's a young man who's recovering from a head trauma and his parents want him home. The doctor will only allow it if they arrange for skilled nursing help. The family is willing to pay a substantial increase on your usual salary. Can you give the doctor a call?"

Chapter 21

"I remember the Corbett affair quite well, thank you." A touch of grey in the voice, not too far away from retirement. Resonant as hell. Marilyn pictured an East Coast Clint Eastwood, out in his skiff on the weekends looking for the big fish. "One of my first cases as Assistant Chief, and quite a deal for this neck of the woods."

Marilyn had Google Earthed the placename as she was calling, and neck of the woods was right. Wendy Corbett had grown up in rural Maine, on a large peninsula of land that tongued out into the North Atlantic and was home to maybe a few hundred souls.

"What happened?"

"Well, the Corbetts were always stay at home types, you know. Mr. C fixed boats and Mrs. C helped people who asked for it. Nothing particular, mind you. Some people would say she was a witch."

"Like, she cast spells and such? Brewed potions?"

"No, nothing like that. Sometimes it was ordinary help, like at a birthing or illness. Sometimes people, women mostly, would go and tell her what they wanted, and she would smile, then awhile later things would work out for them. Magic, you know."

"Uh, no, I don't know."

"Neither do I, but that's what they said. So anyway, Mrs. C

got sick when Wendy was around 14 and stayed that way for almost a year. Wendy stayed home from school, kept up her studies but nursed her mom. Dad was no use in a circumstance like that. Wendy saw herself through the school year and taught herself a lot about nursing. Wanted to be like her mom, you know? Take care of everyone, be compassionate, do the right thing. I guess one day Wendy did the right thing, and Mrs. C was buried the next day."

"How do you know it was Wendy?"

"That's just it. Nobody knows, but they all do. That kind of place. The doctor sure couldn't say anything one way or the other. Looked like a regular death, but it was too early, he said. She still had some time left.

"Wendy and her dad went along for about a year, but her dad was crushed. Useless for work, stayed at home getting thin and ragged. A year after he was diagnosed with heart disease and Wendy cared for him, too."

"Cared for him?"

"That's what the folk around here called it. She cared for him right into his grave. A heart attack, they called it, on account of his broken heart. But everybody knew she was responsible."

"Oh." Marilyn paused, feeling like she was falling down a rabbit hole. "What can you tell me about the dolls?"

The Chief laughed. "Oh, the dolls. Mrs. C was into them. Collected them, made them, had them all over the house. Nice ones, too, none of your plastic crap. That was the scariest thing about this whole mess. When Wendy Corbett moved away to go to nursing school, all she took from the place was two dolls. The spitting images of her folks. Nobody could ever remember seeing them before, but she carried them with her when she left. Spooky, those things."

The Chief paused in his turn, then continued. "The

villagers burned the place to the ground. Nothing we could do to stop them."

"And nothing you could do to stop her?"

Another laugh, deep and resonant, totally without humour. "I think those nursing books taught little Wendy Corbett a thing or two they didn't intend to. There was nothing to pin on her. Courts don't give much credence to local opinion as conclusive evidence, sorry to say. I had to let her go. Good luck, constable. I hope you catch her at it, because that's the only way you'll catch her at all."

Chapter 22

Calls from the Hotel Vancouver rated priority status. Hotel guests wanted their massages now and usually tipped well for the service. When Jackson's cell phone buzzed him away from breakfast he told Carlo at the concierge desk that Room 1214 could expect him within the hour.

Hotel massage was a grab bag. Most people thought it was all glamour and easy work, giving basic rubs to beautiful people. Sometimes yes, and sometimes no. Jackson knew from experience that he could be called in for a relaxation rub and find an overweight, sixtyish multiple heart attack survivor looking for help with a pulled hamstring. Or he could find a statuesque blonde opening the door in her birthday suit who wanted a straightforward relaxation massage. Or anything in between.

As he swung into the parkade Jackson found himself praying for the blonde, or at least a simple session. His rib still hurt from Franklin's poke. Lynn Creek and Leaf flooded his thoughts every other minute. He felt slow and out of sorts. He'd taken another half pill this morning, but no flashes yet. At least that was a relief.

The moment 1214 opened her door Jackson dropped his hopes for the beautiful blonde. Before him, pushing a wide mouth into a sunny smile, was a walking refrigerator of a woman. Six feet at least, with a tower of brown hair that barely cleared the door, she swallowed his hand in hers and gave it a surprisingly gentle shake. "You'll be Jackson, then," she said in a low, strong alto, long on the vowels and thick on the r's. A pleasing blend of almost-Newfoundland and almost-New York accents. "Come in, set yourself up."

She had to step completely around the corner for Jackson to roll his table into the suite on its luggage carrier. He glanced around. Hotel Van standard, heavy draperies matching the thick upholstery on a sofa and two chairs, intricate woodwork on the delicate-looking but solid coffee table and writing desk. Through the connecting door he could see an untouched queen bed and huge mirror. No sign of suitcase or personalization or even mess. The lady must have just arrived.

He busied himself with setup while he went through his patter. "Hi, my name's Jackson, but you already know that. What can I do for you today?"

She laughed, warm and low. "My, but it's been a long time since anyone's asked me that. Usually it's the other way round. My name is Susan, Jackson, and you can help me out by giving me a good massage. Stress relief."

Jackson relaxed the tiniest bit as he pulled his table from the case and snapped it open, swinging the legs into position. It might be a simple massage after all. He had a second's hesitation about whether his portable table would hold her, but dismissed it as he smoothed the thick flannel sheets over top. He'd made sure to get the strongest massage table in the business for days like this. Preparations done, he turned to Susan again, who stood waiting.

"Okay, stress relief. I just have to run through a few questions first." He ran, and she answered, in her rich, soothing alto with that touch of accent and a tug of patient amusement on her lips. No significant medical history, nothing broken or replaced or medicated. He relaxed a bit more. "Last thing, Susan, I need to look at you. Give you the once-over, as it were."

"Gaze away, young man," she replied, still amused.

Jackson gazed. This was really a remarkable woman, he thought, his eyes checking off the landmarks. Six feet, easily 200 pounds. Steady, level brown eyes, small level ears, a face that was as big-boned as the rest of her, with more than a hint of masculinity. A straight jawline, but full, red, luscious lips. Marilyn Monroe lips, in a Robert Mitchum face. His eyes carried the assessment scan lower. Shoulders, hips, knees, all level. Right arm rotated in so her hand swung forward a little. She was right-handed, then. Tiny feet for such a big body. In profile, Jackson saw nothing too extraordinary, except for her sheer size. And strength. He could tell she was muscled like a power lifter.

Jackson blinked and tried to gaze harder, to put it all together. Nothing doing. The switch in his head was turned off.

"Okay. I'll step around here and let you get up." One minute in the bedroom, where he could see one small suitcase unopened on the far corner of the bed, and he heard his table creak. "Ready," she called.

Jackson liked to work his way up in a full-body session, feet to head. The skin on Susan's calves was taut and smooth. The muscles underneath felt hard as granite. The lady was wound up like a cheap clock, he realized. Funny that he hadn't seen that. So this massage would be work after all.

"You have a good touch," she said, her voice muffled through the facepiece. "I'm a little tense these days, be a dear and do what you can for it."

"I'll say," commented Jackson as he worked his thumbs into her gastrocs, trying to smooth them out. "Mind if I ask what has you so knotted up?"

The flannel over her back riffled up and down as she

laughed again. "No, I don't mind at all. Do me a piece of good to talk about it, probably. You see, I'm new in town, but I'm terribly afraid I may have to leave soon. I like it here, the ocean and all, and I really don't wish to."

Her hamstrings felt like a cedar plank. He added oil and brought out his elbow. "Hmm, that's too bad. Your job not working out?"

"Oh, no, that's not it. Not quite. My work is fine, they have no problem with me and I love what I do. No, there's someone who has decided not to like me. It is acutely painful, for them as well as me, I'm sure, and it might be just as well if I moved on. But you see, I don't want to. Thus the – ow! – the tension. Fine work, don't stop."

Light to deep to light. General to specific to general. Jackson ran the Massage 101 litany through his mind over and over again, remembering Franklin's rebuke and falling back on the basics. He sunk into the hamstrings, felt them let go, then smoothed out the leg and moved on. A quick feel through the sheet assured him that Susan had removed all her clothes. Not bashful, then. He flipped the sheet up over her right butt cheek and went to work on the gluts.

"Well, it's a big city," he said, letting his tongue carry on while he focused on the work at hand. "Plenty of room to live and let live."

Another chuckle. The table let out a small creak. "Why Jackson, that's a wonderful way to put it. How perceptive of you. If only it were that simple. You see, my work throws me into occasional contact with this other person, and I am so afraid they'll cause problems for me. So afraid."

Jackson could feel it. Now that she'd said it, the problem was clear. Her legs were full to the brim with the tension of impending flight. Susan wanted to run and was holding herself back by the smallest margin.

"This is really bothering you, isn't it? Much more than you let on to the world."

She rotated her head out of the facepiece. "You understand, then. I knew you would. Yes, it bothers me, as you say. I feel like I've finally come home again, and this one person's hatred might be enough to chase me away." She relaxed into the table again and sighed. "It's a burden."

There was silence for awhile as Jackson finished up and moved over to the other leg, which was the same. He was working up a bit of a sweat; this was like massaging a linebacker. When he'd finished with the legs, Jackson folded the sheet down over her back.

The first sweep of effleurage confirmed what he'd expected. The tension was centered in Susan's legs. Her back held only the usual knots and trouble spots, and underneath an amazing strength. He was certain it had never failed her.

"So, what is it you do, Susan?" he asked.

"I'm a nurse," she said.

He was using his elbows again, working through a mass of erectors that could lift a small car. "I imagine a one-person transfer is no problem for you," he said, trying not to grunt with the effort.

Another soft chuckle. "No, not very much. Which is a good thing, since I often work alone. I do home care." Jackson felt a ripple of tension pass under his fingers, a quick, almost electric shot, there and gone again.

"Do you like being a nurse?"

"Oh, heavens, yes, nursing is my life," she said, her voice slowing down and lapsing more into the heavy r's as the de-stressing started to work. "Has been since I was a girl, long before I actually went to school for it. My Mumma taught me to always care, you see. Have compassion for the pain and suffering of those around you. She showed me by example, helping whoever came to her. Whether it was a healing, or a wishing, or just a good listen-to, she'd figure out what they most needed and give it to them."

"She was a nurse, too?"

Susan laughed. "Lordy, no! My Mumma was a witch. Not the long black dress and the broomstick sort of thing. She was a plain, hardworking woman, but she knew how things worked. She saw things other people didn't see, like how you can work with the energies of things and such. That was how she helped. You know."

Did he? It was a silly idea, but he could feel it take root somewhere deep in his chest. He stayed silent, working and letting his patient talk.

"Well, my Mumma was sick for a time and I got my chance to care for her. I had to listen hard, but I learned a lot. It hurt, too, the caring that needed to be done, but after my Mumma passed on I knew I'd done well. That's what my father said, that I'd done well."

"Sounds like a hard time," Jackson said, his mind on his work. They were talking low now, his fingers drawing lines of redness up the skin of her neck as he smoothed out the complex web of muscles and fascia that held up her head. His face was close to her right ear, and they almost whispered to each other.

"Yes, it was hard, thank you for saying. Then my Dadda got sick, and I had to care for him, too."

"Oh. Did he pass away?"

"Yes, poor man. It was the heart for him."

She pivoted her head to glance back. Jackson stopped, momentarily unable to work on her neck. "You understand, don't you? That kind of suffering? You've seen it before in your line of work, I imagine?"

"Yes," he answered. "Some of my work is in people's houses,

and sometimes all you can do is give them a little peace or a quiet night's rest."

She slipped back into the headrest. "Exactly! You do know. You see the suffering that those poor patients are going through, and the families, and you want to help. You have to feel for them, or you aren't doing your job. You have to care for them."

Jackson paused half a beat in the rhythm of his massage, caught by something that didn't sound right. "Well, you do care for them. Nursing is helping."

He lifted the sheet up over his eyes and Susan turned over. The table did creak this time, loud and long, but it held. He started over on her legs.

"Yes. I help." Susan kept her eyes closed, letting him work. The room was silent for a time. Jackson kept his hands moving, working through the lady's impressive quads, but he was uneasy. Susan sighed. "I only wish he would leave me alone to do my work." There it was, that ripple of electric stress again.

"No way to avoid this person, eh?"

"Well, I hope so. It would solve everybody's problems if we stayed clear of each other. But I'm afraid he won't let this thing rest. He doesn't like the way that I care for my patients, how I take them away from their suffering. Thank you for asking, dear. You're such a doll."

He almost fell down. The shock was a high-voltage wave that started at the floor and came perilously close to blasting him right out of the suite. The only thing that stopped him was the sure and certain knowledge that Wendy Corbett would beat him to the door.

With a huge effort he forced his legs to relax from their wild urge to run and told his hands to keep on moving. The massage continued. It was the only thing he could do.

Caring for them. That was what she called it. It was so wrong, on so many different levels, his mind balked to think of it. She was a nurse, goddammit. Killing patients wasn't part of the deal.

"Maybe the other guy has a point," he heard his mouth say, and immediately pinked up. "What is it about your 'caring for people' that he doesn't like, exactly?"

His mouth was going to get him into trouble one of these days. Wendy – call her Susan, he reminded himself – kept her eyes closed and answered him. "I simply do what must be done, of course. What any good nurse would do. I remove the suffering. I help everyone move on." She sighed again and smiled. "I care for them."

"I see." Jackson's mind was whirling. He finished with the second leg and swung a chair around to the head of the table, dropped more oil onto his fingertips and reached for the nurse's neck. This was the most personal part of his routine, face to face. He wasn't sure he could do this, but his fingers slid under her shoulders and pulled back, lifting Wendy Corbett's head into his hands. It was huge, heavy and repulsively masculine. Jackson turned his own head to the side and let his hands do their thing.

"What I need to know is, what's this person going to do? I love Vancouver, but I have to know that he won't try and make waves. I have to know that we can both work here in peace." There was a note of real sincerity in her voice that surprised him. She meant it. She was calling for an amnesty, sort of. Live and let live. He could go on massaging, she would go on nursing. She would go on killing her patients. Some of them would inevitably be his clients.

More like live and let kill.

"I know it causes him no end of pain, poor dear. He's already tried to make trouble and had rather bad luck of it. I hate to see him suffer so."

A tremble actually made it through his fingertips and into Wendy's massage. He knew a threat when he heard one.

"You could stop what you're doing," he heard himself say. "Maybe he has a point. Maybe your version of caring isn't the right one." The tension in his own legs rose to cramping level. This lady could reach up and snap him like a twig.

She sighed once more. "It's what I do." Simple, straight-forward. Absolute.

He was stuck. The nurse was waiting for an answer. This was why she had engineered this whole thing, to plead with him to let it go. Or else. There it was, and he had to do something with it.

He finished with the right side and carefully switched hands, rolling her huge head over. He could keep on rolling it. One hand on top, one hand on bottom, a quick pull against ligament and bone too fast for relaxed muscles to react, and it would be done. Untold numbers of future patients would be saved. She'd already as much as threatened him with the same treatment.

His hands completed the turn. He wasn't that kind of person. Jackson Teague did not take life. And he would not, could not, sanction anyone else doing it.

"It sounds to me like you and this other person are at an impasse," he said at last. "He can't allow what you're doing, and you think what you're doing is right. Doesn't sound like either of you is likely to change." He let the tips of his fingers sink into the nurse's subocciputals, giving her neck the tiniest bit of traction in his finishing move of the routine. He let her head back down onto the table and the massage was done. Wendy – Susan – sighed once more, and so did he, as he stepped into the bedroom to let her get dressed.

"Ready." She was all the way across the room, easily visible from the bedroom door. She didn't want him to worry about any sudden moves. She was caring for him.

Jackson packed up as fast as he could without seeming to hurry. "That was a wonderful massage, Jackson. I must say, you are quite professional. You are to be commended." She handed him his fee, but without a smile. In fact, she looked as tense as Jackson felt. He took it without a word.

She extended her other hand, and another $100 bill. "Here's a small appreciation for your good work. You earned it, I know how hard this massage was. Buy yourself a treat." Jackson took the tip. Not to do so would be too awkward.

"Thanks, Susan," he said. "If I was to offer any advice, it would be to stop caring so much."

Nurse Wendy Corbett had the last word as the door closed. "Buy that treat soon," she called.

The $100 tip went down a mail chute on his way out of the Hotel Van. The travel case of new pills followed. He hadn't seen anything wrong during that whole massage, in fact it had taken practically a death threat to clue him in. Taking half a pill was no good. He needed to be able to see things. As much as he hated to admit it to himself, he needed some of his condition back.

Three more hours, then he was back on the old meds. There was a week's supply still in the medicine cabinet, more than enough to get him back to Parma's office.

A flash washed through him as he maneuvered his Subaru through the growing tangle of protestors filling up the sidewalks on their way to the waterfront. It was full-force, and in an instant he was immersed in the flow of people and traffic on the busy downtown streets. It was a moment of dangerous joy, but this time along with the awe came a deep bass-note rush of anger. How dare she pull a stunt like that.

One golden and scarlet moment, then the flash was gone. The fury, however, stayed with him.

Three hours to get back home. Plenty of time for a side trip. Jackson pulled up to the next intersection and spun the wheel for Chinatown.

The thick hotel door snicked shut and Wendy sank into the closest chair, shivering with pent-up fear. That had been horrible. Absolutely the very worst idea ever. To lay herself bare before him, body and soul, with no idea what he would do. She'd never experienced that level of terror before.

For what? Did she really expect she could talk sense into the boy? She'd tried. As hard as it was she had put the question. Which was also, by its nature, a fair warning. She could at least be proud of that. Now, for better or worse, she had her answer. The massage therapist would have no truce.

She willed herself into a deep, slow breath. The shaking eased. Which was good, for she had prepared for this and now speed was all-important. The replacement pills were in her purse. Teague's apartment was a short bus ride away. She only had a couple of hours before she was expected at the Palmerstons' to begin her new assignment. She was prepared for that, too. It was going to be a busy day, but at the end of it, if she was careful, she would be free.

His hands had been all over her. Wendy stormed for the

bathroom, dropping clothes as she went. A shower had to come first.

Chapter 23

Jackson drove straight east down Georgia Street, catching the lights until he was across the Viaduct into Chinatown. He kept his pressure on the gas pedal light, though he wanted to be at the nurse's place, tear it apart, find what he knew was there, run it down to the police station and get the lady locked up right now. He watched for cross traffic, kept his patience with the growing streams of protestors and held his anger in check all the way to the little playground.

Three preschool boys were whacking the slide and making roadbuilding noises in the sandbox on top of the rise. Smile and wave, he told himself, and tossed them a passable grimace while giving the entire hill a wide berth. They waved and went back to their playing as Jackson strode into Wendy's back yard.

He didn't look at the main floor windows. Either the family upstairs was home or not. He figured the door into the basement suite wouldn't be fixed yet and by the time any police arrived he would have something.

Anything. Real evidence had to be here. Maybe he would get another flash and his condition would reveal what he'd missed before. With the weirdest sense that the day was getting completely upside-down, he realized he was counting on it. The door was still broken. With a twist of the doorknob he was inside the tiny kitchen.

Flash. The room was trying to shove him back out the door

again, draining any confidence that this wild half-plan would work. The chill almost-wind seemed to blow past his shirt and push directly on his heart. Get over it, he gritted, and forced himself to sweep the room. The apartment was still tilted and subtly strange, from the stove to the drapes. But no, his condition was telling him. What he wanted wasn't in here.

The flash was gone. They were coming faster now. He stepped into the living room and waited.

The dolls stared back at him. The three empty spots were still there, like missing teeth. No breath of sound came in from outside and even the dust motes in the air hung perfectly still. Jackson braced himself.

It was like somebody pushed him through a paper wall into the universe next door. The room came alive. Hundreds of doll eyes glinted at him as if he were shining a flashlight into a darkened, overcrowded kennel. He'd braced himself for a nightmare, but it wasn't like that at all. The dolls looked at him, sure. The room itself was as painfully out of kilter as the kitchen, but the dolls themselves exhaled peace. We will wait, said their eyes. You have work to do here. We have time.

He shook it off. Okay, so the sight of the dolls wasn't going to frighten him to death. He still needed to act fast. A sweep of the living room told him what he wanted wasn't here, either. The flash was still upon him. Hoping to get two for one, Jackson hurried to the bedroom.

There! Two steps into the bedroom the flash dropped away, but he'd seen it. Four suitcases lined the open closet shelf, all of them askew from their neighbours except the last one on the right, which was straight against the wall and pulled out a bit. Hiding something.

One yank brought the suitcase to the floor with a thump. The shelf was a little over Jackson's head but within easy reach. He stuck his hand all the way back to grab the evidence.

He heard the awful snap and the accompanying dry crunch and a full-body reflex threw him back onto the bed before the pain arrived. Jackson knew it was coming. He mashed his face into the bedspread and when the red tsunami of agony arced over from his right hand he let himself scream. Not that there was any kind of choice. The screams were torn from him again and again, the tears leaking out from his face, and the pain almost made him retch into the sheets it was so intense. His rib's complaint at the mistreatment barely registered.

When he got his breath back, Jackson knew he had to look. His right hand was just over there, to the right. Turn, he told his head, and it slowly complied.

The board was thick hardwood. The brass coils of the spring were massive and gleaming, brand new. The long, square business edge of the rat trap was sunk out of sight into the meat of his middle and ring fingers. There was no blood, his skin had held, but the dent went all the way to the board.

It had to be done. Before he could think about it he reached over with his left hand and lifted the thick wire out of his two fingers. He thought he heard a squishing sound, and then he stopped thinking as another wave of unbelievable pain tumbled him back into the pillow for more screaming. Move, was the only command he could give. He let his body do the rest.

He was in his car, with a brief memory of some spooked kids on a playground. He was driving, using his left hand, leaving Chinatown behind. He was going back over the Georgia Street Viaduct, back downtown. Only three blocks away from his destination, as the pain finally ebbed to a Thor-hammer throb, did he realize he was headed for the Saint Paul's Hospital emergency room.

Wendy tossed a sweet thank-you to the young woman who held the apartment building's front door open as she came rushing up the steps. Down the hallway Teague had repaired his door, but one shove from her shoulder and she was inside again.

She knew where to go. The bathroom medicine cabinet held two pill bottles, which was a surprise but not a roadblock. The older one, his traditional meds, she was familiar with. She examined his new pills, worried they might be some strange and exotic shape. Not a problem - they were plain, pink circles imprinted on one side with a star. The star didn't matter; nobody looked at their pills.

She took a flat plastic pill manager out of her bag, five small compartments for each day of the week, 35 little plastic squares in all. This was Wendy's one item that would get her instantly jailed, obtained several years before from a kindred-spirit pharmacist in Detroit. Each square contained pills of a different size, shape and colour, a kaleidoscope of familiar-looking medications. Each pill held a twice-lethal dose of carfentanyl. Wendy had used these pills a few times in the past and they worked splendidly.

Teague's drugstore did things the old-fashioned way. Both pill bottles were padded with a fluffy cotton ball. Wendy pulled the puff of white out of the new bottle, then teased a wisp of it off the main ball and placed it over the pills in the bottom of the container. Then she took a small pair of tweezers, plucked a round, pink pill from her collection and dropped it in the center of the nearly-invisible barrier. The rest of the cotton ball went on top of the one pill.

She doctored the old meds the same way. Then she placed them both back on the shelf. She stepped back to survey the work and called it a job well done. The massage therapist was dead. The rush of heat bloomed inside her as she'd come to expect, but the strength of it watered her knees and caught her breath. Her hands found the sink for support and she told herself to look at the pill bottles again. There they sat on the little glass shelf, Door Number One and Door Number Two, waiting to ensure whatever choice Jackson Teague made was his last.

They were a violation of the Second Rule, so she could continue to serve the First. "Just this once," she said to the mirror. "For the greater good."

The next business, in contrast, would be a mercy. Wendy walked out the front door and down to the bus stop. The trip over the Lions Gate Bridge to West Vancouver was a long one and she had an appointment to keep.

Ahmed was on a call when Marilyn stepped into his cubicle with a file folder that now bulged with notes. He waved her into a seat and finished up. "I'm sure your neighbour won't chop down any more of your trees, but really, it's a city bylaw concern. You need to talk to them." He passed on the city's number and hung up. "There, another one off the list. Looks like you've been busy. What's up?"

Marilyn took a deep breath and dove in. "Jackson Teague might not be crazy. One nurse was present or nearby for all his patient deaths, a Wendy Corbett. I've tracked Corbett's work history from her present employer, a home care agency on the West Side, back through most of the northern States and about 18 years, all the way to her home state of Maine. On the advice of an old coworker I also talked to the chief of police in her hometown. Everybody I talked to – everybody – either has ambiguous things to say about this woman or was asking me if

I'd caught her yet. Ahmed, Corbett is one hell of a nurse. She can work anywhere, help out on any ward, has excellent bedside manner, the whole package. And death follows her wherever she goes. It's never her fault. The death is either expected but early, or unexpected but just one of those things that happens."

Ahmed absorbed it. "The police chief?"

Mathers flipped to the page in her notes. "Wendy Corbett's mother was some kind of village witch. Wendy was forced to leave school when her mother got sick, till Mom passed away a little early. That toasted her dad's health, and she had to take care of him a year later. No proof of anything, but it was too much for the townspeople. They burned her out and she left town with a small suitcase and two dolls, the spitting images of her folks. She's been working as a nurse ever since. All across the continent, always moving on when the suspicion grows. This is her latest stop." Marilyn pulled out her map and showed him.

Ahmed whistled. "Not bad, constable, not bad at all. Pretty damn scary, actually. You know what about all this scares me the most?"

"What?"

"Two things. First, we have twenty years' worth of suspicion and still not a shred of proof. Second," he traced the line from east to west across the map, "it looks like she's out of places to run to. You want a serious fight on your hands, try cornering a wild animal."

"So what's our next step?"

Ahmed stood up. "Our next step is to find proof. Anything so we can get this lady off the streets. Her place, now."

"Don't we need a warrant?" Marilyn was reaching for her coat.

Ahmed shrugged. "Let's look around first. Never know what we'll find."

In between patients Charles liked to swing by the triage desk and scan the waiting room to get an idea of how the day was going. He spotted Jackson at once, scrunched into a corner chair with an ice pack on his hand and a face the colour of overwatered dough.

There were twelve bums in seats, mirroring the eleven charts on the desk and the one Rina was handing him. "Asian female. Scratchy, watery eye, red like the blazes. She can't stop rubbing it. Code 4."

He saw the chart that said Teague on it, close to the end of the line. "What about that one?" he asked, pointing to the corner where Jackson was trying not to be noticed.

Rina, ten years Charles' senior and undisputed queen of the triage nurses, looked up over her desk through the glass. "Broken fingers, just came in. I haven't had time to enter him in the system and pull up his details. Code 5, a simple splint job. He can wait a bit."

Charles put the pink-eye down and fished Jackson's chart out of the lineup. "No he can't, he's in shock. I'll take him." Without waiting for Rina's outrage to find her voice he stepped into the waiting room, pointed a finger directly at Jackson, and said, "You. Come with me." He meant for it to be loud and clear, heard across the noisy room. Maybe it came out with a bit of an edge. Jackson jumped like he'd been slapped, then hustled towards him. People are jittery and sensitive in shock, he berated himself. Take it easy.

There was going to be hell to pay for this. A massage therapist comes in with broken fingers, Charles has an RMT friend. Charles grabs the right chart like he knows the patient's name. Somebody would make the connection, and no one jumped the line at St. Paul's ER.

Hell, Charles thought as he bustled Jackson down the hall, Georgia's look of disappointment still fresh in his mind. Damn the torpedos.

"Hey, guy," he said, as Jackson eased into a sitting position on the bed and he scritched the curtains closed. He began running Jackson's vitals, leaving the ice pack for later. "What's up?"

He expected to hear the one about the car door, or maybe the filing cabinet. Loan shark was unlikely, but not totally out of the question.

"She did it. She did all of it. Those patients. She threw the rock at Leaf. She did this." Jackson's words were lucid but quiet, spoken a little above a murmur. He lifted the ice pack a fraction of an inch off his lap, grimacing as he did so, then let it flop back down.

Oh man. Charles slipped the blood pressure cuff over Jackson's good arm and took a good, long look at his eyes. Jackson was pasty, a fine sheen of sweat standing out on his face, dishevelled, hunched over his broken hand. Definitely in shock. His eyes looked a bit strained, which was to be expected, but clear.

"On your meds?"

Jackson nodded.

"The new ones, or the old ones?"

"The new ones. I'm clear as a bell, Charles. Listen." Charles wheeled over a stool and listened as he gently unwrapped the hand from the ice pack.

"I got to thinking, and I went back to Lynn Creek and looked. I found the place where the rock came from. I saw finger marks where it had been pulled out of the ground. There were footprints in the mud."

"Come on," said Charles, "hundreds of people use that trail. People like to throw rocks all the time."

Jackson stared at him. "Leaf looked up and saw her. 'You're her,' he said, but not in a friendly way. He knew, Charles. Then she chucked that rock and he pushed me. He was right where I was. Get it? That rock was meant for me."

Jackson's middle two fingers were snapped clean in half and swollen up like Vienna sausages. An angry red welt was laid across the top of both proximal phalanges. No examination was necessary, just an x-ray. Which was good, because Charles' head was spinning.

"You'll never guess what she did next. You'll never guess what I was doing this morning."

"So I won't bother. What were you doing this morning?"

"I was working."

"Good. I know things have been a little slow for – What?"

"It was at the Hotel Van. She had it all planned out, Charles. She said it all, without saying anything, you know? She wanted to call a truce. More like a surrender, actually. I lay off, she goes on killing people, we leave each other alone."

Charles checked Jackson's eyes again. As near as he could tell, both professionally and personally, Jackson was telling it straight. There was no lie in his face. Holy man.

"She said this. She said all this."

"Yes." Jackson recounted some of the conversation, and it sounded totally damning without being actionable in any way. Unless he was dreaming the whole thing.

"I went back to her place."

"You went back there? After the police - tell me you didn't go inside."

Jackson shook his head. "No time for the full story. You should see her place, Charles. Remember the dolls I kept talking about? She has hundreds of them. Think of it. A doll for a life. Hundreds. Think of that."

Charles found that he didn't want to. What he wanted to do was reach for the nasal cannula hanging on the wall and give himself a shot of oxygen. What the hell had Jackson done? What if he was actually right? He pointed to the one indisputable fact in this whole mess. "And this?"

Jackson grimaced. "She was expecting me. She left me a present."

"Rat trap?"

"Yep. Placed where my – condition – would lead me right to it."

"Okay. Okay." Deep breath. Charles was an ER doctor, he lived and breathed rapidly evolving situations. He ran through the list of things known and unknown, lined up what he had and what was needed. "Please tell me you found something else."

Jackson shook his head. "I know what you're saying, and no actual proof of anything. It has to be there, but I didn't find it." His voice cracked on the last word. The emotional blanket provided by the shock was shredding, allowing the stress to show. His friend had been through a lot.

"Jackson? You going to hold this together?"

"Can't hold much right now, but I'll try." He managed a weak grin.

"This is pretty big, man. But first things first. You're out of commission on this one, as of now. Got it? We'll fix up that hand, then we'll tell the police what we know. If it convinces me, then it has to make an impression on them. Let them find the proof. Okay?" Jackson nodded.

"Good. I have to go arrange an x-ray for your fingers. It'll only take a minute. You stay put and keep it together." Another nod.

"And Jackson?" Charles paused at the curtain. "I'm really,

really sorry for not believing you the first time." He felt himself blush. From the bed, Jackson waved him off with his good hand.

He left the room and headed for the computer terminal at the nursing station to book Radiology for the x-ray. By the time Jackson went down the hall and around the corner they would have his entire computerized record. No mixups, no concerns. It actually worked pretty well.

He did the password thing to get into patient records, then entered Jackson's patient ID to update his file. He would be doing some of Rina's admitting work since he'd scooped the file before she could enter him into the system. The front page of Jackson's record flashed up with his vital statistics. Then a big, red box flashed over top of it and kept flashing. 'Psychotic Break · Danger to Self and Others · Apprehend and Admit' bleeped on and off, obscuring the rest of the file underneath, impossible to ignore.

Charles' heart fell into his Nikes. Jackson had sounded sincere. Charles had believed him, listened as his friend and not his doctor. Which was another ethical breach to add to Charles' mistakes for the day.

'Psychotic Break · Danger to Self and Others · Apprehend and Admit.' The same message would be flashing at the security station on the second floor. Charles didn't need to do anything except point them in the right direction when they got here. Three, four minutes, tops. Then it was the police, then the secure floor. Maybe for a long time.

What about the crushed fingers? He might never hear the truth about how that had happened. He hadn't asked enough questions, he'd taken Jackson's story on faith. He knew better. Healthy skepticism was an unofficial but essential tool in an ER doc's toolbox. It might as well be inscribed on the wall · Don't Trust Anything.

Don't trust anything. The message was still flashing. Charles tried a couple of keys and nothing happened. He tried some escape commands, tricks the computer guy had taught them to get out of problems with the new system. The second one worked. The message went away and Jackson's chart was there for him to see.

Charles went straight to Recent History. There was his appointment with Dr. Parma and his enrolment in the clinical study. His time in the Lion's Gate ER after the creek accident hadn't been logged because the team had had their hands full with Leaf. There were no other entries since, and only visits to Dr. Parma for the two years before. Charles scrolled through the notes again. Nothing unusual at all.

It was a false warning. Charles felt the hairs on his neck prickle, felt his face heat up with shame for the second time in ten minutes. The nurse had somehow gotten into the system and figured out how to set another trap.

It was all real.

"Check here. I'll go to Emerg." Charles heard the voices at the same time as the footsteps, hurrying down the hall. Security was fast today. He had to be fast, too.

He wiped the screen, backed out of the system and left the workstation. A black uniform came around the corner. It was Harmon, linebacker-huge and always ready to wrestle with the tough cases, holding his radio in one hand. "Hey, Dr. Green, know anything about a patient alert?"

"Nope, nothing here," he called back over his shoulder as he headed for Jackson's curtain. "Try the waiting room." Harmon muttered his thanks and left, speaking into his radio.

That would deter Security for a minute or two. Charles paused at a closet and again at a trauma cart. Then he slipped through the curtains and saw Jackson still seated, ice pack back on his hand.

"The nurse left you a Christmas present," Charles explained, "a detain order in the system. Security is after you. You have to get out of here until I can straighten this out." He threw Jackson a white lab coat. "Put this on."

Without a word Jackson did as he was told. He'd whitened again at the news, then a deep red flush hit his entire face at once, turning him the same colour as his hair. Good, thought Charles, that new adrenalin rush would help counter the last of the shock. "Here." He shoved his cart items, plus a few other things, into a plastic garbage bag. "Splints, tape, some pain meds. Best I can do right now. Ready? Let's go."

The two doctors left the exam room at a fast stroll, Jackson carrying the bag in his good hand and tucking the other out of sight. The front entrance was out of the question; Rina was probably relaying Jackson's description to Harmon right now. Charles led the way to the MD parking lot door.

They passed through Radiology, Nuclear Medicine and Ophthalmology on the way to the back of the building. The building had seen the alert. Charles saw nurses and doctors adjusting their laminated plastic ID cards, part of the security protocol that prevented exactly what Charles and Jackson were doing now. Charles stayed right in front of Jackson, blocking his empty lab coat from view, and stepped around the last corner to the back door.

Another guard was stationed there, a young one Charles didn't recognize. He snapped to readiness as he saw the two approaching and said, "Sorry, we have a situation, nobody's – "

"Only a second, Trevor forgot his badge in his car. That can cause no end of trouble for you guys in a thing like this, so it's best if we just go get it. I came along to let you know it's okay."

The guard – Gull, his nameplate said – was probably on his first alert. "I'm sorry, sirs, but I'm not allowed to – "

Charles waved a hand. "Yes you are. One quick minute, out

and in, and he'll have his ID. Otherwise he'll be bothered every time he turns a corner and we have more important things to do. We're expected in surgery in ten minutes, a woman is having her uterus out." When all else fails, mention the OR. And gynecology.

It worked. Gull turned a bit green and his uncertainty deepened. "But, sirs, I – "

"Thanks, one minute." Charles nudged past the boy and shouldered open the door. Jackson gave the guard the briefest of nods and they made it outside.

The doctor's parking lot had more space for bicycles than cars and opened through a screen of trees onto Thurlow Street. Charles walked Jackson out to the sidewalk.

"Where's your car?"

"One block over."

"Good, go to it. Don't go home, they have your address." He held out an arm and Jackson draped the doctor's smock over it.

"Thanks, Charles. You're going to get in deep shit for this, you know." Jackson's tone was grateful, but his eyes glittered with hard anger.

Charles grinned. "What are friends for? I'm going back to try and explain it all. You hole up somewhere and patch up those fingers. Keep your cell phone close. When I have things cooled down I'll call. Got it?"

"Yeah. Got it. Lay low, cool off." He wasn't looking at Charles. He was staring straight ahead, at something he wanted to strangle.

Charles laid a hand on Jackson's shoulder and spun him around. "Hey, I mean it. You've done enough. You're hurt, call it a day. I'll get the police on this and they can take it from here. This fake alert clinches it. I promise. Got it?"

The glower persisted for a moment, then seemed to go out. "Really? They'll believe you? There's enough to prove it?"

Charles wrapped him in a hug. He could feel weeks of tension leak out of his friend at last. "Find some place to lie down, man. Yes, I believe you. I'm sorry it took so long. This nurse is a stone cold killer and I want you to drop it now. Don't go anywhere near her. Let the cops do their thing. You get some rest. I'll take it from here."

Jackson's shoulders softened, a good sign. "Okay. Okay. I can do that."

"Good. Now I have to go face some music. Keep away from home and keep your cell phone close." He watched Jackson cross the street. Then he turned back to the hospital and stood up straight. At least he had a good story to tell. He shivered. It was a real spine-tingler.

Chapter 24

Louise Palmerston looked pathetic, hovering over the still form of her son and wringing her hands. "Really, you two look worn to a thread," Wendy was saying in her bereaved-family voice. "Your son is just going to sleep the night away. Go on out, for heaven's sakes. Take some time for yourselves."

The father was all for it. "Colin's in good hands, Louise. I watched the doctor grill this lady, she knows her stuff. She'll watch over him better than we ever could. It'll be okay. An early dinner at Chez Michel. What do you say?"

"Call him Leaf," she murmured. "He looks so pale. I hate that bandage. Are you sure this is okay?"

Ever so gently Wendy laid an arm around the skinny woman's shoulders. "Mrs. Palmerston, in the coming days your son is going to need you strong, rested, and ready. But for tonight he's only going to sleep. Trust me, take this opportunity to recharge. Get yourself some food." She gave the tiniest warm squeeze, careful not to let any of her own tension into the embrace, and felt the woman relax. This was so vital, to get the parents out of the house.

"Three hours," she breathed, gazing down at her boy. "I suppose we can leave him for three hours."

Wendy squeezed again. "Good girl. That will be plenty of time."

Twenty minutes later they were finally gone. Wendy had

checked her patient twice in that time, scrupulously following the doctor's instructions. She was a professional, after all. She walked up to the bedside again for the next round. The boy's pulse was slow but fine. "Open your eyes," she said, putting some volume into it. Nothing. She brushed an eyelid with her finger and Leaf's eyes flickered briefly open, then closed. She moved her finger and firmly pushed down on his eyebrow. He groaned and lifted one arm to try and stop her, but with no real effect. About a nine on the Glasgow coma scale, she figured, and noted it in his chart. Her rock had done some serious damage. He would suffer the effects of it for a very long time.

She went to her assigned bedroom and took the angel out of her overnight bag. It would be a startling addition to her collection, but the moment she had seen the clay figurine of the skinny, naked man standing on a surfboard with an outsize grin and shaggy hair flying out behind him, she knew she had the right piece. Even though she'd only seen the boy for a minute, in a hooded wetsuit at the bottom of a cliff, she'd been left with the image of a wild-haired nature lover. How lovely it had been to see the photographs around his bedroom verifying her intuition. The doll was perfect.

She escorted Leaf's angel into the sick room, placed it on the bedside table next to his head and stood back. A wave of sympathy rolled over her at the boy's suffering, and the greater suffering to come. He would never surf again. A depressed skull fracture erased some things, scrambled others. Leaf wouldn't want that. He needed some mercy.

The nitro glycerine spray was in her bag in the other room. It was a potent, immediate vasodilator, untraceable once the spray soaked in under the tongue, that opened up blood vessels to their widest extent. One good shot would drop the boy's blood pressure like a stone, re-rupture every damaged blood vessel in his head, and accomplish Wendy's aim without a fuss.

Leaf's injury would simply kill him, nothing anybody could have done.

She was alone in the cavernous house. The time was perfect. She went to get the spray.

Syren gripped the wheel like it was a life ring from the Titanic as her ancient Buick bucked through the turn onto the Upper Levels Highway and rocketed towards Horseshoe Bay. Her cell phone bounced around on the vinyl of the passenger seat, still displaying the last text. Joe, her Joe, had gotten hurt like she knew he would and was calling for his mother. He was in the hospital now, in Nanaimo. He was across a vast expanse of open water. He needed her.

The Horseshoe Bay ferry terminal was a few short miles away. She wouldn't think about it. A quick shot down the big hill in time for the 4:30 sailing, glide right onto the big, solid, unsinkable ferry and stay in her car while all the crazies went topside to stare at the killer waves. There would be no rocking, no horrible disconnection from solid land, no dreadful realization that the vehicle deck was probably at or even below the waterline where even a pinhole leak would send a million tons of watery death over her in a second and she'd be left sinking down where the crabs and the jellyfish –

Stop it. She gritted her teeth and grabbed the wheel harder. Dr. Parma gave you the pills, you took them, he told you to think happy thoughts, to focus on Joe, now do it. Happy, she thought. Sunshine and sparkles, she thought. Joe, dying in a hospital bed. Sunshine, sparkling off killer waves, daring her to cross. Joe. Dear Joe, she thought. No matter what, I'm coming. Nothing will stop me.

She pressed the accelerator to the floormat and the big Buick shot like a cannonball towards the terminal.

Jackson breathed a sigh of relief as he settled behind the wheel of his Subaru and tossed the bag of splints onto the passenger seat. It was awkward turning the key with his left hand, but he made the effort, telling himself he couldn't rest, not quite yet. He had to get home. Police or no, men in white coats or no. The final half-pill was wearing off and home was where his old meds were.

Flash. Thurlow Street came to life outside his windshield. He was parked in line with the one-way traffic and the next car that passed him, a blue smart car, drew a nearly-visible line through the air that both traced where it had been and hinted at where it would go. He could see the driver's intention to turn left at the next intersection and watched as the car signalled and changed lanes. A bicycle flew past just outboard of his sideview mirror, spokes glinting as the cyclist flowed like water between the cars. Jackson wanted to jump out and run after him. God, the pull was strong.

He picked his right hand up off his lap and firmly placed it down on the dash. The pain was dull and thick now, but there was still plenty of it. He let himself shout out the throbs in the privacy of his own car and the flash was gone.

He had to get home, right now.

No police cars prowled within a block of his apartment building. It made sense - they probably had better things to do than corral one injured massage therapist with a screw loose, what with the entire waterfront jammed with protesters to shout at the Northern Sea Otter.

He grabbed the bag of splints and bandages and went inside. He was through the open door of his apartment and almost to the living room before it registered that he'd walked in through an open door. He whipped around and looked. Sure enough, the jamb was in splinters. Again.

"Don't look at me, it was like that when I got here." He spun around again, completing the circle, and there was Borden standing in the middle of his living room, hands held wide. "Your building security sucks, by the way." He was holding a crumpled strip of duct tape in one hand.

"Borden? What? How the hell - " Cognitive dissonance, said a textbook in his head as the day took another jump on the weirdness meter and he found himself leaning against the wall for balance. Focus on the facts, it said, that will help. He scanned Borden up and down. The guy was scraped, gaunt, and looked half-scorched. His right arm was tucked up in a sling. He looked like shit.

"You look like shit," Borden commented. "That hand needs some ice, probably a doctor. Look, I really need your help again. You know, with that thing you do. Sorry about barging in like this, but I'm in a bit of a time crunch."

"What?" Jackson shook his head, unable to take it all in. Focus, he told himself. First things first. He turned towards the bathroom. "I can't man, I - "

"Like I said, bit of a time crunch." An unexpected steel in Borden's tone made Jackson stop and turn back to the living room. Borden was holding a gun in his good hand. A fucking pistol, exactly like in the movies, black and solid. "And your assistance is mission critical. Now." He waved the thing, and like a magnet it brought Jackson back into the living room. "A ten pound weight, bullet-shaped, launched through a three foot tube. The target is 500 feet away. How much powder do I use and what's the launch angle?" He gestured again, at a pad of paper and a pen sitting on the kitchen pass-through.

This wasn't happening. But one look at Borden's eyes told Jackson otherwise. Before, on the beach, Borden had been edgy but affable. Now he was all edge. A sheen of sweat glittered on his forehead. Then a flash took Jackson full-force, electrifying the room. This time it was all about the gun, the solid red line lasering from the tip of its barrel to Jackson's chest. Its unwavering intent was so apparent to his eye he almost clapped a hand over his heart. He moved back to Borden's face and saw the truth. This wouldn't be the first time the man had pulled a trigger.

"You know that's not how I work. I don't do numbers and graphs. I work by feel. Sorry."

Borden considered for a moment, then stepped to one side. "So you do," he said, and waved the gun towards a backpack on the sofa. "In there."

The thing was heavy; ten pounds, for sure. Jackson reached in and pulled out a grey, snub-nosed cylinder about the size of a large, plastic coke bottle, with three shiny metal ribbons trailing out behind it. Hardened thermite, with magnesium igniters. "Holy fucking hell, man," he said, cradling the thing in his good arm, "what are you going to do, melt a bridge?"

"No, that didn't work out. Now you have it. Do your thing. Tell me what I need to know. Time's ticking." Borden shifted his weight from one foot to the other, obviously impatient.

He was going to use this thing. Jackson wanted no part of it. But he needed to tell Borden something. He knelt down and mimed aiming the projectile to make it look good. "The launcher is a tight fit?"

"Tight as a virgin, get on with it."

The flash was still with him. Despite himself he saw the

trajectory. The thermite was smooth, held together with some kind of plastic. To lob this thing 500 feet ... He jumped up and stepped into the kitchen, a quick move that startled Borden but didn't get him shot. A second later he was back with a bag of sugar and a bowl. It would be an insane amount of powder compared to the few grams he was used to, but ... he poured some into the bowl, then a little more. Then some more. Like a neon rainbow, he saw the projectile's arc head out the window, over the grass across the street and squarely onto the first of the beach sand. "There. This much powder, this angle." The arc blinked out and the flash was done.

"Very good. Put it back in the pack." Borden scooped up the bowlful of sugar. The gun was gone. He threw the pack's strap over his shoulder and headed for the door. "You're going to be famous, kid. And really, the door was like this when I got here." Then Jackson was alone, holding an empty sugar bag and remembering to breathe.

The door. "What now?" he grumbled. No doubt the nurse had set some kind of life-and-death trap for him, but he just couldn't drum up any more dread. First things first. He headed for the bathroom.

The two pill bottles sat in his medicine cabinet, right where he'd left them. The old meds he hadn't touched in a week were pushed into an unused corner of the second glass shelf. The new meds occupied the front and center position on the bottom.

Parma's clinical trial had been worth a shot. Maybe it was helping plenty of people. Not him, though. He fished the old meds off the second shelf and popped the top. One flip of cotton, one shake, and the pill was in his hand. He tossed it in a lazy arc and opened wide to catch it.

Flash. This one was the strongest yet, blazing in its intensity and totally euphoric in its rush as the last of the half-pill left his system. The tiled backsplash behind the sink flowed its lines into the reeded wallpaper above. There was a subtle cross-hatching in the linoleum floor he hadn't even noticed in years. A drop of water hung in a sweet ache of suspended animation from the bathtub faucet and the blades of his razor glinted from the toothbrush cup. Even the old dust on the glass shelves of his medicine cabinet sparkled in the sudden light. And his lips clamped shut, the flying pill bouncing off them and clattering to the sink.

A brilliant, green line shot at him through the dust on the second shelf where the old pill bottle had been dragged through it. Alive in his mind was the vision of no dust on the cap and only one pill falling out of the shaken bottle.

The episode was gone. He examined the bottle and found the cotton trap. He used his toothbrush to flip over the pill in the sink and saw how it was slightly different than the others. He tweezed the top off the new meds with his fingertips and saw the same trap there.

He had the night nurse dead to rights.

Was she smart enough to use gloves or were her prints all over the bottles? It didn't matter. The sudden appearance of a deadly poison – he had no doubt about that – in his medicine cabinet, along with everything else, was solid evidence. It was finally enough for Jackson to dig out Constable Mathers' business card. They would take fingerprints. They would analyze the pills. They would find Wendy Corbett and arrest her and that would be that. Maybe she'd go berserk when she was caught, try to kill them all. Maybe she would break down and confess; he'd like to see that. But one thing was for sure – the killer nurse was enjoying her last day of freedom.

His cell phone rang in the kitchen. Charles, with news. Jackson hurried out to answer it.

Another flash lit up Jackson's life on the way to the kitchen; he was almost getting used to them. His phone was vibrating a jig on the pass-through, then it stopped. It wasn't a phone call, wrong ringtone. It was a message.

Not a message. A photo.

Leaf was awake, barely. He was reaching out, holding his phone, taking a picture of himself. There was a big, white bandage around his head. The bed he was in had brass rungs for a headboard – was he at home? Jackson tried to be delighted to see him conscious, in his own bed, but Leaf didn't look well at all. His face was sunken, strained, his eyes bare slits of awareness. It was draining all the energy he had to take the picture.

Over Leaf's right shoulder was the most hideous thing Jackson had ever seen. It stood a foot tall, spindly and leering from its surfboard pedestal, seeming to reach for the rest of Leaf's life. He cried out at the sight of it.

The nurse was there. She was going to do it. First Jackson with the pills, now Leaf, the boy who'd seen her. She was going to finish what she'd started.

No she was not.

Jackson caught himself at the door of his apartment. The new meds had worn off. The flash wasn't subsiding. He was going outside with a naked mind. He had the old meds, but they would take time to reach his system, maybe hours. Hours Leaf didn't have.

For one terrible moment Jackson was stuck. Then he snatched up the bag of splints, ran to the living room and buried his face in pillows again as he jammed them onto his broken fingers and taped his entire right hand together. Then he was in the bedroom, lunging for his hobby box under the bed and coming out with the Open Sesame and his tin of black powder. Then he ran for the door. No use locking up.

Leaf had saved his life and paid a terrible price to do it. Jackson wasn't about to let the nurse have him. If he had to battle his condition as well, so be it. He might even be able to use it. Might - God help him - even need it.

With his one good hand he pounded out a text to Leaf - I'm coming.

Chapter 25

Wendy Corbett lived in an illegal suite under an Asian family's house. From Marilyn's vantage point on the knoll of a small playground behind the place, it was one of the better situations around. Separate back entrance down seven concrete steps to an old wood door. There was a touch of lace on the one window visible to them. With a pair of binoculars Marilyn could see a glimpse of neat kitchen beyond.

"If she's home?" she asked Ahmed.

"Then we ask if we can come in and start asking her about names and dates. You have a list of the questionable deaths?"

"Yep."

"Good, we'll start there. As soon as she asks for a lawyer we clam up, of course, and take her in. Then we search her place."

"And if she's out?"

"Then we walk around and see if there are probable grounds for entry."

So they advanced on the apartment. It turned out, after two knocks, that Corbett wasn't home. Neither, apparently, was anybody upstairs. Ahmed grinned. "Now let's have a look," he said.

He stared hard through the door's small window, then moved on to the kitchen window. A slow circuit of the building brought them past the bedroom, a tiny frosted one for the bathroom, and around to the living room. The living room window had the drapes pulled, but it was open a crack.

"Let's see what I can do here," Ahmed said, and bent down. He blew into the opening and the drapes moved. "Here, keep doing that," he told Marilyn as he moved to look through the crack.

Marilyn blew deep breaths into the curtains. With each breath Ahmed scanned what he could see. "Nothing," he reported, disappointed. "I don't see – wait, do it again." She puffed one more time. "Whoa! The place is full of dolls. I mean, full."

He stood up; so did Marilyn, a little dizzy from blowing. "Is that probable grounds?"

"Not ordinarily, but in this case I would say so, wouldn't you?" He grinned again, and they made their way around to the kitchen door. One good shove and they were in.

"Look here." Ahmed gestured to the shattered wood on the doorframe that he'd pushed through. "We're not the first ones to come knocking."

Both of them whistled at the sheer number of dolls in the living room. They spent some minutes puzzling over the sprung rat trap next to the damp spots in the bedspread, but nothing overtly incriminating showed itself.

Ahmed stopped in the middle of the living room, a scowl on his face. "These dolls are creeping me out. Do you feel it? Like the place has a hundred eyes watching you. Where's the proof? Come on," he muttered, "where are you? I know you're here somewhere."

They searched harder. From the desk Marilyn called, "Got something." She held up a blank notepad, half the pages torn off. "She's got a heavy hand." Some quick, light work with a pencil shaded over the paper gave a clear impression of the last note. Palmerstons, it said, and gave a West Vancouver address.

"I know that name," Marilyn said. "It was in the news a

couple of days ago. Big family on the North Shore, their son got beaned by a rock. Looks like she has a new patient."

"In here," called Ahmed from the bathroom. "You should see this."

He'd peeled back the kick panel of the bathroom vanity. "I saw scratches," he explained. In the middle of the bathroom floor was a beautiful wooden box perfectly sized to fit the opening. Ahmed had lifted the lid. It was loaded to the gills. Books, bottles, needles, a pill case and other paraphernalia filled the container. Ahmed picked up the top book, Contraindications And Adverse Reactions In Critical Nursing. The missing sheet from the scratch pad was marking a page. Nitro Glycerin, said the heading on the page. A third of the way down was a big swath of yellow highlighter. The text underneath said, 'Strictly contraindicated in all cases of traumatic brain injury. May exacerbate bleeding, hydrocephaly, and cause seizures and death.'

"Here," Marilyn pointed back into the box. In one corner was a blister pack of four tiny canisters with little aerators on top, looking like miniature perfume misters. One of the blisters was empty. "Nitro sprays."

"She's doing it today." After another glance at the address on the paper, and at a nod from a white-faced Ahmed, Marilyn reached for her phone. The West Vancouver Police needed to know about this.

"What have you done?!" There was a cell phone in the boy's right hand and he was smiling. Unconscious, but smiling, as if he knew a secret. Wendy felt a crashing wave of cold dread fill her as she snatched the phone up and worked the buttons. When she saw what Leaf had done, the dread solidified into a knot of fear and despair.

One picture, sent to the one person who would read it for what it was. She sat down hard on the edge of the bed, the nitro spray rolling out of her hand and out of sight under the bed. Run, screamed her mind. There was still nothing anybody could prove and an entire world to lose herself in. Her bag was still packed. The front door was steps away.

The thought was gone before it had fully formed. In its place was anger, real anger like Wendy had not felt in many years, smothering the cold despair with a red fire. She stepped closer to the boy in the bed and felt her hands ache. She could kill him right here and now for his impudence. She wanted to finish the job her rock had started and bash his fool head in.

It wasn't the Second Rule that stopped her, and she registered a small surprise at its passing. She could quite happily tear this boy's life out here and now. What stopped her was cool logic. She would be caught. Leaf's death – now that someone else had been alerted and was on his way – would be bad for her.

The death of Jackson Teague, however, would do her nothing but good. The heat of her fury became a thunderous rush of excitement at the very thought, and she clutched the sheets between her fingers until it passed.

He was coming. In order for Wendy to continue living here, his death had to look natural. It must be an accident. She had work to do.

"Can't help you," shouted Staff Sergeant Robert Campbell into the mic clipped to his shoulder. He was hot, drenched in sweat, and he'd been shouting for half an hour and couldn't seem to stop. "Tell me we've got a serial axe murderer running through an old folks home and we still couldn't help. Every first responder in West Vancouver is at Horseshoe Bay. An old lady with a car like a tank lost control on the hill and plowed through an entire line of parked ferry traffic. It's a disaster down here. We got at least ten dead. Incoming lanes are a war zone, outgoing lanes are full of ambulances and fire trucks. Whatever you got, you're on your own."

"Here you go, Sarge," said a West Van fireman, walking over with his hand out. "Pried it out of the Buick." Campbell took possession of a battered cell phone just as it started to buzz. Joe, the call display said. He forgot the VPD's problems and braced himself for more of his own, then answered the call.

Chapter 26

The cops were doing hero duty down on the waterfront, trying to keep a lid on the protesters. From the driver's seat of his van, halfway over the Second Narrows Bridge, Borden glanced up the harbour towards downtown and the Lions Gate. It was too far to see the waves of placards and people pulsing through the streets, but the radio was full of traffic advisories and updates on the fun. Good. That would keep the boys in blue occupied and out of his way.

The Northern Sea Otter was making her slow, stately run. From far out in the inlet came the boom of that ridiculous foghorn, echoing off the mountains even over the rush of traffic. The radio commentators gushed on about the cryogenic natural gas spheres glowing like the world's biggest golf balls, the whole boat dressed from stem to stern in bunting and nautical flags. The huge tanker would sail under the middle of the bridge with a couple of feet to spare, then swing towards the North Shore as it chugged a deliberate full circuit around the inner harbour. Nice and safe, no natural gas leaks, nothing to worry about from this beautiful new industry.

Borden looked again in the direction of the Lions Gate Bridge and allowed himself a brief regret for an opportunity lost. It would have been magnificent. Then he swung his gaze over to the small Seabus ferry putt-putting across the inner harbour, altering course to swing wide around a freighter headed for the container terminal.

He smiled. Plan B was no slouch, either.

Jackson's determination got him as far as Balsam Street and the Subaru. The street was deserted and there wasn't a breath to stir the branches of the huge chestnuts overhead, but he could feel the potential for movement all around him. His car sat quietly in its parking space like a jaguar in the jungle.

This was going to be a trippy ride.

He idled down the hill to the Cornwall Street intersection and found the crowds. Every able-bodied activist in Kitsilano was headed downtown to protest the LNG tanker parade and the rest of the city was going to watch the show. The cars on Cornwall were crawling. And Leaf was in his bed on the other side of them.

The traffic was impossible. It was also gorgeous. Smooth, neon shimmers illuminated the straight-line course of each driver's intent. A Tesla one block up the street decided to change lanes and Jackson could see the driver's decision and his merge point before the Tesla's front tire crossed the dotted line. He could see the dance.

He could see his way in. A flickering line of possibility blinked into life between the Subaru's front bumper and a space between two oncoming cars. It blinked out as the cars passed, then there was another. Then another, keeping time with the openings.

They weren't openings. They were barely the width of a massage table, but Jackson needed to move. He followed the next flash as it arced into being and slid the corner of his bumper between a Peugot and a Mustang.

Nobody honked. The Mustang let him in and the flow of traffic hardly noticed.

It was no-parking time on Cornwall, which meant two lanes fed traffic into downtown. Jackson saw the same suggestion of a gap in the left lane and took it. Then, like magic, there it was again on his right. He nipped in, three cars ahead of where he had been. Still no horns.

He was using it. He was doing it. Left, right, like a snake through grass, Jackson was threading the needle through rush-hour traffic almost at normal speed. In no time he was on the Burrard Street Bridge, where the lanes opened up under the south parapet and the cars accelerated onto its solid, big-iron construction, speeding into the downtown core.

He needed to focus. There were at least five different ways to get from Burrard to the Lion's Gate Bridge. The best shot on this crazy day was a straight run down Burrard to Alberni Street, then hope he could work some magic on the gridlock to get from Alberni onto the bridge approach. That was a good enough objective for now. Best if he didn't let himself think about the bridge itself.

The sidewalks couldn't hold all the pedestrians and burped people onto the streets, snarling traffic even more. It was a full-on Vancouver protest party. The cops kept an eye on things from each corner, talking into their mics. Jackson saw one tall, bearded guy in army fatigues stride down the sidewalk with an actual replica of the Northern Sea Otter bobbing on his head, looking like it was sailing over a human sea. Others noticed and started to boo him. When he reached an open spot the guy spread his arms and twirled in a big circle, clearing a space, then pressed a button on his jacket. The miniature tanker on his head popped and burst into flames. The crowd roared and cheered as the guy went down under a wave of police.

Jackson nipped into the next nonexistent gap in traffic and left the fracas behind. The image of the burning tanker stayed with him, chilling his heart. Borden was stone cold crazy. He had a thermite bomb the size of a football. Could Jackson's five-second trajectory guess actually work? He'd never seen the launcher. One chance in a million, he thought. He hoped.

Enough of that, he needed to focus. Leaf was in trouble. There were enough cops around the Vancouver waterfront to handle anything.

He checked the car clock as he made the turn onto Alberni Street and saw that less than ten minutes had passed since Leaf's text. Keeping up with the dodge and weave, keeping his attention on the cars and away from the trees and highrises towering overhead, he pushed the Subaru until the storefronts blurred in his peripheral vision. Bidwell Street would be his ticket to the bridge approach that wound through Stanley Park. Then it was a simple matter of getting across to the North Shore.

The tires chirped as he made the turn onto Bidwell. No other cars stood between him and Bidwell's intersection with the six lanes of Georgia Street that serviced the bridge. His condition painted the street ahead in an iridescent, green shimmer, like a cosmic highlighter. Clenching his jaw and placing a totally unreasonable trust in the crazy, he kept his foot on the gas.

The bridge lineup in the far lanes was thick but moving well. Traffic coming into downtown was zipping by Bidwell like angry bees, lighter but taking the opportunity to move fast. There were gaps. Just not good ones.

He was coming up on the intersection full speed. He lifted his foot and headed for the brake, ready to leave rubber behind. He tried to look everywhere at once, plan something that would keep him moving, but it was all too fast. Cars and trucks zipped along all of the first three lanes. He would have to stop.

A thick, green blur laid itself out in front of him, jigged through the oncoming lanes and showed him his neat entry into the bridge traffic. Diagonally left against the traffic to pass in front of a Civic in the first lane and behind a GT-R in the second, snap right to slip between a delivery truck and an F-250, snap left again to slide his bumper into bridge traffic. It was a one shot, one second deal.

He jammed his foot back on the gas and took it.

This time there were horns. There were screeches and at least one curse. His tires chirped again. But no crunch. And when he dared breathe once more he was pointed towards Stanley Park.

"Holy shit, did you see that?" Ahmed exclaimed, grabbing the dash of the Charger as Marilyn wrestled them down Georgia Street. "Guy's a nut case."

Marilyn clamped her teeth together and reached for the lights. "Yeah. Want to know something more? He's our nut case. That's Jackson Teague's car. He knows where the nurse is. Hit the takedown, will you?"

She pulled out of the lineup into the first eastbound lane, forcing an F-250 to move over, to see if she could get a jump on Teague as the siren blipped into life. Somehow, in the thick of bridge traffic, the boy was moving fast.

Jackson's mirror ignited with a blast of primary reds and blues, flashing and dancing in a seductive rhythm he dared not look at, obviously intended to stop him. The police car's siren pierced the Subaru's windshield glass and practically lifted him out of his skin, it was so close.

"I can't stop!" he yelled to no one, and deked into the far right lane with the bumper move that was, by now, second nature. The nurse had already been alone with Leaf for far too long. He needed to keep moving. Maybe the cops could follow him in. If they could keep up.

He scrunched in towards the steering wheel and narrowed his eyes, trying not to look around and certainly not to look up. He was in the middle of Stanley Park. The trees were magnificent.

Corrugated brown trunks powered up through the earth on both sides of the road, many not even sprouting a branch for the first twenty feet. When Lord Stanley dedicated the peninsula in 1889 as a park for the new city, most of the old growth had been logged off except for a few trees that were simply too huge to cut down. After a hundred years of protection, the temperate rainforest of the park was now home to young giants and the occasional mammoth grandfather tree.

He couldn't help but glimpse them as he drove past. The massive pillars spearing out of the ground had been spaced by wind and sun in patterns as intricate as Victorian lace. He could see their sheer strength, each tree shimmering in his peripheral vision. The forest lived and breathed for him, like it had three years before. The living geometry of Stanley Park had pulled him in on that awful day, drawn him forwards to walk in wonder among the giants and toward his downfall.

It was around the next corner. He screwed his eyes as tightly closed as safety allowed, gripped the steering wheel harder with his good hand and got ready. The trees of Stanley Park had nothing on the Lions Gate Bridge.

The other drivers tried. Marilyn split the two bridge-bound lanes as they shuffled and squeezed to left and right in front of her, but there wasn't enough room in the confines of the park's narrow road and too many cars. "How the hell is he doing that?" she wondered as Teague's Subaru disappeared out of sight, making good time.

"The North Shore's a mess, too," said Ahmed, scowling at his cell phone. "The West Vancouver cops are still at Horseshoe Bay and the North Vancouver team's all down at the waterfront sifting the crowd. Everyone's in a lather because one of the traffic cams caught a face."

Marilyn felt her game-on tingle and glanced over. "Really? Which one?"

"The alert says his name's Borden. Says he's an explosives expert. The cam shows him driving an old, white camper van." Ahmed turned to her. "Anything to do with your fun on the bridge last weekend?"

"No idea what you're talking about," replied Marilyn, crossing her fingers on the wheel.

Ahmed absorbed that. "Wow. Crazy day."

"Yeah."

"So it looks like we're on our own with this little situation."

"Looks like it. If we can get there."

"Oh, we'll get there. We'll be first on scene," said Ahmed. He flipped out his keys and unlocked the Remington 870 shotgun from its mount. "Only ones on scene."

Marilyn moved another carlength closer to the bridge.

Chapter 27

There was a commotion at the lions. The walk/cycle paths on either side of the road circled around two stately, crouching, cast-concrete lions that guarded the entrance to the bridge and each lion had a knot of people in front of it. Jackson saw Parks Board uniforms and bicycle cops holding back crowds of pedestrians as he sailed past the lions with the flow of traffic, that was now moving pretty well. They were keeping the bridge open for cars but stopping walkers. No wonder. Most of them held protest signs, and he guessed that more than a few had unpleasant things they wanted to drop on the Northern Sea Otter.

Then the road arched onto the bridge deck. His eyes flew open of their own accord and rose up.

Suspension bridges were built for beauty. Jackson, naked to the full impact of his condition, felt the breath torn from him in a wordless gasp. Twin grey cables thick as elephants emerged from under the lion buttresses and flowed upwards to drape over the first of the bridge's two towers, easily 300 feet above the water. Smaller cables curtained down in pairs to cradle the bridge deck, which rose out of the forest to pass through the first tower. The symmetry was perfect. The power of the thing was unbelievable. The entire structure vibrated, thrumming with a deep, ultrabass chord he could feel in his bones. He didn't so much drive onto the bridge as he was drawn up into its embrace.

His condition, faced with such a sight, left no room in his mind for any kind of resistance. This was what he had felt three years ago, this pull into the sky high above the First Narrows. He was tempting Fate, this was a bad idea. It felt so wonderful just to be on this bridge.

The supporting cables zipping by his side windows in perfect procession slowed their march. Behind him a horn blared. His foot was off the gas pedal. His good hand had been reaching to open the car door.

Not this time, he yelled from a back corner of his mind. Leaf needs me. With the shred of self-control he had remaining, he raised his right hand and let it fall.

The feeling of bone fragments grating against each other under the improvised splints sent a shiver through his spine. The brilliant spike of pain snapped him out of his fascination. Drive, he thought. I can do this. He scrunched up his eyes again and planted his foot back on the gas.

Memories cascaded in on his mind. The forgotten time was unveiling itself as he relived it. He remembered stepping onto the bridge, walking the sidewalk and touching each cable as he passed. He'd bent down to touch the deck. He'd stopped and leaned his back against the first tower, eyes closed, feeling simultaneously the cold steel and the warmth of a power that came from the bedrock far below.

Charles had talked him back from the edge, kept him from jumping. Jackson knew this because that was the official account and that was what Charles had told him. How had he gone from that feeling of amazement to wanting to jump? He'd never asked - not Dr. Parma, certainly not himself. According to the police report he'd stopped all bridge traffic for two hours, tied up a dozen police officers while they activated their 'person in crisis' protocol and tried to talk him down. They had pulled

Charles away from saving lives in the ER to coax Jackson back from the edge, wrap an arm around his shoulders and put him into the back of a cop car. He was remembering all of that now. But still - how had it gone so wrong?

The first tower passed by and the bridge deck leveled out for the final, gentle climb to its apex.

The road ahead pulled him forward. The big cables sloped down in synchronized, graceful arcs to grasp the center of the bridge before ascending to the second tower. The very air crackled in this spot where the bridge's massive strength met gravity in perfect counterbalance. I can do this, he commanded himself. Just keep driving.

Then, from the corner of his eye, he caught the glimmer and was lost. His foot slipped over to the brake. He stopped, turned in his seat and stared as the cars behind him started to blast.

It was a perfect day, warm and blue with only a few clouds in the sky. Far below and stretched out in front of him was Vancouver Harbour, the trees of Stanley Park to his right and the spires of the city in the distance. A half-dozen small boats scurried towards the inner harbour, leaving triangles of wake behind them, and the water glittered with reflected sunlight. The North Shore mountains lifted skyward to the left with the neighbourhoods of North Vancouver looking settled and at home on their slopes. As he watched, a wind rolled in off the ocean behind him and combed the landscape. The clouds scudded inland. The canopy of Stanley Park swayed in a smoothly advancing tide. And the water - it danced with wave after wave of sparkling diamonds as the gust blew past and into the far beyond.

He was dazzled. The sound of the complaining cars all around was nothing to him. There was nothing except this vast, panoramic, breathing view of life. That, and the memory flooding back of the time he'd seen this before.

No way was he stepping out his door for a closer look. With the other lane of cars angrily roaring by so close, that would be suicide, and he had no wish to get hurt. Just as, three years before, he'd had no wish to get hurt either. He knew it now. Jumping had never been part of the plan. All that commotion, all the careful talking and cajoling, had not been necessary. He'd simply been lost in the view.

There was thumping coming from outside, and a warbling tweet. With an effort, Jackson refocused. A handful of police guarded the center of the bridge. One of them was crashing a hand down on his hood and blowing into a whistle, furious that he would dare to stop, waving his other hand in a wild move-on gesture. A cloud breezed over the sun and Jackson forgot the cop, his gaze pulled back to the ever-moving life all around.

Then the air exploded with a sound so deep and loud it practically broke his windows. The spell in his head was shattered. Even the cop jumped back onto the sidewalk. Jackson swivelled around and there was the Sea Otter, big as God and a thousand feet from the bridge, all decked out and moving at a crawl towards the harbour. All the traffic had slowed and all the cops were waving their arms to keep things moving.

Leaf. He hung onto that one thought and left behind the scene of his undoing. Taking away a memory and something that almost felt like forgiveness, he slipped his foot back onto the gas and moved forward. His cheeks were wet and he was wearing a fool's grin. He sped down the slope and around the ramp to West Vancouver, headed for Palmerston Avenue.

Wendy was drenched. It had been years since she'd perspired in uniform. The slippery moisture under her arms and down the small of her back irritated her beyond measure, but she forced it to the back of her mind as she finished the last preparations in the Palmerstons' living room.

It was done. She'd never had to lay traps like this, but she could take pride in her swift and ingenious work. No way would the massage therapist gain access to the house, and if he did then no way would he make it to Leaf's room. He was going to slip from a tortured life into a quick death and it would all be a terrible accident. His friend would be released from a future of pain and suffering soon afterwards. Then Wendy would be free.

Now that the heavy lifting was done, she had time to breathe. She drank in deep gulps from the kitchen tap and allowed herself a moment to marvel at her lack of remorse. Setting the traps was a serious breach of the Rules, but it felt like nothing. A righteous anger and a vicious, delicious heat that curled her toes had subsumed them completely. Jackson Teague was young and healthy, and he was in her way, and that was enough.

This was going to be fun.

Tires squealed from down the block. Wendy hurried to the front windows to watch the show.

Chapter 28

Jackson followed his cell phone's map to a set of ornate black gates, set into a hedge that was taller than two of him and thick as a wall. The gates were brutally utilitarian, made of thick, arrowed bars eight feet high and anchored by stone pillars on each side. The entrance was as forbidding as a dungeon. Should he hit it with his car? Not if he ever wanted to use his car again.

A door, framed into the hedge to the left of the driveway, allowed for pedestrian access to the sidewalk. Made of thick oak planks held together with wrought iron straps, it carried on the menacing, medieval look.

Except it was ajar.

He almost went through it at a run. Its very obviousness stopped him one step from the threshold. Nobody who owned a wall like this would leave the side door open.

He gave the oak planks a kick, swinging the door wide on creaking hinges. A violent red streak of straight-down movement sent him vaulting back into the road as something hit the pavement with a bam and clatter. Rolling down the walk was an old, metal paint can, spilling its cargo of stones all over the place.

He laughed out loud. It was going to be like this, was it? That would have knocked him a good one, maybe even killed him on the spot. Well, the door was open now. He stepped through onto the Palmerston estate.

So this was money. A smooth, gleaming driveway sloped up a respectable hill towards a mansion of a house, lined on both sides by more high and impenetrable hedge that was accented here and there with huge elm trees and scalloped alcoves. Jackson knew about granite countertops, but who had a polished granite driveway? It gleamed in the afternoon sun. The thin, mortared joints made a thrillingly even checkerboard right up the hill to the house. The slope must be heated in the winter or it would be impassable.

Leaf was at the other end. Jackson took off at a run.

He made it two steps before the world upended, his knees and elbows burst into pain and he was staring at flecks of mica in the granite. "Ow," he said, thankful his nose was still in one piece. There was slime everywhere. Jackson thrashed about but couldn't find purchase for his feet or even his hand. His efforts slid him right back down to the wooden door.

Back at the entrance he sprang to his feet, wincing at the fresh bruises. Nothing broken, but he was covered in gunk. He sniffed, then tasted, then looked around for the evidence.

20 feet up the hill he spotted the big can of olive oil thrown against the base of an elm tree. Jackson laughed again, despite his mounting anxiety to be inside that house. She'd slimed him twice now. The nurse was running out of tricks.

He ran outside the gate and dug under the hedge, pulled his shirt into a pouch and filled it with dirt. Throwing the dirt in front of him, he got past the spilled oil.

Pay attention, he scolded himself. Look. Your reflexes might not save you again.

The driveway levelled out and continued for another 30 feet, pooling into a roundabout at the front door of a white, colonnaded, three-storey massif of a house. The feeling that he was storming a castle was inescapable. Bright, yellow sight lines flickered from each window. They were only in his head, but they might as well have been red laser dots. She could see him. He felt her gaze like an itch in the center of his forehead.

The high hedge and thick elm trunks continued, unbroken, up to the front door. Ahead of him was a fancy car parked to one side of the drive and a line of statues on pedestals tucked at pleasing intervals into the scooped alcoves in the hedge.

Jackson felt like he was in a shooting gallery. He needed cover. The car would provide some. On the way he passed an actual armless Venus in white marble and a Henry Moore in shiny bronze. No wonder Leaf felt like he had to get away from this place, he thought. Right next to the car was a Thinker done in dark, brooding iron.

As he got closer he gasped. No wonder the driveway gate was so formidable. The car in front of him was an honest-to-God Aston Martin DB4, a gleaming 60's classic that topped out at 130 miles an hour and a million dollars at auction. He could smell old leather, unburned gasoline and car wax from ten feet away. It was close to the left edge of the driveway. The slim path between it and the Thinker would get him a little closer to the house unmolested. He advanced.

A breeze picked up and he jerked his head down, away from the thick, swaying elm leaves. No time for that. He could control his condition's dangerous fascinations, he knew that now, but it would be hard work. There was not a trace of any buffer in his system. The whole world was alive and alight. He was seeing everything.

Something was wrong. He stopped. It wasn't the car; the lines of the DB4 were a work of art, liquid movement frozen into steel. It was The Thinker. He had one elbow jutting out over his knees. The elbow was out too far, the geometry was awkward.

The sculpture was tilted. The whole statue was rocked

forward on its base, angled towards the car. He could see the tightly-balanced forces of gravity and weight wavering on the edge of calamity. The Thinker was propped up at the back by a rock, ready to fall with the slightest encouragement.

There was the line. Four pound test fluorocarbon fishing line, nearly invisible in the shadow of the car, running six inches above the flagstones to the statue's base. A tripwire, evil and glowing red in the afternoon. If he had rushed, it would have caught him.

He didn't get it. A falling statue, even a heavy one, from five feet away? It might brush his ankle. There must be more to this. The nurse didn't make ineffective traps. He picked up a stick from under the hedge, high-stepped over the line and moved up the driveway till he was clear of the car. Then he tossed the stick behind him.

The base wobbled. The Thinker leaned some more, then fell to the granite with a ringing clang. It really was iron. The impact shattered two flagstones into shiny granite chips and sent a shower of sparks skeeting under the Aston Martin.

A blinding, hot sheet of fire belched out from under it. The car humped up off the driveway then disappeared in a whuff of flames. Jackson sat back hard, scrambling to evade the searing heat. The fishing line was melted, the Thinker face-down in the midst of the burning fuel. No trace of the trap remained. The terrible elegance of it left him breathless. He'd even smelled the gasoline and missed it. The loss of the Aston Martin was a shameful embarrassment. Jackson had forgotten what he was facing.

The sight of the dancing flames was wildly delicious, but he had work to do. He blocked the fire with the wad of his right hand long enough to tear his gaze away and looked around. No more mistakes. He couldn't afford to miss anything. Come on, he told his condition as he scanned the scene ahead, do your thing.

The driveway continued its checkerboard pattern all the way to the house. The statues had been placed with a ruler, marching in file up the drive. A breeze tossed the branches of the elms overhead and caught his wonder until he wrestled himself back down to ground level.

More, he told his mind. Look for the disturbance. The nurse insults the very ground she walks on. Look for it.

Ten steps ahead the driveway levelled out to a flat plain. Ten steps more and the surveyor-straight lines between the tiles refracted, a microscopic change of angle that his mind highlighted in electric blue. It took him a moment to figure out what he was seeing.

The next trap was a puddle of water.

It hadn't rained in days. The puddle was large, extending from hedge to hedge and easily ten feet across, almost to the front corner of the mansion. In order to reach the house Jackson had no choice but to get his feet wet.

The other half of the trap was easy to spot and brilliantly, frustratingly final. A thick, black cable had been ripped out of a junction box beside the front step. Its frayed ends rested in the water. Next to it was a spilled bag of coarse road salt.

Heating coils for a driveway this massive used 240 volts. And 240 volts through salt water was instant cardiac arrest.

He was stopped, mere feet from Leaf. He screamed at the front door in a wordless rage as he saw a side curtain move. Then he ran back down the driveway.

The Aston Martin singed him as he passed, no more than he deserved for torching it. He danced along the dirt track through the oil, went out the hedge door, grabbed the gallon paint can that had tried to brain him and emptied it of the last of its stones. Taking the can and a few of the largest rocks, he ran back up to the water trap. He had one chance to do this and the clock was counting Leaf's time in seconds. Two feet from the water he laid the paint can down on its side, held it still and stomped on it.

Over and over, he rolled and stomped the sides of the old metal can until the opening was a ragged pucker just smaller than his largest rock. This was crude, his mind was yelling, imprecise, awkward, bad geometry. No choice. He pulled out his tin of black powder and set the paint can on the ground.

The black electric cable was resting in the water ten feet away. Not far, but the rock was a terrible fit on the mouth of the paint can launcher. There was going to be all kinds of leakage. Jackson felt the heft of the rock, rechecked the distance it had to travel, envisioned the jets of escaping gas around the sides of the explosion, and emptied most of his gunpowder tin into the bottom of the paint can.

Two other rocks served to angle the launcher. It was his best guess, a shallow arc right at the cable, more like a bullet than a missile. There was so much uncertainty involved that the trajectory looked to his eyes more like a scattergun spray than a solid line. The best he could do was maneuver the rocks so the cable was in the center of probability. He dribbled the last of the powder from the mouth of the can down the rocks and along a thin line till it ran out. Then he flicked his lighter.

The paint can went one way and the rock went the other with a grunt like an old man lobbing a shotput. A grey cloud farted sulphur fumes all over the driveway. Jackson heard the rock ping onto granite, but he couldn't see a thing. The midafternoon air was still. The cloud of smoke was going to take forever to clear. He didn't have that long. Holding his breath, he swiped a toe through the edge of the water.

Nothing happened. He did it again, and the same nothing happened. Gritting his teeth, he ran out into the salt water and got both his feet wet before finding the other side. He kept on running to the front door, catching sight of the black cable as he passed, knocked high and dry up against the side of the house with the rock lying next to it.

He didn't even bother trying the brass latch. One folded slip of cardboard went into the jamb above the hardware, the other one below it, then he lit the fuse and stepped back.

The Open Sesame was high art. The fizzing spark eating the fuse was beautiful. In one second it became two separate sparks and jumped to the papers, the top one a hair faster. P-Pow! went the twin tamped charges. The door shuddered open wide as the jamb neatly cracked. Jackson stepped through into a spacious living room and screamed.

"Police, coming through." Borden hustled down McKeen Avenue and the sightseers got out of his way, convinced by the tactical black jumpsuit, web harness full of gear, coiled earpiece and large, nylon duffel bag at his side.

A line of yellow and black barricades marked the entrance to the pier. A sign on the grey building next to it said, Department of Fisheries and Oceans North Vancouver Dock - Authorized Personnel Only. To reinforce the matter, two guards came strolling out of a door towards him.

That was one too many.

The guard in front was about ten years and twenty pounds past combat readiness but looked sharp enough. Guard Junior was barely out of high school, on his toes and looking to the boss for direction. Their waists were slung with the standard commissionaire gear - cuffs, pepper spray, baton, flashlight - and their uniforms were creased and neat. They'd been turning people away all day.

"No sightseeing here, sorry," said the lead guard, gesturing to Borden's left. "Lonsdale Quay's your best bet, downtown. Uh," he hesitated as he got an eyeful of Borden's getup.

"Official business," Borden ordered, adding to their hesitation and getting him two steps closer before pulling his Ruger, suppressor already attached. Pak! He saw the lead guard's eyes register a drawn firearm just as the slug punched a neat hole through his left cheekbone on its way out the other side, where it wasn't nearly so tidy. The sound was like Rocky Balboa hitting a side of beef. The body, filling with adrenalin but suddenly without any higher control, took three startled jumps back through its own brains before falling over.

Guard Junior froze, his eyes threatening to leap out of his head. Borden said, "That way." He gestured towards the end of the dock, sticking two hundred feet out into Vancouver Harbour. A red and white research ship occupied the left side, blocking the view of the inner harbour. To help the boy get over his shock the Ruger went Pak! again, and a chunk of asphalt smacked the kid in the shin. He turned and half-ran onto the creosote planks, stepping around the mess.

"Drop the equipment belt," said Borden. The kid pressed a clip and the web belt full of gear clunked to the deck.

"Today's your lucky day. Jump and swim. Don't stop, don't turn around till you reach the other side."

The boy was at the edge. He half-turned, facing Borden with a moist face. "Thanks, mister."

Canadians. "Don't mention it. You turn, you yell, you die." He waved the overbalanced Ruger for emphasis and the kid leaped for the waves. As Borden watched he surfaced ten yards out, knifing straight for Stanley Park on the opposite shore. A strong swimmer, eager to take advantage of Borden's mercy.

'Barooom-Ahh!' The boy stopped as the Northern Sea Otter's big-dick horn cracked the sky and he saw his peril. The huge tanker was a few hundred yards away and moving dead slow, but no way could he swim past it before the massive hull would be on him. Borden took careful aim. Pak pak! Two small geysers spooshed on either side of the kid's head, encouraging him. He got back to it, swimming as hard as he could.

Perfect. No way could that tanker stop, not fully loaded. There was only one move left and the skipper took it. A rumble shook the dock as two massive jets of foamy water erupted from the boat's starboard bow thrusters. With aching slowness, the Sea Otter edged five degrees to port, giving the kid a fighting chance.

Instead of passing by the DFO dock a thousand feet into the harbour, it would be at 500 feet when it came level with Borden. Perfect.

He gave himself one last moment to gaze at the world. He'd built contingencies upon contingencies, that was his nature. Still, if the next few minutes went according to plan, this pier, a sizeable piece of North Vancouver, and that hateful fucking bridge were going to vaporize inside a miniature supernova. The only place he'd survive would be in the history books.

Which didn't sound half bad.

Borden bent to his duffel and got busy. This was a makeshift setup. It was going to take every minute he had.

Chapter 29

Wendy sobbed as her giant heart shattered. Her life's work was over. All the beautiful traps had done nothing and the boy was here, inside. There was no possible way she could kill him now and have it look natural.

There was no more thought of running. Instead she crouched. The awful ache that had been in her legs for days was now a rush of strength waiting for release. Because of Jackson Teague she would never be able to care for another patient in pain. She'd never again see her beloved angels, caress them all and remember them each night before she went to bed. All she had left was this one last thing. She was going to love every minute of it.

The boy screamed as he fell into the final trap, the one she'd known he couldn't avoid. She drank in his agony and screamed it back at him as she charged.

The living room burned his mind. Jackson had one gestalt glimpse of fine Italian armchairs done in rich burgundy and ornate black walnut, framed nautical charts down one hall, book-lined walls and more statuary leading to a dining room and spiral stairs deeper inside the house, all over top of layered Persian carpets. The furnishings spoke of elegance and comfort. The nurse had transformed them into a source of excruciating pain.

Bruise-purple rays of wrong pulsed at him from all corners of the compass. He blinked, stunned into place at the doorway, trying to see. Some changes were obvious. A long runner carpet to his right was canted so badly it ran half up the wall. Books had been torn from their shelves and left sideways on their backs, teetering off the edge. Every carpet was misaligned. The sofa and four armchairs didn't talk to each other. The longer he gazed the more he saw.

The statues brought it all into terrible focus. Three terra cotta warriors looked ready to march into a corner. Atlas tried to hurl the earth into the same place. A miniature replica of Joan of Arc pointed her sword there from across the room. All the furniture in the room was aligned to one single spot just left of the sofa, filling the room with a thick web of harsh viridian that only he could see.

He stepped forward, hardly knowing that he did so. The web was drawing him in. It hurt, like someone was taking a steel club to a set of testicles in his mind. He blinked past it, trying to see.

Crouched at the apex of the web, dripping with sweat and glaring, was Wendy Corbett. With a roar like an injured boar the night nurse ran straight for him.

"Whoa, look at that!" Ahmed pointed out the windshield at a greasy, black fireball as they skidded off the bridge mess and up the hill towards Palmerston Avenue. "Since when do massage therapists pack explosives? Looks like the party's started without us."

"Let's hope they're still dancing," muttered Marilyn as she squashed the pedal to the floor.

She was fast. The room's violet haze was a dagger in his mind. The nurse was huge, almost on him. Jackson had no choice but to trust. He took a deep breath and opened the door to his condition wide. "I need you." The dagger gave a massive, agonizing twist and then was gone. In its place he saw. The nurse, three steps away now, burned with a horrible dedication that left room for nothing human. She trailed the lives of her victims behind her like a vapour. There was no stopping a force like that.

'So don't try,' said Toshiko-Sensei's voice in his mind. Wendy was going to knock him off his pins and body-slam him into the next life. Jackson did the obvious thing and made himself not there.

The nurse ran past as he pivoted, grunting with surprise at his sudden absence. His left hand fell onto hers as she reached. He placed his right forearm against her elbow as she passed and rotated smoothly around and down, keeping his splinted fingers free, feeling the alignment of it like a cool breeze in the middle of a baking desert. Wendy grunted again as she found herself upside-down and airborne.

She crashed into a bookshelf and the house shook. Jackson danced away as she leaped to her feet in a surprising show of agility. "Hold still!" she bellowed. "You're ruining it!" She lunged again. He sidestepped deeper into the living room.

"Where's Leaf?" he yelled back.

They circled each other around the furniture, Wendy reaching and Jackson dodging. "The poor boy's not doing so well," she snarled, "I'll be helping him out soon enough."

"Is that what you call it? You kill people, lady."

"I. Ease. Their. Suffering." Wendy lunged again, and got him.

Her grip on his upper arm was crushing, an explosion of red pain, followed by another as her other hand smashed into the side of his head. Jackson tried to shake off the grip, slip down, pull back, but it did no good. She could overmaster any fight he put up. Her fist hit him again. Jackson felt his knees quiver.

She was breaking his arm, pulling him in. He couldn't get away. 'So don't try,' Toshiko-Sensei said in his head. Relaxing again, Jackson switched directions and let himself be pulled into Nurse Wendy's chest.

And turned, and bent over. A simple redirection of energies, from pull to push, from her to him back to her, and the huge woman was airborne again. He didn't feel any of her weight as she sailed over top of him and smacked into the floor; of course not, it was her own overbalancing that carried her. It always had been. It always would be.

He had a breath before the nurse got up again. The stars in his head weren't going away. There was sticky wetness flowing down from his right ear and the beginnings of a headache. That wasn't good.

Wendy looked him over with a hot, savage pity. "Look at that, you've hurt yourself," she said. "Let me fix it for you."

God she was fast, closing in with a wrestler's rush. Or, Jackson considered as the stars in his head grew sharp points and his knees shook, I'm slowing down. That's not good.

She was here, head down, charging. A massive, red tsunami of intent between her outstretched arms was going to crush him where he stood. Jackson did the only thing he could. He stepped in.

He met her before she was ready, melding his energy with hers in an awful embrace he might never be able to forget. His left arm circled around her charging head. He bent and pivoted again, directing her energy down, around, sweeping in a big, perfect curve. Once more the nurse was airborne above him.

Then he broke the curve. At exactly the wrong moment, in a horrifying shattering of the perfect geometry and still holding tight to the nurse's head, he stood up straight.

The great weight of the nurse's arcing body met the sudden stillness of her head with the single, loud pop of her odontoid process snapping off and neatly severing her spinal cord at the first vertebra. It was as final and complete as the hangman's drop. Jackson let go. She crashed to the living room floor and so did he.

The stars were clearing. A hallway led deeper into the house. Leaf was back there, somewhere. He was still alive. Jackson had to get to him, but his legs were inexplicably hard to find. He gritted his teeth and tried again.

Chapter 30

Marilyn and Ahmed made a wide berth around the burning car, eyes everywhere and Ahmed's shotgun at port arms with a chambered round, but their attention was on the house. A loud crash had just slammed the front door shut and now there was incoherent screaming.

"Go!" shouted Ahmed. They rushed the door, splashing through a puddle as another crash sounded from inside.

"Still dancing," Marilyn muttered as they braced the door. "Police!" she shouted, and swung it open wide.

The place was a mess. Teague was in the middle of it, crouching and turning, and – in a sight Marilyn wouldn't soon forget– a mountain of a woman was upside-down above him, swinging around her head in the crook of Teague's arm.

"Oh boy," she whispered as she saw Teague snap to his feet. The execution was perfect. They heard the pop from the door.

The nurse crashed and lay still, gone. Teague crashed, too. He tried to head for the far hallway, but fell again. He was bleeding from the ear. "I'll get him," she yelled at Ahmed, "you find the Palmerston boy!"

Jackson was on the burgundy sofa. He recovered enough equilibrium to sit up straight and found himself staring at a face, a pretty one, full of concern.

"Look at me, Jackson."

"Constable Mathers."

"Pupils are okay. Your ear's cut, but the bleeding has stopped. An ambulance is on the way."

"Leaf! He's in the ..."

Mathers' hand held him down, no great task. "Your friend is fine," she said. "Well, not fine, but unharmed. We'll take him to the hospital, too. The nurse didn't get to him."

"She's – she's -" his words failed him. What next, Jackson thought.

"I know. What you said about her was right on the money. Looks like she's been at it for a good many years, too." Mathers glanced towards the center of the room. "It also looks like she's dead as a doornail. You know anything about that?"

He grimaced. "I might."

"I saw. Nice moves. Don't worry about it. You rest now."

He could do that. With a sigh, he sank further into the couch. "Hell of a day. Did you catch Borden?"

Her attention went from caring to sharp. "What did you say?"

"Borden, the terrorist. Eyes on the big tanker. There's a million cops around, you must have him by now. Right?" He sat up straight again.

Mathers was on the phone. "It's Mathers, no time to explain, what's the situation on the potential North Shore threat?" She listened, then said, "Thanks." Before she could hang up Jackson waved a hand.

"Has anything changed in the last half hour?"

Mathers relayed the query, listened, then nodded. "A suicide swimmer, just this minute. The Sea Otter is altering course to miss."

He jumped up, fighting nausea, and ran to one of the nautical charts on the wall. "Show me. Show me, now!"

Mathers pointed. "The Sea Otter's past the bridge. Here's where it altered course - " she pointed at a spot a little ways east of the bridge - "swinging five degrees towards shore."

Jackson stabbed at a long, grey rectangle sticking out from land. "What's that?"

Mathers looked. "Lions Gate Bridge, Salish reserve lands, industrial - it's the DFO dock. A secured area. There won't be anybody there."

"Except Borden. Let's go." He turned for the door, but Constable Mathers pushed him back.

"Nonsense. Talk to me, Jackson, what do you know?"

He struggled to put the whole sordid mess into a few words. "I can see trajectories. Ballistics, you know?" He demonstrated with a hand, making a whoosh and boom noise for emphasis. "Borden found out and threatened me. He's got a mortar made of thermite. It's big, really big. I - it might actually work, if the ship gets close enough." He jabbed a finger at the DFO dock. "Like right there."

Mathers called it in. She listened, then said, "Yeah," and put the phone down. "The protestors have ramped things up. We've got three fires, a bunch of vandalism, and scuffles on both sides of the water. They can get people to the DFO dock in twenty minutes. I can be there in eight." She rose and called into the house. "Ahmed! Ambulance is inbound, I have to go. You got this?" A muffled affirmative came from down the hall. She turned for the door.

"I can get us there in four."

Mathers turned back. He was powering for the door, angry all over again. For one second she seemed to consider it, then said, "No way. You stay here."

"You know what he looks like?"

She paused again. "I've seen surveillance photos."

"I've had coffee with him. I beat you over the bridge. Four minutes. Come on, we have to go now."

Halfway down the driveway she passed him the keys. "You ever tell anyone about this, Teague, and I swear I'll cuff you and throw you off the bridge."

The Charger was a whole different beast than his Subaru. With the lights, sirens and his mind on fire, he got them to the dock in the promised time.

"White van!" Marilyn pointed at a crappy, camperized Ford parked a block away as Jackson brought the car to a four-wheel skid in front of the barricades. "God, one down!" She gave her radio a staccato update as she bailed from the passenger door and headed for a uniformed figure on the ground a dozen feet away. "Stay here!" she yelled behind her as she went.

Not a problem, he thought. The guard was obviously beyond help, half his skull was splattered over the pavement. The dock stretched out into the water. Perched at the far end, angled out towards the harbour, was a tube on a plank. It had an armadillo look which took him a second to figure out. The tube, probably a cardboard form for concrete posts, had been wrapped with thick, grey wire.

To contain the force of a blast. It was Borden's mortar, mounted and ready to go.

The colourful flags on the nose of the Northern Sea Otter were level with the dock. In ten seconds the first of the four spheres would be lined up with the mortar. From this angle each sphere looked as huge as an observatory. Jackson's gunpoint calculations could be pinpoint accurate or wildly off the mark, it didn't matter. So long as the thermite slug covered the distance it couldn't miss.

Pak! Pak! Two chunks of creosoted wood flew off the end of the dock closest to the pavement. Marilyn, who'd just discovered the uselessness of checking the guard for a pulse, dove down behind the thick body. "Shots fired!" she yelled into her mic, pulling out her own pistol.

Borden crouched behind a white bollard at the end of the dock, swearing and unscrewing the suppressor from the end of his gun. Jackson had seen two red streaks erupt from his hiding place as he fired. Marilyn, prone behind the guard, was searching for a target.

"Last bollard on the left!" he shouted through the open passenger door. She swung her pistol over top of the dead man's gut and zeroed on Borden's hiding place. A wavering red line phosphoresced through the air with her aim, but it wouldn't solidify in Jackson's sight. He'd never seen her gun fire, didn't know its strength. She had the line, but it was a very long shot.

"Teague!" Borden's face was a study in amused consternation. Then he lifted his gun, freed to its full horsepower by the removal of the suppressor, and Jackson saw the scarlet intent of Borden's aim laser directly onto his face.

"Shit!" He dove for the car seat as two handguns roared and the windshield of the Charger spiderwebbed, showering him with glass pebbles. The echoes bounced back from the DFO building.

This was too much. He squirmed over the center console until he could peek around the passenger door. Marilyn was still behind the guard. Her shots had fallen short, he could see the pocks in the wood of the dock. Borden, feeling cocky and feeling the time pressure, had abandoned the bollard for his launcher. The Sea Otter was abeam of the dock, the second of her four tanks passing out of the launcher's range. In another fifteen seconds she would be past. He was digging in a pocket.

Jackson saw the lick of a flame.

"Higher!" he shouted to Marilyn. She took aim again and let fly two more rounds. He saw them this time, sharp lines that flew wide and into the harbour.

"Half down, a sliver left!" She made the adjustments as Borden, irritated, turned and fired. Four reports slapped the air.

He saw Borden jump and heard him yowl as Marilyn shouted, "Fuck!" She let off two more rounds, one wide and one right at Borden's feet. Borden dropped his gun, jammed one hand against his side, grabbed a small cylinder off his belt with the other and rolled off the dock into Vancouver Harbour.

Jackson slid out of the car and ran to Marilyn. A red spray extended back from her right calf, which was bleeding but not spurting. "Look!" She ignored the wound, pointed to the end of the dock. Where a sputtering, smoking ball of yellow flame was eating its way towards the launcher.

They had one second. One shot. He threw himself down across her back, good hand wrapping around her left arm and taped hand supporting her right. He could feel her surprise, rising to outrage, beneath him. His head was next to hers, his eyes and his condition riveted on the launcher.

"Trust me," he whispered.

The line was there, a streak of brilliant light from the end of Marilyn's gun to the far edge of the dock. He steadied the weapon, guided it into position. "Fire," he said, as the fizzing yellow ball disappeared inside the launcher.

Her gun kicked, reinjuring his broken hand. The launcher bellowed, spewing a thick gout of smoke into the air. A second column of smoke and orange flame jetted sideways from the back of the launcher where Marilyn's bullet had punched a hole through the tube's armour. A blindingly white star rocketed out from the mess, eclipsing the sun as it arced away from the dock towards the Northern Sea Otter. Robbed of propellant by the unexpected leak, the thermite shell made it halfway to the ship before dropping into the water of Vancouver Harbour with the sizzle of a thousand angry wasps.

Sirens warbled behind him, cruisers approaching fast from both directions. Maybe he heard helicopter blades in the distance. Maybe it was all in his head. Which really hurt, even more than his hand. The policewoman felt warm and comfortable beneath him. He might have said, "Mind if I go to sleep here?" But probably he just dreamed it.

One Month After

The weather people were calling for a midsummer storm, so Kits Beach was full of Vancouverites soaking up the sun before its arrival. Even the water was crowded with bodies. But it was the ocean; there was always room for a few more. Looking around the tablecloth Jackson grinned and said, "Last one in!"

Charles and Georgia beat him to the waves. The Palmerstons stayed behind to guard the potluck and keep Leaf company in his wheelchair. The three of them were seldom parted these days. Jackson dove into the beautiful, warm water and sliced for the bottom, confident that he would have Harold and Louise in the ocean before the end of August.

The tide was coming in strong, riffling the sand along the bottom and sending deep pulses of delight coursing along his bones. The water was warm enough he could have stayed under forever. He held himself down, feeling the heartbeat of the earth, until his breath forced him back to the surface.

His condition did have some side benefits. Now that he was back on his old meds, freshly adjusted with the help of Dr. Parma, a trace of the special sense was his constant companion. Under check, but available.

Parma had outright goggled when Jackson told him the story. So had the rest of Vancouver, mesmerized by the close call on the waterfront and the revelation of a killer nurse in their midst. It had been a busy and inconvenient month, what with a hospital stay, police interrogations, media interviews and work. That was another side benefit of this whole mess - his phone was ringing off the hook with new clients.

"Hey, man. Tide looks like it's ripping in." Leaf sat between Harold and Louise, who still looked a little awkward with their butts in the sand but were determined to be part of their son's life. The bandage under the rainbow beanie covering Leaf's bald head would be with him for awhile yet. He could walk a few steps away from his wheelchair and was starting intensive rehab to re-establish more control over his body, but everyone told him not to expect too much. It was going to be a long road back, they said.

Leaf and Jackson had talked it over in one of their many conversations and found themselves in complete agreement. Leaf would be slacklining within a year. Jackson was cracking the books again, studying brain injury rehab, and had made sure he was part of Leaf's team.

"Let's see what we have," he announced, taking over as host of the potluck. It took two tablecloths now to hold the feast. Louise had brought fresh butter rolls from a West Van bakery. Harold handed over a jar of stuffed grape leaves, perfect for the summer heat. Charles put down a roasted vegetable quiche next to Jackson's marinated salmon fingers. Georgia contributed a plateful of chocolate-dipped strawberries along with her chilled apple juice.

"Yum," said Leaf. "Let's dig in."

Jackson picked up a roll and winged it at his face. Leaf's right hand flew up and caught it. Reflexes, Jackson's research said. That was where the recovery began. Leaf grinned and took a bite.

"Hey hey," murmured Charles, sitting across from Jackson and staring over his shoulder. "Looks like we have company."

Jackson spun around to see Marilyn Mathers on the paved

path a few feet off the sand, balancing between a pair of crutches. The blaze-orange bikini top and flamingo beach wrap were a definite improvement over the uniform, he thought. She'd had the cast on her leg done in navy blue, with a Vancouver Police crest stuck over top of a forest of signatures, so there was that. They'd shared an ambulance ride after the dock and spent most of the next week at police headquarters being debriefed and interrogated. He hadn't seen her since.

He stood up and waved. She waved back. "Chocolate strawberries!" he called, adding a come-over gesture. She hesitated for a moment, deciding, then her face broke into a sunny grin. Jackson caught a glimpse of something flash between them as she powered her crutches over the sand, a wash of silver so light it was only a shimmer, there and gone almost before it registered. Then she was with the party, levering herself down to the sand on one leg.

His original assessment had been right, he decided. She was fit as a triathlete. Over in his chair Leaf started up with a slow, quiet laugh, amused by God knew what.

"Nice to meet you all," Marilyn said after Jackson's introductions. "The Has-Been shot a chunk out of my tibia, so I'm going to be on these sticks for the rest of the summer. The doc said vitamin D is good for bones and I should try to get some sun. I figured this beach is as good as any."

"Better than some," Jackson said. "I happen to live right over there." Marilyn gave him polite surprise. It lasted about a second before everyone collapsed into laughter. The day, already as good as Vancouver could deliver, brightened.

Talk turned to recent events. The nurse had been shoved into the community graveyard and Marilyn's investigation - now led by Ahmed - was reopening old patient files across the continent. The dolls, after some discussion, had been distributed to family crisis counsellors across the city. The LNG company had apologized for its stunt with the Northern Sea Otter, paid Vancouver a hefty sum for the cost of policing the protest and moved their attention back up to the north coast. Demand for natural gas was growing across the world. The consensus around the picnic was that the industry was going to be a major player in the province's economy.

"At least they won't have the Has-Been to worry about anymore," said Georgia. That was the name the media had given Borden once the police released a few tidbits from his past. As far as Jackson was concerned, the label fit just fine.

"I'm not so sure about that," replied Marilyn, turning to Jackson. "You remember seeing him grab a tube off his belt as he went over the side?" He nodded. "I described it to a police diver. It was a Three-Shot, a three breath microtank. We never found any body."

The sun had started its long, slow fall to the horizon. Rising up to meet it was a line of black clouds, far away but already thick. As Jackson watched they flickered with the first lightning of the summer. It was going to be an electric night.

A cool breeze, vanguard of the advancing storm and already perfumed with the coming rain, blew in over the water. He saw it tickle whitecaps off the waves, grab a towel, toss a young girl's hair, then flip up a corner of their tablecloth on its way inland. He turned and watched it fly up among the trees, feeling the now-familiar thrill. Then he closed his eyes and turned back to the food. His hand was already smoothing out the cloth, the splints on his two fingers glinting in the sun. He'd have to watch for that. Always and forever.

He redirected the hand over to another roll. Charles observed it all; he was wearing a touch of that doctor face again. Jackson flicked the roll at Charles' nose; Charles was fast, but not quite fast enough, which got another round of laughs.

Another breeze rocked in from the storm, cooler than the first. Marilyn untied the beach wrap from around her waist, draped it over her shoulders and leaned in until their shoulders touched.

Afterword

Next time you meet a nurse or care aide, take a moment to thank them for their service. They keep us together when we're at our worst, and do it with compassion, elegance and professionalism. To be clear: Wendy is a singular aberration. While predators of her ilk do, very occasionally, make the headlines, they are vanishingly rare.

Massage therapy is enjoying something of a golden age. Extensive research into the systemic effects of touch therapies, the development of new techniques, and improved training standards are leading to a greater integration of massage therapy in the treatment of illness and injury. In many areas, massage therapists are rightly seen as healthcare professionals; in other places, not so much. Not yet. Perhaps this story, and others like it, will help to tip the balance.

I have taken some minor liberties with Vancouver geography, for which I beg forgiveness. All in the service of a good story.

Spread The Word

Did you enjoy The Night Nurse?

Drop me a line, I'd love to hear from you:
  nightnurse@tonyberryman.com

Rate and review The Night Nurse on:
  Amazon
  Chapters Indigo
  Goodreads
  Barnes & Noble

Tell your world:
  Share Jackson and Wendy with friends and followers

Stay connected:
  https://tonyberryman.com/newsletter/
  https://www.facebook.com/tonyberrymanwriter/
  https://www.instagram.com/tonyberrymanwriter/

Acknowledgements

This sort of thing doesn't happen without help. Huge thanks go out to Deryn Collier, mystery author and editor, for being an expert eye when I most needed her; Bala Zuccarello of One World Press for the invaluable information download and support; Joanna Penn and Suzanne Anderson for hacking into the indie publishing jungle and sending back maps; Shawn Wernig of Eggplant Studios for the awesome cover work.

And, always, thanks go to Juanita Rose Violini of Mystery Factory, ace mystery plot consultant and First Reader. Check out her work at mysteryfactory.com.

CPSIA information can be obtained
at www.ICGtesting.com
Printed in the USA
LVHW031915180321
681863LV00004B/789